He heard shouting in Pashto from beneath his feet. A wooden trap door in the guard tower floor suddenly flew up; Tangretti put two rounds into the head that emerged. Then, as the second tango dropped clear, he pulled out one of the two fragmentation grenades he was carrying, yanked the pin, and sent the small, iron sphere down the opening before kicking the trap door shut.

There was a loud, ringing blast and the door snapped open again. He kicked it shut once more, then picked up the PKM, which was propped up against the inside of the tower wall.

"Charlie One! Two tangos down, center compound!"

He glanced at the south gate, but couldn't see the Ospreys of Fireteam Alfa. They would be sticking to the shadows as much as possible, not charging headlong through the open gate.

But that appeared to be exactly what was happening at the opposite side of the compound. Half a dozen Mujahideen were streaming through the north gate, firing wildly, their AKs on full auto.

Damn it all! So much for low profiles.

SEALS THE WARRIOR BREED Series
by H.J. Riker

ENDURING FREEDOM
CASUALTIES OF WAR
DUTY'S CALL
IN HARM'S WAY
MARKS OF VALOR
MEDAL OF HONOR
NAVY CROSS
BRONZE STAR
PURPLE HEART
SILVER STAR

SEALS

THE WARRIOR BREED

ENDURING FREEDOM

H. JAY RIKER

AVON BOOKS

An Imprint of HarperCollinsPublishers

AVON BOOKS
An Imprint of HarperCollins*Publishers*
10 East 53rd Street
New York, New York 10022-5299

Copyright © 2005 by Bill Fawcett & Associates
ISBN-13: 978-0-06-058597-6
ISBN-10: 0-06-058597-8
www.avonbooks.com

First Avon Books paperback printing: December 2005

Avon Trademark Reg. U.S. Pat. Off. and in Other Countries, Marca Registrada, Hecho en U.S.A.
HarperCollins® is a registered trademark of HarperCollins Publishers Inc.

Printed in the U.S.A.

10 9 8 7 6 5 4 3 2 1

SEALS

THE WARRIOR BREED

ENDURING FREEDOM

Prologue

Tuesday, September 11, 2001

**Lower Manhattan
New York City
0846 hours, EST**

From that moment forward, they would call it 9/11.

At 0846 hours on a beautiful, blue-skied morning of late summer, American Airlines Flight 11—a Boeing 767 with ninety-two souls on board—angled out of the northern sky high above the southern tip of Manhattan and slammed into the 110-story North Tower of the World Trade Center, high above the heart of the city's financial district. Not since the 1945 crash of a B-24 bomber into the seventy-ninth floor of the Empire State Building during a heavy fog had anything like this happened. Observers both on the ground and in the burning tower assumed that they were witness to a similar, unthinkably horrific accident.

Seventeen minutes later, at 0903 hours, United Flight 175–with sixty-five passengers and crew—arrowed into the South Tower, accelerating at the last moment in order to increase the destruction and the casualties. A horrified America, watching live on the news channels, now began to realize that this was no pilot's error or mechanical fault.

This was a deliberate, carefully planned and orchestrated attack against the United States.

Almost exactly one hour after the first strike, American Flight 77 out of Dulles International plunged into the west side of the Pentagon. At 1005, the White House and other key buildings in Washington, D.C., were evacuated. At 1010 hours, a fourth jetliner, United Flight 93, crashed in an empty field in western Pennsylvania. Its passengers, alerted to unfolding events by cell-phone calls from family and friends, had stormed the cockpit to prevent another suicide attack, one aimed at the nation's capital.

The specific flights used in the attacks evidently had been chosen for having few passengers—meaning the hijackers would have fewer problems controlling them—and large fuel loads for their cross-country flights, again to maximize damage. Fires fueled by aviation gas burned fiercely in both towers of the World Trade Center for the next hour, sending a vast pall of black smoke into the brilliant morning sky.

Some hundreds of people trapped in the upper floors of the twin towers chose quick death in a jump to the pavement a quarter of a mile below over burning to death. News cameras caught one man on film as he jumped—evidently someone with skydiving training, for he held perfect free-fall form, smoke trailing from his burning clothes as he fell. Many others were seen to be burning as they plummeted to the street.

A few blocks from the World Trade Center, on Chambers Street, 650 children at Public School 234 were evacuated to safety moments before the towers' thunderous, final fall. One child of five stopped and pointed into the ominous, smoke-darkened sky. "Teacher, look! The birds are on fire!"

The South Tower of the WTC collapsed sixty-two minutes after it was hit, followed by the North Tower eighteen minutes later. Boiling, churning walls of smoke, dust, and debris surged through the skyscraper-walled canyons of the city's financial district.

Though initial estimates were higher, the final death toll of the attacks against the World Trade Center, an icon of capitalism and the West since the 1970s, was 2,792. At the Pentagon, 124 people died on the ground, with another sixty-four passengers and crew killed on board Flight 77. Forty passengers and crew died in the crash of Flight 93. Less the nineteen terrorists on board the four hijacked aircraft, the total number of dead was 3,001, with another 2,337 injured. The fires at Ground Zero on Manhattan would continue to burn for ninety-nine days—the longest burning commercial fire in U.S. history.

Sixty years earlier the Japanese attack on Pearl Harbor had killed 2,403 Americans, half of them the crew of the USS *Arizona*. Only sixty-eight of the dead at Pearl Harbor had been civilians. In comparison, the vast majority of the victims of the attack on September 11 had been civilians, though over five hundred of the total had been firemen, police, or military personnel stationed at the Pentagon.

The new war, born in the fires of the Arabian Gulf, had come home to America in a thunderous roar of terror, flame, and carnage.

The September 11 attacks had been planned and executed by a terrorist organization called al-Qaeda, led by a wealthy Saudi national named Osama bin Laden. As with the aftermath of Pearl Harbor, an outraged America, roused from complacent half slumber, sought a grim and terrible vengeance.

Half a world away, the U.S. Navy SEALs, together with other branches of the U.S. military and intelligence services, responded. . . .

Chapter 1

Asian Star Hotel
Kuala Lumpur
1545 hours, local time

At the moment, Lieutenant Kenneth Mariacher didn't look the part of a U.S. Navy officer. He wore his sandy hair medium long, and affected a mustache that curled down around the corners of his mouth. The bright yellow sport shirt, featuring silhouettes of palm trees and surfers, wasn't exactly Navy issue either.

But he did look the part of an American tourist visiting the capital of Malaysia, and that, after all, was the idea. Both the powerful binoculars he was holding to his eyes and the compact headset with its needle mike positioned before his lips were, if not Navy issue, then *government* issue, and tools of his trade.

Beside him, on the floor in front of the window, MM1 Philip Lehman remained motionless behind the massive length of his Barrett .50 rifle, his eye inches behind the weapon's oversized sniper scope. Behind them, on the bed, an aluminum suitcase was open to expose the AN/PRC-117F satellite communications unit, while the cruciform antenna on its spindly folding tripod rested nearby on the floor. The sixteen-pound unit was powerful enough to acquire a satellite in geosynch even from inside a hotel room in downtown Kuala Lumpur. Although the prick, as field operators called the PRC unit, had its own encryption capabilities, a smaller unit, a KY-99 crypto device, was attached for additional signal security.

The joke within the Teams was that the Agency *always* insisted on using KY with the prick when they were going to screw someone.

Their Agency contact had gotten them this room, though Mariacher would have been happier with a sniper's nest on the roof. Hotel rooms were closed-in places with only a single door. It was too easy to get trapped inside one when things went sour. But the third-story room did give them an excellent view down onto the shabby-looking two-story flat across the street. The Asian Star was a hotel catering to foreign businessmen and tourists in the heart of Kuala Lumpur's Chinatown district, close under the loom of the skyscrapers marking the heart of the city. The place was surprisingly clean, and even had amenities like in-room bathrooms and a hotel staff. The Kelang bus terminal sprawled just across the busy Jalan Sultan to the south, a broad avenue crowded with autos, motor scooters, buses, taxis, and even a few trishaws. The apartment was squeezed in between the terminal and the opening of an alley directly opposite the Asian Star.

A black Mercedes limo nosed its way through the rush-hour traffic, stopping in front of the apartment. Doors opened and several men got out.

"Wheel," Lehman said, his voice soft. "*Got* the son of a bitch!"

"I see him," Mariacher replied, shifting the binoculars

slightly. Their target, a tall, bearded man in a conservative business suit, the traditional Saudi *ghutra* and *igaal* on his head, and carrying a leather brief case, was standing on the sidewalk beside the limo, apparently speaking with the driver. He was flanked by a pair of bodyguards made almost laughably obvious by their sunglasses, black suits, and the way they watched everybody on the street but the man between them.

"Red Dog, Red Dog," Mariacher said. "Forward Blue. Tag on the Green Tiger, plus two tangos. Clear sky. Over."

In the code-rich, guarded terminology of covert ops, *tag* was their assigned target. *Tango* was slang for terrorist. *Clear sky* meant they had a clear view of the target and could drop him at a word. *Green Tiger* was the code name for the mission, and was also the Agency code for the target.

A set of photographs of the man on the sidewalk lay on the bedside table. Mariacher didn't need to check them, though. He had memorized Khalid Shaikh Mohammed's face in long hours of study and preparation for this mission.

Mohammed's ties to international terrorism—and *especially* to al-Qaeda—ran deep indeed. He had been charged in a failed 1995 plot to blow up eleven passenger aircraft on their way from Asia to the U.S., and as a result he was on the most-wanted lists of the CIA, the FBI, Interpol, Mossad, and half a dozen other agencies. He was the uncle of Ramzi Yousef, one of the key conspirators in the 1993 plot to blow up the World Trade Center in New York City. A younger brother had been killed in Pakistan when the bomb he was making exploded, and an older brother was a card-carrying member of al-Qaeda. It was also rumored that he was close to Saad bin Laden, the son of Osama.

And while he hadn't been charged yet with complicity in the 9/11 World Trade Center attacks, it was believed that he'd had a key role in the attack. *Green Tiger* . . .

Mariacher lowered the binoculars and glanced at a small black-and-white TV monitor set up beside the window. It showed the sniper's eye view through Lehman's scope, recorded for later analyses or for use as evidence. Mohammed's turbaned head and shoulders all but filled the screen as he leaned forward beside the limo's open passenger-side front window. The scope's calibrated crosshairs centered just in front of his left ear.

Three pounds of pressure on the trigger and Khalid Shaikh Mohammed would be dead. The round chambered in the Barrett contained enough high explosive to turn a man's head into a thin red spray. Hell, a .50 caliber bullet fired at this range would do that even without explosives.

A dry voice came back over his headset. "Blue Forward, Red Dog. Copy your tag. Wait one. Over."

"Not yet," he told Lehman.

"I heard, sir," the sniper replied. He had his own com headset. "Shit. He's moving."

Mohammed had just turned and was going up the steps of the apartment, followed by his bodyguards. The crosshairs locked onto the center of his back, following him up and through the wooden door.

"Red Dog, Forward Blue, call time," Mariacher said, alerting the team's controllers that the target had just moved out of sight. "Repeat, call time. Over."

"Forward Blue, copy. Over."

He raised the binoculars again, focusing this time on the second-floor window at the corner of the alley and Jalan Sultan. According to the Agency, the entire building had been rented by an international shipping firm that almost certainly fronted for al-Qaeda's financial arm. The upstairs room at the building's northwest corner, in the building plans acquired by the Agency, was an office. At least, that was where the phone lines were connected, and where a large wall safe had been installed five years earlier. It was also the only room in the building with an air conditioner, mounted in one of the two windows above the alley.

Even terrorists like to be comfortable when they're planning atrocities.

Lehman deftly worked the bolt on his single-shot Barrett, ejecting the explosive round. He set the bullet aside, selected another round from an open case on the floor by his knee, and chambered it. "Penetrator chambered," he said. The new penetrator round wasn't explosive, but it would punch through several inches of solid brick.

The office had two windows above the alley and two more overlooking the Jalal Sultan, and through those last Mariacher could see the legs of several men entering the office.

"Red Dog, Blue Forward. Tag in the nest. Over."

"Blue Forward, copy. Wait one. Over."

"Wheel?" Lehman said. "I'm going to Triple-Mike Romeo."

"Do it."

The image on the monitor shifted from black and white bricks and a window to a shifting, abstract flow of blues, greens, yellows, and reds. The sniper scope on Lehman's Barrett .50 operated both at optical wavelengths and by infrared, but also had a special adaptor for picking up millimeter microwave radiation, or MMMR, which included long infrared and short radar wavelengths.

Essentially, vibrating water molecules gave off radiation at these wavelengths—lots of it—and "warm bag of water" was a good if simplistic description of a living human body. The imaging device, still highly classified, built up a picture of the target in the same way as an infrared night-vision device. On the screen, Mariacher could see five distinct human-shaped figures in green, with yellow cores, wavering slightly against the deeper blue of the background.

The technology was brand new, and in Mariacher's opinion damn scary. There were already plans to put it into use for airport security and for terrorist surveillance in the States, and this unit was one of the very few already operating with U.S. special ops forces. Since millimeter radiation easily penetrated some materials, like clothing, glass, and even brick walls, but was blocked by others—metal and human skin, for example—it was the perfect tool for covert surveillance.

But who, he wondered, will watch the watchers?

The computer combined the passive microwave picture with conventional infrared imaging. On the monitor, the air conditioner showed as a bright smear of yellow and white as it dumped heat to the outside; the tangos inside were clearly visible, even through bricks, wood, and plaster, but nonradiating elements—like furniture and floors—remained invisible. One figure folded into a seated position, hunched forward, arms before it, as though leaning on an invisible desk. Two more appeared to hover in midair, as though seated in chairs opposite the desk, while two more were in standing positions in the back.

"Red Dog, Blue Forward," Mariacher reported. "We have gone Triple-Mike Romeo. Five tangos in the nest. Clear sky. Over."

"Blue Forward, copy clear sky. Wait one. Over."

Time dragged through the next twenty minutes. It appeared that the five targets—three principles and two bodyguards, at least—were holding a conference over there.

"Red Dog, Gold Forward," a new voice said at last. "In position. Confirm five tangos in the nest. Clear sky. Over."

"Gold Forward," the dry voice said. "Copy. Wait one. Over."

Gold Forward was the second SEAL sniper team—Chief Bradley and QM1 Osterlee. When Blue Forward, as the advance OP, had reported Mohammed's arrival, they had en-

tered the main building of the Kenang bus terminal, across
the alley to the west of the apartment, and taken up a position surveyed several days earlier. The position gave them a
clear line of sight across a one-story garage directly to the
west windows of the tango office. Although he didn't know
it, Mohammed was now positioned in a deadly cross fire,
from the north and from the west.

"Gold Forward, Blue Forward," Mariacher called. "Can
you ID Green Tiger?"

"Blue Forward, Gold, affirmative. Green Tiger is in a
chair opposite the desk, on the right, as we see him."

Gold Forward's position let them see through one of the
alley windows, the one not taken up by the air conditioner
unit, and get an optical make on the occupants. The passive
microwave radiation showed man-shaped images but no details of faces or clothing. Lehman shifted the aim of his Barrett slightly, bringing the crosshairs to rest on the farther of
the two men seated side by side.

"Roger that, Gold. Got him."

"Shit, what are they waiting for?" Lehman said, eye still
to the scope. "We could *take* the bastard."

"Chill, Phil," Mariacher replied, grinning. Normally,
Lehman was as stone-cold as they came, enough so that
"Chill" or "Chill-Phil" were his handles, a source of jokes
and mild harassment within the Team. "Maybe they want to
pull a snatch-and-scratch."

"Fuck that. I could put a penetrator through Tiger's
legs . . . pop! Just like that. Me and Gold, we take down the
others, two at a time, before they know what hit 'em. Drop a
Little Bird on the roof with a team to bag the tag while we
provide cover, and we have him at a secure facility in Thailand before he even has a chance to bleed to death. The
spooks have their man for questioning, and we cap four
tango bastards in the bargain."

"I'm sure the powers-that-be will be delighted to take up your suggestions at the next planning session, Chill. Right now, we wait."

"Hurry up and wait," Lehman growled. "Even in the Teams, it's hurry up and fucking wait."

Wednesday, September 19, 2001

Miramar Motel
Oceanside, California
0045 hours, PDT

Fifteen forty-five hours in Kuala Lumpur was the middle of the night in southern California. HM1 David Tangretti was comfortably entangled in the legs and arms of the nude young woman soundly sleeping half beneath him when his cell phone warbled, dragging him from a pleasantly exhausted coma. He reached across her left breast, which rolled enticingly with the movement, and fumbled with the phone he'd left on the bedside table. "T'gretti," he said, the word half a mumble.

"Drop your cock and grab your socks, Doc," the voice on the other end said. "Better get your ass back here. Stat."

The words brought him to full awareness. "Fletch? Whatcha got?"

"The base is locking down. All leave and liberty cancelled. Roll call on the grinder at 0430."

David groaned. "Roger that. I'm there." He clicked the phone shut.

"David?" the woman said sleepily. "What time is it?"

"Go back to sleep, hon," he told her. "It's nothing."

He slipped out of bed and began retrieving his clothing by the faint glow of a streetlight in the parking lot that was shining through a narrow gap in the curtains. Boxer shorts, socks, civilian slacks and shirt, shoes . . . all where he'd scattered them on the deck just a few enjoyable hours earlier. He had to sort through her clothing to get his—panties and bra, jeans, MTV T-shirt. No one could accuse Marilyn of being too formal.

She was a toothsome twenty-five-year-old blonde, a waitress he'd met at a nearby Denny's. Tonight she'd gotten off work at seven, he'd taken her to dinner at Applebee's, and somehow or other they ended up in the rack at a motel on Oceanside Boulevard, just off Route 5. He started pulling on his clothes.

David was currently assigned to Alfa Platoon of SEAL Team Three, stationed at the U.S. Navy Amphibious Training Center at Coronado—on the narrow spit of land walling San Diego Bay from the Pacific Ocean. Alfa was currently engaged in a series of training exercises with the U.S. Marine's 1st Force Recon, code-named Operation Mainstay. The exercises, which included a variety of joint training evolutions at sea, in the air, and mostly in the mud, were being carried out at the SEAL training center in Coronado, on San Clemente Island off the coast, and at Camp Pendleton, the sprawling U.S. Marine base located just a few miles north, up the coast from Oceanside. In fact, it had been during his five-day stay at Camp Pendleton two weeks ago that he'd met Marilyn.

The problem was, he technically wasn't supposed to be off-base . . . which, again technically, meant he was AWOL.

Hey, no big deal, he figured. When he didn't actually have duty, no one cared if he slipped out to see his girl, just as long as he was back for roll call in the morning. Things were just in an uproar because of the attack on the World Trade Center eight days ago. Every military base in America had been on alert since then, and people were jumpy.

Even so, he'd kept slipping out to spend time with Marilyn,

and his buddies back at the base continued to cover for him. Fletch's call just now had probably saved his sorry ass. Coronado was a good fifty miles south of Oceanside. If he left right now, he should be back on base by 0230 or so. Plenty of time. But he would leave now because he didn't believe in leaving things to chance . . . or in pressing his luck. It sounded as though they were going to lock down the base, and it would be a *lot* harder to sneak back in once that happened.

"David?" Marilyn called from the bed. "Are you *leaving*?"

"Sorry, honey. I have to, or I'll be in trouble at the base. But I'll call you."

"What, is a Marine hurt or something?"

"Or something." David was a Navy SEAL now, but he'd been a medical corpsman before he'd joined the Teams. Roughly equivalent to Army medics, though with considerably more training, corpsmen provided medical care and support for both Navy and Marine Corps personnel.

In fact, corpsmen and Marines had a long and very special relationship, since it was Navy corpsmen who went ashore with the Marines and looked after them in combat. David's father, Bill, had been a corpsman and a SEAL during the Vietnam War. He'd left the Teams at the end of that conflict, when the U.S. military had begun its postwar cutbacks, but in May 1975, as a Navy corpsman assigned once more to the Fleet Marine Force, he'd been pinned down on the beaches of Koh Tang with the 7/9 Marines during the infamous *Mayaguez* incident.

When he finally left the service, Bill Tangretti went to medical school and became a doctor. His son, determined to follow in his steps, joined the Navy in 1987, trained as a hospital corpsman, and then applied for SEAL training as well. He'd served in Desert Storm, bouncing over sand dunes in a Special Forces DPV—essentially a heavily armed dune buggy—in pursuit of Iraqi scuds.

He'd deployed to Somalia in '93, going ashore with a joint SEAL-Marine Force Recon landing party as a part of Operation Restore Hope, only to be pinned in the glare of camera lights by overzealous CNN reporters. For the seven years since, he'd primarily been engaged in training—both giving and receiving. SEALs trained incessantly, always preparing for the next mission, whatever it might be. In 1999 he'd been assigned to the SEAL training center at Coronado as a proctor, doing his sadistic best to weed out the wannabes and turn tadpoles into a new generation of SEALs. Three months ago he'd been reassigned to Three Delta, a special operations platoon tasked with working with Marine Force Recon.

Marilyn knew none of this. David had told her only that he was a Navy corpsman and that he was currently working with the Marines, both at Coronado and at Pendleton. He always wore civilian clothing off-base, so she'd never seen his SEAL trident.

David preferred it that way; a very few SEALs—and a far larger number of SEAL wannabe imposters—liked to impress the girls by telling them they were in the Teams. That left a foul taste in David's mouth; most members of the Teams were tight-lipped about what they did. It was safer that way. And while it wasn't a breach of security for him to admit that he was a SEAL, he personally preferred the low-profile approach.

Hell, Marilyn had taken him to bed not knowing what he did for a living. Why complicate things?

"You go back to sleep," he told her, picking up the little overnight bag he packed for such occasions. "I'll take care of things at the front desk and give you a call as soon as I can."

She sat up in the bed, letting the sheets fall. Her nude body was gorgeous in the half light. "You know, I was hoping we could go to the beach this weekend."

"I'll have to get back to you on that one," he said. "I don't know if I'll be free."

"You don't even know if you have duty this weekend?" she flared. "Are you trying to avoid me?"

"Did I try to avoid you tonight?" he shot back. "I just don't know what my schedule is yet, is all."

"I dated a Navy electronics guy for almost a year, David. He *always* knew when he had duty! One weekend in four, just like clockwork!"

"Well . . . it's different for me. Look, hon, I gotta go. Honest, I promise to call you." He pulled out his wallet and placed a twenty on the motel room dresser, next to the TV. "Here's for cab fare, okay?"

"What the hell? You bastard, are you *paying* me for what we did tonight?"

David sighed. "No," he said, and slipped out the door. Marilyn seemed determined to turn this into an argument, but he was not going to play.

He found the night clerk on duty at the desk and squared the bill for the night with him, then got into his Civic and headed for the interstate. Twenty minutes later he'd put all thought of Marilyn out of his mind, turning his thoughts to more crucial issues as he sped down Interstate 5.

What the hell was going down back at the base?

Thursday, September 20, 2001

Asian Star Hotel
Kuala Lumpur
2105 hours, local time

Mariacher was a SEAL; and as a SEAL, he was used to waiting.

Waiting, in fact, was one of the primary weapons in the SEAL arsenal. The history of the Teams was full of stories of small groups of Navy SEALs infiltrating enemy territory by boat, helicopter, or parachute, walking for miles to reach an assigned station, and then just waiting there, not moving, not speaking, sometimes for days until the ambush was sprung or the observation of enemy activity had been reported. In BUD/S—the Basic Underwater Demolition/SEAL training that every SEAL endured—they learned *how* to wait, how to assume a deliberately uncomfortable position in order to remain awake hour after hour after interminable hour. They learned how vital patience was in any covert operation, and how outwaiting the enemy invited him to make a fatal mistake.

And so Mariacher waited. He was at the Barrett .50 now, its bipod set on the windowsill, the stock propped up on a bedside table and a couple of Kuala Lumpur phone books. The scope was still set for IR and trained on the office window across the street, but it appeared that no one was home.

Phil Lehman had slipped out an hour ago to check out the area—especially the street—and to get some chow. SEALs were used to waiting, yeah, but at least this time around it wasn't neck deep in icy water, or crouched under a boulder overlooking a valley where Saddam *might* decide to deploy a scud launcher or two.

Waiting. It was necessary. In fact, it made up the largest portion by far of all covert ops, save, possibly, for the training ahead of time.

But he'd also learned the vital need for *timing* in such ops. It was possible to wait and wait and wait . . . and find the target had eluded you.

And Mariacher was beginning to suspect that was what had happened this time. He and Lehman, and their fellow SEALs in Gold Forward above the bus terminal, had been watching that damned apartment across the street for almost five hours now since Mohammed's arrival—and it had been three *days* since they'd rented this room and begun the surveillance.

That, Mariacher decided, was what was making him nervous. Gold Forward had taken up their position only five hours ago, but he and Lehman had set up their OP/sniper's position late Monday evening. Three days in one spot, in one tiny trap of a room, in a city where they didn't dare trust anyone, least of all the clerks at the desk downstairs—hell, yeah, it made him nervous.

"Hey, Mynock?" Lehman's voice said in his headset. The nickname was a play on Mariacher's name, which was pronounced *my-ocker*. Somehow, his Teammates had turned that into the name of a repulsive little energy vampire in one of the Star Wars movies. "Appaloosa. All clear out here. I'm coming in."

Both men were carrying M-biters. The full designation for the 2.7-pound tactical radios each man carried was the AN/PRC-148 (V) Maritime MultiBand Inter/Intra Team Radio, or MBITR—which SEALs and Recon Marines had shortened to the more colorful and less tongue-tangling M-biter.

"Roger that," he replied. "Palomino." *Appaloosa* was both the password and the reassurance that the other SEAL wasn't coming up the stairs with a gun held to his head. *Palomino* was Lehman's assurance that someone unpleasant hadn't moved into the room in his absence. A moment later a key rattled in the door, and Lehman entered with a red and white paper bag in hand—dinner. He locked and bolted the door behind him.

"Chow time," he said. "KFC. I was getting sick of Chinese." The joys of Western civilization. There was a chicken place three blocks from the hotel, and a McDonald's a block north of that.

"That works," Mariacher said. "How's the real world?"

"No problems. I chatted with the desk clerk for a while, long enough to check out the lobby. No one hanging around down there. The guy at the desk spoke good English. I gave him the sob story about two British businessmen who'd missed their contacts in the big city, and had anyone been asking about us. He said no . . . and I'm inclined to believe him."

Mariacher nodded. While their CIA controls had scoped out the place ahead of time, and presumably checked out the staff, the SEALs preferred to rely on their own assessment of the place and its personnel.

"After that," Lehman continued, "I watched the street for a while, and even wandered around back of the hotel, just for a look-see. Lots of people, but no obvious loitering. What's the word up here?"

"No change. The office is still empty." The meeting over there had lasted for well over two hours, but at just past six—three and a half hours ago, now—all five men had left the office. Infrared wasn't picking up any signs of life, which could mean that all five men had simply moved to a room in the back of the building, since the scope couldn't pick up infrared through two walls, or they'd left the building.

They'd not been through the front door. The SEALs had had that exit under surveillance at all times, and no one had come out or gone in.

Which left the back door. There was one, according to the building plans acquired by the Agency, but the two SEAL units had not been tasked with watching it. The back door was the responsibility of Sean Dugan, code name Diamond, and his . . . people.

Dugan was their controller for this op, a CIA officer working out of the U.S. Embassy here in Kuala Lumpur. Purportedly, he had his own team of covert operators for this mission, but he'd requested support from the Navy SEALs in case a sniper action was required, or as backup in case of serious trouble his operators couldn't handle.

Dugan, in fact, was "Red Dog," now comfortably ensconced in his war room in the basement of the embassy over on Jalan Tun Razak. Neither Mariacher nor Lehman liked the man; his affectations—a Texan drawl, cowboy boots, and his hearty "Call me Tex"—all seemed so calculated, so artificial.

"You think Diamond missed something?" Lehman asked.

"I'm beginning to wonder."

"Here . . . you want to eat while I watch?"

"Nah. Go ahead. I got it covered."

He heard the rustle of the paper bag. "Maybe we should check with him."

Mariacher considered this—*had* been considering it for the past hour. Their job was to watch the building across the street, and to cap Mohammed if Red Dog gave the order. Period. It wasn't professional to try second-guessing your controller or to pester him with impatient "Daddy, are we there yet?" questions.

He glanced at the satellite antenna on the deck. The unit packed far more power than an operation of this sort usually required. It was what was known as a UHF DAMA satcom— DAMA for Demand Assigned Multiple Access—meaning several hundred users could share a single narrowband satcom channel. Next to it was a Digital Communications Terminal, or DCT, a small computer, basically, that could compose, edit, transmit, and receive both text messages and graphics. That unit was connected to the television monitor at the moment.

What all of that meant was that as they maintained their surveillance of Mohammed, they had a number of other people—possibly several hundred—almost literally looking over their shoulders. The SEALs hadn't been told who might be watching the op, but it was easy enough to guess.

Langley, of course—the CIA headquarters in Langley, Virginia. JSOC, at Fort Bragg. And the Pentagon. Hell, the president himself could be watching from the White House war room.

No, this was definitely a situation where they would play things by the book. And the book said you didn't second-guess your control.

"I was figuring on giving him another two-three hours," Mariacher said after a thoughtful pause.

"Hell, yeah," Lehman replied. "Wait until the son of a bitch is asleep in bed and *then* call him."

"Besides, if we call for help, we're begging for micromanagement from someone further up the chain of command." He nodded at the satcom unit. "God knows who's listening in."

"Roger that, Wheel," Lehman said. He sat on the edge of the bed, fishing a piece of chicken out of the bag. Mariacher turned his full attention back to the target building across the street.

Wheel. The slang term was SEAL-speak for the lieutenant in command of a SEAL platoon. He was in command even if his Team consisted of himself and one other SEAL.

A knock sounded on the door. Both SEALs spun instantly, pulling their sidearms from the holsters they wore at their backs, hidden beneath their loose-fitting tourist shirts. Mariacher took cover behind the side of the hotel-room dresser, Lehman behind the bed, both men holding their weapons two-handed, aimed at the door. "Who's there?" Mariacher called out, keeping his voice controlled and casual.

"Maid service," a woman's voice, thickly accented, called back. "You want bed turned back?"

Shit. The one problem with a hotel with amenities was keeping the staff at bay. The management tended to frown on firearms in the rooms.

"No, thank you," Mariacher replied. "Everything is fine!"

He thought he heard a noise outside—a rustle of starched material, perhaps, or someone shuffling on the carpet. "Please," the woman called again. "Is maid service. You want towels? You want soap?"

"No," he said, speaking loudly and firmly. Damn it. Her voice sounded . . . tight. Scared, maybe. But was that because she was having trouble with the language or because something else, something more dangerous, was unfolding?

A key turned in the lock, the doorknob turned, and then the door rattled hard against the dead bolt.

Maybe it was a persistent hotel maid with poor to nonexistent English. But maybe . . .

"Red Dog, Red Dog," he said, his voice barely above a whisper. "Blue Forward. We may have a situation—"

The door exploded inward, wood chips flying as the dead bolt was ripped from the wall. Mariacher had an instant's glimpse of a pretty, dark-haired Asian girl coming through first, with some heavy-duty muscle in black right behind her.

Heavy-duty muscle, four gunmen, all wielding AK-47s.

Chapter 2

Thursday, September 20, 2001

Asian Star Hotel
Kuala Lumpur
2121 hours, local time

The gunmen were dressed like professionals, or at least like
Hollywood's idea of what professional hit men might look
like—black trousers and boots, black pull-overs, black
woolen ski masks—but their assault was about as amateur as
it got. All four crowded through the narrow door in single
file, the leader holding the maid by her hair close by her
scalp as he tried to steer her forward while aiming his AK
one-handed past her shoulder.

The two SEALs were ready for company, however. The
first gunman wasn't big, but he was big enough that the girl
he was hiding behind didn't provide him with much cover.
Both SEALs double-tapped the triggers on their SIG Sauer
P226 pistols—a weapon known in Navy SEAL parlance as
the Mark 11. Four 9mm rounds snapped past the maid's left
ear and exploded the gunman's head in a shockingly scarlet
spray of blood, bone, and brain, the fusillade startlingly loud
within the thin-walled confines of the room.

Had SEALs been taking down that hotel room, they would have blown the door and tossed in a flash-bang first, to blind and stun anyone inside. Then two men would have come through, and two only, one rolling left, the other right, while two more covered from the doorway.

The leader continued into the room minus most of his head, the girl propelled forward in front of him by the body's momentum. She was screaming, but the scream was covered by the roar of four more shots from the SEAL handguns.

The second attacker went down and back, rounds slamming into his center of mass. Number three in line collided with number two in a messy tangle of black. Number four was fumbling with his assault rifle, trying to bring it to his shoulder, when four more shots punched him back through the open doorway and into the hall outside.

Number three had just hit the deck and was trying to get clear of number two when Mariacher dropped his aim and put two last rounds into him, one in the chest, one in the head.

The entire action had taken perhaps three seconds, if that much. The relative silence that followed, punctuated by the woman's frantic, asthmatic-sounding sobs, was, if anything, more startling than the gunfire.

"Blue Forward, this is Red Dog! Come in! What is your situation? Over!"

How long had they been trying to get through? "Red Dog, Blue Forward. Wait one." Mariacher took a grim satisfaction in saying that.

Lehman sprang across the bed, went up against the wall next to the door, then rolled around into the hall. Mariacher was right behind him, rolling the other way.

The hall was empty, though sounds were coming from several of the other rooms. A door down the passageway cracked open, then slammed shut again.

Lehman grabbed number four by his ankles and dragged him inside. Mariacher picked up the dead gunman's AK, tossed it on the bed, then turned to the woman.

She lay on the thin, blood-splattered carpet, eyes wide, gasping for breath, clearly terrified.

"Did you know these men?" he asked her.

Her answer was a shrill torrent of . . . it wasn't Malay. It sounded Chinese. She obviously hadn't been party to the intrusion. No one could act that terrified. The gunmen must have seen her in the passageway, grabbed her, and forced her to try to let them in.

"Easy, there," he told her. "Easy. You're safe." He wished he had more than a few words of Chinese.

Well, there was an international language available. Reaching for his wallet, he pulled out a wad of Malaysian paper currency—fifty dollars or so—and handed it to her. Usually, if someone is handing you a month's wages, they're not about to shoot you. The girl's eyes rolled wildly and she was still breathing like she'd just run a grueling marathon, but the sobs subsided as she took the money.

"Go!" Mariacher told her. He pointed at the door and gestured for emphasis. *"Go!"*

She got, in a rustle of starched uniform.

"Let's pack our bags, Chill," he told the other SEAL. He dropped the partially emptied magazine from his pistol's butt and snicked home a fresh one. "It's time to get the hell out of Dodge!"

"You think they had backup?"

"Dunno. We're going to pretend they did, though. Just in case."

Lehman was already breaking down the Barrett and stowing it and the ammo in a suitcase-sized carrying case. Mariacher took a moment to call their control. "Red Dog, Blue Forward. They made us. We're pulling out."

"We copy, Blue Forward. What is your tacsit, over?"

"Four tangos down. You might want to send some cleaners over here. No casualties for the good guys."

"Roger that. Regroup at Point Quebec."

"Copy Point Quebec. Blue Forward out." He switched off the unit and began closing the cases holding their communications gear. They would leave behind most of their heavy equipment—monitor, battery pack, cooling unit for the IR scope—but the DCT, the KY-99 crypto device, and the Prick-117 and its antenna all would have to come along, as well as the rifle. The com gear, and most especially the encryption codes stored in their computers, were classified; as for the Barrett .50, the SEALs didn't like the idea of letting *any* weapon fall into tango hands.

They would also hang onto their M-biters, which they could carry in holsters beneath the tails of their voluminous tourist shirts. They might lose contact with Red Dog, depending on range and the presence of intervening buildings, but they should be able to stay in touch with Gold Forward, and the units were designed to serve as survival radios as well as tactical communications units.

At least, Mariacher thought, they wouldn't have half of freaking Washington looking over their shoulders any longer.

The smaller carrying cases went inside a pair of backpacks. The suitcase with the PRC-117 they would carry as it was, a seventeen-pound white elephant. Mariacher shouldered one backpack and picked up the radio, taking a last look around, while Lehman took the pack and the rifle case. "Let's book."

They already had an escape route plotted. There was a window at the end of the hallway opening onto a fire escape going to an alley in the back, but if the bad guys knew their business, going down that way would be as suicidal as strolling down to the lobby and out the front door.

An intersecting corridor, however, ran past a line of rooms

on the hotel's west side. Mariacher chose one and, pistol in hand, threw his shoulder against it, hard.

The door smashed open and he rushed inside. Incense curled from a bowl on the dresser. Several empty bottles lay scattered on the floor. A naked and obviously excited man lay in bed, tucked in between two equally naked and very young Asian women.

"Kuso!" the man shouted, sitting up in bed. *"Kono yo-gore!"* Both women screamed in shrill harmony.

"Excuse us," Mariacher said, running past the foot of the bed. "Just passing through." He wasn't sure what the man had just called him, but the language sounded Japanese. He must be a Japanese businessman, visiting the notorious fleshpots of Southeast Asia.

"Room service," Lehman added. "Can we do anything to make your stay more enjoyable?"

Mariacher banged open the room's window and took a quick look outside. Behind him the businessman and both girls fled, still naked, into the hallway. Ignoring them, he un-shouldered the backpack, set down the PRC-117, holstered his pistol, and swung himself outside.

The wall was brick, but SEALs were accomplished climbers. More than once Mariacher had competed with other Teammates in scaling brick or stone buildings. His superiors didn't like that kind of activity; they preferred that their SEALs keep a low profile. But once, he'd free-climbed four stories up the outside of a hotel in San Diego.

Besides, it was *only* three floors to the alley below. He picked his way down until he was fifteen feet above the street, then let go, landing with a parachutist's drop-and-roll. He glanced left, then right. The alley was still clear. Holding up his hands, he motioned for Lehman to drop their gear.

Down it came, two backpacks, a satcom radio, and the rifle case, one at a time. He caught each, set it down, then spotted for Lehman as the other SEAL slipped through the open window and started his descent.

"Where to now?" Lehman asked, retrieving his gear. "Did I hear you say Point Quebec?"

"Affirmative. South."

"Roger that."

Point Quebec was one of several CIA safe houses they'd been briefed on when they arrived in Kuala Lumpur. It was located in a neighborhood with the unlikely name of Brickfield, on the far side of the Kelang River a short distance south from Chinatown.

Their descent had brought them to the alley behind the Asian Star Hotel, which opened onto a broad north-south avenue called Jalan Hang Kasturi. They approached the opening onto the street cautiously; if the enemy had the hotel covered on all sides, they would certainly be watching the mouth of that alley.

The main street was not as busy as it had been during the afternoon rush, but there was still traffic, with lots of people on the sidewalks. Chinatown was crowded, the streets brightly lit, the throngs noisy. After a moment's hesitation, the two SEALs stepped out onto the sidewalk, putting themselves in the midst of a large and boisterous crowd of Asian men evidently out on the town. Mariacher and Lehman didn't exactly blend in; the two SEALs were a head taller than the tallest of the men around them, and their Western clothing and features made them stand out. Still, any tango observers would be more likely to follow them than open fire on a crowded street.

He hoped.

"How do you think they made us?" Lehman asked as they cut across Jalan Hang Kasturi.

"Only two likely possibilities," Mariacher replied. "Someone on the hotel staff fingered us. . . ."

"Possible, but I'd bet money against that one."

"Yeah. The place is pretty upscale, and I had a good feeling with the staff people I talked to."

"Same here."

"The other possibility is that Dugan's operation here isn't as secure as he thinks it is."

"Gee. Imagine that?"

They turned north and started up the west side of the street, partly to give any pursuers the wrong idea about where they were headed, partly to put as many buildings and people between them and the area immediately around the Asian Star Hotel as possible.

"Too soon to say which," Mariacher pointed out. "But my money is on Diamond's assets."

Dugan/Diamond would be one of several CIA officers operating in Kuala Lumpur out of the U.S. Embassy, and there would be others behind the facades of other agencies and organizations throughout the city. Officers like Dugan rarely did their own clandestine ops, however. They recruited others to do their work for them—their intelligence assets.

The trouble was, anyone who could be bought once could be bought twice. Worse, the enemy here wasn't the Russians or the Chinese, as had been the case during the bad old days of the Cold War. The enemy was al-Qaeda, an organization that was both very, very wealthy and that espoused fundamentalist Islam. Malaysia was quite moderate, even pretty laid back and relaxed as far as Islamic states went, but there would always be some percentage of any local Muslim population poor enough, dissatisfied or disenfranchised enough, angry enough, or fanatically religious enough to sign on with bin Ladin's jihad against America.

Mariacher was willing to bet that someone in Dugan's local intelligence network was al-Qaeda . . . and that someone had not only tipped off the bad guys to the fact that Khalid Shaikh Mohammed was under surveillance, but the location of the surveillance OP.

Sirens blared in two-tone cadence, the sounds growing closer. "You think that's for us, sir?" Lehman asked.

"We'll assume so. C'mon. Down here."

They ducked left, west, into another alley. Now they needed to elude the local law enforcement agency as well as the tangos. Third World cops being what they were, Mariacher wasn't willing to gamble their lives on the possibility of the local police actually helping them. Besides, if that room at the Asian Star had been a death trap, a jail cell would be far, far worse.

With luck, they were out of the line of sight of anyone watching the hotel. The alley grew narrow, dead-ending at a wooden fence. They scaled the fence, dropped into another alley beyond, then jogged toward the Jalan Sultan Mohammed, a broad north-south avenue running along the river. As they reached the sidewalk and turned left again, they slowed to a walk, moving south now. Nothing attracts attention like a running man.

The full nighttime glory of Kuala Lumpur pulsed and dazzled around them. The capital of Malaysia was one of those modern miracles touted in the commercial guides, a vital, modern, and beautiful city rising from what had been jungle a century and a half before. The heart of the city, the financial district and the Golden Triangle business district, lay a few dozen blocks to the northeast, where the twin spires of the Petronas Towers rose from the forest of shining, modern architecture at what the tour books called KLC, the Kuala Lumpur Center.

Between the towers and Chinatown, the Kuala Lumpur Tower, a needle-slim landmark with a bulge near the top, rose in brightly illuminated splendor from the parks near the city's wealthier section along the Jalan Ampang. On their right, several skyscrapers rose from the city's Central Market district along the west bank of the Kelang River, their lights reflected in the dark water below.

Mariacher scowled at the river. Bad planning, guys, he thought, the sentiment directed at Diamond and the Agency suits who'd selected the CIA safe houses in this damned city. Point Quebec was on that far bank, which meant either they swam, to emerge dripping wet and conspicuous on the far side, or they crossed one of the bridges spanning the river. Up ahead, roughly marking the southern border of Chinatown, a major highway, the Jalan Kinabalu, crossed the river. That span was on one of the city's two or three busiest arteries. It was brightly lit, both by streetlights and the glare of the city all around. Two Americans trying to cross that span on the walkway would make perfect targets.

Navy SEALs trained, and trained hard and constantly, to carry out combat and covert operations in every conceivable terrain and environment. Of all environments, though— jungle, desert, forest, mountain—the toughest was urban . . . and most especially the heart of a crowded and bustling metropolis like Kuala Lumpur.

"Watcha thinking, Wheel?" Lehman asked him.

"I'm thinking river," he said.

"Roger that, sir. Water is the SEAL's best friend."

"Let's get wet."

Wednesday, September 19, 2001

Headquarters
Naval Special Warfare Command,
Coronado, California
0635 hours, PDT

"Gentlemen," the naval officer with the three gold stripes of a commander on his blue jacket began. "Things are moving into high gear."

Turning from the podium, he tugged aside the sheet that was covering a large map set on an easel at the front of the room, and a low murmur of voices went through the room as the audience recognized it.

"The target," the captain continued, "is Afghanistan."

"Big freakin' surprise," BM1 Randy Fletcher said, his voice just loud enough for HM1 Tangretti to hear.

"No shit," David replied. He'd been leaning back in his chair, but he tipped it forward now, arms crossed over his knees, listening intently. He was also trying to see the map better. Tight clusters of triangles and squares were printed on it in green, red, and blue—a grouping near the northern border, others thickly scattered in the south and the southeast, near the border with Pakistan, a lone group in the southwest. He was too far back, though, to be able to read the words printed on the board.

He'd made it back to the base at just before 0300 hours without incident. He'd thought he was going to get hassled when he flashed his ID at the Marine guards at the front gate and they insisted he get out of his car for a thorough check. When they found out he was a hospital corpsman, though, the Marine sergeant just shook his head and said, "Better get your ass inside, Doc. You wouldn't want to be left out in the cold."

Theoretically, he'd had an hour and a half before reveille

to grab a little rack time, but he hadn't been able to sleep. His mind kept turning over the implications for the sudden recall. Sealing off the base could mean only one thing.

The SEALs were going to war.

After their zero-dark-thirty reveille and breakfast, the six-teen members of SEAL Three's Alfa Platoon had assembled inside the basement-level room in the headquarters of the Naval Special Warfare Command Center set aside for secure briefings. The enlisted SEALs—fifteen of them—were seated in folding metal chairs at the back of the room. The big, pol-ished wooden conference table and the softer chairs around it had been reserved for the brass, and there was a hell of a lot of it present this morning, definitely a time to watch all of the p's and q's of military courtesy.

Alfa's wheel, Lieutenant Fred Driscoll, was by far the most junior officer present. David recognized Captain Theodore Cunningham, the CO of Naval Special Warfare Group 1, which was the headquarters unit for all of the West Coast SEAL Teams, SEAL Delivery Team, and Special Boat Squadrons. His boss was there as well, Admiral Clarence McFarland, the current commander of Naval Special War-fare Command, and the man who was, therefore, the senior SEAL in the Navy.

A second admiral sat opposite McFarland. He had been introduced as Admiral Christopher Gorman, one of the Navy's DEPOPSDEPs. The alphabet soup identified him as one of the redundantly named deputy operations deputies headquartered at the Pentagon. Though not a member of the Joint Chiefs of Staff, his boss, the Vice Director of the Naval Chief of Staff, was. That was a not so subtle clue to just how important this briefing was going to be. Both admirals were accompanied by their own entourages of lesser ranking brass, commanders and captains, mostly.

Several officers in the blue dress uniform jackets of the

U.S. Marines were present as well, though the senior officer wasn't wearing his dress uniform at all, but camouflage fatigues. He was Colonel C. Connor Hatch, commander of 1st Force Recon at Camp Pendleton, a man notorious for his unorthodox and independent style.

The man at the front of the room was Commander Dickinson, from Naval Intelligence. There were several suits in the room as well, civilians who hadn't been introduced by name or title, but who were almost certainly CIA, DIA, NSA . . . Intelligence, certainly. *Spooks*.

One thing was certain. The unusually early hour for this briefing—0630 hours—meant that someone had a scheduling bug up his ass and was in a hell of a rush. More than that, though, enlisted SEALs didn't usually get to sit in on briefing sessions with admirals and captains. The time, and the fact that Alfa Platoon was here this morning, meant that something *really* hot was going down.

"Things are coming down to the wire," Dickinson continued. He had a ponderous way of speaking—filled with clichés and an air of drama. It was tiring just listening to him. "Later today, the president will be ordering combat aircraft to bases in the Persian Gulf. Two carrier battle groups, the *Enterprise* and the *Carl Vinson,* are moving to attack stations in the Indian Ocean. Gentlemen, it is official. We are going to war.

"The enemy is al-Qaeda, and the Taliban, the Islamic fundamentalist regime controlling most of Afghanistan. I don't need to tell you gentlemen that this could get nasty. The Taliban has already called for a holy war against the United States if we attack, and al-Qaeda is committed to attacking Americans and our allies anywhere in the world. Rather than sit back and wait for them to strike again, we are taking the war to them. Alfa Platoon of SEAL Team Three will be one of several special operating teams we will be inserting into enemy territory. You, gentlemen, will be among the first ones we have over there, boots on the ground."

That had the SEALs' attention. Most of the high-ranking brass must already know what was going down, but the word hadn't filtered out to the rank and file yet.

"A quick recap is in order," Dickinson said. "Eight days ago, September eleventh, terrorist elements hijacked four civilian jetliners and deliberately crashed them into the two towers of the World Trade Center, in New York, and into the west side of the Pentagon. The fourth airliner, we now believe, was intended to strike the U.S. Capitol Building in Washington. Only the heroic efforts of the passengers on board Flight 93 prevented a disaster of truly terrible and epic proportions."

Oh? Destroying the WTC wasn't epic enough for you? David thought, but he pushed the wry thought aside. The September 11 attacks had been aimed at the *idea* of America, at her *symbols,* as much as at her population. Even though most of the country's senior leadership had been evacuated within twenty minutes of the strike on the Pentagon, and long before Flight 93 could have reached Washington, the destruction of the Capitol Building would have vastly compounded the message the terrorists were delivering to the United States and to the world.

"The attack had a stunning effect on the country," Dickinson continued. "Trading on Wall Street stopped. The FAA halted all flight operations at the nation's airports for the first time in history. Incoming flights from overseas all were diverted to Canada or to Mexico. The military was placed on high alert. President Bush, who was attending a speaking engagement in Florida when the attacks went down, announced that we *would* 'find those responsible and bring them to justice.'

"On the next day, the president called the attacks an act of war, and requested twenty billion dollars from Congress to begin the recovery. Thursday, the president vowed that America will lead the world to victory over terrorism, and called this 'the first war of the twenty-first century.' Secretary of State Colin Powell announced that the prime suspect in the bombings was Osama bin Laden.

"Bin Laden was well-known to the CIA and other intelligence agencies, of course. He was on the Agency's most-wanted list. We knew he was in Afghanistan at the time of the attacks, thanks to several NSA communications intercepts. As far as we know, he's still there, and he is tight, very tight, with the Taliban regime in Kabul. Deputy Defense Secretary Paul Wolfowitz indicated that this would be a sustained military campaign, and not a single strike, unlike *other* retaliatory strikes in the past."

That brought a few grim chuckles from the audience. "Yeah," an aide sitting nearby said, just loud enough to be heard. "No more going after fucking camels with cruise missiles."

In August of 1998, following car-bombing attacks overseas that had killed American citizens, President Clinton had ordered cruise missiles fired at known or suspected al-Qaeda training camps in southern Afghanistan and in the Sudan, a retaliation widely regarded within the military community as somewhat less than effective or appropriate. Twelve people had been killed in Afghanistan, and twenty wounded in what turned out to be a pharmaceuticals plant in Khartoum, Sudan, thanks to faulty intelligence.

The feeble and misguided attack had been widely seen not as a message sent to al-Qaeda and bin Laden, but as a message sent by Clinton to his more hawkish domestic critics, proof that he *was* tough on terrorism . . . at least when he wasn't busy defending himself against impeachment attempts and sex scandals.

Dickinson, checking his notes on the podium, ignored the *sotto voce* comment. "Initial overtures to the Taliban were rejected or ignored. On Friday, September fourteenth, President Bush declared a state of national emergency, and gave the Defense Department authority to call fifty thousand reservists to active duty. The Taliban regime warned of revenge against the U.S. if we attacked Afghanistan for harboring terrorists. On Saturday, the president responded by declaring that American troops would hunt down terrorists in a long and unrelenting war, and stated that the American people not only want revenge, but they demand an end to what he called 'barbaric behavior.' At the same time, the State Department issued a warning that governments *worldwide* would be isolated if they tolerate or assist terrorist groups. I should add that also on Saturday, the government of Pakistan agreed in full to a list of conditions we'd presented to them, regarding a possible attack on Afghanistan.

"Sunday," Dickinson went on, "the president pledged a 'crusade to rid the world of evil-doers.' Vice President Cheney warned that all who harbor terrorists face 'the full wrath of the United States.' The same day, a senior Pakistani delegation was sent to Kabul, Afghanistan, to give them a message: hand over bin Laden to the United States, or face a massive military assault."

David had been following the news as much as any of the other SEALs in Alfa Platoon, and the politics of the unfolding engagement had been an almost constant topic for late-night barracks bull sessions. Like the others, he wondered about President Bush's use of the word *crusade*. If any one word carried a few hundred tons of negative baggage in the Islamic world, it was that one—a reminder of the repeated attempts by Western, Christian kingdoms to take and hold the Holy Land—sacred to Moslems as well as Jews and Christians—between the eleventh and the fourteenth centuries. Many of the people over there had long, long memories; the word crusade was bound to raise hackles throughout the Islamic world.

Had Bush deliberately chosen that word to rattle bin Laden? Or would it end up causing more trouble than it was worth among America's Islamic allies? It felt to David like a public relations gaffe.

"Yesterday," Dickinson went on, again consulting his notes, "September eighteenth, the Taliban called upon Muslims worldwide to wage holy war against America if we attacked them. Defense Secretary Donald Rumsfeld announced that we are now preparing for a sustained offensive against terrorists and *all* countries that support them. The battle lines, gentlemen, have been drawn."

David exchanged a concerned glance with Fletch. Could the United States actually be considering attacking a number of countries simultaneously? Back during the Gulf War, there'd been a lot of discussion about whether the U.S. was capable of fighting two wars at once; the fear had been that North Korea was going to make trouble while the U.S. military was engaged in Kuwait.

The list of states sponsoring terrorism across the globe was unpleasantly long. Iraq and Iran, both. Saddam Hussein was still in power, despite the Gulf War, and the ayatollahs still rattled their religious sabers from time to time. Both countries were thought to be aggressively pursuing nuclear, chemical, and biological weapons research, both had long records of state-supported terrorism, and neither had any love for the West. Syria. Sudan. North Korea. Libya . . . though the rogue government of Mu'ammar Gadhafi had been maintaining a decidedly low profile since the U.S. strikes against that country back in the '80s. Chechnya, though, was usually viewed as Russia's problem.

And where did you draw the line? Colombia wasn't harboring drug-lord terrorists, but the government was widely perceived as ineffectual in handling the problem. Same with Pakistan. Same with the bandit revolutionaries in the Philippines, Somalia, Peru, and a dozen other nations. The United States of America might be the only superpower on the block right now, but even she wasn't strong enough to take on half of the world.

Despite his misgivings, David felt a stirring of approval, even of eagerness at the idea of launching a sustained campaign against the terrorists. *It's about damned time,* he thought. So far as he and most of the other SEALs he knew were concerned, America had been at war for a long time . . . but without most people in America even realizing it. The war with shadowy terror groups like Hisbollah and al-Qaeda, for most Americans, felt more like public relations campaigns, with no kick to them . . . kind of like the war on drugs. People turned on the news and heard about a terrorist outrage—about a jetliner crashing over Scotland or a truck bomb in some African city they'd never heard about—and unless someone among the dead was a friend or a relative, it had little impact.

After 9/11, though, that would change. Every American was a target, so far as the terrorists were concerned.

But now, at least, every American knew there was a war on.

And nothing, David thought, was ever going to be the same again.

Chapter 3

Along the Kelang River
Kuala Lumpur
2145 hours, local time

Despite the lateness of the hour, traffic was still heavy on the Jalan Sultan Mohammed. Since Malaysia was a former British colony, traffic moved on the left, and most vehicles had right-side steering. The two SEALs waited, choosing the right moment, then dashed across the highway to reach the riverbank on the far side. Horns blared, drivers waved angry fists and shouted colorful imprecations in several languages, but the traffic here was slow, bottlenecked somewhat by the entrance ramp to the Kinabalu Highway just ahead.

A taxi screeched to a halt in the southbound lane, inches from Mariacher's leg, horn sounding, driver leaning out of the right-side window and screaming in what sounded like Chinese. A Toyota tapped the taxi's rear bumper, which distracted both drivers. A shrill argument ensued, and the SEALs kept moving, jogging across the more lightly trav-

eled northbound lanes until they were off the pavement and
crouched in the mud beside the dark water.

"Let's hear it for keeping a low profile," Mariacher said.
Other drivers were stopping on the far side of the highway,
and the argument appeared to be growing more intense as
the traffic grew more snarled. "C'mon."

Crouching low in an attempt to stay out of the glare of
streetlights and oncoming headlights, the SEALs slogged
south along a crumbling, muddy bank. The river stank, and
the water's edge was thickly coated by scum and what
looked like laundry suds. "I don't see any no swimming
signs," Lehman quipped. "What about the gear?"

Mariacher looked up, down, and across the river, estimat-
ing angles between several landmarks—the bridge to the
south, a brightly lit red mosque to the north, a slender, blue-
lit spire to the southwest. "We ditch the stuff here," he said.
"In the water."

"Roger that." A large, concrete culvert opened just above
the water, and they hid the radio gear and Barrett .50 in the
mud and litter of plastic and bottles just beneath the outflow.
The cases all were watertight, and Diamond and his people
could recover them later, using a metal detector if they had
to. Even SEALs would have trouble swimming with a
seventeen-pound radio on their backs.

They'd keep their M-biters, though, and their SIG Sauers.
There was no telling what else the night might have in store
for them.

Backpacks and suitcases well-hidden, they began wading
out into the river. Mariacher pointed at the bridge. "If we get
separated, we meet up there, under the bridge, on the west
bank."

Lehman nodded. "Right. Uh . . . I think they're looking
for us, Wheel."

The traffic altercation on the Sultan Mohammed boulevard was still going strong. Flashing blue lights and the two-tone wail of sirens showed the police were arriving, or would be soon. Traffic was bottlenecked enough now that even police cars were having trouble getting through.

But then Mariacher saw movement silhouetted against the light of stalled traffic. It looked like a man—no, two men—moving along the side of the highway above the water.

They might be police, though they weren't in uniform. And they might be the taxi driver and a friend, hunting for the cause of all the commotion.

But it was also possible that they were being hunted by friends of those gunmen back at the Asian Star Hotel.

Whoever they were, they hadn't spotted the SEALs, not yet. After a few more yards, the muddy bottom dropped away and they began swimming, moving slowly to avoid attracting attention, using a side crawl to keep their heads just above the noisome water.

SEAL training, of course, was aimed at making the BUD/S recruits comfortable with the water, *any* water. Ever since Vietnam, SEALs had learned that when they found themselves in a tight spot, the way out led to the water. A man could all but disappear in the water, and very few pursuers would try to come in and get them. Training evolutions popularly called "drown-proofing," which involved tying a recruit's hands behind his back and having him do things in a deep-water tank like retrieve a swim mask, soon dispelled any fear the tadpole might have of the water. Later evolutions in SEAL school were carried out in the thickest, blackest, most stinking, most unpleasant mud the SEAL instructors could find.

Well, *almost* the most unpleasant. Earlier in Team history, SEAL recruits had had to muck their way through the Tijuana River, which, according to scuttlebutt, was literally an open sewer. Enough tadpoles had come down with dysentery and other unpleasantnesses that the powers-that-were had found healthier stinks to play in—the mudflats behind the SEAL training center along San Diego Bay.

The point was that SEALs lost all hesitation about swimming in sewage very early in their training. It was a job skill that had saved quite a few lives over the years . . . including, Mariacher reflected, the life of his father.

And now, quite possibly, his own life as well.

He reached the middle of the river and floated for a while, letting the current do most of the work. The water was midnight black, though it tended to reflect the dazzle of city lights from both banks. The SEALs had the advantage here. While it was possible that someone looking for them from the riverbank would see their heads against a reflection, as long as they each kept one ear in the water they wouldn't look particularly like human heads. Seen in silhouette, they appeared no different than any of dozens of logs or garbage or lumps of less identifiable flotsam drifting with the sluggish current.

Better still, any gunmen searching for them along the bank would have piss-poor night vision by now, with their eyes constantly blasted by city lights and the headlights of oncoming traffic.

Mariacher took another long look at the east bank of the river. He couldn't see . . . no, there. Three human figures, silhouetted against the marquee of a theater. One was holding something to his ear—a cell phone, possibly, or a radio. If the three were looking for them, they didn't appear to have spotted them yet. It looked as though they were searching the mud along the bank, not the water itself.

He caught Lehman's glance and signaled, two fingers toward his eyes, then pointed at the east bank. He brought his forefingers together, then split them apart, and Lehman nodded. They would let themselves drift apart, with the idea that two widely separated random lumps of flotsam drifting in the river didn't attract the eye as well as two pieces of flotsam of the same size drifting close together. They moved slowly, though, trying as much as possible to look like floating garbage. Even if the men on shore weren't watching the river itself, movement or a splash against the reflection of city lights would easily snag their attention.

Most of the light was behind them, however, in the glare of the business and nightlife districts. The two SEALs were approaching the Jalan Kinabalu Bridge, which put them south of Chinatown, and the neighborhoods on both sides were beginning to look considerably less prosperous than the brightly lit sections to the north and northwest.

In the 1860s a group of Chinese miners prospecting for tin had hacked a malaria-infested clearing out of the middle of the Malaysian jungle at the confluence of the Kelang and the Gombek Rivers. They named the shantytown that sprang up along the banks Kuala Lumpur, meaning "Muddy River Mouth."

Thirty years later the shantytown had boom-timed into the capital of the Federated Malay States, and now the city of Muddy River Mouth was considered one of the economic miracles of Southeast Asia.

Economic miracle or not, though, Kuala Lumpur shared with all cities the sharp dichotomy between the very rich and the very poor. While the wealthy districts to the north—City Center, the Golden Triangle, and Millionaires Row along Jalan Ampang—all ostentatiously displayed their affluence, outlaying parts of the city were considerably less prosperous. To the SEALs that meant less light, less chance of being spotted.

Mariacher had to look up now in order to see the traffic on the Kinabalu Bridge. Time to start thinking about getting some dry ground underfoot. The shadows under the bridge pylons were impenetrably black. They would be able to take stock of their situation there.

He shifted to a breaststroke, swimming a little harder,

working his way crabwise out of the river's central current and closer to the west bank. He couldn't see Lehman now. He couldn't see the men on the east bank now either.

Maybe they'd won clear.

But they would still have to be cautious. They weren't out of the woods—or, in this case, the river—yet.

Wednesday, September 19, 2001

Headquarters
Naval Special Warfare Command,
Coronado, California
0705 hours, PDT

His dissertation on the news headlines of the past week complete, Dickinson turned to indicate one of the civilians at the table. "Mr. Kuhlman, of the Defense Intelligence Agency, has a few words about the enemy. Mr. Kuhlman?"

DIA? David had assumed the suits were *C*IA.

The Defense Intelligence Agency employed civilians as well as military personnel. Technically, they reported to the Secretary of Defense, though on the organizational table they came under the Director of Central Intelligence, currently George Tenet, the same guy who ran the CIA.

Dickinson stepped back from the podium, but the DIA suit remained at his place at the table as he began to speak. "Gentlemen, by this time you've all heard more about bin Laden than you'd care to, except, possibly, for news that we got him. We've been after that son of a bitch since long before 9/11."

True enough. Osama bin Laden—his given name was sometimes spelled Usama, and military sources frequently used the abbreviation UBL to identify him in reports—was a figure well known to the SEALs. He'd been *the* most wanted terrorist in the world for several years now.

"But for those of you who came in late, the man is a Saudi national," Kuhlman went on. "He's the seventeenth child of some fifty to fifty-three children—the exact number of siblings is uncertain—in a family that runs the Bin Laden Group, a consortium of the largest construction companies in the Arab world. The bin Ladens, based in Jidda, Saudi Arabia, made their fortune on building projects carried out for the Saudi royal family. We estimate Osama bin Laden's current personal fortune at something in excess of $250 million.

"Bin Laden's support of terrorism started in 1984, when he moved from Saudi Arabia to Pakistan to help Abdullah Azzam. Azzam was the founder of the Office of Services, which was establishing training camps along the Afghan border in order to support their mujahideen brothers in their fight against the Soviet invaders of that country. Bin Laden used part of his fortune to help recruit Muslim volunteers worldwide for the war against the Soviets. Two years later he established his own training camp for Persian Gulf Arabs, which he called Al Masadah, the Lion's Den.

"In 1988, bin Laden's ambitions turned global. Bin Laden and an opium trafficker, warlord, and future prime minister of Afghanistan named Gulbuddin Hekmatyar, together and, ah, with CIA help and money, I might add, founded a group called al-Qaeda, which is Arabic for 'the Base.' They did so secretly, through Pakistan's ISI."

David blinked. He hadn't known that before, though it made sense in a sick and twisty kind of way. During the Soviet invasion of Afghanistan, from 1979 through 1989, the CIA had been heavily involved in covertly supporting the mujahideen, both within Afghanistan and in Pakistan, along the rugged Afghan border, where hundreds of refugee camps provided both cover and recruitment opportunities for the anti-Soviet guerrillas. The Inter-Service Intelligence was Pakistan's equivalent of the CIA, and the Agency had relied on them heavily for channeling money and arms—especially Stinger missile launchers for use against Soviet helicopters—to the Afghan resistance.

"In 1989, when the Russians finally withdrew from Afghanistan, bin Laden returned to Saudi Arabia, where he took up duties within the family business. The following year Iraq invaded Kuwait, and U.S. military personnel began arriving in Saudi Arabia. Reportedly, he was outraged that the House of Saud would permit such a desecration of holy ground. In 1991, when a militant Islamic government came to power in Sudan, he moved al-Qaeda's headquarters to that country.

"After that, things began to move quickly. In 1993 a truck bomb exploded beneath the World Trade Center in New York City, killing six and injuring a thousand people. The mastermind of that attack was Ramzi Yousef, a Kuwaiti revolutionary financed by Iraqi intelligence . . . and by al-Qaeda. There is at least some evidence that there were chemical agents inside the van that was used to carry out the attack. Fortunately, that part of the bomb didn't work. If it had, casualties conceivably would have been much, much higher. Al-Qaeda was strongly implicated in the attack, as was the Office of Services, but no charges were made at that point.

"In September of 1993, during Operation Restore Hope, Somali militiamen trained by al-Qaeda at their camps in the Sudan shot down an American helicopter. They killed eighteen U.S. Army Rangers in the battle that followed, and dragged the mutilated bodies of several Americans through the streets. The incident, which received a lot of play in the media, led directly to the withdrawal of U.S. forces from Somalia.

"In 1994, the Saudi government disowned bin Laden and he was forced to flee the country, to the Sudan. His own family publicly disavowed him, but that didn't even slow him down. In November of 1995 a car bomb exploded in Riyadh, Saudi Arabia, killing seven, five of them Americans. Seven months later a truck packed with two and a half tons of TNT went off in Dharan, Saudi Arabia. The blast killed nineteen American servicemen. Al-Queda was implicated in both attacks. A fatwa issued by bin Laden in September of 1996 called for jihad against all Americans, in retaliation for their 'occupation' of Saudi Arabia. That same year, diplomatic pressure by the U.S. against the Sudan forced him to leave town again.

"In 1998, truck bombs were set off simultaneously in front of the U.S. embassies in Kenya and in Tanzania. Hundreds died, most of them Kenyan civilians on the crowded streets of Nairobi. Again bin Laden was implicated, this time through an organization funded and organized by al-Qaeda, the World Islamic Front.

"In that year, bin Laden moved to Afghanistan, where the Taliban was busy trying to consolidate their hold on that country. They'd taken over in a coup in 'ninety-six, and they owed bin Laden big-time, for financing and for military assistance. There, he started what he called the International Front for Jihad against Jews and Crusaders. It's a kind of umbrella organization for al-Qaeda and all of bin Laden's other international militant groups. The Front for Jihad promptly issued another fatwa, saying it is the religious duty of Muslims to kill Americans—*any* Americans—wherever they can be found.

"In 1999, bin Laden moved to a village called Farmifadda, in Afghanistan, and later to a heavily defended compound outside of Jalalabad. Attempts to infiltrate agents failed. We were able to keep tabs on him, though, through signals intelligence and satellite reconnaissance."

Signals intelligence meant the National Security Agency, that highly secret branch of the U.S. intelligence community that, among other things, eavesdropped on America's enemies through every means from wiretaps to satellites. Bin Laden reportedly used cell phones for many of his activities, and those calls could easily be intercepted from space.

The question, David thought, was why all of that technology hadn't already nailed the bastard.

"In 2000," Kuhlman continued, "the USS *Cole,* a U.S. guided-missile destroyer, was attacked by suicide bombers while docked in the port of Aden, in Yemen. The blast tore a forty-foot hole in the ship's side and nearly sank her. Seventeen American sailors died, and thirty-nine were wounded. Once again, American intelligence had evidence that bin Laden and al-Qaeda were behind the attack.

"Bin Laden and al-Qaeda are now both under the protection of the Taliban, the Wahhabi extremist fundamentalist government that now controls about ninety percent of Afghanistan. The Taliban leaders have repeatedly rejected requests that they turn bin Laden over for prosecution or expel him from the country, claiming that they couldn't possibly think of surrendering a *guest* who is enjoying their hospitality. Clearly, the Taliban has cast their lot in with bin Laden.

"Al-Qaeda remains a deadly organization, well-financed, well-equipped, and absolutely dedicated to attacking U.S. citizens and interests worldwide. Our best estimates are that al-Qaeda now numbers some five thousand trained fighting men, with cells operating in at least fifty countries, including the United States. They have two principle goals. The first is bringing in militants from all over the world and molding them into an international army, with the intent of killing Americans and Jews wherever they can be found, in accordance with bin Laden's fatwa. Their second goal is even more ambitious. They want to use that army to bring *all* Muslims under a single fundamentalist and militant version of the *sharia*, Islamic law.

"At this time, bin Laden and the headquarters of al-Qaeda both remain in Afghanistan, enjoying the, ah, hospitality of the Taliban. We believe they are still in a heavily guarded compound on the outskirts of the city of Jalalabad, close to the Pakistan border. Our best intelligence says that bin Laden is constantly surrounded by about two hundred guards and retainers, all Saudi.

"I don't need to tell you, gentlemen, we want this bastard. Dead or alive, but we *want* him. And that's why the DOD is looking at the possibility of a special covert op to go into Afghanistan and locate bin Laden. Ideally, we grab him and have him on a military flight back to the United States before he knows what hit him. At the very least, we confirm where he is, and our people on the ground zap him with a laser so we can get him with a smart bomb."

Smart bombs, David thought wryly, had been all the rage since the Gulf War, when CNN coverage had been filled with bomb's-eye footage as the things had flown into ventilator shafts, hangar doors, and windows with eerie precision. Most such weapons were "smart" by virtue of a tracking device in their nose that picked up the reflected radiation from an infrared targeting laser being aimed at the target either by troops on the ground or from an aircraft, and used computer-guided stabilizer controls to steer the bomb as it fell. SEALs, with most other members of the military special operations community, received extensive training and practice with the hardware used to lase targets for incoming ordnance.

Still, even the smartest bomb was less flexible, less adaptable, and far less dangerous than an assault by a small and well-trained unit of SEALs.

"Alfa Platoon of SEAL Team Three has been tasked," Kuhlman went on, "to form a special operations strike force, together with Marine elements of 1st Force Recon. This strike force, which will be code-named Task Force Osprey, will be inserted into southern Afghanistan in advance of overt military operations by the U.S. armed services in that country. They will find bin Laden and either extract him or arrange to have him neutralized. Commander Dickinson?"

"Thank you, Mr. Kuhlman. Questions, gentlemen?" Dickinson asked.

Fred Driscoll raised his hand.

"Lieutenant?"

"I just want to see if I understand this, sir," Driscoll said in his easy Texan drawl. "We've just been told that we're going to war with the Taliban and anyone else who harbors terrorists. Now you're telling us that Alfa is going in specifically to get bin Laden. If we can get the SOB with a covert op, why go to war at all?"

"Fair question. Here's a fair answer: We want bin Laden because he's a rallying point for militant Islamic extremists worldwide. We want him so we can make the point that people can't knock down our skyscrapers and kill our people without some very serious payback. It's been pointed out that killing him would just make him a martyr. Well, frankly, we would much rather have him be dead a martyr than a live terrorist. So long as he is alive and free, it looks like the United States is helpless, unable to protect herself or her citizens. Bin Laden is a symbol, and an important one.

"But bin Laden is *only* a symbol. The organization he heads could carry on without him. It's got extensive financial resources of its own now, quite apart from bin Laden's personal fortune. It has an army, five thousand strong. It has a navy estimated at twenty vessels—cargo ships and large yachts, mostly. It has an incredibly tangled network of front organizations, dummy corporations, and false fronts behind which they carry out their recruitment efforts, fund-raising, and military operations across the globe.

"In the coming months, we are going to pull al-Qaeda down. We will freeze their financial assets, seize their ships and equipment, kill or capture their leaders, and put an end to the threat of al-Qaeda permanently.

"At the moment, the majority of al-Qaeda's army and their leadership is in Afghanistan, and we are going in to destroy both. If the Taliban puts itself between us and bin Laden, we will go through them to get him."

"By *we*," Fletch said quietly at David's side, "I think he means *us*."

"You don't think the spooks would be doing their own fighting, now, do you?" David whispered back. "That would be unnatural! Anyway, this is one op I wouldn't miss for the world."

"You're nuts!"

"Hey, I wouldn't be a SEAL if I wasn't!"

He was excited. Damn, this was what all the training and constant practice was all about! This was a chance for the Teams to do what they did best. America was at war, and it was a war that would not be won by smart bombs, satellite reconnaissance, massed air power, or tank divisions. But a small, dedicated, and highly trained unit like the SEALs could go places where tanks could not, execute a surgically precise strike, and *make a difference*.

Thursday, September 20, 2001

Along the Kelang River
Kuala Lumpur
2212 hours, local time

Dripping, Mariacher crawled out of the river and onto the muddy embankment beneath the massive concrete pylon of the bridge. Ahead, a shadow moved, and he froze, reaching behind his back with a hand for his SIG Sauer.

A voice blurred by alcohol or other chemicals called unintelligibly from the darkness. Another shadow appeared, staggering beneath the shelter of the bridge.

Street people. Drunks or dope addicts. As his eyes adjusted, he could make out perhaps a dozen of them. An elderly Malay man with missing teeth swigged from a large bottle. Nearby, a younger man tugged the rubber tourniquet from his arm and let an empty syringe drop in the mud. Another man coughed, the sound rasping and tubercular. As Mariacher emerged from the water, they watched him, some with suspicion, some with dull disinterest.

This, he reflected, was the darker underside of the economic miracle. Malaysia might be an Islamic state, meaning that alcohol and hard drugs were forbidden, but Islamic law couldn't compete with poverty or the need for temporary oblivion.

The man with missing teeth lurched unsteadily toward him, one hand out, palm up, mumbling something in Melayu.

"Tidak!" Mariacher said, his voice sharp. He didn't speak the Malay language, but he had memorized a few words and phrases ahead of time—"Yes," "No," the all-important "Please" and "Thank you." The man blinked at him, evidently digesting the word "No."

Mariacher's hand was on his holstered pistol, but he decided not to draw the weapon. Doing so would definitely cause a stir, and he still hoped to keep things quiet and low-key.

A moment later Lehman crawled out of the water. He looked at the watching homeless. "Friends of yours?"

He ignored the gibe. "Let's move."

The two SEALs backed away from the small crowd. One of them called something out in Melayu. Mariacher shook his head and again said, *"Tidak."*

The crime rate in Malaysia was actually quite low, among the lowest in all of southeast Asia, in fact. The worst crime most Western tourists faced was the occasional purse snatching from the back of a motor scooter or the theft of wallet or cell phone. He doubted that they had anything to fear from these people, but he wasn't going to turn his back on them either. The shoes and clothes the two SEALs wore were valuable enough; the radios and weapons represented a small fortune to people this far down on Malaysia's social ladder.

"If we're being followed, Wheel," Lehman warned softly, "this bunch could finger us."

"Then let's get as far away from here as we can, right?"

"Affirmative."

At the moment, Mariacher didn't even know if they *were* being followed. Those figures on the east bank of the Kelang a few minutes ago might have just been irate motorists looking for the big foreigners who'd caused the traffic jam.

But he wasn't going to make any assumptions along those lines. *Someone* had spotted the surveillance of Mohammed, and been concerned enough to send in that hit squad. If that unknown someone was that determined to neutralize them, they might be determined enough to hunt them down no matter what it took.

They needed to get to the Brickfield safe house as quickly as possible.

"Oh, *shit!*" Lehman said.

"What's the matter?"

"Will you look at where we are?"

Mariacher had been backing up the embankment next to the bridge, keeping his eye on the crowd of vagrants behind them as Lehman led the way up the slope. He turned now and his eyes widened.

"Oh, *shit!*" he said.

Lehman nodded. "Exactly."

Chapter 4

Thursday, September 20, 2001

West Bank of the Kelang River
Kuala Lumpur
2218 hours, local time

Mariacher had seen the tower before from the other side of
the river—tall, slender, and with blue lights running in a
straight line up the side. He hadn't realized what he was
looking at. From this vantage point, however, just across another city boulevard, they had a clear view of the entire complex, nestled away inside of five acres or so of parkland,
diagonally opposite Kuala Lumpur's train station and just
across the street from the Heritage Station Hotel. The spire
rose alongside a large, flat dome with a pleated surface,
looking much like the top of a huge umbrella.

He'd seen photographs of the place during his prep work
for this mission. The complex was the Masjid Negara, the
National Mosque of Malaya. The architecture was modern
and impressive. Those pleats radiating from the center of the
dome formed an eighteen-pointed star, representing the thirteen states of the Malaysian Federation plus the five pillars

of Islam. The dome, which covered the prayer hall, and the tower next to it, which was the minaret from which the faithful were called to prayer five times each day, stood in sharp contrast to the more traditional onion-dome mosques elsewhere in the city.

Brickfield and the CIA safe house were located south of there, between the Jalan Damasara and the railroad tracks. He had been aware that the National Mosque was in this area but hadn't realized it was quite this close. There were people on the street, *lots* of people, many of them in turbans, a few wearing the Saudi *ghutra*. Even this late at night, the mosque appeared to be quite busy, with people coming and going. A train had just arrived, and lots of people, many with suitcases, were on the street.

"Just our luck," Lehman growled. "We come out at raghead central."

"Belay that 'raghead' crap," Mariacher told him. "Most of them are good, decent people. Same as just plain folks anywhere."

"Yeah, but with a very small and very vocal minority that want us dead. You don't run into that with just-plain-folks in St. John, Kansas. Not usually, anyway."

Mariacher let the comment slide. This was hardly the time or place for political correctness lectures.

Still, there was a tendency to paint all Muslims in the colors of those extremist few, like bin Laden or Khalid Shaikh Mohammed, who'd declared war on the United States in particular and on Western civilization in general. It was one of the many tragedies of the war, a polarization that created extremists on *both* sides.

"So how do we get past them?" Lehman wanted to know.

Mariacher considered the problem. They'd both studied maps of Kuala Lumpur before the mission, back in Virginia Beach, and again at the U.S. Embassy here in Malaysia.

They'd learned the locations of four CIA safe houses within the city, rendezvous points Oscar, Papa, Quebec, and Romeo, and escape routes from the Asian Star to each of them.

The memorized route to the Brickfield safe house was across the Jalan Istana Bridge, half a kilometer south of the Kinabalu Bridge. If they'd gone that way, they would have come out close to the south end of the train station and well clear of the National Mosque.

Here, though, they had only two choices. They could go back to the river and swim another half klick to the next bridge, or they could play the part of innocent—if waterlogged—tourists and stroll south past the mosque grounds. If he remembered correctly, immediately south of the National Mosque grounds lay the Islamic Center, and south of *that* the Kuala Lumpur Visitors Center, both directly across the Jalan Damasara from the railway station.

Mariacher turned some other options over in his mind. The other three safe houses were scattered all over the city. The nearest, other than Quebec, was Papa, and that was a good three miles north. The Brickfield safe house was less than half a mile to the south.

They could try to catch a taxi . . . but he doubted that even if they were able to flag one at this hour, the driver would take them on. There was also a hotel here—the embankment had dropped them beside the parking lot of the Heritage Station Hotel—and they might try to go to ground there. The place looked pretty upscale, though, and two westerners soaked to the bone and smelling of raw sewage would not be welcome in the lobby. In any case, the fewer chances they took with locals, whether cabbies or desk clerks, the better.

And there would be friendlies waiting at Point Quebec to take them in and hide them. And fresh clothing. And *showers*.

"We split up," Mariacher said after a long moment. "If

they're looking for us, they're looking for two Americans together. We'll be less conspicuous separately."

"With twice the chance of being spotted, sir."

"And twice the chance of one of us making it back. You
game?"

"Affirmative, sir. It's just . . . the buddy system, y'know?"

BUD/S training hammered into recruits the gospel that
SEALs stuck together, supported one another, and never,
ever left a buddy behind.

"We'll still use the buddy system. I'll go first and take
point. You let me get out ahead, oh, fifty meters or so, and
then follow. You keep an eye on me. I'll keep glancing back
to make sure you're still with me."

Lehman nodded. "Sounds good, sir."

"We walk casual." He nodded toward the brightly illuminated park across the boulevard and the blue-lit minaret.
We're *tourists,* got it? We have a perfect right to be here. We
just don't get close enough to anybody else to let them *smell*
us, right?"

"That *would* raise a stink," Lehman quipped.

Mariacher groaned. "Ahh . . . right. I'll see you at Point
Quebec." He glanced left and right, then stood up and strolled
into the hotel parking lot.

Wednesday, September 19, 2001

Headquarters
Naval Special Warfare Command,
Coronado, California
0720 hours, PDT

David Tangretti yawned. He hadn't gotten much sleep last
night, and when the briefing officer ordered the lights switched
off, it started to feel exactly like attending a slide lecture in

high school, trapped in a boring class first thing after lunch and having been at a late party the night before. The briefing room was in the NSWC headquarters basement; they couldn't even open a window.

Besides, damn it, he *knew* this stuff. The SEALs had been studying these people for years now.

Commander Dickinson had ordered the briefing room's lights out and was now working a laptop computer on the podium, which controlled the photographs projected onto a large movie screen on the wall. At the moment, a grainy, much enlarged newspaper photo of a thin man in a turban and a heavy black beard was on the screen, his face high-lighted to separate him from a number of other turbaned men. A second, smaller photo was inset at the lower left. This one was black and white, and enlarged so much you could see the half-tone dots.

"This one is a real sweetheart," Dickinson was saying. "He's a hermit. We think these may be the only two photos we have of the man. He is Mullah Mohammed Omar, and he is the emir of Afghanistan, the head of the Taliban movement . . . in effect the ruler of the country, though he never leaves Kandahar, and may never have even been to Kabul. His official title is 'Amir-ul Momineen,' Commander of the Faithful. He was a hero of the war against the Soviets. He fought with the Harajat-I Inqilab-I Islami faction of the mujahideen. Reportedly, he was wounded by shrapnel in one eye.

"He has been extremely reclusive. He refuses to meet with westerners, or with the media. We actually know very little about him. We think that he may have close family ties with bin Laden. Supposedly, they like to go fishing together. There are reports that Omar married bin Laden's oldest daughter, and that bin Laden took one of Omar's daughters as his fourth wife. The Taliban has consistently denied this, however."

The photo changed to show a view of dry desert terrain

from the air, looking down on a large, walled compound with a number of buildings.

"Reportedly," Dickinson said, "our friend Omar spends most of his time here, in a facility specially built for him by bin Laden outside of the city of Kandahar. From here, Omar issues the orders that govern the country, and he stays in daily touch with bin Laden, by cell phone."

Interesting, David thought. The NSA must have a whole warehouse full of taped recordings of this guy's phone conversations.

"Omar and bin Laden are tight," Dickinson went on. "Very, *very* tight. The two men fought the Soviets together. Bin Laden's fortune helped put the Taliban in power.

"They share completely a particular interpretation of the *sharia,* which is the body of Islamic law, derived from the Qu'ran. Since the Taliban came to power, in 1996, they've gone way, way beyond what most Qu'ranic scholars consider necessary to obey God's law. More on *that* later."

Another photo came up on the screen, a man with a long, sad face and a shorter beard than Omar's. "This is Mohammed Rabbani. Don't confuse him with Burhanuddin Rabbani, who is the former president of Afghanistan and a member of the anti-Taliban Islamic Unity Party, which means he's one of the good guys. *This* Rabbani is the Taliban's second-in-command, under Omar. He's considerably more moderate than Omar, but we believe Omar has been sidelining him consistently in matters of policy. We also believe that he has been urging Omar to surrender bin Laden and reach an agreement with the United States. Omar, however, will not hear of surrendering his old fishing buddy."

Other faces appeared on the screen, one at a time, as the briefing officer ran through a kind of rogue's gallery of Taliban leaders—Abdul Wakil Motawakil, the Minister of Foreign Affairs; Ubaidullah Akhund, the Minister of Defense; Abdul Razaq, the Minister of Interior Affairs.

One bearded face and description particularly caught David's attention, however. "This is Qari Ahmadullah," Dickinson said, "head of the Taliban's secret police. The group is currently called the National Security Directorate, the *Amaniyat* to locals. It is, in fact, a continuation of the KHAD, the secret police agency set up by the Soviets when they controlled the country. Reportedly, the top leaders have been changed, but the rest of the agency is exactly the same, even down to the personnel, as it was in the eighties under the DRA. Reportedly, they still use the same techniques— kidnapping and torture—to root out threats to the regime."

The faces, the litany of names, went on. Ministers and deputy ministers. The governors of Kabul Province, Nangrahar Province, and Heart Province. The mayors of several cities.

The computer-projected slide show shut off and the room lights came up.

"So, what's the point of this rogues' gallery?" Dickinson rhetorically asked the audience. "To make the point that the Taliban are thugs, pure and simple. They have very little support worldwide, even among Islamic states. Saudi Arabia and the Gulf States support them . . . and Pakistan, which put them in power in the first place.

"They are uneducated, for the most part, except in the Qu'ran, which they claim is all they need to know to run the country. The rulers are religious leaders with no formal training, and no understanding of how government works. Their mismanagement has resulted in the starvation or exodus of tens of thousands of their countrymen.

"They belong to the Deobandi movement, a Sunni Islam sect emphasizing piety, austerity, and the family obligations of men. As extremist Sunnis, they hate Shi'ite Muslims almost as much as they hate Christians, maybe more. They've been committing genocide on the Hazara, a Shi'ite tribe on the central plains. Of course, they've been committing genocide on just about anyone who doesn't agree with them.

"Most of the Taliban leaders are Pashtun. That's the major ethnic group in the country, which comprises at least seven tribes and forty-two percent of the population.

"The Pashtun, by the way, are the largest tribal group left on earth. The border between Afghanistan and Pakistan goes smack through the middle of the traditional tribal territories. Needless to say, the Pashtun don't pay a lot of attention to borders. They don't think that way.

"At this time, only three nations have recognized the Taliban as the legitimate rulers of Afghanistan—Saudi Arabia, the United Arab Emirates, and Pakistan. Their biggest supporter until now has been Pakistan. Back in the eighties, Pakistan was feeling more and more isolated, with India—their longtime enemy—to the south, and a communist Afghanistan with Soviet troops to the north. Pakistan's president, Zia al-Haq, was an international pariah because he'd come to power in a coup and hung his predecessor. He began making overtures to the CIA, and before long he was actively supporting the mujahideen and their war against the Soviet invaders.

"Pakistan had hoped to control Afghanistan through their Taliban clients, but the Taliban leadership has proven to be erratic, unpredictable, and dangerous, to the point that even Pakistan is beginning to reconsider their support of the regime. The Taliban has been promoting jihad among the former Soviet states in southwestern Asia, and Afghanistan is the only country to recognize Chechnyan independence. That has provoked Russian anger toward Pakistan for supporting the Taliban. The Taliban has also been promoting jihad against the Chinese government in Xinjiang Province, which has angered Beijing. When the Taliban first came to power, they marched into the Iranian embassy and murdered a bunch of Iranian diplomats—they were Shi'ites, after all—and that angered Iran. The Taliban has been actively and openly seeking to acquire nuclear materials through sympathetic sources within former Russian territories, which has alarmed everyone in the region, as well as the United States and its allies.

"And so at this point, gentlemen, it's safe to say that the Taliban doesn't have many friends.

"Over the past five years, the United States has made no fewer than thirty distinct, formal requests to the Taliban that they turn bin Laden over to the United States for prosecution as an international terrorist. Each request was ignored, refused, or countered by an untenable counteroffer.

"And so, gentlemen, and as I said earlier, the Taliban is going down. Our principle targets remain, of course, bin Laden and al-Qaeda, but the Taliban is sheltering them, and we *are* going to dismantle the Taliban in order to get al-Qaeda.

"That concludes my portion of the briefing. Are there questions?"

"Yes, Commander," Admiral McFarland said. "Several times this morning you've mentioned Pakistani support of the Taliban. You've emphasized that this support may be eroding, but we all know that alliances don't switch off overnight. How big a problem is that going to be for us?"

"That's hard to tell at this time, sir. Officially, Pakistan has decried the 9/11 attacks and has been calling for bin Laden's surrender. In fact, they've been our main channel to the Taliban in attempts to talk with them.

"At a local level, however . . . well, we know that many members of Pakistan's ISI are ideologically committed to the Taliban. ISI agents have been working with and fighting alongside the Taliban for years. The current military leader of Pakistan, General Musharraf, is reportedly trying to rein in the ISI. The ISI's leader, however, Lieutenant General Ahmed, remains a strong Taliban supporter. It could be a problem, yes, sir. How bad a problem it's going to be, well, we just don't know yet."

"I think it's safe to say that our people on the ground will have to operate independently of the locals," McFarland said.

"Well, as far as is practical," Dickinson replied, "yes, sir. But they will *have* to have local guides, interpreters, and intelligence contacts.

"The ten percent or so of Afghanistan that is not controlled by the Taliban is run by a loose association of warlords and political groups called the Northern Alliance. Their political leader is former president Burhanuddin Rabbani, who, as I said, leads the Unity Party. However, the real Northern Alliance strength lies with their army—about fifteen thousand men. These were under the leadership of General Ahmed Shah Massoud, a former mujahideen commander, but two days before 9/11, Massoud was assassinated by al-Qaeda suicide bombers working for the Taliban. The new leader is Mohammed Fahim Khan. We don't know yet if Fahim can hold the Northern Alliance together.

"However, the Northern Alliance has a large and well-established network within Taliban-controlled territory. Our people will be able to draw on these assets to carry out their missions."

The question and answer period carried on for several more minutes, but David's mind kept turning on the whole question of intelligence. SEALs—those who were operators, at any rate, the men who actually worked out in the field—tended to be suspicious of intelligence claims made by the

CIA or any of the others in the alphabet-soup zoo of U.S. intelligence. They preferred developing their own intel sources.

From Dickinson's description of the situation, Afghanistan was a jungle of groups, spooks, tribes, ideologies, and treachery, and it was going to be a nightmare for American operators to sort out whom to trust.

Still, how tough could it be? From the sound of things, America's intelligence agencies were well on top of the situation, knew the players, and even had a good idea as to where bin Laden was hiding. It should be a simple matter to put together a plan to send in covert strike teams to simultaneously hit all of the places bin Laden might be hanging out and grab the bastard.

He smiled grimly at that thought. He was under no illusions as to the ability of the brass, the spooks, and the politicians to turn a simple operation into a class-A cluster fuck. The briefing was a case in point. The enemy, as he understood it, was al-Qaeda and Osama bin Laden, and yet most of the session had been focused squarely on the Taliban.

Okay ... the Taliban was sheltering bin Laden, wasn't playing by the rules, and consisted of annoying bastards. Dangerous, annoying bastards. But the target was bin Laden. Simple as that. Grab him, and worry about the rest later.

He had the unpleasant feeling that much of the briefing had been designed to rationalize the decision to invade Afghanistan.

Dickinson adjourned the briefing session with the promise that things would resume at 0900 hours, when they would begin covering specific plans for field ops in Afghanistan. David wondered if it would be worth trying to grab an hour's sleep before then.

Probably not.

He did step outside the SpecWar headquarters, however, with Fletch and four of the other enlisted SEALs. If sleep wasn't an option, then a cup of coffee at the mess hall across the grinder certainly was.

The morning sun was brilliant, the air warm. Thunder rolled as a flight of Navy F/A-18s carved their way through the bright September sky.

"So," Fletch said. "We're going to Afghanistan!"

"Yeah," RM2 Lawrence Karr said. "Task Force Osprey! Man, we're gonna kick some serious raghead ass!"

"Roger that!" Chief John Nolfi said. "Bin Laden's gonna learn the meaning of the word *payback.*"

"Looks that way," David said. "I wonder if we'll have to grow beards, to fit in with the locals?"

"Nah," Fletcher said. "Probably they'll drop us in and have us just sneak-and-peek. Leave the spook work to the Agency."

"Maybe," Nolfi replied, "but . . . Ah! Atten-*hut!* Attention to colors!"

The six SEALs came to a sharp halt and snapped to attention. Thirty yards away a morning colors detail was gathered at a flagpole. At 0800 hours exactly, the Star Spangled Banner blared from a loudspeaker, and the detail began hoisting the American flag. David and his companions saluted, holding the salute as the national anthem played through to the end.

The flag only went halfway up the pole, however—half-mast, for the more than three thousand Americans murdered at the World Trade Center, at the Pentagon, and aboard Flight 93.

David felt conflicting emotions, but the one that stood out most clearly was a sense of being honored. Right now, a lot of people in America wanted *revenge,* wanted to strike back at the monsters who'd slaughtered so many civilians in the name of religion.

And the Navy SEALs would be among the select few who would actually get to deliver it.

Thursday, September 20, 2001

Brickfield District
Kuala Lumpur
2239 hours, local time

Mariacher kept his pace down to an almost casual stroll. He attracted a few glances from passersby, but no one seemed excited or suspicious.

He didn't exactly fit in with the local scene, and the fact that he was still dripping wet didn't help. Most visitors to this area were here to see the National Mosque, and that meant that most were Muslim and wore conservative clothing—unlike the bright hey-I'm-a-tourist sport shirt Mariacher was currently wearing.

It was customary for Muslim visitors to a new city to go immediately to a local mosque and pray. There were facilities there for ritually washing oneself, and even beds for those who might need a place to stay. That was why the train station was so close to the Masjid Negara—a matter of convenience for Muslim visitors to the city.

But that meant there were lots of Muslims in and around the station, gathered in the park and crossing the street to the mosque. Mariacher felt out of place and unpleasantly conspicuous. What bright bulb at the CIA had decided to put the safe house for this op practically across the street from Kuala Lumpur's premier Muslim tourist attraction?

Every few moments he glanced back over his shoulder. Lehman was there, half a football field back. He was easy enough to see, even when the street was especially crowded, standing head and shoulders above the locals in his brightly colored shirt. Possibly, Mariacher thought, their prominence was a form of camouflage. They were so damned obvious they couldn't possibly be up to no good.

South past the railway station, then a left off the Jalan Brickfield, the neighborhood dropped a point or two in social status; the buildings smaller and shabbier, their facades in need of paint or repair. American zoning laws didn't apply here. Houses appeared to be mingled indiscriminately with small shops and stores—a small market, several shops selling bric-a-brac and souvenirs, all closed, with iron bars over doors and windows. There were few people here, compared to the crowds at the train station.

But he felt himself being watched. SEALs tended to develop a sixth sense about that, when they were in danger or a tight situation. He could feel a growing sense of unease, of danger, a prickling at the scalp, a growing itch to pull out his SIG Sauer and find cover.

Ah. There they were. Several Malaysian men in sleeveless T-shirts sat on a badly weathered porch, smoking cigarettes, watching him. He smiled, nodded, and gave a small wave as he walked past, looking for a reaction. Their gaze followed him, flat and empty of emotion.

Damn. How was he supposed to tell the good guys from the bad? Since the events of 9/11, *all* Muslims—for some Americans, at least—were now suspect, and Lehman's attitude, expressed back at the bridge, was not unusual among Mariacher's Teammates. On the other hand, he knew at least one SEAL who was a Muslim.

Assuming that a man was a terrorist because of his religion or culture was decidedly not an attitude Mariacher shared, but he certainly understood the temptation. In a situation such as this one, survival often required taking on just a touch of paranoia and looking at everyone he met, save for his own Teammates, as a possible enemy.

The men on the porch watched him pass but made no hostile move. Ahead, twenty yards down the street, he could see another house, another weathered porch, but recognized details of the windows and door from photos he'd studied at the embassy.

It was Point Quebec, the Brickfield safe house.

He was on the south, left side of the street, which meant he was walking with the traffic. A battered white panel truck came up behind him, tires squealing, then lurched to a halt as the back and side doors banged open. Four men jumped out, while a fifth sat at the wheel.

Unlike the gunmen at the hotel, these attackers were unmasked. They appeared to be Malaysian, and quite young, probably in their early twenties. Two waved handguns like John Wayne wannabes, while the other two wielded short, heavy truncheons resembling billy clubs.

After the gunman with AK-47s at the hotel, this seemed almost ridiculously easy. SEALs are well-trained in hand-to-hand combat, particularly in the Korean martial art form known as hwarang-do. A kid with a Browning Hi-power reached for his arm; Mariacher grabbed his wrist and fell backward, moving with the attacker's movement, pivoting, striking hard behind the ear as the gunman fell past.

Releasing the falling man's wrist, he continued the pivot, slamming his elbow into the throat of the next thug, who was crowding in close with an upraised club. Twisting, he rolled clear. The second gunman was holding a revolver two-handed, trying to get a clear shot, but the other club wielder was in the way.

Hwarang-do emphasized the balanced play between *um*

and *yand*—the Korean equivalents of the Chinese yin and yang—one moment using one's opponent's own movement and force against him, as in jujitsu, the next striking hard and with deadly precision, as in various schools of karate. Mariacher turned his pivot into a roundhouse kick that connected squarely with the club wielder's chest and sent the kid stumbling back into the gunman. They collided and the two went down in a struggling tangle. Mariacher stepped across, turned, reached down, and snapped the gunman's wrist.

The first gunman was just rolling onto his back, reaching for his Hi-power, which he'd dropped, and trying to get a clear shot. This was no time for an exhibition of martial arts prowess or for fair play. Mariacher reached up behind his back, drew his SIG Sauer in a swift, fluid motion and put two rounds into the man, one through his throat, the second into his skull.

As the twin cracks from his pistol echoed across the neighborhood, the driver in the truck floored the accelerator and peeled out, tires shrilling. One of Mariacher's opponents was trying to get to his feet, and he snapped a hard kick into the side of his head, sending him sprawling out into the street.

Lehman ran up a moment later, gun in hand, but the fight was already over. One the would-be abductors was dead. Of the other three, one was unconscious; one rolling on the ground clutching his throat, trying to breathe through a crushed trachea; and the third sat on the sidewalk, cradling his wrist and screaming.

Lehman surveyed the carnage. "Can't leave you alone for a minute, can I, sir?"

"Watch for shooters," Mariacher said. He turned, scanning their surroundings. A well-organized attack would have backup somewhere, possibly a sniper, possibly more gunmen. Where? *Where?*

But he didn't see any other attackers. Twenty yards away, however, the men he'd seen smoking on the porch had stood up and were watching. Then one began applauding, followed a moment later by the rest, and then they were cheering. Mariacher wasn't sure what to make of that. Either the attack represented a welcome bit of diverting entertainment in this neighborhood, or they didn't like tough kids trying to abduct foreigners around here.

He decided it must be the latter. The attack clearly had been an attempted kidnapping rather than a hit. Otherwise they would have just opened up on him with automatic weapons from inside the truck. Malaysia had few kidnappings these days, political or otherwise, but the neighbors would be assuming they'd just seen an abduction thwarted by the victim.

Two men came out of the safe house, a Malay and a westerner, looking singularly obvious and out of place in a sport coat and tie. "Get inside!" the westerner snapped. He sounded angry. "So much for a low fucking profile!"

Mariacher picked up one of the pistols dropped in the street, while Lehman grabbed the other. "I didn't have much choice in the matter," he replied.

"At least we have someone to question," Lehman pointed out.

Several more Malaysians appeared from the safe house and began dragging the abductors, alive and dead, into the house. One walked down the street to have a word with the neighbors. Mariacher and Lehman, after a last look around, went up the steps into the house.

For a safe house, Mariacher thought, it somehow didn't feel all that safe.

Chapter 5

Brickfield District
Kuala Lumpur
2245 hours, local time

The tango with the crushed windpipe was choking. His face was blue, his movements weak and uncoordinated. He lay full-length on the entryway floor alongside his dead or unconscious friends, knees drawn up to his chest, hands clutching at his throat.

"What the hell were you thinking of, mister?" the man yelled, seconds after they were through the front door. "Brawling on the doorstep! This is supposed to be a safe house, damn it! Not a combat zone!"

"You might want to talk to these guys about that," Mariacher replied, kneeling next to the choking man. "You have a knife on you?"

The man blinked, uncomprehending. "A knife? Why?"

"Because this tango is going to choke to death in another minute or two if you don't get me one!" Mariacher snapped. "Now move it!"

One of the Malaysian kids handed him a folding pocketknife. Opening the blade, Mariacher found a spot on the injured man's throat two fingers below the shattered hyoid bone and punched the knife through the trachea. Turning the blade sideways, he opened the cut wide. At once, the tango sucked in a deep breath.

"I need a tube of some sort," Mariacher said. "PVC would be great, if you have it. No more than an inch or so in diameter."

"A tube? What for?"

"I'm trying to save this tango's life, damn it!"

"Hey . . . are you a doctor?"

"No, but I play one on TV," Mariacher replied, parodying a line from an American television commercial. "Now will you go and— Ah! Thank you."

The Malaysian who'd given him the knife had vanished, then returned with a white plastic box marked with a large green crescent—the equivalent, in Muslim countries, of the red cross. The box held an emergency surgery kit and included a length of translucent soft plastic tubing and a roll of white surgical tape.

The incision was bleeding—not heavily, but enough to threaten to fill the opening and drown the wounded man. Mariacher slipped the end of the tube into the hole past the blade of the knife, withdrew the knife, then swiftly taped the tube in place. The injured man lay quietly now, conscious, his eyes wide as he watched Mariacher's face. His face was returning to its natural color.

"Looks like he's gonna make it," Lehman said.

"Oh, yeah. He'll be up and around in no time," Mariacher said. "In fact, you'd better get cuffs on him. Looks like he's recovering pretty fast."

"Slick work."

"I know a couple of SEAL medical corpsmen back in the States," Mariacher said. "If any of them were here, they'd probably criticize my technique. But hey, it's good enough for government work."

The wounded man, his eyes still locked on Mariacher's face, reached up suddenly. Mariacher started to brace for a block . . . but the guy only gripped Mariacher's hand tightly, clinging to him for a moment in what looked like a rush of intense emotion—*gratitude*.

"Looks like you have a new friend, there," the westerner said.

"Yeah, but we're still going to cuff him."

The man tried to say something but all that came out was a rasping gurgle. "Take it easy there, guy," Mariacher said, squeezing the man's hand in return. "You'll be okay."

"Will he be able to talk?"

"Depends on how badly I smashed up his voice box," Mariacher replied. "But I imagine so, eventually. He needs to get to a hospital, though. He needs a doctor."

The Malaysian kid returned with a handful of plastic zip ties and began using them to bind the prisoner's hands behind his back. The tango rolled on his side and offered his wrists, without even an attempt at struggling. Al-Qaeda was known for its use of fighters willing to commit suicide to carry out their missions. This one, however, didn't seem interested in becoming a martyr.

Mariacher, meanwhile, checked the other two prisoners. One was still out cold, but the other sat against the wall, cradling his broken wrist and whimpering. After a brief examination, Mariacher took a roll of gauze bandaging and splinted the man's wrist by the simple expedient of tightly binding the broken right arm to the intact left forearm. That would keep the break immobilized, and served at the same time to secure the prisoner's hands.

"So . . . you're not a doctor?" the westerner asked, sounding uncertain.

"Negative. But all special ops forces personnel get pretty heavy-duty training in emergency first aid and field medicine. You never know when you're going to need a doctor, and the closest one is a few hundred klicks away."

"Well, I'm glad you could save him. We're going to want to question all three of these guys closely." He pulled a cell phone out of his jacket pocket and turned away.

Mariacher looked at the kid who'd helped by fetching the medical supplies and zip-ties. He didn't look older than sixteen, but he seemed to have a lot on the ball, and certainly had been more helpful than the other guy. "You speak English?"

"I do, honored sir."

"What's your name?"

"Najid, honored sir," the kid said. "Najid Syed Sirajuddin."

"Forget the 'honored sir' crap. I'm Ken. Thanks for the help. You did real good."

"It was a pleasure, hono— It was a pleasure."

"Who's this guy?" he asked, nodding at the westerner.

"My name is Wheeler," the man said, snapping his phone shut and turning back to face them. "Jerry Wheeler. CIA."

Mariacher nodded curtly. "Mariacher," he replied. He didn't like using his rank when he was still effectively under cover.

"I know. And you must be Lehman."

"Guilty, sir."

"Welcome to Point Quebec. Since you blew our cover, though, we're going to have to move, and fast."

"Hey, we didn't blow anything," Lehman said. He nodded toward the men on the floor. "Talk to *these* guys. They're the ones who chose the fucking ambush site, not us!"

Another Malaysian teenager holding an Uzi submachine

gun stood by a front window, peeking through the venetian blinds.

"Anything?" Wheeler asked him. The reply was a sharp negative shake of the head, and the CIA man seemed to relax a bit. "Maybe the tangos didn't have backup."

"You hire them pretty young, Wheeler."

The CIA man shrugged. "Hard to get good help these days, you know? These guys live in the neighborhood, no families, they were unemployed, and they needed money. So they work for us."

The tangos who'd tried to grab him weren't much older. Modern warfare, across the world, tended to consist of old men arming children and telling them whom to kill.

"Anyway, Gold Forward will be here soon. And Diamond is on the way as well. We'll have these people on a plane for Mactan in two hours. Our people will interrogate them there."

Mariacher nodded. Officially, the United States military had pulled out of the Philippines after the Filipino government refused to renew the lease on the naval base at Subic Bay in 1991. As the war on terrorism began heating up in the late 'nineties, however, a renewed American presence had been established on the island of Basilan, and at a facility near the city of Zamboanga on Mindanao. In addition, an aviation and intelligence support facility was located on Mactan. Initially and officially, those bases had been built to help the Filipinos in their terrorist war against Abu Sayyaf, a terrorist organization with proven links to al-Qaeda. Lately, though, there'd been talk about expanding those bases to provide the United States with an advance staging area for antiterrorist campaigns throughout southeast Asia. The topic was a hot button for Filipino politicians and anti-American protest groups, but if enough money was involved, Mariacher knew, Washington would get what it wanted.

He caught himself feeling sorry for the prisoners, however. The several hundred American personnel on Mactan and Basilan were supported by several thousand Filipino soldiers, and those guys were not known for their compassion or their mercy when it came to captured terrorists.

"Wouldn't it be better getting them all the way back to the World?" he asked, using the military slang for the United States.

"It's out of our hands, Mariacher. We might get them in the U.S. after Mactan is done with them. You guys, however, are on your way to Utapao, tonight."

Mariacher raised his eyebrows. "Tonight? What about our debriefing?"

"You'll debrief there. Diamond is going with you."

"Why the hurry?"

"You mean besides the fact that you exposed our safe house here, and someone wants you out of the country as fast as they can give you the boot? I don't know."

"Listen, suit," Lehman said, angry. "You'd better lay off that shit. We didn't expose anything. The tangos *knew* we were coming down that street. Understand?"

"My friend here is right, Wheeler," Mariacher said. "We evaded the bad guys at the river. If they were able to send a car to try to snatch us off the street, it was because they knew *exactly* where to go."

"I just wonder why the hell you put a safe house smack up next to the National Mosque," Lehman said.

"*That* doesn't mean anything," Wheeler said. "C'mon, everyone in Malaysia is Muslim . . . unless they're Buddhist or Hindu or Christian." He jerked his thumb over his shoulder. "The Holy Rosary Catholic Church is right over there, just a few blocks from here. We leased this place because it was cheap, and because it was close to the train station."

"Still," Mariacher said, "if I were you, I'd check out how many of the Agency's Muslim assets knew about this place.

Somebody tipped off the bad guys and let 'em know that we were after Khalid Muhammed. They knew just where to send a team to try and take us out. After we got clear of the surveillance area, they were searching for us, but we were able to give them the slip. But then they just happened to have a truck on hand and five operators to try to grab us before we could get to the safe house."

He glanced at Najib, then at the other three Malaysian teenagers, who were watching the street outside from the front window. The leak might be there. More likely, though, it was higher up in the local Agency network. Najib and the others wouldn't have known anything about the op to nail Mohammed.

"I'll keep that in mind," Wheeler said, a sarcastic edge to his voice. "Is that your plan, then? To blame your failure on the Agency?"

"We're not blaming anyone, Wheeler. If you have a leak in your operation, you need to know about it, find it, and plug it."

"There's no leak!" Wheeler shouted. Najib looked up, startled.

"Ri-i-i-ight . . ." Lehman said, drawing out the word.

"We're not going to argue with you, Wheeler," Mariacher added. "But you people had better tighten up your security unless you want a car bomb parked on your doorstep."

"Sir!" one of the boys at the window called. "Two men . . ."

Seconds later a knock sounded at the door. Najib opened it, revealing Chief Bradley.

"Autumn Mist," Bradley said, giving the password.

"We know who you are," Wheeler said. "Get inside before someone sees you!"

Bradley entered, followed by Charles Osterlee. "Hey, Lieutenant," Bradley said, seeing Mariacher. "Lehman." He looked them up and down. "Looks like somebody's been hitting the old swimming hole."

"E and E, Chief," Lehman said. "The bastards sent a hit team after us."

"So we heard. What the fuck happened to the target, anyway?"

"I don't know, Chief," Mariacher replied. "We had him in our sights. Diamond told us to hold . . . and nothing. Somehow, he slipped out of the building and we never saw it."

Bradley nodded. "I think our friend 'Tex' is going to have some explaining to do. I'm wondering about the guys he was supposed to have on the alley out back."

"My thoughts exactly, Chief." He glanced at Najib. "But let's save it for the debrief."

"Roger that, sir." He shook his head. "Not one of Team Six's better days, though."

"Not one of *my* better days, Chief."

"C'mon," Wheeler said. "There's a room upstairs. You can all grab a shower and get into some clean clothes, at least."

"Great," Mariacher said. "Some of us need it."

"You can say that again," Wheeler told them.

Wednesday, September 19, 2001

Headquarters
Naval Special Warfare Command,
Coronado, California
0925 hours, PDT

The briefing had resumed a few minutes past 0900 hours. Tangretti and Fletch were back in their seats, the assembled admirals and captains and commanders back in theirs. Facil-

itation of this portion of the briefing had been assumed by
George Kuhlman, the DIA officer.

"The name 'Taliban,'" Kuhlman was saying from behind
the podium at the front of the room, "comes from the Arabic
talib, meaning a student, or a seeker of truth; specifically a
seeker of religious truth. After the Soviets left in 1989,
Afghanistan pretty much fell into anarchy. The communist
government—the Democratic Republic of Afghanistan—still
held power in a few major cities, but in the country, local warlords were fighting one another for control and settling old
debts. They'd united against the Russians . . . but Afghanistan
is an incredible hodge-podge of cultures and languages, and
with the common enemy gone, they went after each other."

The lights were off again, and a photograph was projected
up on the screen. It showed a number of bearded, turbaned
kids in the back of a truck, holding aloft AK-47s and a couple of RPGs. Above them a flag streamed in the wind—pure
white, with green Arabic script across the center—the flag
of the Taliban.

"According to one version we have of the story, in 1994 a
mujahideen warlord stopped a family on the road at a checkpoint near Kandahar, robbed them, and kidnapped their two
young girls to keep his soldiers entertained. The girls' parents went to a nearby *madrasa,* an Islamic school, and
pleaded for help from the mullah there, Mohammed Omar.
Omar rounded up thirty students, rescued the girls, and hung
the mujahideen commander.

"An alternate story says the commander was kidnapping
teenage boys, forcing them to submit to mock marriage ceremonies, and then raping them. Whatever the truth of the
story, the Taliban owe their initial success to the support
from local civilians. These guys were seen as heroes, routing
the bad-guy warlords, and their services became very much

in demand. They were warriors of the Faith, supporting the downtrodden against all comers. Better than Hollywood.

"This story about Omar and the warlord is a little too neat to be entirely true. It leaves out the fact that in 'ninety-four Omar and bin Laden enlisted the help of their old friends in the Pakistani secret service, the ISI. Seems that Pakistan had been backing Gulbuddin Hekmatyar's faction in his bid to control Afghanistan. They figured if Hekmatyar controlled Afghanistan, they could control Hekmatyar.

"Hekmatyar was one of *the* big heroes of the Soviet-Afghan War, but, as mujahideen go, he was pretty incompetent, and his campaign to unite the warring Afghan factions was stalled. The mujahideen controlled the countryside, but the cities were mostly still held by the DRA . . . the guys the Soviets left behind when they pulled out. Late in 1994, Pakistan was hiring the Taliban to protect their convoys along the border, and they decided to switch their support to Omar. Two years later the Taliban, with *lots* of Pakistani and Saudi help, took Kabul. They invaded the U.N. compound where the DRA leader was hiding, castrated him, and hung him in the city square. Omar became what passed for a national leader.

"The Taliban *did* restore order and impose moral restrictions on the lawless elements. They disarmed many of the warlords, and put some of the worst of them out of business. They stopped the worst of the kidnappings, rapes, and murders. They even cut the country's poppy production. Until recently, Afghanistan was *the* world's major exporter of heroin.

"But all of this came at a terrible cost to the locals."

The picture on the screen changed. Bodies lay in a dusty street, as bearded men standing nearby waved their weapons in the air.

"The Taliban now enforces a religious dictatorship with absolute control over the population. They continue to depend on Pakistan and Saudi Arabia for support, both for money and for weapons and personnel. There were reports of whole busloads of adolescent Pakistanis going across the border to fight with the Taliban after being given a day or two of training. We believe that perhaps fifteen percent of the Taliban military now consists of Pakistani and Saudi troops. During the past few years, eager young fighters from all over the world have been flocking in to Afghanistan to fight under the Taliban banner of holy war. While al-Qaeda is not technically a part of the Taliban, AQ fully supports the Taliban government, and we consider them to be the best-trained, the most fanatical, and the most dangerous of the forces available to them."

Another picture. This one showed what appeared to be an enormous statue, set back within a deep recess in the face of a cliff. A group of men in the photograph, tiny figures clustered near the feet of the monument, gave an idea of the scale.

"As Commander Dickinson said earlier, the Taliban is not making a lot of friends on the international scene. Last March the Taliban achieved a degree of notoriety by blowing up two giant statues of the Buddha at a place called Bamiyan northwest of Kabul. Huge, *huge* monuments . . . the one shown here was 183 feet tall, carved into the side of a mountain over fifteen hundred years ago. They were a priceless cultural heritage for the country, and the Taliban called them idolatrous and blew them both to bits."

The photo changed again. This time it showed several Afghans in the street. They appeared to be wrestling a man to the ground, while a crowd watched impassively.

"They have created an arm of the government called, believe it or not, the Ministry for the Promotion of Virtue and the Prevention of Vice, a kind of religious police that now numbers an estimated thirty thousand. Under the Taliban's view of Islamic law, radios, videotapes, VCRs, television, computers, and even the flying of kites are all banned, with the idea that such things distract people from the proper worship of Allah. The law is rigorously enforced by the religious police. Men are required by law to grow a beard at least as long as a clenched fist, and they can be beaten or arrested if their beards are deemed too short. Reportedly, members of the Ministry of Virtue and Vice have authority to go into private homes, looking for violations."

Another photo appeared. A man, shirtless, his hands tied behind his back, hung by the neck from some sort of crane or gantry. His face was black, his eyes wide open. Again, the crowd watched without visible emotion.

"Penalties for crimes are harsh and medieval. Adultery is punished by public stoning. Homosexuals are crushed under brick walls. Thieves have their hands cut off, sometimes hands and feet both. Murderers are publicly killed by relatives of the victim, often by having their throats cut at center field of a packed soccer stadium. Many who commit relatively minor infractions are summarily hanged in public, and often their bodies are left on display for days. People suspected of working for the CIA, for the Russians, for Iran, for women's rights organizations . . . they tend to disappear, probably into Amaniyat prisons. Afghanistan is now under a rule of terror."

Another picture. A person in a blue garment that completely covered the body knelt on the grass. A robed and turbaned man stood behind the figure holding an AK-47 to the back of the person's head. A blur around the faceless figure's head suggested that the photo had been taken at the instant the man pulled the trigger.

"The plight of women has been especially bad under Taliban rule. They're not allowed to be seen in public, hold jobs, or go to school if they're over eight years old. They are required by law to wear a garment called the burka, which covers them completely, head to toe, with a heavy mesh panel over the face through which to breathe and see. It's against the law for them to wear white socks or shoes—the color of the Taliban flag—or to wear shoes that make noise when they walk. This photo shows the public execution of a woman accused of murdering her husband. Her trial appears to have amounted to an accusation by the man's relatives. She was not allowed to speak in her own defense. Women are not permitted to speak in public."

Another photo. A woman in a blue burka crouched on the ground as two turbaned men stood over her, truncheons raised high.

"If a woman shows any skin, if she even makes any *noise,* she can be publicly humiliated, beaten, and arrested by the religious police. They may only appear outside the home in the company of a husband or a close male relative. The windows of any house with women living inside must be painted black, so no one can look inside and see them by accident. For a time they were not allowed to go to the hospital or seek medical care, because that would require exposing their bodies to the view of male medical personnel.

"That situation, especially, caused an uproar within international circles, and some hospitals were rearranged to provide separate female wards, but women are still often refused medical treatment. Reportedly, the only hospital in the Kabul area allowed to take in women has no electricity or clean water, and only thirty-five beds. Taliban spokesmen say Afghanistan has more serious problems than educating its women or providing them with health care."

David Tangretti watched the slide show, but with a growing sense of restlessness verging on irritation. Yeah, the Taliban were thorough-going SOBs, granted. They enslaved their women, brutalized their citizens, and blew up priceless archeological treasures. But why the lecture? He wanted to hear about al-Qaeda. *They* blew up American buildings with thousands of people inside. *They* were the self-declared enemies of America, and the ones he wanted to get in his sights.

"Lights, please . . ."

Kuhlman looked out over his audience. "Until 9/11," he said, "the Taliban was not considered a major threat to Western security. They were harboring the AQ, but Washington was willing to continue pursuing channels in dealing with them. In fact, the United States didn't even have a contingency plan for going to war in Afghanistan. Now, however, that is going to change. President Bush has authorized planning for Operation Infinite Justice—the invasion of Afghanistan, the removal of the Taliban from power, and the destruction of al-Qaeda."

David suppressed a groan. Operation Infinite Justice? Who the hell had dreamed up *that* moniker? For the past twenty years military operations had been given code names that, more often than not, seemed designed more for public relations than as simple designations. Just Cause in Panama. Allied Force in Kosovo. Restore Hope in Somalia. Restore Democracy in Haiti. And now . . . Infinite Justice?

Still, he understood the feeling behind that choice in code names, and perhaps that was the real reason for going after the Taliban, rather than trying to take out bin Laden surgically. Americans wanted to strike back, and they wanted to strike back *hard*. Three thousand Americans murdered would not be avenged by a covert police operation.

Infinite justice. Infinite revenge. Two sides of the same coin.

"The Department of Defense is now drawing up several operational plans to achieve these ends," Kuhlman went on. "Options range from conducting an air war exclusively, to limit American casualties on the ground, to a full-scale ground war of the same scale and scope as the one attempted by our Soviet friends a few years ago." Kuhlman grinned. "Obviously, the idea would be to have this war be somewhat more successful in its prosecution and outcome.

"One thing the DOD is *very* cognizant of, however, no matter what the final shape of Infinite Justice might be, is the need for small, elite units on the ground. B-52s can't locate bin Laden and bring him back to the U.S. for trial. Stealth fighters and smart bombs can't go inside caves and bunkers to find hard intel on al-Qaeda plans and whereabouts. And that is where Task Force Osprey, and other covert operational units like you, will come into play."

At last, David thought. *Let's get to the good stuff!*

His tiredness forgotten, his irritation at the bureaucratic mentality forgotten, David Tangretti leaned forward to hear what role the SEALs might play within the ancient mountain fastnesses of Afghanistan.

Chapter 6

Utapao had been a major U.S. airfield during the Vietnam War, when combat aircraft of all descriptions had departed its 11,500-foot runway to carry out their missions over North and South Vietnam, and neighboring Laos and Cambodia. Today the air base was known as Rayong-Utapao International Airport, and served as an important hub for Bangkok Airways.

The American military still maintained a presence here, however, albeit low-key compared to the massive buildup during the Vietnam conflict, when something like seven thousand Americans had been stationed here, or in the Satahip complex along the coast of the Gulf of Thailand. Mariacher was standing in front of the building housing the headquarters for U.S. special ops, watching an unmarked C-135 Hercules circle in for a landing, and wondered if some of his buddies were on board that aircraft.

Cobra Gold was an annual multinational training exercise, the largest in Southeast Asia, which included military forces from the United States, Thailand, and Singapore. The main exercise generally took place in the spring, but bilateral training with elements of the U.S. Navy SEALs working with their Thai SEAL counterparts, under the designation UNDERSEAL, took place twice a year, during the main Cobra Gold event, and in the fall. Training was intense, as were all SEAL exercises. Josephus had said of the Roman army two thousand years before that their exercises were bloodless battles, their battles bloody exercises, and the same concept held true now for the Special Forces—except that for the SEALs, even training exercises occasionally resulted in injury or death.

The Herky Bird touched down with a lightness that belied its considerable bulk, engines thundering as it slowed, and then taxied to a halt. The rear ramp lowered with a whine, and sixteen men filed down and onto the tarmac beneath the aircraft's tail, falling into two ranks of seven. The remaining two appeared to be calling the roll. He couldn't recognize faces at this distance, and couldn't even be sure they were SEALs as opposed to other Special Forces personnel, but chances were they were either SEALs or EOD personnel arriving to practice mine disposal out in the Gulf of Thailand.

Mariacher wondered who they were, where they were arriving from. Were they just arriving to take part in UNDERSEAL, or returning from a training exercise in some other part of the country?

If the latter, he sincerely hoped their exercise had been more productive than the cluster-fuck in Kuala Lumpur.

"Hey, Lieutenant?" Chief Bradley called from the top of the steps behind him. "They're ready for you."

"On my way, Chief."

Why, he wondered, did these sessions always feel like damned interrogations?

Lehman, Osterlee, and Bradley had already been in to see the op handlers. They'd deliberately saved him for last. The debrief was in a conference room on the ground floor, with a large portrait of President Bush on one wall, a computer terminal and several monitors in front of another. Two men in civilian suits sat at one side of the brightly polished mahogany conference table; one he didn't know, but the other was Dugan—his handler in the Kuala Lumpur op. Mariacher was relieved and happy to see Commander Daryl Warren next to them. Warren was DevGroup, like him, and while technically not his commanding officer on this op, he did serve as a liaison with the SEALs and with the Navy. Mariacher didn't like working for the CIA; things tended to get too strange too quickly, and you never knew where you stood with them.

"Lieutenant Kenneth Mariacher, reporting as ordered, sir," he said, coming to attention. He was still wearing civilian clothing—slacks and a sport shirt he'd been given at the safe house—and the familiar military litany felt strangely out of place without a proper uniform.

"Have a seat, Mr. Mariacher," the unknown civilian said. "I'm Karl Mitchell. Mr. Dugan and Commander Warren you already know."

"Yes, sir."

Mitchell pulled a PDA from his shirt pocket, opened it, and used the stylus on the screen. "I will remind you that everything said in this room is deemed Top Secret. Suppose you just go ahead and tell us your take on Green Tiger. From the beginning, if you please."

"Aye aye, sir. I received my preliminary briefing four weeks ago, and was asked if I wished to volunteer for an

SMU deployment to Southeast Asia. I said yes . . . and the next thing I knew my team and I were on a commercial flight out of Dulles for Kuala Lumpur."

He kept his recitation short and to the point, a listing of places and times, of people met and orders received. Green Tiger overall had actually been fairly typical for the Sea Ghosts—a classified unit operating under the Navy's Development Group: SEAL Team Six—which now carried out SMU missions for JSOC. Headquartered at Fort Bragg in North Carolina, JSOC drew covert operations teams from all of the military services, including the Army's Delta Force; Rangers; 160th SOAR, the Air Force's Special Tactics Squadron 1; Marine Force Recon; and the Navy's Development Group, or DevGroup. Special Mission Units, or SMUs, were drawn from the JSOC pool as needed and deployed where needed. Generally, those missions were carried out under the aegis of the Department of Defense, but frequently one-shot SMUs were assembled and deployed under the heading of officers working for the Operations Directorate of the Central Intelligence Agency. Such had been the case for Operation Green Tiger.

Mariacher and the other Sea Ghosts had met Diamond—Sean Dugan—in Kuala Lumpur, in his office at the U.S. Embassy, and been briefed on the details for the mission. The operational parameters were simple. Take a particular building under surveillance from a room already rented on the third floor of a hotel across the street and from the roof of a bus station nearby, and watch for the arrival of Green Tiger—Khalid Shaikh Mohammed. Upon receiving a go from their handlers, they were to terminate the target . . . the charming euphemism for killing the man.

"We had the target in our sights," Mariacher told the listening men. "We had an easy shot while he was on the street, a window of, oh, maybe thirty, thirty-five seconds. After that we had a clear shot while he was in conference inside the building. We would have had to punch a round through a brick wall to get him, but it was still a good shot. The window this time was open for two and a half hours.

"After that, Green Tiger and the men with him left the room. We did not see them exit the building, and we received no further updates from Diamond." He glanced at Dugan. The man was sitting at the table, hands clasped in front of him, not meeting his eyes.

"The operation went back to standard surveillance procedure. Because we wondered whether the target had been alerted to our presence, Blue Forward Two performed a recon of the area, both inside the hotel and on the street, but saw no indication that we'd been made.

"A few minutes after his return to the stakeout room, however, at approximately 2120 hours, four tangos used a maid's key to gain access to our position. We took them down, reported the situation to Diamond, and then performed an E-and-E to get clear of the operational area."

He then briefly described their movement through Chinatown, their swim across the river, and concluded with the attempted abduction outside the safe house.

"You feel certain that tango elements didn't follow you from Chinatown, then?" Warren asked him.

"Affirmative. We saw what might have been a search in progress on the east bank of the river, but saw no indication that we'd been spotted. We were seen by civilians on the river's west bank—under the bridge, and on the street opposite the National Mosque."

Mitchell looked up from his PDA. "The report faxed here by Wheeler at Point Quebec, um, rather strongly suggests that terrorist elements followed you all the way from Chinatown, possibly by interrogating the civilians along the way who did see you."

Mariacher sighed. "It's possible, sir. *Anything's* possible. However, it took us no more than half an hour—less than that, really—to get from the river to the safe house. We saw no sign of pursuit. It's my feeling that the truck that tried to grab us in front of Point Quebec had been alerted by radio or phone, and that they were waiting for us to show up."

"Which suggests that the local tango network knows where the Brickfield safe house is," Commander Warren pointed out. "At least they know the general area, and had elements already in position when you came along."

"Yes, sir." He hesitated, glancing at Dugan, who was still avoiding eye contact. "There's another aspect to the op, though. Perhaps Mr. Dugan can clarify some points."

Mitchell snapped his PDA shut and pocketed it. "Actually, there's no need to go into other aspects of Green Tiger. Your story tallies with what we've already heard from the other members of your SMU. You carried out your part of the mission to the best of your ability, and—"

"Begging your pardon, sir, but this mission was screwed from the git-go, and there are holes in this thing big enough to drive a truck bomb through. Operational security was compromised form the beginning, and—"

"Thank you, Lieutenant. That will be all."

"No, sir, I don't think it is all. We were told that we were to cap Green Tiger. Then we were put on indefinite hold until the target had escaped. We were told other exits from the target building were covered by another SMU. We were not given contact information for this other SMU and could not coordinate our part of the mission with them."

"Lieutenant Mariacher—"

"Green Tiger did not come out of that building on the side we had under surveillance. That either means he went past

Mr. Dugan's SMU, whoever they were, or he went into hiding somewhere else in that building—the basement, possibly. Either way, Blue Forward was compromised. They *knew* we were there, which room we were watching from, and that means a security breach of dangerous—"

"Lieutenant Mariacher, that is *enough*!" Mitchell slammed his open palm down on the mahogany tabletop. "You are dismissed!"

"The boy's got a point, Karl," Warren said. "My people's lives were put at risk. JSOC, DevGroup, and I all would very much like to know why."

"I couldn't give authorization," Dugan said, speaking for the first time. "I was told to put a hold on the op by Magic Carpet."

Mariacher didn't know that code name, but could easily guess. Magic Carpet would have been one of those other listeners over the mission's communications net—the Pentagon, possibly, or, more likely, someone in the Operations Directorate at Langley.

Mitchell scowled. "Sean, let's hold this conversation for a moment, shall we?" He looked at Mariacher. "I remind you again that what you may have heard in this room is classified Top Secret. You are dismissed. Wait outside."

"Aye aye, sir." He smiled. Mitchell was reminding Dugan that he, Mariacher, didn't have the security clearance necessary to discuss Magic Carpet. Dugan had just screwed up, big-time, and from the look on Mitchell's face, he was about to have a new one torn.

It couldn't happen to a nicer fellow, he decided.

He found Lehman, Osterlee, and Bradley waiting just down the passageway outside the briefing room, at a lounge area that had a sofa and some chairs, and a counter with a coffee mess—lifeblood of the Navy.

"How'd it go, Wheel?" Bradley asked him.

"About like we expected, Chief," he replied, pouring himself a plastic cup full of rather noxious looking black liquid. "Someone screwed up and they're looking for a scapegoat."

"Would that be you, Lieutenant?"

"I don't think so, Chief." He grinned. "Not this time, anyway. Commander Warren is having words with them as we speak."

"I don't know Commander Warren, sir," Osterlee said. "Is he new to DevGroup?"

"Relatively new. He ran a platoon for Team Two, and then was in training command for a while. I understand he volunteered for DevGroup after he got his third full stripe. That was maybe a year ago or so."

"He seems like a good guy."

"He is."

"I just want to know why they stopped our shot yesterday," Lehman said. "I mean, I had the bastard, I *had* him." He held out his hand, open palm up, then closed it into a tight fist. "Right here."

"My thought is that someone decided they could grab him instead," Mariacher said.

"Like I was sayin'?" Lehman asked. "Kneecap him, and send in a helo to bring him in."

"A lot would have depended on what they already had prepped and ready to go," Bradley pointed out. "You can't put something like that together spur of the moment."

"I don't know about that," Lehman said. "The tangos did pretty good, at Point Quebec."

"No way." Mariacher shook his head. "We're here, and the tangos who tried to grab us are on Mactan. That's not what I would call 'pretty good.'"

"The lieutenant's right," Bradley said. "Sending a truck-load of guys out to snatch someone off the street without fire support or proper backup is not exactly what you call your careful planning."

"So who made the call?" Lehman wanted to know. "Dugan? Or somebody back at Langley?"

"Good question," Mariacher said. "Our friend Tex Dugan is doing some serious ass-covering right now, I think."

Half an hour later the door down the passageway opened and Warren and the two civilians walked out. The civilians appeared to be in the midst of a restrained but angry discussion, one that stopped as soon as they realized that the SEALs were watching them. The two of them hurried out the front door. Warren watched them go, then walked down the passageway to where the SEALs were waiting.

Mariacher stood up. Warren was giving nothing away by his expression. "It couldn't happen to a nicer fella," Mariacher said, keeping his voice light. "Coffee, sir?"

Warren gave him a sharp look, as if to ask what Mariacher knew or had heard. In fact, Mariacher was performing the verbal equivalent of reconnaissance by fire—tossing a provocative statement out to see what might come back. He didn't know that Dugan was being censured somehow, but it seemed a reasonable possibility, based on what he knew and what he'd just seen.

"Our friends in Virginia," Warren said slowly, referring to the CIA's headquarters at Langley, "are a bit sensitive right now. They are about to take delivery of one very large ass-load of shit, COD. They feel a bit exposed, and I don't mean to incoming from al-Qaeda. There are some people back in Washington who would very much like to know why AQ caught us so completely by surprise on 9/11. Yes, I'll take a cup. Thanks."

Lehman was already pouring it. "Pollutants, sir?"

"Negative. I take it straight."

"Why *did* AQ catch us with our pants down, Commander?" Mariacher asked. "I assumed we just weren't looking in the right direction. Did the Company know something and drop the ball?" *Company* was field slang for the CIA.

"That is what Congress is going to be asking soon," Warren said. He accepted the cup from Lehman, took a sip, and made a face. "Shit. How long has this crap been on the hot plate?"

"Since about halfway through the Truman administration, would be my guess, sir," Bradley said.

"Actually, the Agency *was* watching al-Qaeda. Bin Laden is on their most-wanted list, has been since the mid-nineties. They knew he was behind the embassy bombings in Africa, the two bombings in Saudi Arabia, and the bombing of the *Cole*. They knew his money, at least, was behind the Yousef attempt on the WTC. They have a whole office at Langley devoted to following bin Laden and what he is up to."

"I've been wondering," Mariacher said, "if they didn't have their underwear in a twist because of Bojinka."

Warren took his time replying to that. He sipped his coffee, then took a seat with the others. Mariacher sat down beside him.

"I wouldn't wonder about that too loudly," he finally said. "That's the sort of sensitive information that the Company is a bit touchy about right now."

"Well, well," Bradley said. "The pigeons are coming home to roost, eh?"

"Yeah," Lehman added. "Time to wake up and smell the plastic explosives."

Warren sighed. "You guys didn't hear this from me," he said, "but the word is that the Agency wanted to have the credit for nabbing Green Tiger. After Bojinka, well, they kind of have a special-case hard-on for this guy, you know?"

Mariacher nodded. "I can imagine. Bojinka hit them where it hurts."

Project Bojinka had been conceived and planned by none other than Khalid Shaikh Mohammed—Green Tiger—a terrorist strike against the West of truly monumental proportions. It had been exposed early in 1995, when a fire in an apartment in Manila led to the discovery of sophisticated bomb-making equipment and material, including nitroglycerine. Philippine police had soon arrested and tortured Abdul Hakim Murad and learned details of the plot. While information obtained under torture was always suspect, those details were unexpectedly confirmed a few months later when Ramzi Ahmed Yousef, the mastermind behind the 1993 WTC attack, was captured in Pakistan and turned over to the American authorities. According to classified reports Mariacher read during his briefings for Green Tiger, Yousef had actually boasted about Bojinka to the FBI agent escorting him back to the States, confirming everything Murad had said, right down to the code name.

Bojinka was an Arabic word meaning "explosion." Yousef and Murad had shared that apartment in Manila, turning it into a bomb-making factory in preparation for an attempt to smuggle bombs onto either eleven or twelve airliners at airports all over eastern Asia, their timers set to detonate simultaneously while the United States–bound aircraft were out over the Pacific. As an extension of Bojinka, two private aircraft were to have been loaded with explosives. One was to be flown into the Pentagon. Murad himself had already received flight training, to fly the second plane into the headquarters of the CIA at Langley, Virginia.

Murad had been extradited to the United States, and his testimony helped convict Yousef. Both were now serving life sentences in prison.

At various times other high-visibility attacks had been incorporated into Bojinka, including a plan to assassinate President Clinton and a plot to kill Pope John Paul II when he was scheduled to visit the Philippines later that year. The centerpiece of Bojinka, however, remained the plan to destroy a dozen trans-Pacific airliners, coupled with kamikaze-style strikes against Langley and the Pentagon.

At a press conference three days after the 9/11 attacks, the director of the FBI had spoken of reports that the hijackers received flight training in the United States, called this "news," and added that had this been known ahead of time, perhaps the September 11 attacks could have been averted.

The problem with this statement was that U.S. authorities *had* known that men with ties to terrorist organizations—including al-Qaeda—were attending flight schools all over the United States; at least ten different schools in Texas, New York, North Carolina, Oklahoma, and Louisiana. Investigators found a business card for the Schenectady-based Richmor Aviation flight school in the Manila apartment shared by Yousef and Murad.

Official concern at the time had centered on the 1996 Summer Olympics in Atlanta. The idea of terrorists flying suicide missions into a packed stadium remained what one official had called "a nightmare scenario." All civil aviation had been required to stay at least three miles away from the stadium. Planning for the 2000 Olympics in Sydney also focused on the possibility of a terrorist spectacular involving a fully loaded jetliner crashing into the opening ceremonies in front of live TV cameras.

And yet, there'd been no heightening of security by the FAA, no warning, no precautions taken to prevent what actually happened—the simultaneous hijacking of four airliners by flight-trained fanatics and the murder of three thousand people. One official had pointed out that despite a lengthy list of people with ties to al-Qaeda and other known terror groups taking flight training, there'd been no way to connect the dots between that and the possibility of hijacking jetliners for use in kamikaze attacks into American buildings.

"We know Mohammed was the mastermind behind Bojinka," Warren agreed. "He was a freelance terrorist at the time. And before that he was involved with the 'ninety-three attack on the World Trade Center, through his nephew, Yousef. Apparently he didn't actually join al-Qaeda until 'ninety-eight or 'ninety-nine, but when he did, they made him head of the organization's propaganda arm. The Agency would like to talk to him, obviously."

"We were tapped to hit Mohammed a month ago," Osterlee pointed out. "Two weeks before 9/11. Last week, when we got to the embassy in Kuala Lumpur, we were told he had a part in the attacks. But the plan was still to kill the bastard, not try to bring him in."

Bradley shook his head. "Sounds to me like people weren't talking to each other back at Langley," he said. "Typical."

"It might have been someone in the field too," Mariacher said, "trying to pull off an impressive coup. A live Green Tiger would make an impressive trophy back in Washington."

He was thinking of Dugan. The CIA officer struck Mariacher as a cowboy, the sort of operator who shot from the hip, who made up the plan as he went along, the very sort of technique that SEALs tried to avoid. The way things had actually gone down, though, it seemed more likely that someone back in Langley put a hold on the assassination attempt at the last moment.

Warren sighed. "Well, we'll never know the whole story. *Somebody* screwed up and Green Tiger got away. The important thing is that you guys carried out your part of the operation perfectly. No one's blaming you."

"No, sir," Mariacher said, "the important thing is that that bastard got away clean. Maybe the Agency bungled things back home, or maybe Dugan wanted his own people to nab AQ's propaganda chief, but one way or another, Mohammed escaped. The CIA aren't the only ones who want to nail that son of a bitch."

"Does that mean you're volunteering?" Warren asked.

"Volunteering? For what?"

"We think that Green Tiger caught a private flight out of Malaysia before dawn this morning. We don't know the aircraft's destination . . . but we think he may be trying to get back to either Pakistan or Afghanistan. And Sea Ghost has been tasked to go find him."

"Outstanding!" Bradley said.

"Yeah," Mariacher said. "I'm volunteering." He looked at the others. "We *all* are."

"Good. Because things are about to get very hot in that part of the world. It's not official yet, but the word is that the U.S. is going to hit Afghanistan. And we're going to want our best people over there, boots on the ground."

Thursday, September 20, 2001

TGI Friday's Restaurant
Oceanside, California
2050 hours, PDT

Boots on the ground. The term had been bandied about a lot lately, especially within the U.S. Special Forces community. There were a fair number there who felt the Rumsfeld Doctrine was running just a few cold ones short of a six-pack, and that the military should go back to certain basics. Afghanistan, all agreed, would be a testing ground for the philosophical debate now raging over just how modern war should—or *could*—be fought.

For HM1 David Tangretti, SEAL Team Three, there was no question. There was no possible way to fight a war without getting your hands dirty.

Secretary of Defense Donald Rumsfeld was well known in the military community for his stress on clean, surgical, and all but bloodless warfare carried out by the almost magical array of smart bombs, spy satellites, and high-tech weaponry available. In fact, the name "Rumsfeld Doctrine" was being applied more and more to this type of war . . . the sort of video-game conflict Americans had been used to seeing on CNN ever since the Gulf War.

Well, satellites could spot what might be terrorist training camps in the mountains of Afghanistan, but they couldn't prove that terrorists were being trained there. They could photograph individual people on the ground from 250 miles up, but they could not identify a single man as bin Laden or prove whether he was dead after a cruise missile strike. Smart bombs could fly into a targeted window in Baghdad's Air Defense headquarters, but they couldn't capture Saddam Hussein. Sophisticated electronic eavesdropping equipment could listen in on a cell phone conversation in Afghanistan from the comfort of an office at Fort Meade, Maryland, or Langley, Virginia, but to positively identify and kill or capture the men responsible for carrying out a terrorist attack against American citizens, you needed *men,* highly trained and dedicated men, on the ground and in the know. Critics of the Rumsfeld Doctrine called it "boots on the ground."

And in just a few more days, Tangretti knew, he was going to be on the ground . . . high up in the mountains, halfway around the world.

First, though, he had to square things with Marilyn.

"What do you mean you're being shipped out?" she demanded. "Where are they sending you?"

"I'm . . . not allowed to talk about it, actually," he said.

He looked around the restaurant, which was fairly crowded tonight.

Once again, he wasn't supposed to be offbase. Fletch was covering for him, though he'd had to promise that this was absolutely the *last* time he would pull anything as hare-brained as this. Tangretti had agreed. As a sign of good faith, he wasn't even going to sleep with Marilyn tonight. He'd gotten her to meet him at the restaurant so he could tell her good-bye . . . and then it would be straight back to the barracks at Coronado. *I promise!*

He'd wondered how easy it would be to keep that promise. Marilyn was absolutely fantastic at the art of coital de-cerebration . . . a phrase Tangretti had coined to describe the happy experience of having your brains fucked out. As a temptation, she was tough to resist. As it turned out, though, she was making that part easy for him. She hadn't forgiven him yet for running out on her in the middle of the night yesterday, and was convinced he was lying about his Navy responsibilities.

Well, he wasn't lying exactly. He just hadn't told her the whole truth.

"Bullshit," she told him. "When I was dating John, he *knew* when he was going to sea. And he knew about when he was coming back. You told me you were working with the Marines at Pendleton. They're not going anywhere."

"Not yet," he told her. "Look—"

"What's your ship?"

"I beg your pardon?"

"If you're going on sea duty, you have to have a ship. Which one?"

He hesitated, caught between telling her the truth—that he didn't have a ship, but was being temporarily assigned overseas—and making something up. The former would raise more questions. The latter could be checked on . . . and he disliked lying on principle.

But the hesitation alone was enough to give him away.

"You don't have a ship," she said. "You're lying to me. Who is it?"

"What?"

"You're seeing someone else, right? Who is it?"

He sighed. "I'm not seeing anyone else. Look, I'm not even supposed to be off-base. I snuck out anyway to tell you. Would you rather I'd just vanished on you?"

"Maybe you should have!"

"I want to see you again," he told her. "I want to see you when I get back. I just, well . . . I just can't say anything about it, is all."

"When I was dating John—"

"Maybe you should go back to John instead of seeing me!" he snapped.

"John was a bastard. And you are too!" Her eyes widened, and she looked past his shoulder. "Oh, God . . ."

"What?" He turned to see what she was looking at. Friday's was one of those restaurants that had televisions hanging from the ceiling at strategic locations. Usually, they were tuned to sports channels for the game currently in season, but at the moment every television showed the face of George W. Bush.

"Hey, hey, hey!" someone in the bar shouted. "Pipe down, everyone! This could be important!"

Usually, Friday's was noisy to the point of distraction, but the whole restaurant fell completely silent. Everyone, at every table and booth, was watching one of the TV monitors.

"Aw, he was on the tube earlier," another voice called out in the silence. "This is an instant replay!"

"Well shut up anyway," the first voice replied. "Some of us ain't heard it!"

Someone turned the sound up so all could hear. According to the caption at the bottom of the screen, this was an address given by the president to Congress just a few hours ago.

"We have seen the state of our union in the endurance of rescuers working past exhaustion," the president was saying. "We've seen the unfurling of flags, the lighting of candles, the giving of blood, the saying of prayers in English, Hebrew, and Arabic. We have seen the decency of a loving and giving people who have made the grief of strangers their own. My fellow citizens, for the last nine days the entire world has seen for itself the state of our union, and it is strong.

"Tonight, we are a country awakened to danger and called to defend freedom. Our grief has turned to anger and anger to resolution. Whether we bring our enemies to justice or bring justice to our enemies, justice *will* be done. . . ."

"You're going," Marilyn said, her voice almost a whisper. "You're going someplace overseas to fight the terrorists!"

And all he could do was silently nod.

Chapter 7

TGI Friday's Restaurant
Oceanside, California
2104 hours, PDT

"On September the eleventh," the president continued, "enemies of freedom committed an act of war against our country. Americans have known wars, but for the past 136 years they have been wars on foreign soil, except for onc Sunday in 1941. Americans have known the casualties of war, but not at the center of a great city on a peaceful morning. Americans have known surprise attacks, but never before on thousands of civilians. All of this was brought upon us in a single day, and night fell on a different world, a world where freedom itself is under attack. . . ."

Marilyn reached across the table, laying one hand on his wrist. "David! Are you a frogman?"

"Actually, I'm a SEAL," he told her. "Most of us don't like the name 'frogman.'"

"That's so *exciting*!"

"The evidence we have gathered," Bush said, "all points to a collection of loosely affiliated terrorist organizations known as al-Qaeda. They are some of the murderers indicted for bombing American embassies in Tanzania and Kenya and responsible for bombing the USS *Cole*. Al-Qaeda is to terror what the mafia is to crime. But its goal is not making money; its goal is remaking the world and imposing its radical beliefs on people everywhere."

"Are you going to the Middle East?"

"I really can't talk about it, Marilyn."

"The terrorists practice a fringe form of Islamic extremism that has been rejected by Muslim scholars and the vast majority of Muslim clerics—a fringe movement that perverts the peaceful teachings of Islam. The terrorists' directive commands them to kill Christians and Jews, to kill all Americans, and make no distinctions among military and civilians, including women and children. . . ."

Marilyn closed her eyes and gave a little shiver. "Ooh! I'm sleeping with a Navy *SEAL*! . . ."

"Actually, you're just having dinner with one. I have to get back to the base right away. But I wanted to say good-bye."

"Well, not without another stop at the Miramar Motel, right?" She was clinging to his wrist now, possessive, even demanding.

"Sorry, hon. I can't."

"The United States respects the people of Afghanistan— after all, we are currently its largest source of humanitarian aid—but we condemn the Taliban regime. It is not only repressing its own people, it is threatening people everywhere by sponsoring and sheltering and supplying terrorists."

"Afghanistan!" Marilyn exclaimed, loudly enough that several of the patrons at the bar nearby glanced at her. "You're going to Afghanistan!"

"By aiding and abetting murder, the Taliban regime is committing murder. And tonight the United States of America makes the following demands on the Taliban. Deliver to

United States authorities all of the leaders of al-Qaeda who hide in your land. Release all foreign nationals, including American citizens, you have unjustly imprisoned. Protect foreign journalists, diplomats, and aid workers in your country. Close immediately and permanently every terrorist training camp in Afghanistan. And hand over every terrorist and every person and their support structure to appropriate authorities. . . ."

The president, David thought, was on a roll now. Personally, he didn't like Bush, Jr. that much. Since he hadn't cared for Gore either, he'd voted Libertarian in the last election as a personal protest. Now, though, as Bush stood at the rostrum before Congress, an immense American flag at his back, he appeared tough, determined, and presidential in a way David hadn't seen him be in the past.

September 11 had changed a lot of things . . . and a lot of people.

"These demands are not open to negotiation or discussion," Bush said. "The Taliban must act and act immediately. They will hand over the terrorists or they will share in their fate.

"I also want to speak tonight directly to Muslims throughout the world. We respect your faith. It's practiced freely by many millions of Americans and by millions more in countries that America counts as friends. Its teachings are good and peaceful, and those who commit evil in the name of Allah blaspheme the name of Allah. The terrorists are traitors to their own faith, trying, in effect, to hijack Islam itself.

"The enemy of America is not our many Muslim friends. It is not our many Arab friends. Our enemy is a radical network of terrorists and every government that supports them. Our war on terror begins with al-Qaeda, but it does not end there. . . ."

Watching Bush try to reach out to Muslims worldwide, to reassure them that the United States wasn't on a crusade against all of Islam, David thought it was interesting that Washington's biggest nightmare—aside from the very real possibility of another 9/11 style attack—must be that attacking Afghanistan would polarize the entire Muslim world against the United States.

If that happened, al-Qaeda and bin Laden would have won. As simple as that.

"Now, this war will not be like the war against Iraq a decade ago," Bush said, "with a decisive liberation of territory and a swift conclusion. It will not look like the air war above Kosovo two years ago, where no ground troops were used and not a single American was lost in combat. Our response involves far more than instant retaliation and isolated strikes."

"Ah, we should go in and nuke the friggin' raghead bastards!" someone yelled from the bar.

"Damn straight!" another called out.

Talk about polarization! Most Americans were pretty ignorant when it came to foreign countries, foreign politics, or religions that they saw as out of the American mainstream. David had heard about a number of ugly incidents during the past week, as Americans took out their rage and frustration and out-and-out fear against Muslims—most of them U.S. citizens—or simply against people who *looked* different.

Bush had differentiated a moment ago between Arabs and Muslims. Sadly, most Americans were unaware that there *was* a difference.

"Americans should not expect one battle," Bush went on, "but a lengthy campaign unlike any other we have ever seen. It may include dramatic strikes visible on TV and covert operations secret even in success."

"Did you hear, David? Covert operations! That's what *you'll* be doing, right? And that's why you couldn't tell me!"

"Shh. I want to hear this."

"And we will pursue nations that provide aid or safe haven to terrorism. Every nation in every region now has a decision to make: Either you are with us or you are with the terrorists. From this day forward, any nation that continues to harbor or support terrorism will be regarded by the United States as a hostile regime. Our nation has been put on notice. We're not immune from attack. We will take defensive measures against terrorism to protect Americans. . . ."

David remembered what they'd said at the briefing yesterday. Bush was as much as announcing to the world that Afghanistan would not be the last country to feel America's wrath. The purveyors of terror would be hunted down and destroyed no matter where they tried to hide.

But "any nation that continues to support terrorism" took in a lot of territory. There was a long list of those. Syria. North Korea. Iran and Iraq. Libya. The Sudan. And, of course, one nation's terrorist was another's freedom fighter. There were nations with active terrorist groups or ongoing revolutions that might not be supporting terror but would take a dim view of an American invasion to take those groups down. Egypt. Pakistan. Jordan. Saudi Arabia. The Philippines. Indonesia. Colombia. Even Mexico.

The United States simply could not take on the entire world all at once.

"And tonight, a few miles from the damaged Pentagon, I have a message for our military. Be ready. I have called the armed forces to alert, and there is a reason. The hour is coming when America will act, and you will make us proud."

"Yeah!" one of the guys at the bar shouted. "We're gonna kick some freakin' raghead terrorist ass!"

"This is not, however, just America's fight. And what is at stake is not just America's freedom. This is the world's fight. This is civilization's fight. This is the fight of all who believe in progress and pluralism, tolerance and freedom. We ask every nation to join us. . . ."

"Hoo-yah," David said, very softly. It was the SEAL battle cry.

After dinner he stood with Marilyn in the restaurant parking lot. She stepped up close to him and put her arms around his waist, looking up into his face with a most persuasive let's-go-to-bed expression.

"So, Commando," she said. "You didn't mean what you said about having to go back to the base right away, did you?"

"I'm afraid I did."

She reached down with one hand and squeezed his crotch. "Are you *sure*?" she asked, oozing seductiveness.

He reached down and, firmly grasping her wrist, moved her hand away.

"Look, there's nothing to discuss. I have to get back to the base right away. But I want to see you again, okay? I'll call you as soon as I can." He would be going to an advance base before actually inserting into Afghanistan. There would be satellite hookups there, and the chance to call home periodically.

"When are you leaving?"

"Tomorrow." Actually, he wouldn't be leaving the United States for another two weeks. Tomorrow he was on his way north for a stint of mountain training in the San Bernadino Range, south of the Marine training area at Twentynine Palms.

But it would be simpler just to say good-bye now and leave it at that.

"I wish you wouldn't go."

"Hey, I *have* to! You heard the man on the tube. I have to be ready. It's what I signed on for."

"I mean, just for tonight. You could make it back to base before reveille again."

He kissed her, then drew back. "Sorry, hon. But I'll be back!" To tell the truth, he was looking forward to a full night's sleep . . . *alone,* and in his rack. "See ya!"

He turned away before she could throw anything else at him, unlocked his car and climbed in. He gave her a jaunty wave as he keyed the ignition, then peeled out of the restaurant parking lot.

Man! His thoughts were disjointed as he drove south again on Interstate 5. Did he even want to see her again? Maybe he was leaving at a good time in the relationship. He definitely needed to think about things before seeing her again. Marilyn was hot, but sometimes she could be too damned persistent, as tenacious as a hungry shark.

But there was something disturbing about the way she'd been coming on to him when she found out he was a SEAL. Damn it, he didn't want her to like him because of his *job*. *That* made him no better than the jerks who went around bragging about being SEALs in order to get the girls into bed with them.

And what did that make *her*? A celebrity junkie? An adrenaline addict? A SEAL groupie?

As he entered the northern outskirts of San Diego, the Inland Freeway split off and Interstate 5 became the San Diego Freeway. As he passed the exit for Balboa Park and the San Diego Zoo, it hit him.

Marilyn didn't have a clue as to what a SEAL was or what it was they did. What she *thought* she knew was the product of Hollywood and of a popular culture that tended to glamorize the Teams, turning them into two-dimensional macho

action heroes who ran around blowing the crap out of stereo-
typed bad guys.

As a SEAL operator, he had done his share of killing bad
guys, sure. Hunting scuds in the Iraqi desert had been no
picnic, though the idea was to carry out your mission with as
little gunplay as was possible. In the world of the Teams, for
the most part, a mission that ended in a firefight was a mission that had failed.

Aw, the hell with it. People had been acting crazy in all
kinds of ways ever since September 11.

There was trouble waiting for him at the main gate to the
Naval Amphibious Warfare Center. As he drove up to the
gatehouse, he could see Marines—more Marines than were
usually present—and they all were turned out in full combat gear, camo BDUs, M-16 assault rifles, and Kevlar hel-
mets. He pulled out his wallet to flash his ID, but a big
gunnery sergeant he'd never seen before motioned him out
of the car.

"Hey, Gunny. What gives?"

"Please step out of your vehicle, sir."

In times past, if there was any question from the guards at
the gate, he'd told them that he was a corpsman on his way
up to Pendleton, which usually was true. This time, however,
it didn't look like he was going to be able to talk his way
through.

The gunnery sergeant studied his ID card, then handed it
to another Marine.

"Hey! What's the idea, Gunny?"

"We're just going to check your name against the list of
base personnel."

"Hey, Gunny. I'm a Navy corpsman. It's cool. I just had to
make a special run up to Pendleton."

"I doubt that, sir. Camp Pendleton's locked down tight too."

The Marine returned a moment later with the ID and

whispered to the gunnery sergeant. "Well, well, Doc," he said. "Navy SEAL, huh?"

"Yeah."

"You belong here, all right. But you do *not* belong off-base. I'm going to have to put you on report."

"C'mon! There's no need for that! There's this girl, see—"

"Save it," the Marine said. He shook his head, almost sadly. "I hate to tell you, Doc, but you are in a world of shit."

Friday, September 21, 2001

Brickfield District
Kuala Lumpur
1140 hours, local time

His name was Qazi Lal Hanif, and he'd been preparing for this day for a long time. Born in the city of Kandahar, in south-central Afghanistan, he'd killed his first Russian when he was twelve, in 1987. Six years later he joined Khalid Shaikh Mohammed, serving as one of his personal bodyguards.

He'd known all along that one day he would be a martyr for the cause, a living weapon aimed at the enemies of Allah: the mighty, the just. In 1994 he'd gone with Mohammed to Manila, in the Philippines, to plan a major blow against the westerner enemies. He was to have boarded a United Airlines jetliner in Manila, carrying on board a small but powerful bomb that he would hide under his seat during the first leg of the flight, to Tokyo. He would have gotten off the plane in Tokyo, leaving the bomb on board. Had the plan worked, that aircraft and eleven others all would have exploded in the sky above the Pacific at the same time, hours later.

The attack, at one blow, would kill perhaps two thousand passengers on twelve aircraft. More important, aviation authorities would certainly ground all flights worldwide. The cost to Western businesses would be incalculable, and the Americans would know that the Base was a powerful force indeed, a mighty weapon in the hand of Allah, His name be praised.

The plan, unfortunately, had been exposed when police raided the bomb-making center in Manila, and one of the fighters, Abdul Hakim Murad, had been captured and tortured. Mohammed and those with him managed to flee the country, returning to al-Qaeda's main base in the Sudan.

Almost at once Hanif had begun training for other missions at a camp outside of Kassala, learning techniques of reconnoiter, security, and the manufacture of explosive devices. One day soon, he knew, he would be driving a vehicle loaded with explosives. One brilliant, fierce flash . . . and he would be in Paradise with Allah and his Prophet, blessings upon his name.

Somehow, though, those missions had never materialized. Others were accepted for the attacks in Saudi Arabia and, later, against the American embassies in Kenya and Tanzania. He'd remained within Mohammed's entourage, visiting brothers throughout Afghanistan, Indonesia, the Philippines, and finally in Malaysia. There was talk, endless talk, about a truly spectacular strike, one that would bring the hated Satan America to its knees. There was talk of brothers attending flight school in America, learning to fly the big jetliners that would become al-Qaeda's version of cruise missiles in this new phase of the struggle.

Most of Hanif's life had been driven by two all-consuming understandings—of the Islamic obligation of jihad, or holy war, and of the Pashtun ethic of Pakhtunwali, the code of honor that defined who and what a Pashtun was.

Under Pakhtunwali, a true Pashtun would sacrifice every-thing, including his life, to safeguard his honor, the honor of his family and clan, his women, and his faith. Every insult was to be avenged, with interest. As an old Pashtun proverb put it, "He is not a Pashtun who does not give a blow for a pinch." The Islamic world—or at least Hanif's understand-ing of the Islamic world—had been at war with the West and with the Satan America for decades now. It wasn't that Hanif wanted to die for the cause, but rather, that his living or dy-ing simply wasn't important, save in how Allah, the merci-ful, the beneficent, could use him.

He was a tool, a weapon. He was honored to be a weapon in the Hand of Allah.

Early that morning the order had come down. A martyr was needed for a very special strike against the American Satans stalking Mohammed. Was there a volunteer?

There were many, of course, but Hanif had been chosen.

His death would benefit many, and in many ways. His family, his father and five brothers back in Kandahar, would receive a special payment from al-Qaeda's treasury. Their life had been hard since the Great Jihad War against the So-viets, and the money would ease their life. More, his name would be remembered as one of the holy ones, a true mu-jahideen: a warrior of God.

So now he drove the battered and ancient Toyota down the Jalal Brickfield, searching for the landmarks he'd been given. Past the Masjid Negara . . . turn left . . . yes! There it was, exactly as he'd seen it in the photographs.

He drove past slowly, checking for obstacles or any sign that defenses had been mounted against an attack . . . bunkers, concrete pylons, anything to block his strike. He saw none. He continued driving slowly—it would not do to be stopped by Kuala Lumpur's police *now,* with the backseat of the car filled with two large drums packed with fertilizer.

He came around again on the Jalal Brickfield once more, then turned again onto the side street. His foot pressed down on the accelerator. Faster . . . still faster. His heart was pounding now, his fists clenched on the steering wheel. In his right hand, between his palm and the wheel, he clutched a small, spring-loaded trigger connected to the car battery on the floor beside him and to the drums of fertilizer explosive in the back. A dead-man switch. When he released the switch, it would close, detonating the explosives.

That way, even if he were killed or rendered unconscious in the crash, the bomb would detonate.

Still faster. Several Malaysian men standing in the street leaped out of his way as he roared toward his target, and he heard them shouting curses at him. No matter. *Nothing* mattered, save only that he reach his target, *inshallah,* God willing.

Swerving at the last moment, he swung the car off the road and across the sidewalk. He hit something hard—the steps, perhaps—and the car jolted heavily, then crashed through the front of the building in a shattering spray of broken glass and flying brick.

Hanif's chest slammed against the steering wheel. Pain burned through his lungs and he almost, *almost,* lost consciousness. Somehow, though, he held onto consciousness, and still clung to the trigger in his hand.

Blood streamed down his face. Looking up through the shattered windshield, he saw a Malaysian man—a boy, really—moving toward him through the shattered front room of the house, a submachine gun in his hand.

There was no more time. For an instant Hanif realized something shocking. He was *afraid.* He didn't want to die after all.

But he was more afraid of capture by the Satans. He released the trigger.

The searing pain in his lungs stopped, as did everything else in his world. . . .

Friday, September 21, 2001

LearJet 35
Above the Bay of Bengal
1410 hours, local time

His name was Davlot Iskanderov, but very few indeed of his fellow fighters would ever know that. To them he was Asef Khan, a nom de guerre, and a far safer name in most parts of Afghanistan than the obviously Russian Iskanderov.

He leaned back in the leather seat and tried to stretch his long legs. He still disliked flying, especially in small aircraft like this one, but it was a necessary part of his job—and he did enjoy the glamour, the prestige, the *perks,* as westerners called them, that went with the position. He was, after all, chief military advisor to some of the most powerful and dangerous men in the world.

Davlot Iskanderov was a Tajik, born in the city of Dushanbe in what at the time had been the Soviet Socialist Republic of Tajik and was the Jumhurii Tojikiston, the Republic of Tajikistan. The eldest son of a well-to-do family within a desperately poor SSR, he'd gone to college, then joined the army, where he was selected for special training and eventually became a colonel in the GRU, the Soviet Directorate of Military Intelligence. He'd served in Afghanistan for three tours, beginning in 1980, working with the DRA in Kabul. He'd helped them set up KHAD, the DRA's intelligence service, and worked with them closely.

It was ironic . . . and amusing, really. He'd swiftly learned to despise Afghanistan, and especially to despise the fanatical and mindless devotion to Islam espoused by so many of that pitiful country's inhabitants. Though his parents had been of Tajik-Muslim heritage, Iskanderov had been raised atheist. In the Soviet Russia of the sixties and seventies, atheism and membership in the Communist party were vital to anyone hoping to advance his fortunes. The more he saw of Islam, both in Afghanistan and in his own homeland, the more he respected Marx's dictum—that religion was the opiate of the people, a means by which the rich kept the poor contentedly enslaved and ignorant of their own miserable condition.

"Abu Akbar!"

He looked up toward the front of the aircraft, where his traveling companion was acting as his own muezzin, reciting the call to Salatu-l-Asr, the mid-afternoon prayer of all devout Muslims.

"Abu Akbar! Abu Akbar! Abu Akbar!"

God is great.

The Learjet Model 35 had been designed with seats for eight passengers, but two had been removed from this particular aircraft, creating a small, clear forward area where the devout could offer prayer even while in flight. Their current course was northwest, and so Iskandar's traveling companion was facing toward the left front of the cabin, the direction, near enough, of distant Mecca.

The venerable passenger jet—owned and operated by a Saudi investment firm that was one of al-Qaeda's front organizations—had a maximum range, with reserves, of just over four thousand kilometers. That meant they'd had to make the flight in two legs, with a stop for refueling at Allahabad, before their second leg into Kabul.

It also meant they would be spending most of the day in

the air. There were shortcuts allowed for Muslims who were traveling, but in general, *salaah,* or prayer, was required five times each day as one of the four pillars of Islam known as Ibadah. Being Muslim meant accepting the responsibilities of Ibadah, including with prayer the obligations of *saum, zakah,* and jihad.

At least, he thought, he had the jihad part covered.

"Ash'hadu an laa ilaaha illallaah! Ash'hadu an laa ilaaha illallaah!"

I bear witness that there is no god but Allah.

For Iskanderov, there was no god but money. As much as he'd hated Afghanistan, his service there had eventually made him rich . . . *very* rich. Through KHAD he'd made contact with several of Afghanistan's extensive drug-smuggling networks, and even helped establish an efficiently working pipeline from Afghanistan into Tajikistan, from which high-grade heroin could be shipped throughout the Soviet Union and to the West. He'd felt no particular remorse for his part in what was widely perceived as a "dirty" entanglement. His contacts paid him very well—as much in a month as he could expect to earn in five years as a colonel in the army.

"Ash'hadu anna Muhammadar-rasulullaah! Ash'hadu anna Muhammadar-rasulullaah!"

I bear witness that Muhammed is the Messenger of Allah.

He'd retired from the army in 1987 a reasonably wealthy man. By that time he knew that the war in Afghanistan was lost. More, however, he was convinced that the Soviet Union itself was tottering into its final days. The army was a hollow shell, poorly armed and equipped, indifferently led, paralyzed by drug and alcohol abuse, the men often unpaid for long stretches of time. The old days of Soviet might and international respect were long gone. Glasnost and perestroika had gutted the nation and left her bleeding and weak, prey to the wolves gathering within and without.

Long before, however, Iskanderov had decided that his best chance lay with being one of the wolves.

"Haya 'alas-salaah! Haya 'alas-salaah!"

Come to prayer.

He watched Khalid Shaikh Mohammed's back as he continued to call the faithful to prayer. Iskanderov didn't *need* to join him. He could claim—like the aircraft's pilot—that he was ritually impure and would need to engage in *gusl,* a complete ablution, before he could properly pray. It wouldn't even be a lie. He'd had that delightful interlude two nights ago with a Malaysian prostitute, and the Qu'ran made it clear that a full-body ablution was necessary for a man after sexual intercourse or a wet dream. The *gusl* was much more than a quick shower; it was a complete ritual bathing that included mouth, nostrils, and head, all performed with the intent that the act be one of purification and worship. Technically, he was unclean.

But there were times when the *show* of religion was of vital importance, to solidify his position with his new employers. This was Friday, the Muslim sabbath. If a mosque had been available, he would have been expected to attend the *juma,* the congregational prayer that replaced the usual afternoon prayer. As it was, because they were traveling, the traditional noon and afternoon prayers were being combined as one.

With only a small inward grimace, he rose from his seat and joined Mohammed at the front of the cabin.

Mohammed nodded at him, a brief acknowledgment, and completed the call to prayer. *"Laa ilaaha illallaah! . . ."*

There is no god but Allah.

They began the formal prayers together, in the *qiyam,* or standing posture, raising their hands to their ears, then folding them, right over left, upon the breast. Then they dropped to the *ruku,* bowing and placing their hands upon their knees, each move dictated by the Qu'ran and long, long tradition, as the Learjet continued to drone its weary hours across the Bay of Bengal.

Iskanderov's mind was less on the ritual, however, than upon their physical destination. He would have to be careful with this formality once they reached Afghanistan, where, under the Taliban, the proper observance of *salaah* was quite literally a matter of life and death.

Afghanistan. That was the one unfortunate part of his current employment. Occasionally he was forced to return there, to meet directly with bin Laden and his lieutenants, or with the country's Taliban masters.

The money was good. *Very* good. But—by Allah—he despised that miserable, benighted wasteland.

Frankly, he thought, they deserved whatever the Americans decided to give them.

Chapter 8

Special Forces Operations Center
Royal Thai Navy Airfield
Utapao, Thailand
1525 hours, local time

"I guess," Mariacher said slowly, "we can rule out infiltration by sea."

The four SEALs were in the small motel-like facility at the Utapao RTNA that served as a barracks for visiting American forces during Cobra Gold. They were supposed to be relaxing. Their hosts had provided a small refrigerator filled with beer and soda, and a kitchenette pantry well stocked with various snack foods and munchies, including candy—"pogie bait," as it had long been known in the Navy. The front door led to a veritable paradise: lush tropical vegetation, palm trees, and a short walk to a pristine beach. It was right off the front of a vacation postcard. There were even women here, lovely, uninhibited, sensual, and by all accounts fascinated by American men. The place was, in short, an R&R dream.

But at the moment the four SEALs were gathered around

a large map of southeastern Afghanistan and the northwest Pakistan frontier, spread out on the kitchenette table.

"Damn," Osterlee said, snapping his fingers. "I figured going in by sub was a cinch."

The others laughed, though Mariacher was concerned at the brittle edge to the laughter. They all were running way short on sleep. They'd been up all night with the military flight out of KL to Utapao, and then there'd been the debriefings that morning. They'd caught a little rack time after lunch, but now they were up again, discussing their new assignment and speculating about an infiltration into Afghanistan. So far, they'd been told almost exactly nothing, save that the Company was interested in seconding the DevGroup cell into a large-scale operation it was mounting in Afghanistan and neighboring Pakistan, and that their mission area would be near the city of Khowst, in Afghanistan's Paktia Province on the border with Pakistan.

The SEALs had worked closely at times with the CIA in the Vietnam conflict, and it was a relationship that continued to the present day, especially in the case of DevGroup.

The Special Forces Development Group had been started in 1980 in the wake of the Iranian hostage crisis. At the time, it was called SEAL Team Six, and it swiftly made a name for itself in the new and vicious war against international terrorism.

A SEAL Six team had been on the point of launching a strike against the cruise ship *Achille Lauro,* which had been hijacked by Abu Nidal's terrorists and was sitting in Alexandria harbor. When the terrorists struck a deal with the Egyptian authorities and boarded a passenger airliner before the raid could be carried out, Navy fighters forced the jet to land at Sigonella, in Sicily, and SEAL Six operators had been on the ground to surround the aircraft and take the terrorists prisoner. Unfortunately, the Italians intervened, surrounding the SEALs who were surrounding the aircraft, and the situation came within an ace of a firefight until cooler heads prevailed and the situation was defused. Though the SEALs themselves considered the op a failure—the politicians had intervened and their prey escaped—the incident made SEAL Six something of a legend within the special warfare community.

Perhaps too much of a legend. SEAL Six had carried out a number of highly professional and successful ops throughout the eighties, most of them successful and, therefore, completely unknown to the public. Unfortunately, the unit's leader—a flamboyant and at times abrasive individual who paid little attention to the political toes he was stepping on at any given moment—came under official investigation for misappropriation of funds.

In fact, the attack on SEAL Six had been part of an ongoing war within the battlefields of the Pentagon and elsewhere inside the Washington Beltway over the whole idea of Special Forces. Many high-ranking military officers, including men who pulled enormous political power, felt that *all* Special Forces—Army, Air Force, and Marine, as well as the Navy SEALs—stole the best weaponry, the bulk of the funding, and the best, most experienced men from the regular services. SEAL Six, with its in-your-face commander, happened to be an especially easy target. SEALs had a long history of going outside the rules to procure the equipment they felt they needed. Commercially available swim fins and masks, for instance, had been better at the time than those issued by the government. The rules of procurement were broken. The SEALs hadn't played by the rules.

And so SEAL Six had come under detailed and devastating scrutiny. The errant commander was court-martialed and served some jail time. The entire Team was reorganized.

But what emerged was, in many ways, stronger and better than the original. The name "SEAL Team Six" was far too well-known for a unit that depended on secrecy for its survival and its success. So the vague and innocuous term "Naval Special Warfare Development Group"—DevGroup for short—was coined. Rather than operating in standard sixteen-man platoons, DevGroup operators deployed in cells, with as many men in a cell as were necessary to carry out the mission.

Except for the U.S. Marines, who'd chosen to retain full control of their own Special Forces assets—Force Recon and their scout/sniper units—all Special Forces now came under the operational jurisdiction of the U.S. Special Operations Command. Within SOCOM, certain "black" military units—so-called because of their highly covert nature—came under the Joint Special Operations Command, or JSOC. DevGroup was among these secret units. The CIA drew on JSOC personnel when mounting special missions abroad, and they drew on former Army Delta Force and Navy DevGroup personnel for their own Special Activities Staff, or SAS.

Which was how the Gray Ghost cell had found itself tracking an al-Qaeda bigwig in Kuala Lumpur's Chinatown. And now, their target somehow alerted and fled, they were being redeployed to Afghanistan.

But they hadn't yet been told just how they were going to get there.

Afghanistan was just possibly the toughest place in the world to enter right now. As Mariacher had just jokingly reminded them, it was completely landlocked. Paktia Province, where they'd been told they would be operating, was 650 miles north of the Pakistani port of Karachi, on the far side of some of the most forbidding mountain and desert terrain on earth.

"It's got to be on foot," Bradley pointed out. "We get to Pakistan by available military flight, and we cross the border on foot."

"What about a HAHO insertion?" Lehman asked.

"No way." Mariacher moved the top of his forefinger across the map. "See these mountains? The Hindu Kush. The Himalayas' little brothers . . . but they run anywhere from three to six thousand meters above sea level. Right here, the Khyber Pass cuts through them a thousand meters above sea level. And just a few miles to the west, south of Jalalabad, it's forty-four hundred meters. The terrain here is all up and down."

"But we could fly in at fifty thousand feet, pop our chutes high up . . . say, eighteen thousand feet. That's well above the highest mountains in this area. We could even drop over Pakistan and paraglide across the border and into the LZ."

"Negative. We'd have to jump at night, to avoid drawing attention. There's just too much that could go wrong with a night jump in rugged terrain like that. We could slam into the face of a cliff or get caught in an updraft. We could be scattered to hell and gone, maybe come down in separate valleys miles apart."

"HALO would be even worse," Bradley said. "We'd have to depend on our altimeters, but those read altitude based on the pressure at sea level. If we're on target, we pop our chutes a thousand feet above the ground. If we're just a little bit off, we auger into the top of a mountain range and never even pull the cord."

"Yeah, but on foot?" Lehman said. "With as much equipment as we're going to be packing? We'll stand out like . . . hell, like tourists."

"You know," Bradley said, "we just might be able to do it the old-fashioned way. Buy tickets on Pakistan International Airlines or Saudi Airlines and fly straight into Kabul with Swedish or German visas. The Company could fix us up that way."

"I don't know," Mariacher said. "Right now the Taliban doesn't like *any* outsiders. We'd certainly be closely watched, and we wouldn't be able to carry anything suspicious in our luggage. No friendly embassy to take delivery of our weapons or other hardware." He shook his head. "Not many options. No good ones, anyway."

"The simplest way to deploy would be helicopter," Osterlee said. "Sneak in over the mountains, drop us off in the middle of nowhere, sneak back out. Piece of cake."

"Not with the Afghan radar sites along the border still operational. We need to get in without alerting the whole damned country."

"All that leaves is boots," Bradley conceded.

"Yeah, and we're going to need local help too," Mariacher added. "I imagine Mr. Mitchell will be able to help us in that area."

"How's your Arabic, Lieutenant?" Osterlee asked.

"Not bad," Mariacher replied. The Sea Ghosts had all gone through a crash course in the language two years earlier, and Mariacher picked up quite a bit of practice in Saudi Arabia and Iraq during Desert Storm. "Rusty, but not bad. Trouble is, not that many people speak Arabic in Afghanistan."

"So what do they speak?" Lehman asked. "Afghanistanese?"

"Actually, they speak maybe thirty different tribal languages," Bradley said. "Pashto and Dari are the main ones, I guess. Those two are the official languages, anyway, and just about everyone knows at least one of them."

"Russian may work," Osterlee said. Most SEALs had gone through the Russian language programs offered to U.S. special operations forces at one time or another.

"It may work if we want to talk to guys who used to support the DRA," Mariacher pointed out. "But for the rest of them, the old mujahideen, it might get you shot. The Russians still aren't the most popular fellows around in that country."

A knock sounded at the door. "C'mon in, it's open!" Bradley called out.

Karl Mitchell walked in. He was carrying a briefcase and wore a troubled expression on an already long face. "Gentlemen," he said. "Sorry to intrude."

"No intrusion, sir," Mariacher said as the others cleared the map off the table and pulled up an extra chair. "Whatcha got?"

Sitting at the table, Mitchell opened the briefcase and handed each of the SEALs a sheet of hardcopy. "First off, I thought you'd like to see the text of President Bush's speech to Congress. He delivered it a few hours ago."

They read through the speech. "Sounds like he's putting us all on notice," Bradley said. "The U.S. is going into Afghanistan, and it's going to be soon." He looked up at Mitchell. "Any idea when?"

"That hasn't been released yet. There's . . . something else you should know."

"Go on," Mariacher said. Something about Mitchell's bearing carried the weight of something very wrong.

"We just got word here. Jerry Wheeler, the CIA man at the safe house in Kuala Lumpur?"

"Yes."

"He's dead."

"My God," Mariacher said. "What happened?"

"We're still trying to get a clear story, but it sounds like a car bomb. Witnesses saw a car moving at high speed down the street, then veer and slam through the front of the building. There was an explosion and fire. The word is four people inside the house were killed, and five more were wounded out on the street."

"Four dead . . ." Mariacher thought about the Malaysian teenager. What was his name? Najid, that was it. Najid, and the other two Malaysian kids, must have been caught in the blast as well.

"Wheeler was pretty bent out of shape by the ambush outside that house," Lehman said. "He seemed afraid that we were attracting attention."

"It wasn't your fault," Mitchell told them. "As you two said yourselves, the bad guys had to have known about the place, and must have had it under surveillance. I'm just glad you guys got out when you did."

"What about the prisoners?" Mariacher asked. "They were still there when we left."

Mitchell nodded. "The tangos may have been trying to kill them before we could get them out of the country. Instant martyrdom. But the word I have is that they're on their way to Mactan, safe and sound. The attack took place—" He stopped and checked his watch. "Only about three hours ago. The prisoners were pulled out while it was still dark."

"You know," Mariacher said, thoughtful, "this is a new pattern."

"What do you mean?"

"Up until now, the tangos haven't usually tried to hit us back directly. I mean, they always go for the high-profile targets, the ones that will kill a lot of Americans and grab some time on the nightly news. They haven't bothered trying to kill us—the SEAL operators or CIA agents—except in self-defense. I think they're upping the ante."

"Could be," Mitchell said. "Of course, one part of Bojinka was supposed to be an attack against CIA headquarters."

"Sure, but that would still be a high-profile target." Mariacher grinned. "Your secret HQ isn't exactly secret, you know. I've seen the road sign." He was referring to the large highway direction sign on the George Washington Memorial Parkway in northern Virginia indicating the exit for the CIA.

"I did think it was unusual that the opposition sent that team to your hotel room in Kuala Lumpur," Mitchell said.

"Roger that," Bradley said. "Most people try to *avoid* combat with SEALs."

Mitchell nodded. "The usual tango MO is to scatter and run when they know they've been spotted. It suggests a whole new way of waging war for them."

"They may just be trying to make us pull back," Mariacher suggested. "They know we want to avoid collateral damage, getting civilians caught in a cross fire. Maybe they figure that if they hit us back directly, especially in residential areas or the heart of a city, we'll back off."

"It could also mean they're scared because we got so close to one of their major leaders," Bradley said. He held up his thumb and forefinger, an inch apart. "We were *that* close to nailing Mohammed, Green Tiger. If Dugan had just given us the word . . ."

"But he didn't," Mitchell said. Opening his briefcase again, he removed a file folder and passed out more sheets of hardcopy. "I needn't remind you that this is classified Top Secret, gentlemen. It's your mission profile."

Mariacher read through the first paragraphs. Gray Ghost cell was again being seconded to the CIA. They would fly to Pakistan, where they would meet a CIA case officer and an ISI agent. With local help, they would infiltrate by foot into Paktia Province. There was a long list of mission objectives. High on the list was contacting an Afghan in the city of Khowst who used the code name "Ali Hassan." The Agency hoped to use Hassan to start an anti-Taliban resistance movement in the region; he might also be able to tell the

SEALs the whereabouts of a number of key al-Qaeda and Taliban leaders.

There was also a list of ground targets the SEALs were to observe, photograph, and report on—Zhawar Kili on the Afghan-Pakistan border, and Kur Zhowt, in the mountains north of Khowst. Both were believed to be terrorist training facilities and logistical centers for al-Qaeda.

One of the listed AQ leaders was Mohammed.

"So . . . any word yet on where Green Tiger got to?" Lehman asked. "Is he back in Afghanistan?"

"We're not sure," Mitchell admitted. "We think he may have caught a private jet at KL International, but we weren't able to track him. Our best information, though, suggests he'll be headed back to Afghanistan. All the AQ big fish are going to Afghanistan. I think they know the Taliban won't give them up, and they figure the United States won't hit the Taliban to get at them."

"Man," Osterlee said, shaking his head. "Are *they* ever in for a surprise!"

Friday, September 21, 2001

Kabul International Airport
Kabul, Afghanistan
2130 hours, local time

Davlot Iskanderov descended from the Learjet. Kabul Airport was in darkness—though whether because they expected an attack by the Americans or because the power was out again, he wasn't sure. He and Mohammed were met on the tarmac by a small army of Taliban militia, armed and nervous. Light was provided by an ancient wreck of a bus, its engine filling the cold mountain air with diesel fumes as it noisily idled.

"Papers!" one long-bearded warrior demanded, speaking Pashto and holding out a leathery hand. "Who are you?"

"God willing," Iskanderov said, speaking Pashto, "I believe you will find these in order." He handed the man a packet containing a Saudi passport; a letter from Mullah Abdul Jalil, one of the Taliban's deputy ministers of foreign affairs; and a bundle of fifteen thousand afghanis—about eighteen Saudi riyals, or roughly five dollars U.S. at the current exchange rate, but still a respectable bribe here. Offering a bribe to Taliban officials was always risky; some of them could be straight-laced indeed, and could interpret an attempted bribe as an insult. On the other hand, not that many of them could read the letter from Jalil, which gave him free passage through regions controlled by the Taliban, but *everyone* could read folding high-value denominations.

The official leafed through the packet with narrow, suspicious eyes. When he handed it back to Iskanderov, the money was gone. "Everything *appears* to be in order," he agreed. "But you are a foreigner."

"I am Tajik," he said. "And I have the blue eyes of the Greeks. But more than that, I am a slave of Allah. I am also with *him*." He nodded toward Mohammed, who was talking with other militiamen nearby.

"It is good. You may pass. Get on the bus."

"Thanks be to Allah."

Many in this part of the world claimed ancestry either from the Greeks of Alexander—Iskanderov's Russian name meant "Alexander's son"—or from the Mongols of Genghis Khan, as marks of prestige. In fact, and despite their paranoid suspicion of *all* outsiders, the Taliban had been admitting many foreigners lately. Recruits to the jihad were flocking into the country in expectation of the final confrontation with the American Satans.

Mohammed encountered no difficulties with his papers.

The militiamen recognized him and ushered him onto the bus with many genuflections and exclamations of God's goodness.

Iskanderov carefully shuttered his emotions from the rabble. They could be useful, but they were also dangerous. He took a seat facing inward, and Mohammed took the seat opposite. Taliban militia brought their suitcases onboard, then took up positions in the rear of the bus, watchful and alert. Iskanderov could not be entirely sure whether they were along for the ride as a guard of honor or as guards for the foreigners.

Both, most likely.

During his time as a GRU officer operating out of Kabul, he'd made a number of contacts with the locals, and even established friendships of a sort. Afghanistan was a bizarre country of warring, tribal feudalism and ever-shifting alliances. None of them were to be trusted, ever . . . but at least they *could* be understood, and their fanaticism, their irrational pride, and their poverty all could be used against them. His connections with the local drug network had made him wealthy in the first place and ultimately led to useful contacts within the several competing organizations known to the world at large as the Russian mafia.

Popular wisdom might hold that drugs contaminated everything and everyone they touched. Iskanderov could only smile at that. After all, drugs had done nothing but make him wealthy.

Lately, however, his fortunes had abruptly changed. Alliances within the Russian mafia were as changeable as alliances in Kabul. Worse, though, a particularly obnoxious band of fanatics had come to power in Afghanistan the year before—the Taliban. At first they'd maintained the flow of drugs through the Tajikistan pipeline, since they needed the cash to buy weapons. Last year, however, they'd all but shut

the trade down, hanging, beheading, or shooting the peas-
ants who grew the poppies from which opium was derived.
Since eighty percent of the world's heroin supply came from
Afghanistan, his Tajikistan pipeline had dried up.

Another man might have simply retired on what he'd already made—perhaps taken up the life of a millionaire
playboy in the Levant or the Riviera. Or he might have
railed against the Taliban and their meddling, and perhaps
found a way to strike back at them. Iskanderov hadn't lied
to the Taliban customs official. His ethnic roots were indeed within the ancient tribal heritage of the Tajiks, dangerous men who never let even the slightest wrong go
unavenged.

But Davlot Iskanderov was, above all else, a survivor. He
prided himself on his ability to shift with changing circumstances . . . and to seize new opportunities when they presented themselves. In the late 1980s he'd made the
acquaintance of a number of wealthy Middle Eastern businessmen, cultivating these contacts as personal friends. One
of these had been an unprepossessing Saudi national, the
scion of a billionaire family and a construction empire,
named Osama bin Laden.

Money attracted money. Bin Laden was wealthy, far
wealthier than Iskanderov, especially now that his own financial empire was tottering and his Afghan contacts were
either being killed or converted. Through Qari Ahmadullah, one of his old KHAD associates, Iskanderov had met
a year ago with one of bin Laden's lieutenants—Khalid
Shaikh Mohammed—and offered his experience in military intelligence to the organization bin Laden headed: al-
Qaeda.

The alliance was perfect. An accomplished linguist,
Iskanderov already spoke Pashto, Dari, Arabic, and Punjabi,

as well as Russian, Tajik, and English. His knowledge of both military tactics and intelligence techniques, and his specific knowledge of *American* military tactics, was proving invaluable to al-Qaeda, an organization that, while well-funded, often displayed a certain naiveté when it came to operating in the real world. And Iskanderov continued to draw a *most* handsome paycheck for his services.

And all he had to do was tolerate these fanatical idiots. It was the ultimate joke, really. He still detested Afghanistan, still detested religious fanatics of every stripe, yet he'd been in the right place at the right time, able to step in and provide the fanatics—the same fanatics who'd deprived him of his livelihood—with the professional help that enabled him to keep the rubles coming in.

"What are you smiling at?" Mohammed asked, scattering his thoughts. He spoke English, which the militiamen would not understand.

"Nothing of importance," he replied in the same language. "I was thinking that if these reports are accurate, if the Americans do invade Afghanistan, they will find themselves in the same trap they fell into in Vietnam."

Khalid Mohammed looked at Iskanderov through half-closed eyes, an unreadable expression. "They will find themselves in the same trap into which you Russians fell, on the plains and high mountains of Afghanistan."

"You are right, Excellency. Except for the fact that I am not Russian."

Mohammed shifted in his seat. "Save your fictions for those who require them. Your past is of no importance to me. Your loyalty to the cause, however, is."

"Excellency, I should think I've proven that loyalty by now."

Mohammed sighed, then looked away, staring out the window at the pitch-darkness beyond. "I know. You have.

You were right, back in Kuala Lumpur. You may well have saved my life there, and I am grateful."

"It's what you hired me for, sir."

"Indeed. Still, *all* loyalties will be put to the test in this coming struggle, especially loyalties to gold. We face a deadly enemy. The United States will not rest until we are all hunted down and destroyed. It is *badal* on a global scale."

Badal was the *Pakhtunwali* notion of revenge for any slight upon a man's honor, the driving force of the feuds of murder and revenge that had bloodied the region for centuries. Americans had killed Pashtuns, Pashtuns would kill Americans, on and on without end.

"As I've explained, Excellency, the advantage we hold over the Americans is their lack of political will. It is what undid them in Vietnam . . . a war that they won on the battlefield but lost at home. Their politicians will not long endure the casualties this kind of war will inflict. They will invade Afghanistan. They will, I feel sure, destroy our Taliban hosts. They will declare victory . . . and they will go home. But al-Qaeda will endure."

"And how dedicated are you to the Base?"

"I am a good Muslim."

"That doesn't answer my question." He glanced at the back of the bus, and Iskanderov thought he read in those dark eyes a look of disdain, even of contempt. "We *all* are good Muslims here."

He wondered about Mohammed's true feelings. That he was dedicated to the cause of al-Qaeda, there was no doubt. But how fanatical a Muslim was he? In the modern world, in the *real* world, one was forced to balance one's responsibilities to the dictates of Islam and to the need to live in that real world. Outwardly, Mohammed was as devout as any of these fanatics. However, he often showed a cold, calculating, and realistic side to his personality . . . as cold and calculating as Iskanderov himself.

"Then put it this way," Iskanderov said. "I am a tool of Allah, the gracious, the munificent. Allah has placed me in your hands, a weapon with which to protect yourself from the Americans. If the weapon is well-forged, if it does what you expect it to do, if it kills your enemies . . . then its loyalty is not in question. It is a thing to be used, nothing more; and so you use it, and give thanks to Allah for having provided it."

"I'm not questioning your loyalty," Mohammed said at last. "But the Base will require the very best of all of its . . . tools. Our survival depends upon it. Our victory depends upon it."

Iskanderov leaned forward in his seat slightly, giving a *salaam* in the Saudi custom. "In me, Excellency, you have the very best, I assure you."

"I am sure that is true, my friend. However . . . while in this place, it would be good for you to examine closely your motives and what you truly believe. These people know and understand duplicity, and they know sincerity. You will not put them off with a few pious formalities."

It was, Iskanderov realized, a warning. Mohammed might not care how devout he was in his daily devotions, but the rabble *did* care. If he made a slip, even his personal and political connections with Mohammed, with Ahmadullah, with bin Laden himself, would not save him.

"I understand, Excellency. Thank you."

Mohammed nodded. After a long silence he said, "And . . . do you have any objections to my making that phone call now?"

Iskanderov smiled. "None, Excellency. In fact, better now, while we're moving, than when we reach Zur Kowt."

At the beginning of their flight, soon after they were airborne, Mohammed had pulled out his cell phone and been about to make a call to bin Laden. Iskanderov stopped him, reminding him that the Americans were capable of tracking cell phone calls through their network of communications and spy satellites. He was convinced that many of the top-ranking al-Qaeda officers had already compromised key locations by their overreliance on the damnable cell phones they loved so much. At the moment, though, he was more concerned about the possibility that the Americans were still trying to track Mohammed as he fled Kuala Lumpur. They had at least one carrier battlegroup in the Arabian Sea; it was not impossible that they would scramble a flight of interceptors to force the corporate Learjet to land or shoot it down outright.

Mohammed placed his call, carefully using code phrases and circumlocutions to avoid compromising himself. The rest of the uncomfortable journey was completed in silence, save for the ratcheting of tortured gears and the cough and whine of the bus's motor.

It was a long drive to their destination . . . not so much in kilometers, but in time. The Zur Kowt camps were only 120 kilometers from Kabul by road, but that road was narrow and winding in places, and often blocked by traffic or by militia checkpoints. In fact, it took as long to reach Zur Kowt from Kabul as it had taken for them to fly the entire 4,800 kilometers from Kuala Lumpur to Kabul—six and a half hours in the air, plus another three hours on the ground from Allahabad, in central India.

The sun was rising when they reached their destination.

How long, Iskanderov wondered, before the Americans were here as well?

Chapter 9

The unmarked C-130 descended toward a tortured landscape of ocher sand and boulders. Mariacher couldn't see a lot out of the small window in the big transport's cargo compartment, but what he could see looked bleak and inhospitable. Nowhere was there a sign of life— no animals, no trees, no buildings. They had to be getting close, though. The whine and thump of the aircraft's landing gear as it came down and locked was loud enough to penetrate the roar of the transport's powerful engines.

"Any sign of a welcoming committee, Wheel?" Chief Bradley asked from the other side of the aircraft. He had to shout to make himself heard above the racket.

Mariacher shook his head and turned away from the window. "Mitchell said we were going to have to blend in with the locals," he shouted back. "I think that means we disguise ourselves as scorpions or something."

Bradley grinned. "I could go with that. Scorpions are cool

critters. They can survive, even flourish, in places that would kill anything else. They're quiet. And they're deadly. Well, some of 'em, anyway."

"They also hide in people's shoes," Osterlee pointed out.

"Yeah," Lehman added. "You just find yourself a nice, cozy empty home, smelling of sweaty feet and foot powder, and in comes this five-headed monster."

"So you sting the son of a bitch," Bradley said. "Serves him right for not knocking."

Mariacher leaned back against the board-hard padding of his seat and listened to the banter. They all seemed in good spirits, ready to take on this latest challenge with a genuine eagerness to strike back at al-Qaeda. Sea Ghost cell didn't quite look the part of Navy SEALs at the moment. They were wearing nondescript desert-camo BDUs and fatigue caps, and might have belonged to any branch of the service. None wore any insignia of rank.

With a stomach-wrenching drop, the C-130 Hercules descended sharply, and moments later the wheels squealed on the runway. After a brief taxi, the Air Force sergeant in charge of the cargo deck called out, "Here you are, gentlemen! Beautiful downtown Dalbandin! Hang onto your wallets!" He pressed a button on the forward bulkhead, and the transport's rear hatch lowered with a whine.

"Dalbandin all hope, ye who enter here!" Mariacher called out, eliciting groans from the others. They trooped down the ramp and emerged into the blazing white heat of the desert.

Dalbandin was a small city located in the Balochistan Desert west of Quetta, and just thirty miles from the Afghanistan border. The Afghani city of Kandahar—the heart and soul of the Taliban movement—lay only 125 miles to the north. Technically, the airport at Dalbandin was not a military facility. However, the Pakistani Air Force had landing rights there, and Mariacher noted with interest a line of Pakistani F-5s parked alongside one of the taxiways, wingtip-to-wingtip, in front of some military-looking hangers. The facility had surfaced frequently in recent military planning sessions. When the invasion of Afghanistan began in earnest, the base would be ideal as a staging area and as a logistical hub, and there'd even been some discussion of the possibility of getting Pakistan to turn the whole facility over to coalition forces.

That hadn't happened yet, however, and the U.S. government wanted to exercise extreme caution not to inflame the already volatile passions of the locals. The people in this part of Pakistan shared ethnic, social, and religious kinship with the people of Kandahar, and there were many Taliban supporters within the local population.

The airport facilities appeared surprisingly modern, and a Pakistani International Airlines 747 was parked in front of the civilian terminal. As the four SEALs looked about, seabags on the tarmac at their sides, they saw two jeeps approaching from the direction of the military hangers.

The jeeps pulled to a halt, and the drivers, in Pakistani khaki uniforms and berets, began loading the SEALs' seabags onto one of the jeeps. A third Pakistani wore the uniform of an army major. It was the fourth member of the reception committee, however, who held their complete and undivided attention.

He was clearly American, wearing civilian clothing, a photographer's vest, expensive hiking boots, a Jack Daniel's ball cap, and $150 Oakley sunglasses. He also wore leather shooting gloves and carried an AK-47 slung over his shoulder.

"Your papers," the Pakistani officer said.

Mariacher handed him their orders, and he appeared to read them carefully.

"You are the American Navy SEALs we were to expect."

Despite the thick accent, he managed to convey a sense of disapproval.

"Lieutenant Mariacher, sir."

"I am Major Ghulam ul Qadi. Welcome to Pakistan." His manner seemed less than welcoming.

"Salaam," Mariacher said.

Qadi gave a pale smile. "I appreciate the polite gesture, Lieutenant, although I speak Punjabi, not Arabic."

"I was given to understand that the word is considered a greeting in most Islamic countries, sir."

"True. Unfortunately, this is not a time of peace. Your country seems determined to . . . to press the situation here."

"This isn't the time to discuss politics or religion, gentlemen," the American said. "Let's get out of here. This is too damned public for my taste."

"And you are? . . ." Mariacher asked.

"Call me Raptor," the man said. He appeared to be working on a beard, though at the moment it simply looked unshaven. The four SEALs all were sporting three-day facial growths as well.

This, evidently, was the Company paramilitary they were supposed to meet here. They'd been given no contact information, no passwords. Mitchell had simply grinned and said, "Oh, you'll know him when you see him. He's a contractor. One of the best."

"Contractor" was the slang term for paramilitary operators working for the CIA. They were mercenaries, pure and simple, albeit mercenaries who for the most part still maintained a powerful allegiance to the United States and its interests. Before signing on with the Company, nearly all had been members of various U.S. elite military units—Delta Force, Rangers, Army Special Forces, and, yes, Navy SEALs.

Mariacher had known a few contractors during his time in the military so far. Many had been recruited while they were still in the service, so that they in effect received their discharge one day and began working for the CIA the next. Most had combat experience; all were superbly trained. The word was that they went through some pretty tough additional training after leaving the military, tuning up their existing skills and adding some new ones. Tradecraft—the skills used by spies—was taught in an eighteen-week program at Camp Peary, the ten thousand acre facility near Williamsburg, Virginia, popularly known as "the Farm." Additional paramilitary training took place at Harvey Point, North Carolina, and at Special Forces training facilities down in Panama.

They piled into the jeeps and headed for town, Mariacher and Osterlee in the back of the lead vehicle, Bradley and Lehman in the other. Their driver mashed down the accelerator and careened off the tarmac, bumping across open ground to reach the highway.

There was a fair amount of traffic on the two-lane road into Dalbandin, Mariacher noted. Vehicles in Pakistan, as in Malaysia, moved on the left . . . but observance of this custom appeared to be at the whim of the driver. Mariacher realized this when he looked up and saw that their jeep appeared to be locked on course for a head-on collision with a garishly painted bus, which in turn was trying to pass an overloaded Russian Zil truck.

"My God!" he said, gripping the side of the jeep and wondering if he should jump. Their driver appeared to have entered a high-stakes game of chicken, holding neither to the left lane nor the right, but keeping to the middle, unwilling to yield to either bus or truck.

Horns blared and the jeep driver half stood in his seat, screaming Punjabi invectives and shaking his fist. Somehow, even standing, he managed to press the accelerator pedal to the floor.

Since neither truck nor bus appeared willing to yield to the other, collision appeared imminent. Mariacher realized he couldn't jump for it, since he would land in the road directly in front of the oncoming Zil. At the last possible moment the truck swerved enough to the right that the jeep was able to pass between bus and truck with almost a foot to spare on either side. Mariacher had an instant's glance up at the bus, which was festooned with hubcaps and other pieces of metal jangling and clattering with the vehicle's motion. Bearded passengers looked back at him, some indifferent, some shouting and waving fists or, in a few cases, AK-47 rifles.

Their driver swerved to clear the back of the bus. Turning, Mariacher saw the bus pull ahead of the lumbering truck and cut it off so closely he could have sworn the bumpers clashed. The second jeep had swerved off the left side of the road, and was able to swing back in a spray of dust and gravel, its driver screaming and gesturing at both vehicles.

Mariacher looked at the contractor, who was sitting in the left-side front passenger seat. He appeared unconcerned. Turning, he gave Mariacher a half shrug, then looked away. "You'll get used to it!" he said, shouting to be heard above the wind.

That, Mariacher decided, was unlikely. He'd picked up an interesting factoid back in Thailand, to the effect that the road accident rate in Pakistan was the highest in the world— ten thousand fatalities a year in a population half the size of the U.S. After seeing this display of driving, he was surprised that the casualty rate was that *low*.

He'd been trained to handle combat, but that training hadn't prepared him for the experience of weaving at high speed through heavy traffic, apparently in defiance both of local law and physics.

Or common sense, for that matter.

Eventually, though, they arrived at a mud-brick building on the outskirts of Dalbandin. The emptiness of the country-side seen from the air during their approach to the airport seemed to be in stark contrast to the reality of the city—bustling, crowded, and noisy. The streets were filled with people, most of them men wearing the baggy trousers and calf-length overshirts called *shalwar kameez*. A few women were in evidence, some carrying bundles or parcels on their heads. They were recognizable as women only because of their burkas, which covered them head to foot and left only their eyes, hands, and glimpses of their sandaled feet visible. Mariacher reflected that this could as easily be a scene in a city in Afghanistan, under the Taliban. Social custom and morality were tightly ruled here by a strongly fundamental-ist interpretation of Islam.

Mariacher stepped down from the jeep, resisting a manic urge to kneel down and kiss the ground. Osterlee swayed a bit as he got out of the jeep. "Steady, there," he warned.

"Man, and I thought the drivers in New Jersey were crazy!" Osterlee said.

"I have heard of the traffic in your New York," Qadi said with a tight smile.

"New York was never like this," Bradley replied, looking at the thronged streets. A bus had stopped in the middle of the street nearby, blocking traffic in both directions. Passen-gers were trying to simultaneously get on and get off, result-ing in shoving, curses, and heated debate. "Somehow, I wasn't expecting such a crowd out here in the sticks," he said. "God! What a mess!"

"You would find it worse in India," Qadi said. "You will stay here for the night. Tomorrow, before dawn, we catch a military transport for Bannu, and from there we will go by truck to Kaka Ziurat. My men will help you with your things."

A few minutes later they were settled into a small room with four bunks and sparse furnishings. Qadi and the Pakistani soldiers had left, but Raptor remained.

"A friendly word of advice," he told the SEALs. "Do *not* criticize these people or the way they do things. Do not talk about the crowds, or the traffic, or politics. These people are incredibly proud, and they will take offense if they think you are criticizing the way they do things." He looked pointedly at Bradley. "And most especially do *not* discuss religion, or use the name of God, as you just did, in a disrespectful manner. There are places here where you would be shot out of hand for saying 'God' like you just did."

"Okay," Mariacher said. "Admonishment noted. What's the plan from here?"

Raptor placed a hand on his shoulder and raised a forefinger to his lips. "We make it up as we go," he said. "Right?"

"Right," Mariacher replied. The warning that the room was bugged was crystal clear.

"For now, get your rest." He hesitated, looked at Mariacher, then jerked his head toward the door. "You'll need it."

Mariacher nodded, and silently followed Raptor out the door.

Outside, the heat of the desert beat down on the noise, dust, and crowded street. Raptor led Mariacher deeper into the heart of the town, past outdoor stalls where turbaned merchants shouted the praise of their wares. It would have been an exotic scene out of the Arabian Nights, Mariacher thought, except that the tales of Scheherazade were never quite this crowded.

The contractor seemed to guess what Mariacher was thinking. "Yeah, it's crowded. Take over half of the population of the United States and put 'em all in a country about twice the size of California . . . except that over half of the country is either uninhabitable desert or uninhabitable mountains. The space left over gets pretty damned tight. . . . In here."

They stepped off the main street and into a narrow alley between two large shops.

"So I see." He was surprised. Raptor had said few words until his lecture in the room a few minutes ago.

"The upside is that we can't be overheard here. The house back there is almost certainly bugged."

"So I gathered."

"I needed to talk with you alone. Do not, repeat, do *not* trust Qadi."

"Back at Utapao they warned us not to trust any of the locals," Mariacher admitted. "I got the idea that out here loyalty is a highly marketable commodity."

"That's one way of looking at it." He was interrupted by a sudden burst of full-auto gunfire. Several turbaned men were in the street, firing their weapons into the air. They appeared excited, even jubilant.

Mariacher was reminded of Kuwaitis celebrating the liberation of their country ten years ago, the wild shooting into the air in complete disregard for the laws of physics. What went up *would* come down, and in these crowds it seemed almost a certainty that innocent bystanders were going to be hit by falling bullets.

"What's that all about?" Mariacher asked.

"Who knows? Most of these people are . . . visitors."

"Oh? From where?"

"Lots of places. There's been a mass exodus across the border out of Afghanistan, of course, ever since it became clear that the U.S. is going to attack them. At last report they were coming across at the rate of four thousand a day. But lots of others are flocking here to join the jihad. The word is that bin Laden put out a call just this morning, asking for volunteers from Pakistan to fight off what he called the

American crusade against Islam, and declared jihad, a holy war, against any Americans who try to attack Afghanistan. Tensions are running a mite high just now."

"I see."

"But even before Li'l bin Laden put out the call, jihadists have been coming here from everywhere. Pakistan, especially, but also Saudi Arabia. Egypt. Morocco. The Philippines. The Sudan. According to the mullahs, this is going to be the Day of Judgment."

"What, like Revelations, in the Bible?"

"Same idea. Satan and his armies are supposed to try to take down God, but the armies of the faithful will gather together and wipe out Satan and all of his host. In case you didn't get the program, we're Satan's host, they're the armies of the faithful. Got it?"

"Got it."

"Keep it in mind. You will find rational thought in extremely short supply out here."

"What about Major Qadi?"

"Qadi is ISI."

Mariacher raised his eyebrows. "Inter-Services Intelligence. Pakistan's CIA?"

"The same. I don't know if he's really an army major either. I doubt it. But his loyalties are *not* for sale. He's almost certainly working with al-Qaeda."

"Shit. I thought the Pakistani government was supposed to be on our side. Whose side are they on?"

"That is . . . let's just say that's a complicated question. The United Arab Emirates withdrew recognition of the Taliban two days ago. That leaves Saudi Arabia and Pakistan as the only two world governments who support the Taliban. Pakistan is trying very hard to stay on America's good side. They've been acting as intermediaries between Washington and the Taliban, you know."

"So I've heard."

"The Pakistani government wants to help us. At least, they don't want us to declare them to be enemies too. President Musharraf pledged support for the U.S. right after September eleventh, but pro-Taliban elements have been staging mass demonstrations ever since. The people here are mostly fundamentalist Islam, and that means they're pro-Taliban.

"As for the ISI, they helped the Taliban get started in the first place, shipping them money, guns, and volunteers. They also helped create al-Qaeda, to train Muslim fighters to fight the Russians. They have a vested interest in what's going on over the border in Afghanistan, and one thing they do not want to see is a government that might be hostile to Pakistan. In fact, rumor has it that the ISI put the Taliban in power just so Pakistan had someplace to go if things heated up with India."

"Jesus." India and Pakistan had fought and lost three major wars since Pakistan had separated from India in 1947, and ongoing border disputes, especially over Kashmir, continually made another war not only possible, but likely at any moment. Since 1998, Pakistan had been a member of the world's nuclear club, which meant that both India and Pakistan had nuclear weapons.

"Some of the people in the ISI," Raptor went on, "are pro-Taliban and pro-al-Qaeda, no matter what orders come down out of Islamabad. The ISI has been called a government within a government. Its head right now is Lieutenant General Mahmood Ahmed. He's anti-American, a fundamentalist fanatic, and he commands extraordinary loyalty throughout the intelligence service.

"Some ISI people are Islamic fundamentalists. Some hate the Jews and see this as part of the struggle to finish what Hitler started. Some simply have their careers dependent on pro-Taliban policies."

"Which one is Qadi?"

"As near as I can tell, all three. There's something else, though. Remember when we hit some terrorist training camps in Afghanistan, after the *Cole*?"

"Sure. A cruise missile strike. Didn't do much good."

"Among the people killed at the target were several ISI agents who happened to be at one of the camps. One them was Qadi's brother."

"Damn. This just gets weirder and weirder."

"I hear you. Thing is, he's been assigned to us as guide, bodyguard, translator, and babysitter. Our contract with the Pakistan government says we're not supposed to go *anywhere* without him. Between you and me, the minute we're across the border, we ditch the son of a bitch. One way or another."

"Thanks for the heads-up."

"Any time. The rules of the game right now are simple. We don't upset the locals. That means we do what Qadi says, and we keep a low profile. Don't do anything to attract attention. Our enemy isn't here, whatever *they* might think." He nodded at the noisy, heavily armed Pakistanis in the street. "It's across the border, in Afghanistan."

"Our orders are to join Task Force 5 and try to track down Khalid Shaikh Mohammed."

Raptor nodded. "Among others. Once we shake Qadi, we can give you a complete briefing."

"Maybe you can start by telling me what this Task Force 5 is supposed to be."

"Special direct action initiative. It's a network of special operatives—Special Forces, Delta, Navy SEALs . . . and CIA contractors. We are to infiltrate the country, gain intelligence for the upcoming invasion, and take down high-profile targets of opportunity."

"By which you mean bin Laden."

"And Mullah Omar, and Khalid Mohammed, and quite a

few others. Part of *my* mission is to find a man in Paktia Province, in Khowst, and talk to him about organizing an anti-Taliban resistance in the region."

"Ali Hassan?"

Raptor nodded. "That's his code name, anyway. He used to work for the Agency."

"We were told he might be able to give us information about where the big fish are."

"He should be able to. In any case, our primary target is going to be a training camp in the mountains north of Khowst. Langley believes it may be a headquarters for Mohammed and some others. It's called Zur Kowt."

"It will be nice," Mariacher said, "to know who the bad guys are."

The contractor shook his head. "It's not that easy out here, separating the good guys from the bad guys. But you'll learn."

Friday, September 21, 2001

Headquarters
Naval Special Warfare Command,
Coronado, California
1625 hours, PDT

Captain Theodore Cunningham, the CO of Naval Special Warfare Group 1, sat behind his desk, reading the report, then slowly looking up at Tangretti. He looked sad, almost fatherly. The base master-at-arms, a master chief petty officer named Brannigan, stood to Tangretti's left and behind him.

"Tangretti, I expected better of you. Your father would have expected better of you."

Damn. Always his father. The fact that Bill Tangretti had been one of the first Navy SEALs, one of the plank owners of the Teams and something of a legend for some of his exploits in 'Nam, was something that the younger Tangretti could never quite escape. But he remained rigidly at attention, wearing crisply pressed dress whites, and kept his eyes fixed on the flag-flanked portrait of President Bush at Cunningham's back.

He'd been restricted to base for the weekend. Well, that was no surprise. Everyone was restricted since the latest alert. But the Marine had written him up—put him on report—and that meant he had to face the captain's nonjudicial punishment, more often called simply "captain's mast." Back in the old days of wooden ships and iron men, they'd called it captain's mast because the ship's captain would sit forward of the mizzenmast to hear complaints and petitions and to sit in judgment of infractions to the Navy rules and regulations that governed all life at sea. "*Nonjudicial* punishment" meant that unless the captain decided that the crime warranted it, it wasn't a court-martial. As long as the accused agreed to accept whatever punishment the captain meted out, everything was cool, and there were no permanent black marks on the man's record.

Of course, Tangretti could have requested a court-martial instead. He also knew he would be nuts to do so. He was guilty, pure and simple. The best thing he could do was take his licks like a man.

"Do you have anything to say for yourself?"

"Sir, no sir," he replied, before adding the time-honored, "No excuse, sir."

"The Marine at the gate said you claimed you'd been out with your girl."

"Yes, sir. I'd just found I was shipping out, first for training, then for Afghanistan. We'd had a fight, and, well, I didn't want to just walk out of her life, y'know? She might not be there when I got back."

"There are such things as telephones, Doc. This *is* the twenty-first century."

"With respect, sir, have you seen the lines at the exchange?" He was referring to the phones reserved for the use of enlisted personnel. Sometimes, especially on the weekends, the lines to use them could be pretty bad. There were other phones available, but . . . why complicate the discussion?

"Anyway, sir," he went on, "this was the sort of thing I needed to say face-to-face."

Cunningham was silent for a moment. "I am not unsympathetic, Tangretti. However, I'm sure you've heard the old expression, 'If the Navy had wanted you to have a wife, they'd have issued you one with your seabag.' That goes for girlfriends too, you know."

"Yes, sir."

"What that means is that your responsibility first of all is to the Navy. And to the Teams, and your Teammates. You can't go AWOL just because it's convenient. Or possible. And I have a responsibility too. I can't ignore this kind of blatant irresponsibility. It would not be good for discipline, or for morale. Do you understand me?"

"Yes, sir."

"In that case, I find you guilty of being AWOL, but not to the degree that would require you to face court-martial. Unless you choose to exercise your right to a formal court?"

"No, sir. I'll accept whatever punishment you have for me, sir."

"You are fined one hundred dollars per month for the next three months and are reduced one grade in rank. I am being this lenient with you, Tangretti, because of your excellent service record so far, and because I do believe there were extenuating circumstances in your case."

"Thank you, sir."

"You are dismissed."

"Aye aye, sir." He hesitated.

"Yes?" Cunningham demanded.

"Uh . . . sir? Just one question. Will this stop me from deploying with the rest of the guys?"

"Why? Do you want it to?"

"No, sir! Absolutely not, sir! I want to ship out with Team Three when we go. I just . . . well, it occurred to me that they might not be taking E-5s."

Until that moment Tangretti had been an HM1, which meant a pay grade or rank of E-6. Now he was an HM2. Some billets, especially those for covert or special-ops deployments, specified only enlisted personnel of E-6 and higher—first class petty officers and chiefs.

Cunningham glanced at the MAA, and smiled. "I'll have a word with your platoon commander. I don't believe there will be a problem."

He let out a pent-up breath of relief. "Thank you, sir!"

"Now get out of here."

"Aye aye, sir!" He did not salute. Navy personnel did not salute uncovered indoors. He turned smartly on his heel and strode out the door.

Normally, at least in Tangretti's experience, being a SEAL was like being in your own private navy, without the sheer mountain of spit-and-polish that surrounded so much of traditional Navy service. They expected SEALs to be responsible, mature individuals, and they were cut a certain amount of slack.

Every once in a while the real navy, of black shoes and inspections, of seabags and weekend duty, intruded. At times like that, David found himself envying his buddy Mark Halstead, who, the last he'd heard, anyway, had left the Navy and was working for the CIA's Direct Action Directorate. *That* must be a blast, and not just the kind you could arrange with a block of C-4. Right now, if he wasn't at Little Creek or Camp Peary, he was out somewhere chasing terrorists, knowing what he was doing and why, who the bad guys were and what to do about them, and *not* worried in the least about rules and regulations.

Tangretti wished he were with him.

Chapter 10

The local term for the region was *ilaga ghair,* which Raptor said meant the land beyond Pakistan's laws. "Think of it as Dodge City," he said with a cold grin, "but without Wyatt Earp."

The town of Kaka Ziurat was a ramshackle collection of single-story buildings and one-room shops, crowded along either side of a road that was more pothole than pavement. Like every other town along the border that the SEALs had passed through in the last thirty-six hours, Kaka Ziurat, was as crowded as New Orleans at Mardi Gras . . . assuming Mardi Gras involved bearded, turban-wearing men sporting AK-47 assault rifles.

The men were most in evidence, wearing *shalwar kameez* in a variety of colors—from blue to green to white to brown—that did nothing to dispel the sense of almost monotonous conformity. There were women too, but they were almost invisible in their form-swaddling burkas, most in blue or shades of dark gray. Mariacher saw several anonymously swaddled forms sitting on the side of the street, surrounded by children, a male companion always in evidence.

The streets were a continuous honking traffic jam of overloaded buses and trucks, Volkswagen minivans, bicycles, donkeys, horses, and men on foot. With all of the animals, Mariacher reflected, it did look a bit like the Old West, though he doubted that Dodge or Tucson were ever quite this packed with gunslingers.

"Where the hell are they all coming from?" Lehman asked, echoing his thoughts.

"Most of them are Afghan refugees," Raptor said. "They've been coming across the line ever since Bush said we were going to attack. But lots are coming to join the jihad. Pakistan. Saudi Arabia. Iraq. Egypt. Hell, maybe even the United States."

Mariacher chewed on that for a bit. The thought of U.S. citizens coming here to fight U.S. troops in a religious war seemed so bizarre he didn't want to credit it. Still, people did some pretty loopy things in the name of religion.

He was looking at some of that loopiness now. A large crowd was gathered in the street, completely blocking traffic, listening to a Muslim cleric giving an impassioned speech. Every once in a while the crowd would shout en masse, *"Allah Akbar!"* and send long bursts of automatic gunfire into the sky. Mariacher didn't understand Pashto, but Raptor assured him that the sermon involved joining the jihad against America and the Jews. Nearby, someone had spray-painted messages on the walls of several buildings, in several languages. "Jihad is an obligation, like prayer," one read in English. "Victory or martyrdom," another proclaimed, in an eerie near-echo of Patrick Henry. A surreal third read, "Telephone now for military training," and gave a phone number.

"That one looks like the Pakistani version of a late night television spot," he said, gesturing toward the message with the phone number. " 'Call in the next ten minutes, and we will send you a brand new AK-47 assault rifle, absolutely free!' "

Raptor gave a dry chuckle. " 'But wait! There's more!' "

"It's not funny," Bradley said. "Jesus! Has anyone checked on that number to see if it's a lead to al-Qaeda?"

Raptor looked around, then seemed to spot Major Qadi haggling with a street vendor some distance away.

"The number is probably ISI," he said. "They're still doing a lot of the actual hiring, screening, and organizational work."

"You're shitting me," Lehman said.

"Nope. It's not *official* ISI policy, you understand. President Musharraf has been trying to reign in the ISI, and there are even rumors that pretty soon he's going to sack Ahmed, the ISI's chief. But the rank and file ISI boys in the field? Most of them are solidly pro-Taliban and pro-al-Qaeda."

The four SEALs and their contractor guide walked through the crowded market. Though they stood out from the majority of the locals, they were wearing Pakistani army uniforms provided by Major Qadi, including natty tan-colored berets, so most of the people in the crowd glanced at them curiously and then ignored them.

Bradley pointed at a stall as they passed. "Is that shit what I think it is?" The bin was filled with plastic Baggies, each holding a quantity of black mash.

"Opium paste," Raptor said. "Yeah, it's sold openly here. Pakistan grows a lot of poppies . . . but most of this stuff is coming across from Afghanistan."

"I thought the Taliban was cracking down on opium production," Mariacher said. "That's what they told us in the briefing back at Utapao."

"Well, it depends on what you mean by 'cracking down.' Also depends on who you talk to. When the Taliban first came to power, they left the drug networks pretty much alone. They probably needed the money to get themselves established, buy arms, buy off warlords, that sort of thing. Then they decided that drugs were evil, so they started shooting and hanging the traffickers and the owners of the larger poppy farms, but they didn't touch what was in the warehouses, or the high-level traffickers who were already part of the government." He shrugged. "Anyway, there's too damned much of the stuff to stop it all, and too many growers to control. They've shut down the major pipelines, but this nickel and dime stuff still keeps coming across the border."

The vendor at the opium stall had noticed their interest. He pressed forward, showing a toothy smile through his beard. "Ah! Soldiers!" he said in broken English. "You like? You buy? For your soldier friends!"

Mariacher shook his head and moved on. The vendor pursued them for several yards, despite sharp words in Punjabi from Qadi. Eventually he returned to his stall.

Other vendors, however, seemed aware now of the small group of what seemed to be Pakistani soldiers, and they began closing in from all sides, eager for a sale. Opium. Rugs. Baskets. Leather goods. Bottled green tea. Watches. Mountaineering equipment. Silver tea services. China. Hiking boots.

Ignoring the press of persistent salesmen, Mariacher turned to Raptor. "Those are good boots," he said, indicating the display to his left. "Brand name stuff. Where do *these* people get it?"

"From rich mountain climbers, of course. You see, lots of

people come to Pakistan to climb mountains. K2 is the second highest in the world, after Everest. But mountain climbing is definitely a rich person's sport. It costs ten thousand dollars, American just to get the permits to do K2, and that's a real bargain. Permits for climbing Everest cost something like fifty thousand. So only rich people can afford it, right?"

Mariacher nodded.

"So some of these entrepreneurs go through the luggage at rich people's hotels and come up with only the finest climbing gear for sale." He pointed at his own feet. "Hey, this is where I got mine. I recommend you all do the same."

Military-issue boots were good, but these were better. Mariacher found a pair of Asolo mountain boots in his size that would have cost two hundred dollars back in the World, but were on sale here for the equivalent of about sixty dollars. He wondered who the original owners were and if they ever made it to their mountain.

Fifty minutes later, their purchases hanging by the laces around their necks and shoulders, the SEALs turned a corner on the street and entered a new part of the bazaar. Lehman stopped, his eyes wide. "Oh, my God . . ."

Fortunately, no one heard him—no one who spoke English, at any rate. Here, stall after stall after stall was devoted to guns.

And more guns. And more . . . and plenty of ammunition to go with them. Mariacher had heard about places like this in the Northwest frontier, but the reality was astonishing. The sheer variety of military hardware was staggering. Most of the stalls trafficked in assault rifles, but he also saw land mines, hand grenades, RPG launchers, swords and knives of every description, and even rocket launchers. Most of the weapons were either Russian or close Pakistani copies, knockoffs from shops all over the Northwest Province; but he saw Chinese, Indian, Eastern European, and American firearms as well.

Or were they copies? It was hard to tell, the workmanship was so exact. One vendor blocked Mariacher's path with yet another toothy smile, holding up what looked like a brand-new Russian AK-74 assault rifle, still slick with packing grease. "Is good! Is good!" the man shouted into his face. "Only twenty thousand rupee!"

"Another bargain," Raptor said, grinning. "That's about three hundred dollars. An original would set you back four times that amount."

"Any Stingers for sale?"

Qadi, standing behind them, heard that comment. "No!" he said. "All Stingers are gone! Selling them is not permitted!"

"Just curious," Mariacher said, surprised at the man's vehemence.

When Qadi was again out of earshot, Raptor leaned close. "Don't be too curious about the Stingers," he warned. "Another sore point."

"Because we tried to take them back?"

"Exactly."

It was yet another part of the torturous history of U.S. foreign policy in this part of the world, and the aftermath of the Soviet War across the border in Afghanistan. After the Russians had invaded Afghanistan in 1980, the American CIA began funneling aid to the mujahideen resistance, covertly at first, but then more openly. The CIA used the Pakistani ISI as a kind of front organization, through which they sent hundreds of millions of dollars in aid, agents, and weapons.

Among those weapons had been the FIM-92A Stinger, a man-portable, shoulder-fired antiaircraft missile; a single-shot fire-and-forget weapon with a passive infrared homing system and a range of up to eight kilometers. An estimated twelve hundred Stingers had been shipped to Afghanistan for distribution among the mujahideen guerrillas. In a war where the Soviets and their DRA clients depended on helicopters for resupply and deployment, and in terrain where the operational ceiling for those helicopters was often below the tops of nearby ridges and mountains, the Stinger had come into its own. Some observers credited it with winning the war; it was an exaggeration, but the weapon had been a vital part of that conflict.

After the Soviet withdrawal, however, CIA agents had gone into Afghanistan, offering cash incentives to the mujahideen warlords to turn in any unused Stingers. They also began searching for a number of Stingers that had somehow vanished in Pakistan en route to the Afghan war. In a region where everything had a price, the offer was repeatedly refused, and that refusal led to a serious break between the CIA and the ISI. There'd been serious concern in Washington that Stingers might fall into the hands of terrorists—and that was years before the rise of the Taliban, or al-Qaeda's relocation to Afghanistan.

And, somehow, Washington simply couldn't understand why the warlords wanted to keep the deadly, modern weapons in their inventories when they could have cash instead.

Stingers remained an issue in the region. There could be no doubt that both the Taliban and al-Qaeda had them. How many and where they might be hidden was anybody's guess. Plenty of local warlords had them as well, simply for the prestige of owning them, since helicopter targets were relatively scarce now.

That scarcity, Mariacher reflected, would be ending soon. He wondered if American helicopters and strike aircraft were going to suffer the same sort of combat attrition the Soviet aircraft had faced. Technology had improved in ten years . . . but the Afghan terrain had not.

Bradley pointed. "I do see some rocket launchers for sale, though. Not Stingers. What are those . . . Redeyes?"

"Probably local knockoffs," Raptor said. "Although the

Pakistani government's trying to curb the really heavy offensive armaments up here. Used to be you could buy a locally manufactured version of a Strela-2 for twelve thousand dollars."

"And now there is a 500,000 rupee fine for attempting to manufacture these weapons," Qadi said, rejoining the conversation once again. "The local gunsmiths have stopped manufacturing all heavy weapons. It is the law."

"But they're still selling missile launchers openly, sir?"

"The gunsmiths have stopped manufacturing all heavy weapons," Qadi repeated. "It is the law."

"Right," Mariacher said, drawing out the word. He was beginning to understand what Raptor had meant by "Dodge City without Wyatt Earp." The Northwest Frontier appeared to be a small nation all its own, with its own customs and its own laws . . . or rather, its *lack* of laws. The locals were taking no notice of the handful of men dressed as Pakistani soldiers in their midst, save to try to sell them things.

Eventually they made their way through the gun market and found the man they were looking for, a short and wizened Pashtun selling Kazakhs—the small, short-legged, shaggy horses favored in this part of the world. Looking at the animals, which were penned just off the street, Mariacher could imagine that they were direct descendents of the Mongol ponies Genghis Khan's hordes had ridden when they swept through these mountains eight hundred years earlier.

Insertion into the combat zone on horseback. This had to be a first for the Navy SEALs.

At least, he thought, they wouldn't be riding in on the backs of camels.

After haggling over the price of a string of ten horses— the four extra mounts would carry their supplies—Qadi motioned them off the street, to a mud-brick house behind the corral. The structure looked as decrepit as the rest of the village, but inside there were rugs on the floor and sparse but modern-looking furniture. They were warmly greeted by a gangly, bearded man who introduced himself as Haji Ahmad Afridi, who offered them chairs and strong, green tea served by two veiled and robed women who vanished silently when their serving chores were complete.

"My wives," Afridi said with evident pride, speaking excellent English.

Afridi was evidently a reasonably wealthy man, at least for this neighborhood. His name, Mariacher knew, showed that he was a member of the Afridi clan of the Pashtun. The Haji in his name meant that he'd been on pilgrimage to Mecca, which implied that he could afford to make that trip. He smiled a gap-toothed grin and clapped his hands together. "I am told you are looking for an escort across the Durand Line," he said. "I am your man, without a doubt! But first . . . the tea, yes?"

As was customary for this culture, they sat and drank tea and discussed unimportant things for perhaps twenty minutes. Mariacher had the impression, however, that Afridi was carefully taking their measure. Several times, they were interrupted by men who came in, dropped to their knees, and questioned Afridi in hushed, respectful tones, speaking Pashto. He replied and they departed. Mariacher wasn't sure if this was part of Afridi's regular workday or if the interruptions had been arranged to impress him with Afridi's importance.

Perhaps it was both.

Most of the conversation, actually, was between Afridi and Qadi, discussing men in the area they both knew, a blood feud between two families, and the political situation in Islamabad. The ISI man had been the one to set up this meeting, claiming that they needed both a guide and an armed escort if they were to make it safely into Afghanistan. Qadi had provided payment too, a thick wad of Pakistani rupees.

Mariacher realized that if they couldn't trust Major Qadi, they wouldn't be able to trust this character either. Still, there was something engaging about Afridi, something that set him apart from the cold and glowering ISI officer. He was friendly and affable, and seemed particularly intrigued by the fact that they were Americans. He was clearly a rogue, but a likable one.

"So what is it you *do,* sir?" Mariacher asked him directly after a time. "You're obviously an important and powerful man here. Are you a village leader?"

Afridi's smile widened. "Oh, I sit on the local *jirga,* of course, Allah be praised, but I am a simple businessman. But I tell you I do know the tracks between here and Khowst very well indeed, and can take you where you need to go. I could take you all the way to Jalalabad, or even to Kabul . . . though there is very little left of that city. I will take you where you need to go, and provide you with the men and arms to guarantee your safety."

Businessman, Mariacher reflected, almost certainly meant *smuggler*. Guns? Drugs? Most likely both.

"We will be visiting a number of places in Paktia Province," Raptor told Afridi. "There is a man in Khowst we must talk to. And there are some . . . places up in the mountains we wish to observe."

"What places, my friend?"

"Zhawar Kili."

"Ah! Yes, I know that area well! And the man you wish to meet?"

"Ali Hassan," Mariacher said, giving their contact's code name. "We have an address in Khowst where we might find him."

"And I can take you to him!" Afridi sounded almost obscenely proud of the fact.

"Thank you," Mariacher said. "I must ask, however . . . why are you helping us? Surely not just for the money."

"Oh, the money is good, the money is good." He laughed and winked at Qadi. "But many of us love you Americans still, despite the . . . the troubles of late. What happened in New York, America, was a terrible, terrible thing. A great crime. I and my men are delighted to help you!"

Mariacher thought about the calls to jihad painted on the walls of houses around the corner, and the gun-waving crowds listening to the mullahs on the street. Who was the jihad directed against if not Americans?

"Mr. Afridi was one of our more important contacts in this region fifteen years ago, when you Americans were trying to help the Warriors of God fight the Russians," Qadi said with a shuttered expression.

Afridi nodded, then leaned forward, glancing left and right in a melodramatically conspiratorial fashion. "You see, my friends, I tell you a secret. I worked closely, *very* closely, with American CIA!"

Mariacher did some fast estimation. Afridi's age was tough to guess, perhaps forty, perhaps fifty, though his wind-weathered and leathery skin made him look ancient. But subtracting fifteen years would mean he'd been a teenager or in his twenties during the Russian war, no older. Working closely with the CIA probably meant he'd been a local Company asset, used as a guide or a message courier.

Like Najid, the teenager back in Kuala Lumpur.

"I mean no disrespect," Mariacher said carefully, "but some of the men outside sound as if they don't like Americans very much right now."

"Ah," Afridi said. "That may be true. Bin Laden has again called for jihad against the Jews and the Americans, everywhere they may be found. And from what I have heard here, three hundred thousand dedicated Taliban are even now taking up positions on Afghanistan's borders, to defend against you Americans when you invade. And . . . you must understand. We Pashtun do not think of the Durand Line as a border. The Pashtun in Afghanistan, the Pashtun in Pakistan, they all are Pashtun. Most within the Taliban are Pashtun. An attack against the Taliban is an attack against *all* Pashtun. You understand?"

"Yes, I do. What I don't understand is why you, Mr. Afridi, are helping Americans when your cousins outside want to shoot us."

"The Pashtun are one tribe," Major Qadi said, "but there are divisions as well. I've heard it said that Pashto is the only language in the world where the word for 'cousin' is also the word for 'enemy.' "

"So . . . a blood feud?" Raptor asked.

"Let us simply say," Afridi said after a long and thoughtful moment, "that I owe certain *cousins* of mine within the Taliban some . . . what is the word you Americans use? Payback. Yes, I must give them some payback, and this is a convenient means of doing so." He grinned. "Besides, the money *is* very, very good!"

Afridi clapped his hands twice, and one of his wives appeared in the doorway, bearing an ornate silver teapot. Her husband gestured sharply, and she began to make the rounds of the room, filling the guests' cups first with more pungent green tea.

Mariacher had been warned of Pashtun possessiveness when it came to their women, and he was careful not to look directly at her. Afridi's affable manner might well vanish in an instant if the man thought he was watching her.

Her garments weren't as severe as those of women under the Taliban. He did get a glimpse of her eyes, unveiled, though the rest of her face was covered. Her burka was relatively lightweight, though it still reduced her body to a shapeless mass that was difficult to identify as *human*, much less female.

When she moved in front of him and started to pour for him, the hem of her burka, dragging on the floor, snagged against his boot. He pulled back sharply, wishing to stay out of her way, and she lurched a bit, sloshing hot tea onto Mariacher's thigh.

He heard her gasp. Afridi was on his feet in an instant, bellowing something at her in Pashto. The woman spun away from Mariacher, ducking her head, but Afridi swung his arm, his fist connecting with her shoulder. She cried out, and replied in a rapid-fire barrage of Pashto before fleeing from the room. Afridi was about to follow, but Mariacher rose to his feet. "Mr. Afridi! It was nothing!"

"This," the angry man replied, "is between me and my woman." The way he said "my woman" sent a chill down Mariacher's spine. Afridi left the room like a fast-moving storm cloud. A moment later the waiting SEALs heard more angry voices, a sudden, burka-muffled thud and a woman's cry of pain.

"Damn it!" Mariacher said, starting forward. Chief Bradley started to get up as well.

But Qadi was on his feet, blocking their way. "No!" he said sharply. "Mr. Afridi is right. This is between him and his wife."

"Bullshit! He can't just go in there and beat her!"

Raptor was up as well. "Stand at ease, SEAL," he snapped. "This isn't the time or the place. You hear me?"

Mariacher wasn't so sure about that. Several more blows sounded from the other room, along with the crash of breaking glassware.

"That woman didn't do anything wrong! He has no right—"

"Excuse me, Lieutenant," Qadi said, "but he *does* have the right. This is Pakistan, not America."

"Leave it, Lieutenant, This isn't the time or the place," Raptor told him again.

Another heavy blow sounded from the other room, followed by a scream, then silence. Afridi reappeared a moment later, smiling as though nothing had happened. "Forgive my wife, please," he told Mariacher. "She is clumsy, that one."

"It was entirely my fault," Mariacher insisted. "You mustn't blame her!"

Afridi scowled for a moment, then brightened. "I believe we were discussing giving the payback to my cousins across the Durand Line," he said, apparently deciding to ignore the entire incident.

Both Qadi and Raptor were glaring at Mariacher, as if warning him to stand down. Reluctantly, he raised his hands, nodded, and returned to his seat. Clearly, there was nothing he could say to make things right, and many things he could say or do that could make the situation considerably worse. If he insisted that the woman had stumbled on his boot, he would only confirm her "clumsiness." If, on the other hand, he insisted that he had tripped the woman, even accidentally, Afridi's pride and anger might well turn against him.

It was also a country—a *culture,* rather—that did not take kindly to foreigners telling them how to manage their private lives.

An hour later Mariacher and Raptor were outside once again, looking over the horses they had purchased for the trek across the border. Raptor leaned close. "I know that really griped you earlier, when Afridi was beating his wife."

"Yeah. Yeah, it did. I knew the Taliban was supposed to be really rough on women. I wasn't expecting it here."

"Keep this in mind, Lieutenant. The people here, the people across the border, they're the same. They're Pashtun, and they may be the most stubborn and contentious people on the face of the planet." He hesitated. "You know, there's a phrase in Pashto, a name for a man who does not beat his wife *regularly,* every day. It translates, roughly, as 'a man with no penis.' Do you understand me?"

"Afridi thinks he's not a man if he doesn't beat his wife?"

"More to the point, his neighbors, friends, and family would think he's not a man. There's no caste system among these people. He wouldn't just lose face and lose status. He would lose *everything.* He would have to leave, maybe go be a janitor in Karachi or something."

"Well, isn't that just too bad. Serve the son of a bitch right."

"Among the Pashtun, under the dictates of Pakhtunwali, three and *only* three things are absolutely vital—the three z's. Those are *zan, zar,* and *zamin*—women, gold, and land. A man proves his . . . his *Pashtunness* only if he can protect his three z's. You follow me?"

"I follow."

"Women under the Taliban have it worse, believe me."

"I'm sure that's of great comfort to women in Pakistan." He shook his head. "I don't get it, though. Malaysia is a Muslim country. I saw women there. Some were veiled, but a lot of them weren't, and they sure as hell didn't get beaten up every day."

"What you're seeing here is not Islam," Raptor told him. "The Pashtun identify themselves strongly with Islam, of course. In fact, they claim they are direct descendents of Qais, one of the Prophet's companions. It's their interpretation of Islam that causes problems. They interpret Islamic law through their old tribal code. You know, under Muslim law, a woman can inherit property. That is unthinkable to a

Pashtun. In the Qu'ran, women are commanded to observe *hijab*. The word is sometimes used to mean the veil, but it actually means either a physical or a spiritual barrier, and refers to dressing modestly. In countries like Turkey or Malaysia or even the United States, that means Muslim women dress conservatively for those cultures and don't use dress—or the lack of it—to call attention to their bodies. Among the Pashtun, it means covering everything except the eyes. For the Taliban, it means even the eyes should be covered by a kind of mesh, so the woman can see out—sort of—but men can't see in."

"Why so much emphasis on what men see or don't see?"

Raptor shrugged. "Seeing a woman is supposed to enflame men's lust. The veil is actually seen as a way of protecting women from being degraded, or being seen as sex objects. And I'd have to say that the majority of Muslim women prefer it that way."

"You have got to be shitting me," Mariacher said. "They *want* to wear those damned tents?"

"Depends on the country. Like I said, in Turkey, a conservative business suit is fine. Out here, they cover everything except the eyes and the hands. It's not Islam. It's how Islam is interpreted by the local culture."

"Fine," Mariacher said. "It's not Islam. But the fucking Pashtun have a lot to answer for."

"Save it for the TAQ," Raptor told him. "Taliban and al-Qaeda. *They're* the enemy. Not the Pakistanis."

"I'll try to remember that."

Chapter 11

Two days later the SEAL caravan left for Afghanistan. Mariacher's horse was a shaggy, white-coated animal named Bhutto. "Bhutto the Bitch," Afridi told him with a broad grin. "None of us liked her, but *this* Bhutto will serve you well!"

The reference, Mariacher knew, was to Madam Benazir Bhutto, who'd been prime minister of Pakistan between 1988 and 1990, and again from 1993 to 1996, the first woman to hold a position of leadership in any Islamic country. She'd been removed from power, however, accused of corruption, and forced to flee to exile in England. By all accounts, Mariacher thought, she must have been a brave and determined person to attempt to rule in a country so devotedly, so fanatically, so enthusiastically and determinedly *male*.

They rode north from Kaka Ziurat at sunrise, following the narrow and winding road at first, then leaving the road at a bridge to follow instead a fair-sized mountain stream descending through a narrow and steep-sided valley. Mariacher had assumed that the boundary between Pakistan and Afghanistan followed the crest of the mountain barrier between the two countries, but he found that this wasn't always true. Kaka Ziurat existed in a river valley on the north side of a low mountain slope. The river valley descended through myriad twists and turns into a broad, open bowl fifty miles across and completely ringed by the encircling mountains.

The city of Khowst lay at the center of that bowl, one of the two largest cities of the Afghani province of Paktia. Immediately beyond Khowst the mountains reared high, rugged, and snowcapped, the highest of them almost eleven thousand feet above sea level. Major Qadi had told them that those mountains were part of the Safed Range extending east and south from the famous Khyber Pass, a spur of the far higher and more formidable Hindu Kush, which reared to almost twenty thousand feet just 150 miles farther to the north.

Those mountains dominated the northern horizon now, rising bleak and rugged, pale against a deep blue sky. Closer at hand, the terrain looked a bit like southern California, Mariacher thought—rugged, the sere hillsides dotted with clumps of brush, with trees visible in the valley below. On either side, rock cliffs thrust skyward, the strata running up and down rather than side to side, as if to bear testimony to the orogenic violence that had created these mountains millions of years ago.

The path along the hillside descending above the left bank of the stream was narrow enough that the caravan had to proceed single-file. In the lead were Afridi and three of his men, followed by Raptor, then Mariacher. The other three SEALs and three more of Afridi's men trailed behind, along with three packhorses, with the dour Major Qadi bringing up the rear. The SEALs had discarded their Pakistani uniforms in favor of nondescript and rankless camo utilities, fatigue caps, and goggles. The temperature wasn't cold—it was in the low fifties that morning—but the wind was stiff and chill enough that all wore field jackets.

They were also now armed, which was definitely an improvement, as far as Mariacher was concerned. Going around unarmed when it seemed as though every local man was carrying an AK had been an unpleasant exercise in maintaining a low profile. However, their equipment on the C-130—weapons, radios, laser designator, and other gear—had arrived in Kaka Ziurat early the day before on a Pakistani army truck, and it didn't appear that anyone had rifled through the stuff during the journey, a definite plus. The troops who delivered the equipment must have been under very definite orders not to go through the shipment . . . or else Qadi had managed to put the fear of Allah into them ahead of time.

In any case, Mariacher was now carrying an H&K MP5-SD slung over his shoulder, a reliable weapon with a built-in sound suppressor, notable because it did *not* require subsonic ammunition. All of the weapons in the H&K MP5 series were popular with modern special ops teams—"the best thing to come out of Germany since Mercedes, beer, *und fräuleins*," as one old SEAL chief of Mariacher's acquaintance once put it. Raptor, he noted, was still carrying his AKM, as were Afridi's bodyguards, while Qadi was armed with an MP5-A2. Pakistan manufactured a number of weapons in the MP5 series under license, and they were much favored by the country's commando and paramilitary units—including the ISI.

Mariacher urged his horse forward enough to let him speak with Raptor without shouting. "So . . . exactly where is the border, anyway?"

The contractor laughed. "Your guess is as good as mine. We may be past it already."

"I haven't seen any markers."

"And you won't, except maybe at checkpoints and official border crossings. Nobody knows for sure where the Durand Line is."

"What's this Durand Line people keep talking about? The border?"

"Yeah. Back in the late 1800s, the Brits were having a lot of trouble with the Pashtun—the 'wily Pathans,' as Kipling called them. They tried to extend the Raj beyond the Hindu Kush a couple of times but never made it stick.

"Finally, around 1893, a Foreign Office secretary by the name of Sir Mortimer Durand sat down in his study with a map and drew the border between the British Raj and the wilderness beyond—the Durand Line, as it was called.

"Trouble was, he used the Hindu Kush as a rough boundary, which is really pretty vague, geographically, and managed to put his line smack through the middle of the Pashtun tribal lands."

"Ah," Mariacher said. "A light dawns."

"Right. The Pashtun have never accepted the border. They wanted the British to recognize them as a separate state—Pashtunistan. The British rejected that in 1901, and the Pakistanis rejected it when they partitioned their country from India in 1948. As a result, about half of the Pashtun live in Pakistan now, and the other half are the largest single group in Afghanistan."

"Which is why there's so much support for the Taliban up here, even on the Pakistan side of the border."

"You got it. Pashtun like Afridi up there still think this is all one, big Pashtun state. In a way, they're right. This area is pretty much outside of Islamabad's direct control—*ilaga ghair,* remember? Tribal law is what counts. The net effect is that a lot of people like Afridi make their living smuggling stuff across the line—guns, drugs, people, whatever. Want to know a secret?"

"Sure. Shoot."

"Back in 1975 or thereabouts, Pakistan sent the first mujahideen guerrillas into the Panshir Valley north of Kabul in order to destabilize the regime of Sardar Daud . . . who happened to be a rather outspoken advocate of Pashtunistan. That caused a civil war, and led directly to the Soviet Union intervening late in 1979."

"Ah. So the Russian invasion was largely Pakistan's doing?"

"Pretty much. Of course, Pakistan was a staunch U.S. ally during the Cold War. They had to be, since India was gravitating toward the Soviets in the seventies. When Russia invaded Afghanistan, that put a real squeeze on Pakistan, almost completely isolating them. That's why they were so willing to be the conduit for U.S. covert aid to the mujahideen during the eighties, and worked so hard arming and training them. When the Taliban came along, Afghanistan was actually on the way to becoming a colony of Pakistan."

"What do you think is going to happen now?"

"After 9/11? Beats me. Pakistan is trying to stay balanced in the middle, friends with us, friends with the Taliban. Not a good place to be, y'know?"

"Yeah," Mariacher said. "Shit, if we end up kicking the Taliban's ass, Pak is going to have to do some serious reevaluation of their foreign policy."

"Roger that. Either that or . . ."

"Or what?"

"Or they'll end up deciding to join the Taliban. Against us."

Mariacher turned in his saddle, peering back up the length of the caravan until he spotted Major Qadi, a good hundred yards away at the end of the column. The politics of this bizarre region were getting more and more twisted, so far as he could determine.

And where it would end, only Allah knew.

Wednesday, September 26, 2001

Zur Kowt Training Camp
On the Afghan-Pakistani Border
Paktia Province, Afghanistan
1515 hours, local time

Davlot Iskanderov stood atop a granite outcropping the size of a house, part of a cliffside rising above the Khowst Valley. Nearby, barracks and bunkers had been chiseled into the wall of the cliff itself. It wasn't much, he thought . . . but it *was* home. At least for now.

Zur Kowt was a small village of mud-brick and stone houses clinging to the side of the cliff in the mountains roughly two-thirds of the way from Gardez to Khowst. Gardez was behind him, northwest of the towering Safed Range. Khowst lay directly below him to the southeast. In fact, the narrow ravine of a mountain stream cutting down past the Zur Kowt camp leveled off on the plain and ran directly through the city of Khowst, roughly twenty kilometers away.

He raised his Russian-made binoculars to his eyes and scanned the city. Khowst was less than impressive—mud-brick and plaster one- and two-story buildings shimmering in the afternoon sun, with only a few more modern concrete block structures, probably built by the Russians fifteen years

ago. The range was too great for him to make out individual
people. Under the Taliban, though, there was remarkably little coming and going among the locals . . . unless there was
something special going on, like a public execution. The
quiet that blanketed Afghan cities these past few years was
like the silence of the tomb: heavy, oppressive, and bearing
with it a hint of deadliness. He remembered what the cities
had been like when the Soviets were in the country. At least
then the cities had been lively . . . sometimes *too* alive, when
the mujahideen launched one of their rocket attacks.

He lowered the binoculars. From here, with the naked eye,
the city nearly vanished . . . little more than a pale blur on
the expanse of ocher wasteland.

Nearer at hand, the valley dropped in a series of cascades
toward the Khowst plain, the bareness of rock, gravel, and
cliff broken by clumps of small trees and scrub. The cliffs
were pocked in places by cave openings. This region was
renowned for its caves, a geographical fact long used by the
local population to its advantage.

The area had been used as a training ground for guerrilla
cells for many years. Bin Laden had set up some of his first
al-Qaeda camps in the region during the Russian war. Directly south of Khowst, right on the Durand Line, was the al-
Badr II camp at Zhawar Kili, part of the Zhawar complex
that had been one of al-Qaeda's principle recruiting and
training facilities until 1998. On August 20 of that year the
Americans had sent seventy-five cruise missiles into the
camps in retaliation for the bombing of the U.S. embassies
in Tanzania and Kenya. About twenty-five people were
killed, including three Pakistani ISI advisors. The camps had
been abandoned since, but they remained both as warnings
of America's technological reach and, paradoxically, as a
monument to al-Qaeda's triumph.

Ali Ahmad Sadeq came up behind him. "The heavy machine guns have been placed as you directed, Colonel Khan."

Iskanderov turned and looked at the man. Like all of the recruits up here, he was dirty and unkempt, his clothing ragged, and he stank of goat. The AK-74 slung muzzle down over his shoulder, however, was meticulously clean and brightly oiled. That had been Iskanderov's first order upon arriving at the camp. Weapons would be cleaned and kept clean.

"Good," he said. "Have the First Company assemble on the firing range. I wish to see how well they use their weapons."

Sadeq drew himself up straight. "We all are expert marksmen . . . *sir*." His hesitation and the way he stressed the Pashto honorific confirmed for Iskanderov much about the man's attitude. He was cocky and self-sure, overly reliant on his religious superstitions. It was also possible that the man had guessed his former nationality, despite the Khan war name. The Tajik, like many of his kinsmen, had pale blue eyes and a Caucasian appearance. While many of the non-Afghan fighters of al-Qaeda looked Caucasian, most of the Afghans and Pakistanis—the Pashtuns, especially—were still suspicious of anyone who looked obviously foreign. Getting these goat herders and mountain bandits to actually trust him was proving to be one of Iskanderov's biggest challenges.

"This is their chance to prove it," Iskanderov told him. "I will be there shortly."

Sadeq turned and left, without even a sketch of a salute. This damned stiff-necked Pashtun sense of independence from all authority save God's . . . it was enough to try any man's patience, a virtue for which Iskanderov had never been known.

Mohammed had sent him to this Allah-forsaken outpost,

however, to inspect this and other nearby camps and make certain the fighters here were ready.

When the Americans came—and they would come, of that he was certain—they might invade from the north, where they would have the help of the armies of the so-called Northern Alliance, or they might come from *this* direction, from the south, through a politically weak and divided Pakistan. Of the two possibilities, Iskanderov favored the southerly approach. Any invasion from the north would have to be staged through one of the former Soviet republics bordering Afghanistan to the north—Turkmenistan, Tajikistan, or Uzbekistan—and the political likelihood of *that* happening was, in his opinion, nil. Pakistan, on the other hand, while a powerful ally of the Taliban, and with powerful allies of al-Qaeda in the government, would cave in to American demands for military basing in that country. Islamabad needed the Americans to protect them against the Indians, which meant that in the long run they would end up as American puppets. That had certainly been the case during the Soviet war, when the American CIA had almost openly used the ISI to create a guerrilla resistance in Afghanistan against the Russians.

Two days before, on the twenty-fourth, the Taliban government had announced to the world that they were dispatching 300,000 fighters to the borders of Afghanistan to repel any invasion of the country by the Americans. At the same time, Osama bin Laden himself had called upon all Pakistanis to join together to fight what he called "the American crusade."

But Iskanderov put little faith in rhetoric. U.S. and Pakistani officials had been meeting for the past two days in Islamabad, and al-Qaeda spies at those sessions had reported that Pakistan almost certainly would support America's demand that bin Laden's organization inside Afghanistan be dismantled. Pakistan, inevitably, would side with the Americans, no matter what her Pashtun minority on the Northwest Frontier might have to say about that.

It didn't help either that there'd been a riot in Kabul just a few hours ago, with religious mobs storming the abandoned U.S. embassy there. Such theatrics helped no one, and cast the Taliban cause in a quaint, almost pathetic light on the world stage . . . as pallid imitators of the Iranian militants who'd stormed the American embassy in Tehran twenty-two years ago and taken the occupants hostage.

No, riots didn't help, and neither did rhetoric. When the Americans came, they would have to be stopped *here,* in these forbidding mountains along the border.

And it was up to him—to Asef Khan, rather—to figure out how best to do it.

Wednesday, September 26, 2001

Zawar Kili
Paktia Province, Afghanistan
2240 hours, local time

Mariacher lay on his belly atop a boulder, face pressed against the eyepieces of his binoculars. The device combined the body and image tube of an AN/PVS-7-D night-vision device with a five-power lens strong enough to let him zoom in among the stark and empty-looking buildings scattered along the ridgetop two hundred meters away.

The caravan had followed the river until the land leveled off on the low-lying plain southeast of Khowst and the river vanished under the soil and gravel. The water-carved channel of the river remained, steep-sided and only a dozen meters wide, which made it an ideal place for an ambush. The

SEALs and their guides had dismounted and led the horses up a smuggler's path cut into the side of the embankment, however, getting clear of the dry gulley and into the rolling foothills and boulder fields that marked off the southern rim of the Khowst Valley.

They'd proceeded west throughout the rest of the afternoon and into the evening, crossing the road they'd left that morning and proceeding cautiously, always sticking to the cover of the immense boulders that littered the ground along the northern base of the mountain slope.

Altogether today they'd managed almost twenty miles— five down the river valley crossing from Pakistan into Afghanistan, ten more along the foothills of the mountains until they were due south of Khowst, and the last five steadily climbing once more, to bring them over a spur in the mountains to the rugged ground above a box valley, its open end pointed south, toward Pakistan. They'd set up their camp in a hidden gully half a mile from this overlook; from there they would be able to establish satellite communications with the Pentagon Op Center and relay information about their objective as they collected it.

The place was largely unknown to the outside world. Their objective was called Zhawar Kili on the maps, but was known to U.S. Intelligence and special ops forces as the al-Badr II camp. Three years before, a rain of Tomahawk cruise missiles had come shrieking in low over the mountains from Pakistan, flown up the canyon, and slammed into the three interlinked compounds that made up the Zhawar Complex. The controversial attack had killed a handful of al-Qaeda terrorists and trainees as well as some Pakistani ISI men, but missed bin Laden and the other AQ big fish who'd been visiting the camps earlier that day.

From this vantage point, Mariacher had an excellent view of the entire surface facility, which consisted of a surpris-

ingly large number of single-story mud-brick buildings behind an adobe wall, enclosing a flat area cut into the side and
along the top of the canyon wall. The area was huge, an entire village, really, located near the top of the mountain
ridge. At first glance it appeared abandoned, but using the
night-vision scope from a point a bit higher up along the
mountainside to the south, he could see several men standing near the various gates in the wall, armed men—
obviously guards.

Closer study revealed other indicators. Several trucks,
parked here and there within the compound. Horses in a corral inside one wall. Stacks of crates that might hold ammunition or weapons. The last intelligence anyone had from this
site was that it had been deserted since the cruise missile attack three years ago, but clearly someone had moved in and
begun setting up housekeeping once again.

Several of the buildings showed what looked like bomb
damage, and there were heaps of rubble here and there that
might be all that was left from some direct hits. Zhawar Kili,
however, was known to consist of at least three separate
bases, one aboveground—this one—and two constructed
underground within the extensive cave systems known to
honeycomb these mountains. Originally built by the mujahideen with Pakistani and CIA help during the Russian
war, it was known to be a logistics, training, and com-
mand/control center for al-Qaeda, though it was possible
that the Taliban now planned to use it as a fortress in the defense of their borders.

"Okay," Mariacher said, whispering into his M-biter's mi-
crophone. "Let's tag it."

"Roger that," Lehman said. He was lying in the darkness a
few yards to the left, holding a Rockwell PLGR96 GPS receiver, a satellite-linked device better known in the field as a
"Plugger." He read the exact longitude and latitude coordi-

nates of their ridgetop observation post off the GPS screen. Mariacher checked the precise range and bearing to the center of the target area, using the built-in laser ranging device in his binoculars. Those two pieces of data together would give the mission controllers back in the World precise coordinates for the base.

Chief Bradley, meanwhile, was a few yards to the right. Like the rest of them, he'd blacked out his face while they were at the camp, and his eyes and lips seemed startling in their contrast to the grease paint. He was holding a Canon digital camera to his eye and snapping off shots through its powerful night-vision lens. The camera was a part of the team's SIDS, or Secondary Imagery Dissemination System. Once they returned to their camp and erected their satcom gear, they would be able to feed these images back to Langley and the Pentagon. The pictures would help them pinpoint high-value targets for future bombing runs or cruise missile attacks.

"This is Gold One," he said over the M-biter channel, identifying himself. "I have all the primary targets catalogued."

"Copy. Good."

Bradley edged closer to Mariacher so he could whisper without using the radio channel. He'd pulled his night-vision goggles back down over his face, giving him the look of a weird cross between insect and robot. He nudged Mariacher. "What the hell's that one big building just east of the town center?"

"I think it's a mosque," Mariacher replied. "Those are about the only buildings in Afghanistan any more with towers on 'em."

"Figures. What you wanna bet they have lookouts up there?"

"They're called muezzin, and they call the faithful to prayer."

"Yeah, and it doesn't hurt if they have a heavy machine gun up there with them, just in case the big bad American Satans show up."

Mariacher continued to study the village carefully. "You seen any weapons?"

"Outside of the small arms the guards are packing? No."

"Neither did I." Mariacher lowered the binoculars. "I'm wondering if that's even a military installation anymore, or if we're looking at a few militiamen."

"Kill them all and let D.A. sort them out," Lehman volunteered, crawling up the sloping top of the boulder beside them. He was referring to damage assessment, the process of gathering intelligence about a target after an attack, to see how badly the enemy had been hurt.

"Yeah," Bradley added. "Frankly, I don't see a thing down there that a couple of Tomahawks wouldn't take care of in real short order."

"Clinton tried that, remember?"

Frankly, the whole walled compound didn't look like it was worth a cruise missile. The Tomahawks that had thundered down on this target three years ago cost around $1.4 million apiece. The targets—mud-brick structures with unknown contents—simply weren't worth the money. If the seventy-five Tomahawks fired at Zhawar Kili had managed to tag bin Laden and end the war on terror—especially if killing him in 1998 would have prevented the attack on the World Trade Center, it absolutely would have been worth it. But over a hundred million dollars to kill twenty-five anonymous tangos? That just didn't make sense no matter how you rationalized things.

That was the supremely, hellishly frustrating part of this war. The United States possessed incredible technology and resources, but she remained vulnerable to attacks by fanatically dedicated mountain tribesmen who could simply vanish into the background of their own country and people, and who didn't possess an infrastructure that made using all of that expensive technology cost-effective. There were a few alternatives. They could try going after their international bank accounts, for instance. Two days ago, in fact, President Bush had signed an order freezing the assets in U.S. banks of twenty-seven individuals and organizations in an attempt to financially cripple al-Qaeda, and he'd demanded that foreign banks do the same. Or the U.S. could try going after the enemy leadership—either covertly, as with the attempt on Mohammed, or by trying to force other governments to hand al-Qaeda leaders over to American justice. Washington had been trying to get the Taliban to surrender bin Laden for years now, and especially during these past couple of weeks.

There weren't a whole lot of options, however, and few of those held much likelihood of success. Of them all, putting special ops teams like the Gray Ghosts on the ground to find high-value targets and eliminate enemy leaders and assets seemed like the best possible course of action by far to Mariacher.

How the hell did you bomb someone back into the Stone Age when they were already there?

"Okay," he said over the M-biter channel. "Blue One to all Grays. Make a special note of anything that looks like it has military value."

"Roger that," Osterlee replied from his overwatch position twenty yards away. "Do rocks count?"

Mariacher chuckled. "Negative on the rocks."

"Gray Ghost, Raptor," a different voice called suddenly, urgently, over the tactical channel.

"Raptor, Blue One," Mariacher replied. "Go."

"Trouble," Raptor said. "Qadi split. He's gone."

"Shit . . ."

Major Qadi had been the topic of several quiet and private

discussions over the past couple of days, both with Raptor and among the four SEALs of Gray Ghost cell. There was a distinct possibility that he was there to set the team up, lead them into an ambush, or sabotage the mission in some other way. Even if he simply alerted Taliban or AQ forces in the area to the SEALs' presence, it could seriously jeopardize the mission, and even force the SEALs to extract.

"What about Afridi and his men?"

"They're still here with me."

"Our gear?"

"Still secure."

"We need to get back there, sanitize, and move," Mariacher decided.

"Affirmative," Raptor said. "I'll keep an eye on Afridi and our stuff. You guys hustle it. We could have an Afghan patrol up here in no time."

Damn! "Okay, Gray Ghosts," Mariacher told the others. "You heard the man. Pack up. We're moving out."

He'd been sure from the start that trusting Qadi was a mistake. The trouble was, there'd been no way to avoid having him along, not if they wanted to operate out of Pakistan.

Politics. The perfect recipe for screwing the mission, and for getting themselves killed or captured.

Their path to their encampment led back over the ridge that made up the back wall of the Zhawar Kili canyon and down the other side, descending into a broad wadi sheltered by large boulders, cliffs, and rock ledges. They used their night-vision goggles to illuminate the way, which turned the world around them into a vivid green and white picture of highly amplified starlight. Lehman was on point, with Mariacher, Bradley, and Osterlee strung out at ten-yard intervals behind—close enough together to stay in sight of one another, but spread out enough to make ambush difficult.

They were less than a hundred meters from their camp

when Lehman stopped abruptly, one hand held high, then went to ground, invisible among rocks and scrub brush. The other SEALs copied him, dropping flat. In the tense silence that followed, Mariacher distinctly heard someone cough up ahead. It might be one of Afridi's men, but—

Gunfire erupted in the night, muzzle flashes stabbing and flashing among the rocks ahead and to the left, between the SEALs and the camp. "Ambush!" Lehman's voice called over his M-biter. "Take cover!"

An instant later Mariacher heard the click and swish of boots running across gravel to his right. He rolled, bringing his H&K to bear on a half-glimpsed green figure racing toward him . . . a bearded figure wearing a turban and the unmistakable bug-eyed mask of a set of Russian-made night-vision goggles. Mariacher squeezed the trigger on his weapon; the sound-suppressed H&K gave three quickspaced tapping sounds, like a finger slapped against a tabletop, and the running figure twisted, toppled, and vanished.

And for the next several seconds gunfire cracked and thundered out of the night across the Afghan ridge.

Chapter 12

Wednesday, September 26, 2001

Zawar Kili
Paktia Province, Afghanistan
2258 hours, local time

The first rule when you're caught in an ambush is simple: *keep moving*. The ambush, most likely, was triggered when you entered the enemy's kill zone, and the very worst thing you can do is stay put.

Mariacher started crawling on his belly toward the right and the body of the man he'd just shot, keeping flat on the wadi's gravel bed as AK rounds cracked and whined overhead and full-auto gunfire continued to crackle in the night. He checked the body first. The man was dead, with three close-grouped holes high in his chest, just below where his collarbones met. Mariacher was intensely curious about the man's night-vision goggles. Nothing in any of the intelligence he'd seen had indicated that al-Qaeda or the Taliban possessed that kind of equipment. That disturbing fact would bear some investigation.

But later. For now, he kept crawling, all too aware that the advantage SEALs usually possessed in night combat—the ability to see in the dark—was not exclusively theirs this time.

Keeping flat, he slipped over a low line of limestone boulders and worked his way up a narrow gully against the cliff face beyond. Ten yards up the slope he peered over the top of the gully's rim and saw two hostiles crouched behind a boulder, their backs to him. Raising his H&K to his shoulder, he tapped off two quick rounds into one man's back, shifted slightly and put two rounds more into the other. Combat was no place for chivalry or playing fair. The two went down together in a tangle of outflung legs and arms. The suppressor built into the muzzle of his weapon guaranteed that the shots were unheard, and there was no muzzle flash to give away his position.

"Blue One," he said over the M-biter, identifying himself. "Three tangos down on the right. Moving three-one-zero."

By telling the others which way he was moving, he was alerting them to check their fire. The last thing the SEALs needed was to begin scoring their own goals, as they were known, through friendly fire. He began crawling farther up the gully, parallel to their original path.

"Gold One," Chief Bradley's voice said over the tactical channel. "Two tangos down, left. Moving three-two-zero."

"Gold Two!" Osterlee called. "Fire in the hole!"

Mariacher dropped behind a boulder, covering his face. Two seconds later a deafening boom sounded from ahead and to his left as Osterlee's hand grenade detonated, the blast reverberating off the surrounding rocks and cliff faces. The volume of gunfire dropped immediately, from a steady, crackling thunder to quick, sharp bursts. Ahead, a turbaned man dropped into Mariacher's sheltering gulley, then started scrambling up the cliff to the right. Mariacher dropped him with a close-spaced triplet of rounds. "Blue One. Tango down, right. Moving."

The ambushers were fleeing, most of them running north-west, up the wadi toward the SEAL camp. A moment later a fresh crackle of gunfire sounded, mingled now with screams and shrill, yipping cries.

"Watch your fire," Mariacher warned. "Afridi's people are up there."

Afridi and his six men had been left at the encampment, along with Raptor, ostensibly to guard the horses and the equipment, but practically to keep them out of the way during the initial reconnaissance of al-Badr II. From the sound of it, the fleeing attackers had blundered into the men at the camp, who must have been alerted by the sudden flurry of gunfire.

The volume of gunfire dropped off once again, and moments later three men appeared in the SEALs' night-vision imagers, running wildly back down the wadi. The hunters had become the hunted, trapped between the SEALs and the gunners at the encampment farther up the slope. Smoothly, in perfect concert, Lehman, Bradley, and Osterlee each dropped one with short bursts from their MP5s. Mariacher held the overwatch position, scanning the entire area, looking for more tangos. After a long silence, however, it began to look as though the ambushers were either all dead or gone.

"Everybody okay?" he asked.

"Okay."

"Affirmative."

"No problems."

"Raptor, Blue One. You people okay?"

"Copasetic, Blue One. The bad guys ran right into our kill zone."

"Check your fire. We're coming up."

"Come ahead."

A few minutes later the four SEALs entered the camp, which was little more than a depression in the flat stone crest of the ridge, with their packs and equipment piled up to one side, their horses tethered on the reverse slope.

Afridi met him first. "Praise Allah that you are unharmed!" the Pashtun tribesman exclaimed. "You know I did not trust that ISI pig. An hour ago he asked me and my men to join him, to betray you! He even offered money! . . ."

Mariacher looked at him curiously. "Why didn't you take him up on that?"

"But, Lieutenant!" Afridi exclaimed, his eyes growing large. "You are my *friend*!"

Mariacher wasn't entirely sure what friendship meant here on the Afghan border, where allegiances were matters of convenience and changed more regularly than clothing. Afridi might be Pashtun, but there were factors other than tribal loyalties driving the man. As for Qadi, he'd represented the Pakistani government, and Mariacher knew by now how little that meant to the inhabitants of the Northwest Frontier.

"Pack everything up," he said. "We have to get out of here before Qadi leads the Taliban to us."

Raptor was a short distance down the slope, kneeling next to a body. Mariacher joined him. "Who were they?" he asked. "AQ?"

"There's no way to know," the CIA operator said. "I'm pretty sure this one is Pashtun: Afghan or Pakistani, there's no difference. Not Arab. Might be Taliban. His beard's long enough." He stood up. "They might even be dacoits."

"What are those?"

"Bandits. The Brits called them that a century ago, here and in India. Comes from an Urdu word, *dakuu*. A lot of the hill people out this way are completely apolitical and could care less what religion we are. But they'd love to get their paws on our weapons, ammo, and electronic gear."

"You're saying these guys just tried to mug us."

Raptor smiled. "I guess you could say that."

Mariacher looked at the man at their feet. His eyes were wide open, staring up at the stars. "Some of the bad guys back down the hill there were wearing night-vision optics. Looked Russian."

Raptor gave him a hard look. "Yeah?"

"Do your dacoits pack that kind of hardware, usually?"

"No. And neither do the Taliban."

"But Papa bin Laden is rich, so the AQ have all the latest toys. I'm thinking these are AQ."

"I have to agree."

"And our Major Qadi set us up."

"I think," Raptor said, "I'm going to enjoy a little chat with the major when we find him."

"You and me both." Mariacher studied the night for a moment. "You know, we have a decision to make now. We've been spotted. We have the option of pulling out."

"Negative," Raptor said. "Right now, the bad guys don't know squat. These guys could've blundered into dacoits or anti-Taliban rebels or even Pakistani troops. That happens all the time up here. Everybody thinks they know where the border is, but no one is really *sure*."

"Qadi'll put them straight."

"You want to pull out now?" Raptor asked.

"Hell, no."

"Good. Because we have a lot invested in Ali Hassan. We need to find him."

Mariacher nodded. "Aye aye, *sir*."

Raptor gave Mariacher a sharp look. Technically, Mariacher was in command of the SEAL Team element, but Raptor, a civilian, was in command of the overall mission. In Kuala Lumpur, Diamond had been the team's handler and given the orders, but the actual details of the mission were up to Mariacher. Here, the politics of the situation were a bit more delicate and a lot less clear.

A very great deal depended on how much he actually trusted Raptor, and Mariacher wasn't sure yet of the answer to that question. The man had performed well so far and clearly had military experience, but . . .

Bradley joined them. "Gear's packed, horses loaded up, Wheel," he said. "And we've sterilized the area."

Mariacher nodded. "Let's move out. Tell Afridi to keep it *quiet*. We may have other AQ patrols out up here."

"Roger that."

Silently, the SEALs and their allies began moving higher into the mountains.

Wednesday, September 26, 2001

Zur Kowt Training Camp
On the Afghan-Pakistani Border
Paktia Province, Afghanistan
2315 hours, local time

Within the deeper recesses of the compound's main cave, Davlot Iskanderov sat at his crude desk—a couple of planks laid across two upright RPG cases—working under the uncertain light of a kerosene lantern when Ali burst in. "Colonel Khan!" he exclaimed. "Al-Badr reports an enemy attack!"

Iskanderov looked up sharply. "Where? When?"

"Less than an hour ago, sir. They report they are under heavy attack! Many casualties!"

"An air strike?"

"No, Colonel! Soldiers. Many soldiers!"

"How *many* soldiers?"

"They did not know. Their radioman just said many Americans, and that casualties were heavy. Sir, they are asking for reinforcements to hold off the American attack!"

Iskanderov frowned. Pashtun tribesmen were easily excited and they tended to exaggerate. When the Americans attacked, it would not be with ground troops. Their first onslaught would be by air, using cruise missiles, attack planes off their aircraft carriers, and their stealth fighters and bombers. Their first targets would be Afghanistan's military infrastructure—defense radar stations, antiaircraft batteries, and communications and command centers. That was how they'd opened the attack against Iraq ten years ago, and there was no reason to think they would change those highly effective tactics this time.

Intelligence showed plenty of American air activity in the region. In fact, for the past four days Taliban forces had been trumpeting the fact that they'd brought down some kind of unmanned reconnaissance drone in the north, clear evidence that the Americans were preparing for their inevitable attack. But outside of reports of a few small ground force units moving into Uzbekistan, the Gulf States, and elsewhere, there was nothing like the incredible buildup of conventional ground forces like the one that had preceded the Gulf War. If that earlier conflict was anything to go by, it would be months yet before the Americans could launch a ground war in the region.

And if an air offensive against Afghanistan had begun, Iskanderov would know about it. He had direct communications lines open at all times to Kabul, Kandahar, and Peshawar, as well as the radar and antiaircraft facilities at both Khowst and Zhawar Kili.

So . . . who were the troops al-Qaeda fighters were tangling with at Zhawar Kili?

He sighed, put aside the files he was working on and stood up. Knowing these people, they could well be fighting bandits, or, more likely still, each other. But it would be best to investigate things himself.

"Have them ready my helicopter," he said. "I'm coming."

Tuesday, September 25, 2001

Naval Special Warfare Training Area
Off Catalina Island, California
1520 hours, PDT

Tangretti surfaced, his head emerging from an oily swell in the glare of southern California sunshine. He pushed back his mask, dropped his mouthpiece, and turned off the O_2 flow valve on his LAR-V Mark 25 rebreather. The water was bone-numbingly cold despite his wet suit, and exhaustion tugged at his muscles, but he still felt focused and in the groove. A few yards to his left Marine sergeant Dennis Tomajczk, his swim buddy for this evolution, surfaced as well.

The two combat swimmers exchanged thumbs-up hand signals. Tangretti then reached down to his belt and pulled up the MUGR unit tethered there, checking their location.

On land, special ops forces used the Plugger GPS for navigation. For missions that required navigating underwater, however, SEALs used the Miniature Underwater GPS Receiver, or MUGR, a rather forced acronym inevitably pronounced "Mugger." The device weighed 1.2 pounds and was completely watertight. It could pick up GPS satellite transmissions down to thirty-three feet—the safe-limit operating depth for rebreathers—and for deeper work it could use a floating antenna.

According to the satellites, they were less than a hundred

meters off-target after their long swim south from Catalina. Not bad at all.

Turning to face the west, he waited until the next passing swell carried him to its crest. The waves were gentle, only a couple of feet, but that made a lot of difference to a man in the water. Sure enough, there, fifty yards away, so distant he could only see them from the top of the wave, two more swimmers were hauling themselves aboard a rubber duck.

He pointed and Tomajczk gave a clenched-fist acknowledgment. Together, they started swimming.

They were a hell of a long way from the training grounds in the San Bernadino Mountains. They'd deployed to the mountains for two days, then been brought back to Camp Pendleton. This training evolution had begun at zero-dark-thirty that morning with a helocast from a Marine CH-53 helicopter over the waters of the Catalina channel and an underwater swim to the island. There, six SEALs and six Marines had infiltrated a mock-up of a terrorist compound, taking down a number of Marines playing the role of tango sentries along the way, then carried out an assault against the headquarters building—during which they killed a number of lifelike dummies.

Next they'd infiltrated the island's naval gunnery range and set demolition charges on a number of targets, including a mock-up of a reinforced cave entrance, moved back to the water, blown the charges, and swum out to sea in twos.

The entire exercise was fairly routine as training evolutions went, but Tangretti found it amusing. He'd been the one to point out the obvious to Lieutenant Fred Driscoll during the pre-op briefing the afternoon before: "Sir . . . why are we training to infiltrate Afghanistan by sea? The largest body of water in the whole damned country is a well dug in somebody's backyard!"

Driscoll's answer had been short and to the point. "Tangretti, the point of this operation is to practice working in close concert with the Marines, and there is *nothing* like a splash-and-smash to teach us how to work together as a team. You copy?"

He'd copied. SEAL training started in BUD/S with each tadpole assigned to a rubber duck boat crew, and during the next several weeks they grew closer than brothers to the others in their crew. Later they paired off with swim buddies, with the constant admonition that you *never* left your buddy and you *always* watched his back—just as he watched yours.

Marine training for Force Recon was similar in many respects. In fact, West Coast Marines trained at the same Coronado facility as their SEAL brothers. Assignment to a Recon Indoctrination Platoon, or RIP, was much like BUD/S training, and was compared by some Marines to the SEALs' Hell Week—not as brutally intense, perhaps, but lasting a lot longer.

After a three-hour swim south from Catalina, the muscles in his arms and back felt like someone had worked them over with a baseball bat, but he maintained a strong sidestroke and kept moving. Tomajczk had moved slightly ahead of him, and he increased his pace. The guy might be his swim buddy, but he was damned if *any* Marine was going to outpace him in the water.

He could see the second duck now and more members of the mission team. The sturdy little CRRCs—Combat Rubber Raiding Craft—had been dropped in the sea earlier as a double duck, as an airdrop of two lashed together was known. Each boat, manufactured by Zodiac, was fifteen feet long, heavily reinforced, and could carry up to eight SEALs and their gear. Originally known as an IBS—for Inflatable Boat, Small—it normally was used to carry an assault team in from over the horizon. This time around, though, it was the swimmers who were going over the horizon, and the CR-RCs that were waiting to pick them up.

Leave it to the Navy to do things bass-ackward, he thought as he crested another swell. *Training us for Afghanistan by dumping us in the ocean.*

Had they been pulled out of the San Bernardino training session for security reasons? Or simply because some admiral or general higher up on the chain of command had gotten a hair up his ass and decided to give them all some more dive hours? If the parameters of this training exercise had been designed solely to test the participants, to push them to their limits, they were succeeding admirably.

He and Tomajczk reached the nearer of the two ducks more or less together. Ready hands were waiting to help them roll onboard. He lay against the side of the craft for a moment, breathing hard.

"What's the matter, old man?" MN1 Pollock said with an evil grin. "Too hard for you?"

"The only hard day," Tangretti replied between breaths, "was *yesterday*." It was an old SEAL training credo out of BUD/S.

One more Marine-SEAL pair came aboard—Lieutenant Driscoll and Staff Sergeant Hennessy. With six swimmers retrieved, Pollack took the tiller on the duck's outboard motor, throttled up the idling engine and began steering southeast. The other CRRC followed moments later. All operators recovered. Good . . .

Tangretti was wedged between Tomajczk and BM1 Randy Fletcher. Fletcher nudged him in the ribs, hard.

"So, what's the word? You been hanging out with that girl anymore?"

"Fuck you, asshole." The traditional Navy riposte was mildly good-natured.

"Hey, I was just wondering if she was worth you getting busted."

"What do you think?"

In fact, Tangretti hated the idea of having been busted back to third class, and he knew he'd be feeling the pinch in his wallet for the next few paydays, but the outcome of the captain's mast hadn't affected his personal life that much. Hell, all of the SEALs at Coronado had been confined to base, not just him—and training exercises like this one gave him plenty of opportunity to get out and stretch, metaphorically speaking.

Tomajczk turned and gave him an appraising stare. "Man, you got busted over a piece of ass?"

"This Romeo's been sneaking off-base for a month, man," Fletcher told him. "A case of true love!"

"Shit, man," the Marine said with a shake of his head. "No fuckin' bitch is worth that! Was she any good in bed?"

Tangretti gave him a tired but knowing leer. "She was good."

He felt mildly guilty about Marilyn. He'd promised to call and had not. The truth was, he was becoming more focused on the upcoming deployment to Afghanistan and didn't want the distraction.

That was what Marilyn was—a distraction.

"Hey, man!" someone called. "There's our ride!"

Tangretti looked off to the east. A black MH-47E Chinook, a massive helicopter with fore and aft rotor blades, had appeared above the horizon and was rapidly coming closer. It flew past them to the north, close enough that Tangretti could read MARINES painted in dark gray on the side. The helicopter slowed, turned, and settled toward the water west of the two CRRCs. Pollack put the tiller over and started motoring toward the hovering aircraft.

This particular recovery mode was called "Delta Queen,"

and had been pioneered by the 160th SOAR Nightstalkers, the Army's special ops aviation group. The Marine MH-47 hovered with its tail toward the two Zodiacs and its ramp lowered. Gently, an incredible sight, the big twin-rotored aircraft lowered itself to the water until its belly touched the surface, then, amazingly, actually began to settle into the water, sinking until the cargo deck was awash.

At that moment the two CRRCs raced forward at full-throttle and the Marines and SEALs onboard hunched over against the hurricane lashing from the twin rotor blasts. The maneuver was tricky with the sea running this heavy a swell. The helo was now pointed into the oncoming swell, and the rotor blasts tended to flatten the sea around it, but the pilot still had to be damned good to keep the aircraft from being completely swamped.

The CRRC motored into the partly submerged cargo deck, where members of the flight crew waited, secured by safety lines against the possibility of being washed out of the aircraft, their boots in the water. The SEALs and Marines piled out of the CRRC and hauled it the rest of the way into the fuselage, lashing it down with tethers as the second CRRC came aboard. Moments later, their gear secure, the SEALs and Marines grabbed hold of the canvas webbing covering the interior fuselage bulkheads. The MH-47 lifted slowly, ponderously, clear of the sea, sending a Niagara of water pouring out of the cargo hold, over the ramp and into the ocean below.

A creature of the sky once more, the helicopter banked left and accelerated, angling toward the east and Camp Pendleton.

"Hey, there's some juicy scuttlebutt, people!" the Marine crew chief called to the tired and wet operators a few minutes later as the MH-47E roared back across the Catalina channel. "Word just came through from CNN! Saudi Arabia has just cut diplomatic relations with the Taliban!"

Despite the deafening chatter of the twin rotors overhead, the cargo compartment rang to the mingled war cries of the men—"Hoo-yah!" from the SEALs, "Ooh-rah!" from the Marines. The United Arab Emirates had cut their ties with the Taliban on September twenty-second. Now that the Saudis had followed suite, only Pakistan still recognized the outlaw regime in Kabul.

Tangretti leaned back against the back of his hard and narrow seat, eyes closed. Damn it, when were they going to get to deploy? He felt like a prize-winning racehorse that had been training endlessly. When would he get to *go*?

Patience. SEALs were supposed to know patience, a far more formidable weapon in their arms locker than an M-60 machine gun or a raft full of high explosives.

Tangretti thought about Marilyn. For him, in a way, she represented what this war was supposed to be about.

He'd been giving it a fair amount of thought since that evening at TGI Friday's. At the moment, American civilians—like Marilyn—still didn't know they were at war, not deep down, at gut level. Several ominous pronouncements had come out of Afghanistan recently, from Osama bin Laden or from the Taliban. Most recently, al-Qaeda had announced that wherever there were Americans or Jews, anywhere in the world, they would be targeted. Marilyn might have the hots for him because he was a Navy SEAL, but the war for her was a distant abstraction. Judging from interviews he'd seen on CNN during the past week or two, Americans wanted to strike back at al-Qaeda for 9/11, but at the same time they were having trouble coming to grips with a crucial question: Why did *anyone* on the planet want to kill *them*?

Americans as a whole tended to be a laid-back and forgiving bunch, tolerant in a parochial way. Foreigners might act in peculiar ways, but that was their business for the most part. Why anyone would hate Americans just because they were Americans was an unfathomable mystery to nearly everyone. The fact that violence against innocent Muslims on home soil was on the increase merely underscored the fact that Americans as a whole neither understood Islam nor the motives of the fanatics who viewed them as legitimate targets of jihad.

Weirdest of all, from Tangretti's perspective, were those few Americans who—inevitably, perhaps—had begun looking for motives for al-Qaeda's hatred in American actions. Well, American foreign policy hadn't always been a beacon of light and reason, that was true, and there were plenty of people in the world with reasons to hate the United States. But even so . . . three thousand Americans dead, most of them civilians, in a vicious sneak attack, and it was *America* that was to blame?

No fucking way.

For him and his fellow operators the issue was a simple one. The motives of the Islamic fundamentalists were, at this point, unimportant. What was important was that America was under a deadly and concerted assault, and he and every other serviceman and -woman was oath-bound to defend America and her citizens from attack. Osama bin Laden and his cronies had decided to declare war on the United States. He and his Teammates would humor him and take the war to him, wherever he might be hiding, ending his threat to the safety of America and Americans once and for all.

He just wished the damned training would be over with, so he and his teammates could show al-Qaeda just how monumental a mistake they had made.

Chapter 13

Saturday, September 29, 2001

**On the Outskirts of Khowst
Paktia Province, Afghanistan
2110 hours, local time**

Mariacher sat beside the campfire alone, his MP5 within easy reach on the ground next to him. The night was dark, without even the keek of insects to break the silence. Beyond the fire and down the hill, he knew, lay the city of Khowst, but there were no lights to mark its location. He as easily could have been still up in the mountains on the border instead of here, a mile outside a fair-sized city.

Three full days had passed since the ambush at Zhawar Kili. The sudden increase of military activity in the area—including frequent overflights by Afghan helicopters—had forced the DevGroup cell to fade farther back into the mountains.

They'd established a new camp, on a ridgetop with excellent visibility both to the north and southeast, into Pakistan. Their supplies and equipment were stored in a shallow cave—little more than a rock overhang, really, which they'd

then camouflaged with slabs of fallen rock. There was little
shelter or forage for the horses, however, so Raptor and
Afridi, with the Pashtun entourage, had taken them down
into the Khowst Valley. There was a man there, Afridi
insisted—a cousin of his—who would stable the horses and
might know the whereabouts of Ali Hassan, the CIA contact
man in Paktia Province.

That had been yesterday. Last night Raptor had contacted
them by radio. The SEALs were to meet with him tonight on
a hilltop just outside of the city of Khowst. One of Afridi's
men would lead them to the rendezvous. They would know
the guide was from Raptor because he would use the password "Mountain spring."

"Shit!" Osterlee had exclaimed when Mariacher told the
others. "This could be another ambush!"

"So, we take precautions," Mariacher replied.

Afridi's bodyguard had showed up early that morning and
given the password. Mariacher and Osterlee would go with
him; Bradley and Lehman would follow, but far enough
away to remain out of sight. They would have to rely on directions relayed to them over their M-biters, but the deployment meant that if there were an ambush, Bradley and
Lehman would be in a position to come to the rescue.

Their guide had led them to this hill overlooking Khowst
from the west. After checking the area thoroughly for signs
of Taliban or AQ presence, they sent the man back into
Khowst and settled down to wait. Even now, though, they
were prepared against the possibility of another double-
cross. Mariacher sat alone by the fire, while Bradley, Osterlee, and Lehman remained hidden among the rocks and
ledges around him, night-vision devices in place, M-biter
channels open, silent, still, and watching.

Mariacher didn't like being this reliant on the locals, especially after Major Qadi's betrayal. The SEALs had little choice in the matter, however. All of them had been growing their beards to better fit in with the local population, but none of them had achieved the fist length from the chin necessary to let them pass inspection by the Taliban's religious police. Their clothing gave them the scruffy look of Afghan militia, and the colored scarves they all wore could be pulled up over the lower part of their faces if they needed to risk being seen in daylight. They even had a cover story prepared, just in case they were suddenly confronted by local militia or other hostiles. They were volunteers from Egypt, which would explain both their foreign look and the fact that they all spoke the Egyptian dialect of Arabic but not Pashtun.

But the best defense they had was to stay out of sight entirely, and that meant they needed to contact locals to get them in touch with Ali Hassan. To do that they needed to trust Afridi . . . and the CIA man who called himself Raptor.

That trust did not come easily for Mariacher. The CIA, in his experience, tended to play complex games where right hands had no idea what left hands were doing, and one team could find itself working at odds with another. Alliances among CIA operators and assets could be as shifting and as complicated as alliances among the Pashtun. He still wondered what the full story had been in Kuala Lumpur, and how Green Tiger could have escaped them.

A low, two-tone whistle sounded in the night, just beyond the ragged edge of the firelight. Mariacher dropped and rolled in a smooth, flowing motion, snatching up his MP5 and aiming it into the darkness. "Manhattan!" he called over his radio.

"Payback," came the response.

"Come on in."

Raptor stepped into the firelight.

"You alone?" Mariacher asked him.

"Yeah. Afridi's cousin will be coming up here for a chat in thirty mikes." He glanced around the fire. "Where's the rest of you?"

For answer, three ruby-red pinpoints of light winked on, dancing against Raptor's chest and on each side. Raptor glanced down at the aim point on his chest, then grinned. "I see."

"Kill the light show, boys," Mariacher told the others over his radio. "Pull up a chair, Raptor. Make yourself comfortable." He kept his H&K in his lap.

"You're not taking any chances. Good."

"We decided it would be better if I met this guy with just you," Mariacher told him as the contractor sat down. "Just in case. We know Qadi has friends down here."

"Roger that. I've had a long talk with him, though, and I think he's legit. His name's Afridi too, by the way. From the same tribe. Abdul Mohammed Afridi."

"Another Mohammed. Great."

"No different out here than naming someone Matthew, Mark, Luke, or John back in the States."

"I know. They just take the religion thing so seriously out here. I don't like fanaticism. Of *any* stripe."

"I'm with you."

They were quiet for a long time, with only the crackle of the campfire to break the night silence. Mariacher was intrigued by Raptor. During the past week he'd shown impressive skill as an operator, and what he'd done just now—sneaking all the way to the edge of the light from the campfire without being spotted by three very good SEALs hidden among the rocks—was nothing short of amazing.

"Can I ask you something?" Mariacher asked.

"Sure. I don't promise to give you an answer."

Hell, Mariacher thought. *Even if he answers, he's still a Company man. He could be lying like a rug.*

"Who are you?"

"Eh? What do you mean?"

"You're an operator," Mariacher told him, "and a good one. Anyone who could sneak up here past my men without being spotted is *damned* good. What's your background? Delta? The Green beanies?"

Raptor sat in silence for a few moments more, as though considering what, if anything, he should reveal. "Actually," he said at last, "I'm a SEAL."

"No shit!"

"No shit."

"You used the present tense."

"C'mon. You know the Teams. It's the same as the Marines. There are no *ex*-SEALs. Just former active-duty SEALs."

"Once in the Teams, always in the Teams," Mariacher agreed. He felt himself immediately relaxing somewhat. The one person in this country—hell, the one person in the whole goddamned *world*—he could trust was another SEAL.

"I'm supposed to keep this all on a strictly professional level," Raptor said. "Code names only, and all that. But the name's Halstead. Mark Halstead."

Mariacher extended a hand, and Halstead took it. "Halstead? I know that name," Mariacher told him. "Medal of Honor?"

"Actually, that was my dad," Halstead told him. "Vietnam."

"You looked a bit young."

Halstead grinned. "Just a little. I enlisted back in 'eighty nine. BUD/S in 'eighty-nine and 'ninety. Team Three."

"Desert Storm?"

"Scud-hunting. Yup."

"It's a pleasure to meet you. What brings a SEAL like you way the hell and gone out here?" Mariacher gave a malicious grin. "I don't see any water."

"I carry all the water I need right here in my canteen,"

Halstead replied, giving the standard SEAL answer to that often asked question. He hesitated another moment. "The Agency approached me in 'ninety-nine," he continued. "They do that. It's how they recruit good people for their paramilitary direct action units. Sometimes they use active-duty military personnel, like you. More often, though, they draw on their own people. They approach likely looking candidates in the SEALs, Delta Force, Army Special Forces, Marine Force Recon—the very, *very* best there are. They arrange for them to move straight over to the Company as soon as they retire from the military."

"You only had ten years in," Mariacher said.

"Yeah, well, I'd enlisted for four, then shipped for six. It was coming on time for me to go lifer, but—well, things happened."

"Like what?"

"Women."

"As in one particular woman?"

"Two, actually. The first was my mother, Wendy."

"I didn't know SEALs had mothers," Mariacher joked.

"Yeah, well, this one did. She and Dad were close. I mean *real* close. But not long after Desert Storm, well, she had a stroke."

"I'm sorry."

"Shit happens. She pretty much made a physical recovery, but, well, it kind of changed her, y'know? It was like she didn't love my dad anymore. She went really crazy a few months after the stroke. My dad had to call the cops on her, put her in the hospital on the locked ward. It—well, it . . . crushed him."

Mariacher hadn't expected this personal a revelation. He remained silent, respectful.

"Mom got out, got on meds, and tried to live with him, but she threw him out a year later. Said she couldn't stand living with a SEAL. Never knowing where he was or if he'd be coming back. He managed to stick it out after that, he retired after thirty, but it was like all the life was gone, know what I mean? For a while, there, he was ROAD."

"Retired on Active Duty. Shit." That was so counter to the spirit of the Teams, Mariacher had trouble imagining it of a SEAL.

"He's been coming back . . . but it's been tough. I think it would have killed anyone else. Anyway, then Mom started working on *me,* trying to get me to leave the Teams."

"That sucks."

"Yes, it does. She ended up moving in with some kind of weird religious cult after that. She still likes me, and we stay in touch, but she hasn't really been the same in the head since the stroke."

"Is that why you left the Teams after ten? So you could tell your mother you weren't a SEAL anymore?"

"Partly, I guess. There's more to it than that."

"There always is. You said 'women,' plural."

"Yeah. While all this was going on with my mom and dad, I met a girl named Cynthia. The demon-bitch goddess from hell. She knew I was a SEAL going in, right? I think she liked the glamour of it all. After we were married, though, she got on this kick about me being called out on deployments at a minute's notice, about weekend duty, about my not being able to talk about stuff, like where I was going or where I'd been. She didn't like being a Navy wife, especially an enlisted man's wife. Didn't like base housing. Didn't like moving every year or two. So she started in on how I needed to get out of the Navy and do something productive. She left me after we'd been married four years." He snorted, a dismissive sound. "I think my mother got to her, actually, and they got to conspiring together. In some ways, I think Cynthia was as crazy as my mother."

"Sounds like it. So . . . why'd you get out, then? If it were me, I'd stay in the Teams just to prove I was my own man. And . . . maybe for my dad." He regretted the words as soon as he spoke them. He hadn't intended to criticize Halstead's actions.

But the CIA man didn't seem to take it as criticism. He shrugged. "I needed a change. The Teams had been my home for a fair chunk of my life, but after the home-front wars, I needed to get clear and start over, you know what I mean?"

"I think so."

"In the Teams—even in DevGroup—you're operating under a tight chain of command with neat little barbed-wire fences around you called Rules of Engagement. Restrictions. Regulations. Everything you do is scrutinized up the ass. Cap a tango and you spend the next month filling out paperwork."

Mariacher smiled. It wasn't quite that bad, but he knew the feeling.

"And I swear, sometimes Navy regulations come down and smack you between the eyes, and they're as insane as my mother ever was."

"You're not going to tell me that you don't have reports, regulations, and ROEs in the Agency."

"No. We do. Of course we do. But there's a lot more independence. It's more . . . I don't know. Free-form."

"Cowboys."

"I know. People call us that. But this is one fucking shithole of a fucked-up world, and there are people in this world who need killing. I'm not a religious nutcase like my mother . . . but I do believe in *evil*. I've seen it. I've fought it. The Company gives me the chance to go out in the field and try to kill them before they manage to kill American civilians . . . like about three thousand of them with a couple of hijacked airliners."

"Welcome to the New World Disorder."

"Roger that. Dammit, sometimes you have to be able to step outside the rules."

They were silent for a time longer as Mariacher digested what Halstead had told him.

"How about you?" Halstead said.

"What about me?"

"I've heard your name before too. It's not a common one."

"No, it's not."

"Your father?"

"My uncle, actually. He was a SEAL in Vietnam too. He went on to help form SEAL Team Six after Eagle's Claw."

There'd been a scramble in all branches of the U.S. military after the failed hostage rescue in Iran, in 1980. SEAL Six had been the Navy's entrant in the hostage rescue team line-up.

"I thought so," Halstead said. "*That* Mariacher. The guy's a living legend, you know."

"He also stepped on way too many high-ranking toes. Not healthy for your career, if you know what I mean."

"And you're in DevGroup, after the way they railroaded your uncle? How come? They put the guy in jail, for Christ's sake!"

"Maybe I thought Team Six—DevGroup, now, rather—was still a good idea. A *necessary* idea. Highly trained and well-equipped operators who can take the fight to the enemy, no matter where he's hiding. That's the name of the game nowadays."

"True. But when they turned SEAL Six into DevGroup, they brought in all those new rules and regulations. Oversight committees. Fiscal reports. The way I heard it, you can't scratch your balls without ten different permission forms and requisitions."

"They don't want any more cowboys," Mariacher replied. "Not like my uncle." *Or like you, Raptor,* he added in his head.

"Or like me," Halstead added, as if reading Mariacher's thoughts. "You ever think about coming to work for us?"

"The CIA? Not really."

"Give it some thought, man. Good pay. Good people . . . well, the ones in the field, anyway. And we get to track down evil in its lair and destroy it, without filling out a ton of paperwork afterward."

"I don't know. I don't care for the paperwork on my side of the fence, but I tend to think some rules are necessary. Otherwise, with no checks and balances, you've got real trouble. 'Who watches the watchers?' "

Besides, he had worked with the Agency and wasn't all that impressed. They liked to play cover-your-ass more than the Navy brass. But he kept his thoughts to himself.

"So, did any of that answer your question?" Halstead asked. "Or was it TMI?"

"It wasn't too much information, no. Thanks, Halstead."

"Call me Mark . . . but not until *after* we extract, okay? I'm still 'Raptor' while we're on the op."

"I hear you." After a long silence, Mariacher added, "Can I ask you something?"

"Shoot."

"What was your rank when you got out?"

Halstead smiled. "I was a boatswain's mate first class. I'd passed my test for chief, but the promotion hadn't come through yet." He gave Mariacher a sidelong glance. "Is that a problem . . . *Lieutenant*?"

"Hell, no! Everyone knows it's the senior petty officers who really run things in the Navy."

Halstead relaxed.

It *was* a bit on the weird side . . . a SEAL officer taking orders from a former P.O. first class. SEALs tended to be less rank-conscious than other branches of the military, however. If a man was right for the job, then he was the *man*. The fact that Halstead had been a SEAL and in combat meant far more to Mariacher than the rank he'd held when he was in.

More minutes passed. Bradley's voice sounded in Mariacher's ear. "Hey, Wheel. Gold One. We have movement, front. Looks like one man. He's armed."

That last was no surprise. In Afghanistan it often appeared that every male was carrying. Supposedly, the Taliban had disarmed the civilian population, but there were so many men in the militia that fact hardly seemed to matter.

"Only one?" Mariacher asked Raptor.

"Haji was going to stay in town, looking up some more of his cousins. I asked Abdul to come alone."

Mariacher rose and moved out of the firelight to the right. Raptor moved to the left. Several minutes later the lone man, bearded, small, wearing a blue turban and carrying an AK-47, emerged from the darkness at the crest of the hill and stepped cautiously into the light. "Hello?" he said in uncertain English. "You are here?"

Raptor stepped back into the light. "We're here, Abdul. Please, have a seat by the fire."

"Thank you, my friend." The man sat but continued to hold his weapon. He was wizened to the point of looking frail, Mariacher saw, and many of his teeth were missing. The leathery look of his skin, though, spoke both of hardship and a hidden strength. Mariacher decided not to judge the man's ability until he knew him better.

"Lieutenant Mariacher," Raptor said, "this is Abdul Afridi. He may be able to tell us something about the people we're looking for."

Mariacher stood and moved back to the fire. Abdul appeared startled by his silent appearance, and gripped his AK more tightly. The knuckles on his hands stood out starkly white. He's scared, Mariacher told himself. Scared men do stupid things.

It helped knowing that the other three SEALs were somewhere in the night close by, both watching Afridi and on the lookout for any more nighttime visitors.

"Hello, Abdul," Mariacher said pleasantly. "Can we offer you something to eat?"

"If it please Allah! . . ."

The man's eagerness surprised Mariacher. He pulled an MRE from a backpack nearby and opened it. The supply of Meals, Ready to Eat, the SEALs had brought with them had been selected carefully so as not to give offense to Muslims—no pork. Even so, he couldn't help wondering in a gallows-humor way whether offering their campfire guest three lies in one, as MREs were known in the service, would turn a potential friend into an enemy.

Abdul began devouring the package's contents, however, starting with the high-energy Hooah bar. When he began trying to figure out how to get at the contents of the FRH, Mariacher reached over and lent him a hand, showing how adding water turned the Flameless Ration Heater into an exothermic chemical heater to warm the entrée—in this case a slice of beefsteak in mushroom gravy.

Americans, Mariacher decided, might make jokes about the edibility of military rations, but Abdul clearly wasn't so picky or spoiled. He devoured the contents so quickly that Raptor broke out a second MRE for him.

"Raptor says you are looking for the one called Ali Hassan," he said after a time, around a mouthful of peanut butter cracker.

"That's right. Do you know him?"

"I know him, yes. But you will not find him."

"Why not?"

"Two days ago he was taken. By the Amaniyat."

"The National Security Directorate," Raptor said. "The KHAD under the Soviets."

"I know. Abdul? Do you know where they took him?"

A shrug. "One does not ask too many question in this country these days."

Raptor reached inside a pocket of his journalist's vest and extracted a wad of currency. "We can pay for the information, Abdul. If you need to ask around . . . perhaps bribe someone . . ."

The money quietly vanished into Abdul's *kameez*. "Oh, I can tell you where they probably took him. There is a warehouse on the edge of town. Where they keep the . . . the . . . I have not the words. The truck boxes."

"Truck boxes?"

Abdul nodded but did not elaborate. "Normally, prisoners would have been taken to the police station, in the center of the city, but . . . since the Taliban came to power, there are too many for that. The man you seek would almost certainly have been taken to the warehouse for questioning . . . unless someone decided to move him to Kabul instead."

Raptor and Mariacher exchanged glances. If the CIA asset was in Kabul, there was no way to reach him. But a warehouse in Khowst might not be as tough a target. At the very least they could do a surreptitious sneak-and-peek to try to find their man.

"Abdul, would you excuse me and my friend a moment? We need to discuss something."

"Might your hospitality extend to another of those dinners in a box?"

Mariacher bit back what likely would have been a blasphemous exclamation to Abdul's ears. MREs were complete 1,200-calorie meals. Abdul had just knocked back two in rapid succession and was eager for more. The man must have an iron stomach . . . or else he was very hungry.

"Of course." Their supply of the things was not inexhaustible, and these would have to last them until they could arrange for local food or begin receiving helicopter or airdropped deliveries of fresh supplies. But food appeared to be a better social lubricant here than money.

Mariacher and Raptor moved a dozen yards back from the fire.

"What do you think?" Raptor asked him.

"I think I don't want to just cut and run, and leave our contact to the KHAD."

It wasn't just the information Ali held. The man had been working for the CIA for years, and had probably ended up in prison because that fact was known. The Amaniyat's love of heavy-duty torture was well known and documented. Mariacher didn't like the idea of leaving anyone to their mercies without at least trying to rescue him.

"His capture means our mission is compromised."

"Shit. We were compromised by Qadi. If he's in tight with the Taliban, he's down there right now telling them everything he knows about us."

"Yeah. Of course, he knows we're supposed to pull out of the country if we're spotted too. And after that firefight the other night, I'm thinking Qadi has already told them we're back in Pak."

"The question is, what does Ali know?"

Raptor sighed. "He knows Task Force 5 is operating in the area. He knows passwords, radio frequencies, and he knows people like Abdul, here, and Haji. He even knows our principle recon target is Zur Khowst, since he was supposed to lead us up there."

"In other words, if he talks, he'll compromise a lot more than just us and our mission."

"And he *will* talk. You know as well as I do that it's only a matter of time before he tells his interrogators every damned thing they want to know. He'll be volunteering information on his own father just to make the pain stop."

Mariacher studied Raptor. It was up to the CIA man to make the decision—stay or run. Knowing Halstead was a former SEAL made things easier, though. Mariacher trusted the man now, as much as he trusted any of the SEALs on his team.

"We can't just leave the poor bastard," Mariacher prompted.

Raptor was watching the hungry man by the fire. "No. No, we can't."

"And we were supposed to scope out Khowst anyway."

"Yeah. You know, I was just thinking. There are a lot of foreigners down there—Arab volunteers for the jihad. Since they're not looking for us particularly—not yet, anyway— we could probably slip in for a quick reconnoiter, and maybe find where they're holding him. It would at least give us something to go on."

"We could phone home for instructions."

"Fuck, and have the Pentagon second-guess every move we make?"

Mariacher grinned. "Cowboy."

"Yippee-ki-yi."

The question, of course, was whether four . . . no, *five*— SEALs could effect a rescue without compromising the rest of their multitiered mission. The more objectives you piled onto a given mission, the more likely that the mission would fail. Worse, hostage rescue operations were not things to be cobbled together at a moment's notice. They needed to gather intelligence, plan the assault, work out multiple paths for E&E, rehearse the assault . . .

Well, one step at a time. The first was to gather intelligence on the objective, and that they could manage easily enough.

Mariacher felt one nagging doubt, however. The team was supposed to pull out of Afghanistan if their presence was discovered. Right now they had some wiggle room. They didn't know for sure that the bad guys were aware of them yet.

But the moment they tried to take down a police station to liberate a prisoner there, the proverbial cat would most decidedly be out of the bag. Leaving the questions of Qadi's betrayal out of the equation for the moment, a skirmish with unknown forces up in the mountains was one thing. An assault on a police facility in a large city was something entirely else.

"Let's do it," Mariacher said. "Sir."

"Roger that."

Chapter 14

Khowst
Paktia Province, Afghanistan
0825 hours, local time

Abdul Afridi lived with his wife and two sons in a mud-brick dwelling on the north side of Khowst. During the night, he led Raptor and the four SEALs down off the hill and to the house, where he formally extended to them the welcome of *melmastia*.

The word meant, roughly, hospitality, but within the complex etiquette and interactions of Pakhtunwali, *melmastia* meant more than simply welcoming the five Americans and his cousin Haji into his house. The SEALs had shared their food with Abdul on the hilltop; now he was honor-bound to share his food with them.

The six of them—Haji's men were somewhere out in the village, Mariacher was told—were invited to sit down around a small, wooden table to eat the morning meal. There wasn't much—a thin stew of a strongly flavored meat that was either mutton or goat, mixed with some vegetables that had been boiled until little remained to reveal their ancestry.

The food was served by a woman—Haji's wife—who was completely veiled in a blue burka that made her look as if she was wearing a heavy wool blanket over her head, with only a thick mesh, like heavy cheesecloth, through which to see and breathe.

"Thank you," Mariacher said as she set a bowl in front of him. He heard a startled intake of breath behind the mesh, but she said nothing. Raptor gave him a hard look from the other side of the table—a warning. *Don't talk to the women.*

It was a reminder of the cultural gulf between the Paktun and the West. Mariacher noted that the single window in the house's front room had been painted over completely black . . . and he remembered hearing about the Taliban's law that made it a crime for a woman to be glimpsed through a window in her home, even by accident. In many homes, he knew, women wouldn't even be permitted in the same room with men, even as servants.

Abdul and his two teenage sons refused to sit at the table while the SEALs and Haji ate. This too was part of the law and practice of *melmastia*—a mark of respect and courtesy to honored guests. According to the briefings Mariacher had received in Thailand, *melmastia* actually required a host to give refuge to *anyone,* even an enemy, for as long as they were inside the home. This code was bound up with the Pakhtunwali concept of *nang*—of honor. Abdul gained honor by serving his guests . . . but upholding that honor meant that he had to be willing to die to defend them.

The thought of this wrinkled little character putting his life on the line to protect five strong, well-trained, and heavily armed Navy SEALs seemed a little bizarre, to say the least. But the man's dedication to his personal code was impressive.

As they ate, Mariacher thought about bin Laden as a guest of the Taliban. The Taliban leaders were, for the most part, Paktun, and would observe the same code. No wonder they'd repeatedly refused to turn bin Laden over to the United States, or else professed not to know where he was at the moment. They could not accede to America's demands without losing honor, and, by the stark all-or-nothing code of Pakhtunwali, losing one's honor quite literally meant that life was no longer worth living.

"The meal was wonderful, Abdul," Mariacher told their host when they were done. "Thank you!"

"It was nothing, and all thanks belong to Allah!"

"Well, I'd still like to show some appreciation." He signaled to Lehman, who grinned and went over to the Team's packs, which were piled up along the wall next to the front door. Picking one up, he opened it and removed the contents, which he placed on the table in front of Abdul. "Here ya go, friend. With the compliments of the U.S. government."

The pack contained twenty of the team's MREs.

"Allah is merciful!" Abdul cried. Turning, he embraced Mariacher in a surprisingly strong bear hug, then, standing on tiptoe, he kissed Mariacher full on the mouth. "The blessings of Allah be upon you, my friend!"

"And on you."

Abdul kissed Raptor, then turned to embrace Lehman. The SEAL managed to gently deflect the assault into a handshake. "That's okay, Abdul. Blessings on you, buddy."

"You are most generous," Haji told Mariacher as Abdul and his wife carried armfuls of MREs to a wooden cabinet in the corner and stashed them away. From the way they handled the packages, they might have been storing gold. "I know the supplies you brought with you are limited."

"Hey, it's the least we can do," Mariacher replied. "These people are putting their lives on the line for us."

"Indeed. Food has been scarce in some regions lately. The Taliban is most particular in the way they protect the souls of men. They are not so efficient when it comes to distributing food, however."

"We're going to be changing that," Raptor told them. "The Taliban has been helping America's enemies. The friend of our enemy is also our enemy. We intend to see to it that the Taliban is replaced by a democratically elected government."

"If by this democratically government, you mean the *jirga*," Abdul said, nodding, "we welcome it. The Taliban, most of them, mean well, and do no more than uphold God's laws. A few, however, have seen fit to put themselves above the rest of us, and *that* we will not tolerate!"

Frankly, Mariacher wondered if these people understood even the most basic aspect of democracy. Well, they would learn. First, though, the Taliban had to be kicked out.

"So tell us," Mariacher asked, "how is it you know Ali Hassan?"

Abdul snapped something in Pashto at his wife, and the woman silently left the room. "Politics," he said then, in English, "are not for a woman's ears."

"Your relationship with Ali is political?"

He shrugged. "In this country, *all* relationships are political . . . and all politics involve relationships. Ali's true name is Hafez Tayed, and he is my friend. He is also my son-in-law. His second wife is my daughter."

"I see."

"Ah, but there is more to it, you see. Hafez has been talking for a long time about organizing the men of Khowst into a rebellion against the Taliban. This has been no more than a dream . . . until the American CIA began promising us help. With men, with weapons, with radios and other equipment, we could easily take our land back from these—these fanatics, and their foreign army."

"By 'foreign army,' you mean al-Qaeda?"

"The Base, yes. Arabs, most of them. Some Tajik. Even some Americans. Not Pashtun. We will *not* have foreigners telling us what to do or how to live."

Mariacher had heard that there were Americans with al-Qaeda. He'd hoped, frankly, that it was only scuttlebutt—rumor and wild stories—but he knew better than to count on it. A fanatic's take on religion could make him do some strange things.

But the thought of Americans working with those monsters was horrifying.

He shook off the unpleasant thought. "I gather Hafez ended up talking to the wrong people."

"It could be. He recruited many into this resistance he hoped to create, myself included. Someone may have told the Amaniyat."

"With Hafez in jail, just who's the leader of the local resistance?" Mariacher asked.

"You're looking at him," Raptor said.

Abdul thumped himself on the chest. "I have that honor!" He hesitated, then added, "In truth, our group is led by a small *jirga* . . . a council of leaders. Hafez's brother is on this *jirga*. And three others. But I—I am the richest, the most powerful!" He thumped himself on his chest. "My voice is the loudest!"

"I can believe that. How many men can you drum up on short notice?"

" 'Drum up'?" He looked puzzled, his head cocked to one side. "Ah! I see! One hundred armed men, easily! Perhaps two hundred more without weapons! And they will eagerly take weapons from the Taliban who are killed, or from the martyrs who fall in our cause!"

"And now the Americans are here!" Haji said, catching Abdul's excitement. "They will free our friend Hafez! The fighters will rise, and together we will bring freedom to our land once more!"

"Whoa, there," Mariacher said, holding up a hand. "One step at a time. First thing we need to do is have you show us where you think he's being held."

"This we can do," Abdul told them.

"I'd also like to show you some photographs. There are quite a few of the Taliban's leadership and members of al-Qaeda we need to find. We were hoping Hafez could help, but perhaps you can as well."

"I will do my best!" Abdul exclaimed. "I know everyone in this city!"

For the next hour and a half Mariacher showed Haji and Abdul his photo album. Actually, it was a plastic waterproof pouch with a stack of photographs inside. He removed the photos one by one, laying them on the table for the two Pashtun to examine. The house was close and dark with the windows painted over and the only light coming from oil lamps. Abdul brought one of the lamps over to the table, though, and by its light the two men studied each picture, each face, closely.

The first was of a thin, bearded face—it might have been the face of a kindly college professor, except that college professors rarely hold AK-47 assault rifles. It was the face that had been unknown until three weeks ago, and now was the most hunted face on Earth. "Osama bin Laden," Mariacher said.

"I know of this man, surely," Abdul said. "But I have never seen him. There were rumors that he was visiting the camps in Paktia Province only a few days ago."

"I heard he was in Kandahar," Haji put in. "He is a ghost, that one. Never in the same place on two successive nights. He fears the American CIA."

"How about this one?" Mariacher laid out the one available photo, grainy and out of focus, of Mohammed Omar, emir of Afghanistan and leader of the Taliban.

"I have never seen him," Abdul said. "Rumor has it that he never leaves his compound in Kandahar."

"That city is the heart and soul of the Taliban," Haji added. "Its spiritual center, and the place that gave it birth. Many of the biggest leaders are there."

Other photos followed, all with negative responses from the two Pashtuns. The Mullah Abdul Jalil, Deputy Minister of Foreign Affairs. Mullah Ubaidullah Akhund, the Minister of Defense. Mullah Abdul Razaq, the Minister of Interior Affairs. Mariacher laid down yet another photo. Abdul started and grabbed Mariacher's arm. "This one I have seen! Right here, in Khowst!"

"Well, well," Raptor said. "Qari Ahmadullah, the Minister of Security."

"KHAD's number one spook," Mariacher added. "When did you see him?"

"Two, no, three days ago. I was, how do you say, downtown. With Hafez Tayed."

"Ali Hassan."

"The same, yes. We had gone down to the central police station to inquire after his wife's brother."

"Wasn't that a bit reckless?" Raptor asked.

A shrug. "We had no reason to believe the authorities were interested in Hafez. Ahmad had not been home for several days, and we were concerned. We were in the front room, talking to the captain there, when a helicopter landed in the courtyard outside. A moment later a number of soldiers came in and made all of us stand off to one side. This man," he tapped Ahmadullah's photo, "then walked past us, along with another man, a foreigner, and several others. They went into the police commander's office, and we did not see them again."

"I see."

"The police came to Hafez's house late that evening. They took him, both of his wives, a daughter, and one of his sons."

"Do you think the two were connected?" Raptor asked. "Ahmadullah's arrival and Tayed's arrest?"

"I don't know. It is possible. Often, orders come down to local authorities from higher up, to make arrests, to question people. I think it is just to keep them busy."

"Sounds like the Navy's bureaucracy," Bradley said.

"Maybe," Mariacher said, "but in the Navy, people don't disappear in the night. How about this other man . . . what did you say? Your wife's brother. Did you learn anything from the police?"

"Alas, no. They knew nothing. Or they said nothing. Many people have disappeared lately and are not seen again. It may be the police. Or the army. Or even the jihad. The Base has been known to conscript men and boys, to give them weapons and order them to fight. The jihad is gathering a large army, a very large army, to fight the Americans when they come."

"But you're sure it's the police who have Tayed."

"As I told you, honored sir, they came in the night, and when they took Hafez and his son, they took his wives and daughter as well. The Base recruits only men between the ages of twelve and fifty."

"Why would they take the women?" Osterlee asked.

"To use as tools to make Hafez talk, of course," was the dark reply.

If Afghanistan's security minister was in the area, Khowst had just taken on a new importance for Task Force 5. They needed to learn more.

"What about this foreigner you mentioned?" Raptor asked.

A shrug. "There have been rumors of a military expert

brought in by the Base. Some say he is Tajik. Some even say he is Russian." Abdul turned his head and spat viciously on the floor. "They call him Colonel Khan. He is said to some- times be in Khowst, sometimes in Kabul or Kandahar. And he is said to have a headquarters in the mountains north of Khowst."

"Zur Kowt?"

"That is the place."

Mariacher continued showing photos to the men. When he finished with the rogue's gallery of Taliban photos, he be- gan laying out photographs of known members of al- Qaeda—bin Laden's lieutenants and associates thought to be in Afghanistan. Again, Haji and Abdul were unable to iden- tify any of them, until Mariacher laid down a photo of a round-faced man with a heavy black beard.

"That one I have seen!" Abdul exclaimed. "He was with the foreigner, Colonel Khan, and with Qari Ahmadullah at the police station. Usually, he is in Kandahar, but there are rumors he is at Zur Kowt now!"

Mariacher looked into the familiar face for a long mo- ment. "Green Tiger," he said. "Well, well, well."

Raptor nodded. "Khalid Shaikh Mohammed. Looks like we didn't come up dry after all. You saw him? In Khowst?"

"Yes, sir! And there is much talk about him in the streets. It said that he planned the attacks against your New York, that he was . . . how do you say? The mastermind."

"That's what we've heard," Mariacher said. "I think we need to have a closer look at this police warehouse you told us about, Abdul. We need to find Ali Hassan—I mean, Hafez Tayed."

"I can take you there now, honored sirs."

Leaving Bradley, Lehman, and Osterlee in the house, his wife's honor amply defended by his two sons, Abdul took Mariacher, Raptor, and Haji out into the streets of Khowst later that morning. They went armed, though Mariacher elected to leave behind his MP5-SD, an unusual weapon in the region, and carried Bradley's MP5-A2 instead, a weapon popular with Pakistani volunteers, with Egyptians, and some others. The thin, cold sunlight as they stepped through the door was blinding after the lamp-lit gloom of Abdul's living room.

"You must be careful!" Abdul warned them as they started down the street. "Keep your scarves over your faces, and do not show too much interest in what you see. Speak to no one! If you should see a woman, look away. You do not want to attract the notice of either the Amaniyat or of the Amro bil Mahroof!"

"The Amaniyat I know," Mariacher told him. "What was that last, though? The police?"

"The religious police, yes."

"The Ministry for the Promotion of Virtue and the Prevention of Vice," Raptor told them. "In a lot of ways they're more dangerous than the KHAD ever was."

"I'll be good," Mariacher promised.

The four men walked deeper into the city, as the streets became narrower, the buildings larger. Abdul's house was on the western outskirts of the city, only a couple of miles from the hilltop where they'd met him. The police holding area, their guide explained, was on the eastern side of Khowst, which meant they had to travel through the center of town.

It was not a pleasant walk.

Mariacher was aware of the smell first, the unmistakable, sickly sweet stink of dead bodies left to rot in the sun. They saw them a few moments later . . . six men hanging by their necks from streetlight poles along the main street leading into the center of town. Their hands were bound behind their backs, their clothing, what was left of it, ragged and black with blood. Mariacher couldn't tell how long they'd been hanging there, and maybe what he was seeing was simply the effects of decay, but all of the bodies appeared heavily bruised and battered, and two were missing eyes, ears, and noses. That, he thought, *might* be the work of carrion birds, but more likely those men had been tortured before being hung.

He was glad of the scarf he was wearing, wrapped several times across his nose and mouth. It didn't cut all of the stench, but it at least helped him breathe.

At first there were no living inhabitants of Khowst to be seen. By the time they reached what Abdul assured them was the center of town, though, they'd begun seeing other people. Most were men, wearing either military-looking fatigues or *shalwar kameez*. He noticed one woman, though, muffled in a brown burka, sitting on a street corner with one slim hand showing, a toddler beside her. A man passed and, without looking at her, dropped several bills at her feet.

"Many women have lost their husbands," Haji explained quietly. "First to the Russians, then to the warlords, and now to the Taliban. Begging in the street is their only recourse."

"What's going on up there?" Raptor asked.

There was some sort of commotion in the street. A large number of men were gathered in front of what appeared to be a market storefront facing onto the broad, open space of the town's central square, shouting and waving both fists and weapons. There were more bodies hanging from lamp poles along the streets here, and several from the arm of a large, heavy crane parked to one side of the square. The mob's focus, however, was on something else.

"Wait here, my friend," Abdul said. "I will find out."

He merged into the fringes of the crowd ahead, then returned a few minutes later. "It is nothing," he told them.

"What kind of nothing?" Mariacher asked.

Before Abdul could reply, a woman in a black burka

shoved her way through the crowd, closely pursued by four
Afghan men, all armed with truncheons. One raised his club
and brought it down hard across the fleeing woman's back.
She dropped to her knees, then collapsed as the men closed
in, trying to cover her head with her arms.

"*Please,* Lieutenant," Haji said, seeing the look in Mariacher's eyes, a look mirrored in Raptor's eyes as well. He appeared terrified. "I know this is not your way, but listen to
me! *This is not your fight!*"

The crowd of shouting spectators had followed the four
men with clubs, and closed in once again around them and
their victim, twenty yards away and across the street. Mariacher could see the clubs rise and fall behind the heads of
the onlookers, could hear the sickening thud of the clubs
against the woman's body.

"What the fuck did she do?" Raptor demanded.

Abdul shrugged. "Who knows? Perhaps she walked too
loudly."

Mariacher gripped his borrowed H&K more tightly. The
idea that a person could be beaten for having squeaky shoes
was, on the face of it, absurd, but he also knew that Abdul
was not joking.

Haji put a warning hand on his shoulder. "My friend, let
us move away from here. It is not . . . safe to be here."

Meaning Haji was afraid he was about to do something
stupid. His SEAL training was better than that. However, the
temptation to say something, to *do* something to help that
poor woman, was almost overpowering.

Abruptly, he turned away and began walking back up the
street, away from the crowd. The others followed. At the
next intersection, Abdul again took the lead, guiding them
along side streets and alleys that would bypass the mob
scene at the city square.

Mariacher's training had included a fair amount of classroom study on other cultures and people, and the training had been backed by deployments all over the world— Thailand and Malaysia, the Philippines and the Sudan, South and Central America, Japan, and other far-flung countries as well. He possessed an innate and genuine respect for other cultures, other religions, other ways of life. Just because a custom was strange didn't mean it was wrong.

But this . . . this persecution of one-half of an entire nation's population wasn't just wrong. It was *evil*.

He thought about what Raptor had told him the night before, about fighting evil. Maybe it wasn't his job, his *fight*, to right the wrongs he was seeing in this miserable shithole of a country, but by God, America, and the U.S. Navy SEALs, he was going to be glad to see the Taliban kicked out and some kind of justice restored.

And if he got to do some of the kicking, so much the better.

Sunday, September 30, 2001

Khowst Satellite Police Facility
Paktia Province, Afghanistan
1340 hours, local time

Qari Ahmadullah was a patient and very thorough man. The prisoner, he thought, was quite strong. He still had a lot of screaming left in him.

Ahmadullah walked closer, bending over to bring his face close to the swollen, bloody mask that was what was left of the prisoner's face. "I'm sure you can remember, my friend," he said gently. "I'm sure you *want* to remember. You want to tell me."

The prisoner was hanging upside down in a tightly bound ball, his knees hooked over a horizontal pole, his wrists tied to his ankles, his ankles lashed to his thighs, his head lashed between his knees. He'd been stripped naked, and alligator clips had been clamped to his penis and scrotum. Wires dangling to the floor connected the alligator clips to a car battery and to the switch in the hands of one of the questioners.

Gently, with plastic-gloved hands, Ahmadullah prized a blood-soaked tennis ball from the prisoner's mouth. "Where were you to meet these American spies?"

"They . . . were . . . to contact . . . me," the prisoner rasped, his voice a cracked whisper. Fresh blood streamed from his nose and mouth and dripped to the cement floor below. "Please . . . please . . ."

Ahmadullah replaced the ball, then took a step back. He nodded to the man with the switch. There was the soft snick of the switch being thrown, and shrieks echoed through the warehouse.

A long time later, Ahmadullah again removed the tennis ball, which kept the prisoner from biting through his own tongue, either by accident, while he was spasming, or deliberately. "Let us begin again. Your name is? . . ."

"Hafez . . . Tayed."

"Your code name was? . . ."

"Ali Hassan."

"Your mission was? . . ."

"To . . . to help organize fighters against . . . against the Taliban."

"And how were you going to do this?"

"American . . . spies. They were to contact me. Give me money. Give me weapons and radios. Help me . . . help me recruit others."

"What others? Who did you talk to?"

"My . . . my brother-in-law, Abdul Afridi. His cousin, Haji Afridi. My brother, Rostam . . ." The list went on for several minutes.

"Very good, my friend. And where were you supposed to meet these American spies?"

"I . . . don't know. Please, I don't know!" The man's voice rose to a shriek. "I swear I don't know!"

Ahmadullah replaced the bloody tennis ball and stepped back.

A long moment later he removed it once more. Tayed was having trouble breathing. His nose had been broken during a savage beating the day before, and his head was congested with blood from hanging head down for so long. With the tennis ball in his mouth, it was almost impossible for him to draw a breath.

"I wonder, Hafez," Ahmadullah said to him, "if we don't need to change our approach again. What do you think?"

The man gave a low, burbling moan. Ahmadullah wasn't even sure he was still conscious. They'd taken him pretty far this time.

"We could let you sit up in the chair for a while, let you breathe. Would you like that?"

Again there was only a moan for an answer.

"Of course, if we did that, we would bring out your wives and daughter again. All three of them at once this time. You could watch as my friends here amused themselves for a few pleasant hours. What do you say to that?"

He reached over and pried one of Tayed's eyelids back. Yes. He was unconscious.

Ahmadullah sighed. "Take him down."

The man Ahmadullah knew both as Colonel Khan and as Iskanderov stepped out of the shadows. "You press him too hard."

"You are a *military* expert, I believe," Ahmadullah said,

the words close to a sneer. "You should stick with your own area of expertise and allow me to tend to mine."

"You idiot!" Khan snapped. "This man is a valuable prize. Every time your people throw that switch, you risk killing him, or turning him into a mindless slab of meat! You could lose everything he knows with your thug tactics!"

Ahmadullah sighed. "Just why are you here, Colonel?"

"As I told you the other day . . . to oversee your questioning of this prisoner. He may have information of a *military* nature which we need to have."

"You will have your information if you let the experts do their job!"

"Experts? You forget I was GRU. I taught your people how to interrogate prisoners! And I taught them better than *this*!"

"You Russian pigs never had the heart to do what was necessary! That is why you did not win with your invasion . . . why you returned to the north with your tails between your legs!"

Iskanderov appeared to be trying to control his temper. Ahmadullah saw his gloved hands flex as though he wanted to strike something.

"My word," Iskanderov said after a moment, "carries a great deal of weight with your government. I recommend that you take care not to destroy this man. It seems clear that he has told you what he knows . . . and that he *doesn't* know where the American commandos are."

"If he has told me everything," Ahmadullah replied, "then we have no further need for him. If he dies, we lose nothing. I intend to be *certain* he has told us all."

Iskanderov glared at him for a moment, then turned on his heel and stalked away.

Good riddance, Ahmadullah thought. If he wants to run to Mohammed, let him. I rule here!

His assistants had untied Hafez and laid him stretched out on the concrete. Ahmadullah knelt next to him. The prisoner groaned, twitched, and appeared to be on the point of coming around. "Put him in the chair," Ahmadullah said. "And go get his women. We need to show him just how much honor he has lost."

The prisoner was close to breaking. From long experience, Ahmadullah was certain of the fact.

Chapter 15

Khowst
Paktia Province, Afghanistan
1530 hours, local time

On the east side of the city there were rows of drab, concrete buildings that must have been built by the Russians—factories, assembly plants, warehouses, and other anonymous industrial structures. The area appeared deserted, however, as though all of the businesses had closed. Perhaps they had. Most of the city's population appeared to be in the city square at the moment, holding a religious rally.

According to Abdul, the government had been calling for days for more volunteers to take up arms against the American crusade. A lot of Afghan civilians had been fleeing the country too . . . as many as four thousand a day according to some reports. Many businesses must have closed simply because all of the employees were gone, especially in regions close to the border.

Besides, there was a widespread belief that when the Americans came, it would be with a rain of bombs that would level the factories across the nation. Better, it was argued, to meet a holy martyr's death in battle, a weapon in your hand and the name of Allah on your lips. But that meant that the day-to-day work of the cities had come to a halt. Reportedly, the religious police forced all businesses to shut down during each of the five times for prayer throughout the day, but the deserted air to this part of town felt like something more: something deeper and longer-lasting.

At least there were no more bodies hanging from light poles or crane gantries, or women pursued by club-swinging thugs.

A brick factory next door to the warehouse gave Mariacher and Halstead a good vantage point from which to observe the facility and make their plans. The warehouse itself was a long, low, flat-roofed cinder-block structure, with garage doors and loading docks for trucks. A guard stood on the roof, pacing slowly. The building sat in the middle of a large yard surrounded by a ten-foot-high chain-link fence and cluttered with empty wooden crates, fifty-five-gallon drums, and piles of rubble. Several ancient cargo trucks—old Russian Zils, they looked like—rusted away near one end of the building.

Most significant, though, was an old Russian helicopter parked in a vacant field on the far side of the warehouse. The aircraft was a Mil Mi-8, a variant known to the West as the Hip-C. About forty of those aircraft had been given to the old communist regime in Kabul, and many Soviet Hips had been captured at the end of the war. Western intelligence believed that the Taliban didn't have the resources to keep many of the old machines flying; clearly, though, a few were still in service. Through binoculars, Mariacher could see two uniformed guards sitting in the shadow of its fuselage.

Much closer at hand, just on the other side of the chain-link fence and not far from the front gate, were several large, rectangular transport containers, sheet-metal boxes of the sort that were carried onboard cargo ships, then offloaded directly onto diesel truck flatbeds. One was offset from the others, green paint fading. A single militia guard stood in front of it, smoking a cigarette and looking bored.

What was stored in a transport container that required a guard? Mariacher wondered.

A careful survey over the course of two hours showed that there were three outside sentries at the facility, not counting the two by the helicopter—one on the roof, one by the transport container, and a third standing by the front gate. All three appeared to be Afghan militia, ragged and unkempt, without even a pretense at a complete uniform. The men guarding the Hip were probably regular army, but were too far away for Mariacher to make out details. None appeared particularly alert. The two guards near the front of the yard spent a lot of time in conversation. The guard on the roof spent a lot of time smoking, and much more time sitting on a crate with his head nodding—dozing, perhaps, after a late night hate-America rally. When the wavering, eerie call to Salatu-l-Asr came from the minarets of Khowst at around 1530 hours, two of the three guards broke out prayer rugs, faced east, and went through the gestures and movements of formal Islamic prayer. The guy up on the roof did not, though whether that was from a lack of religious devotion or simply because he was asleep, Mariacher couldn't tell.

There would be no problem whatsoever penetrating the facility. The question now was whether to go in soft . . . or hard.

Going in soft—sneaking in without being seen and without killing anyone—was preferable for gathering intel. If they went in hard, they would make noise, break things, and kill people, and the bad guys would definitely know that Task Force 5 was in the area.

Mariacher wondered if there was a way to take the place down and pin the blame on someone else. Rebels? Dissidents? The trouble was, there *were* rebels—Abdul Afridi and the others his brother-in-law had talked to. Blame them, and the Taliban police and military would come down on them like the wrath of Allah.

Of course, if and when Hafez Tayed broke under torture, he would spill everything he knew about a local resistance movement anyway, if he hadn't done so already.

Mariacher and Raptor were on top of the brick factory's roof, lying on their stomachs behind the low wall that surrounded it. Age, erosion, and lack of maintenance had resulted in some of the bricks in the wall falling out, and they were able to watch the warehouse grounds unobserved through the hole. Haji and Abdul were on the ground, somewhere inside the deserted brick factory, well out of sight.

"I'm thinking a soft recon," Mariacher said, his voice low. "If we go in hot, the Taliban might level the whole damned city."

"Well, if they don't, we will," Raptor replied.

"You're cold, Raptor."

"I'm a realist. Abdul and Haji both want to go in and wipe the place out. They say they can raise a hundred men by tonight. They're ready to get this revolution rolling."

"The Tals will walk all over them."

"Maybe. According to Abdul, though, there are a lot of men in the local militia who are sick of the Taliban. He says they'd defect if they were given the chance."

Mariacher thought about this. According to the latest they'd heard over the satcom unit, it would be at least a week before the United States was ready to launch its attack against Afghanistan . . . and longer than that before ground troops would actually enter the country.

The report had also mentioned heavy fighting in northern Afghanistan. The Northern Alliance, the coalition of anti-Taliban Afghan forces that still held about ten percent of the country along its northern border, had engaged the Taliban, and by all accounts were winning.

"The big question," Raptor said, "is who does that helo belong to?"

"What are you thinking? Bin Laden is paying a visit?"

He was being facetious, but Raptor apparently took him seriously. "I doubt that. We don't have any reports that OBL is in the area. But the Afghans don't have many helicopters. It has to be someone important—maybe a high-value target."

"Well, we know two TAQ HVTs were in Khowst within the past couple of days, Mohammed and Ahmadullah."

"There's also this mysterious foreigner Abdul told us about, Colonel Khan."

"If it's Mohammed, I *want* that bastard," Mariacher said.

"Sounds personal."

"It is. He got away from my team once. Not again."

"Uh-oh. Hold it. Who's that?"

A door in the front of the warehouse had opened, and several men walked out. Mariacher focused his binoculars on them.

"Militia . . . but pretty well-dressed," he said. "And who's that?"

The militia appeared to be a bodyguard for a man wearing fatigues but carrying only a holstered sidearm. His hair was light brown, almost blond. "That guy doesn't look Afghan," Mariacher said.

"Colonel Khan?"

"I'd be willing to bet on it. He doesn't look too happy."

They watched as Khan and his entourage left the warehouse compound through a side gate in the fence and walked across the empty lot to the waiting helicopter. The two guards jumped to attention and waited as Khan and his bodyguards boarded the aircraft, then followed him aboard. Moments later the helicopter's powerful twin Isotov TV2 turboshafts began spooling up and the big, five-bladed rotor started turning.

"Let's get under cover," Raptor said. The two men backed away from the wall, still on their stomachs, and took shelter among a pile of empty crates, pallets, and sheets of wet cardboard on the brick factory roof. In another minute the sound of the rotors increased in pitch, and the Hip rose from the field, became momentarily visible above the wall, then banked out of sight, flying rapidly toward the north.

"Toward Zur Kowt," Raptor said.

"Or Kabul."

"If that is Colonel Khan's personal transport, they must have a helipad at Zur Kowt. That's supposed to be his headquarters, right?"

"We'll have to check that out. Right now, what are we going to do about this place?"

"Outside guards are down from five to three. I say we bring in the rest of your team and take the place down. Hard."

"And let the resistance take the fall?"

"We'll see what Abdul has to say. My guess is we could cause so much confusion, they won't know who hit them. Abdul might be able to take his people and hide out in the mountains until our guys get here."

"It's worth a shot. Let's do it."

They crawled back out of their hiding place to a trapdoor and a ladder leading to the main floor of the brick factory. There, among ranks of cold and silent kilns, they found Haji and Abdul waiting for them patiently.

"You have checked out the target, yes?" Abdul asked, his eyes alight. "When do we strike?"

Mariacher sat down next to the man. Disconcertingly, Abdul took his hand and held it, like a lover. The SEAL did not pull back. Other people, other ways, he thought.

"Abdul . . . you know that if we attack, the Taliban is going to think that your resistance is behind it. Even if they know we're here, that we attacked their police station, they must assume that you helped us. *Especially* if we're able to rescue Hafez. They'll assume the resistance is trying to break their leader out of jail."

"Major Qadi will have told the Taliban about us already," Haji said. He spat into the dust on the floor angrily. "Qadi would have told them you were here to meet with a guerrilla leader in Khowst. I believe they arrested Hafez when Qadi told them about him."

"How did they know his real name?" Mariacher asked. "Qadi knew him as 'Ali Hassan.' "

"Basic intelligence work," Raptor said. "They know there's a rebel leader in Khowst meeting with American agents, and they know Hafez has been talking about organizing a rebellion. They put two and two together. These people might be religious fanatics, but they are *not* stupid."

"Abdul, I just want to make sure you know what we're starting here," Mariacher said. "There's just the five of us here right now. There will be no American ground troops to help you for weeks yet, maybe for months. If we attack this police station, you're going to have to head up into the mountains and carry out your rebellion from there."

"My friend, you underestimate how much my people hate the Taliban! We will do what is necessary. We will fight from the mountains if we have to, just as the mujahideen fought against the Russians. But we *will* fight!"

"Then pass the word to your men, Abdul," Mariacher said. "Just the ones with weapons. We're going to need a little diversion . . . tonight."

"A diversion? For what?"

"We're going to hit the warehouse, and we're going to bring your people out."

Abdul launched himself at Mariacher, grabbing him around the neck and hugging him close. "Allah be praised!"

Sunday, September 30, 2001

**Khowst Satellite Police Facility
Paktia Province, Afghanistan
1720 hours, local time**

"Sir! We have finished!"

Qari Ahmadullah looked up from his paperwork. "The women?"

"Are back in their cell, sir." The guard gave a gap-toothed leer. "It is . . . *safe* for you to return!"

Vile creature. He began gathering up the papers—reports of refugees streaming across the borders into Pakistan and Iran—and putting them in a folder. "Did the prisoner offer to talk?"

"No. He screamed and called us names, a lot. He still has a lot of fight, that one."

"Return him to the bar. I will be there momentarily."

"Yes, sir!"

Ahmadullah placed the folder neatly in a filing cabinet. He had two final reports on his desk to read. He picked up the first and began skimming through it.

The report was two days old, dated September 28. The American president, Bush, had declared in a televised interview that the United States was in "hot pursuit" of terrorists. A related news item included a quote from an unnamed source in Bush's administration to the effect that the United States had already conducted scouting missions in Afghanistan. And, finally, the United Nations had, on September 28, approved a U.S.-sponsored resolution demanding that all member nations take sweeping and meaningful action against terrorism.

Those three pieces of news strongly suggested that Bush was moving on from mere intimidation and saber-rattling to something more serious; that the Americans would, indeed, be attacking very soon. The first two items were justification to the world that America was serious about entering Afghanistan's borders to find bin Laden. The third was an attempt to prove to the world that such an invasion would be more than an outraged United States lashing out in vengeance; that their invasion of another country was in fact some sort of moral crusade.

Crusade. Ahmadullah smiled at that. The American president had used that exact word in several of his addresses lately, and the Arab world had seized on it immediately. Al-Qaeda had gotten a lot of favorable coverage from Arab television and radio—especially the widely broadcast al-Jazeera news network—and the word "crusade" had figured prominently in that coverage lately. To Arabs, to all Muslims, the word carried the hateful image of invading Western armies, of the wholesale pollution by infidels of the holy places of Islam. The ranks both of al-Qaeda and of the jihadist forces flocking to join Afghanistan in her hour of need had swollen mightily.

Yes. America and Bush would launch their crusade. And they would be stopped as completely as the mighty Saladin had stopped the original Crusaders of Europe eight hundred years ago.

The second report was dated yesterday, the twenty-ninth, and this one contained good news indeed. Bush had announced in a national radio address that America's counterattack would "aggressively and methodically" disrupt and destroy terrorism. More saber-rattling, that. However, there were also truly encouraging reports of thousands of people rallying in Washington, D.C., in San Francisco, in Barcelona, Spain, all protesting armed retaliation against either Afghanistan or al-Qaeda. Hundreds more had gathered in peace demonstrations in Austin, Texas, and in Athens,

Greece. Furthermore, the United Nations had announced that it was resuming food shipments to prevent starvation in Afghanistan . . . an obvious rebuke of America's attempt at isolating the Taliban by blockading all shipments to Afghanistan and deliberately starving her population.

Allah, the merciful, the munificent, all praise be to you!

The Americans would come, yes, but they would find their support eroded at home, just as they'd found it eroded thirty years ago during the war in Vietnam. The so-called coalition they were attempting to create would collapse, and the American attempt would be seen for what it was—the use by Jews and Christians of naked force against the Muslim world.

With the help of Allah, the invaders would be crushed, and their bodies would rot upon these snow-clad mountains. So many invaders had failed to overcome the people of these mountains in the past; from the Russian invaders twelve years ago all the way back to the time of Alexander and the Greeks. Let them come with their bombs and their tanks! They would flee like whipped dogs.

Ahmadullah took another look at the first report. This confirmed what his agents, both here and in Pakistan, had already told him—that American Special Forces were already here. The prisoner in the next room had already admitted that the CIA had military forces here in Khowst, or very close by.

If some of those soldiers could be killed—or, better still, captured—they could be paraded before the Arab world as proof both of American evil and of Allah's mercy. Perhaps the sight of an American commando having his throat slit on al-Jazeera TV would so sicken the American public—they had no stomach for the reality of war—that the peace demonstrations would grow and spread, and Bush the crusader would be forced to back down in public humiliation and shame.

The Taliban needed a victory now, and badly. For the past three full days the so-called Northern Alliance had been fighting Taliban forces in the north, and despite the news being released from Kabul, the fighting was not going well. The Taliban was losing territory. The public exhibition of captured American invaders would dishearten the northern tribes and rally still more of the devout to the banner of jihad.

The problem, of course, was finding these Americans. They were probably in the mountains on the border with Pakistan—the al-Qaeda troops at al-Badr had clashed with them several nights ago. However, they could be here in Khowst.

The thought sent a prickle of anticipation up Ahmadullah's spine. If they were here, they could be led into a trap. He had plenty of forces at his disposal, and that Tajik colonel, much as Ahmadullah disliked him, could be here in minutes with air support if necessary.

He needed to give the idea some thought . . . a means of drawing the Americans in and snapping them up.

First, though, he needed to further question Tayed, the rebel prisoner, to see what other information could be wrung from him. Forcing him to watch—yet again—the abuse of his wives and daughters might have softened him further.

He made a sour face. The guard's insinuation that it wasn't safe for him to watch that part of the interrogation still rankled. Not all of the warriors within the Taliban's militias or in al-Qaeda were as pure in heart, mind, and body as he or others within the Taliban's leadership. There were many among even the faithful who would commit rape and other unclean acts and claim them proudly as marks of their devotion. Most of the leading mullahs agreed that this was unfortunate, but accepted the fact as part of each individual's personal, inner jihad, his struggle to find his place with God.

Perhaps he should arrange for the police officers engaged in interrogation to be rotated more frequently to postings

elsewhere. Some, he feared, like the man who'd just been in
his office, had grown to enjoy the questioning too much.

For himself, Ahmadullah wasn't afraid of contamination,
but he did know that the sight of a naked woman—worse, to
actually touch her, to *lie* with her—would render him unclean. At the same time, he acknowledged that such acts
were at times necessary in the pursuit of a larger truth, a
greater justice. Torture, even of infidels, was never pleasant,
save to the truly sick of mind and soul; but it was necessary,
a sacrifice to the greater glory of Allah.

Enough. He needed to complete the breaking of Hafez
Tayed.

The man was close to breaking. He could feel it.

And that made him feel surprisingly good—able to take
satisfaction in a job well done.

To Allah's eternal glory and praise.

Sunday, September 30, 2001

Khowst
Paktia Province, Afghanistan
2145 hours, local time

The sun had set long ago, and the city of Khowst was
cloaked in a darkness unrelieved by city lights. Electricity
was still available from the central power station, but apparently someone had decided to black out the entire city, probably in anticipation of American air attacks.

A few buildings had their own generators, though, and
cracks and threads of light showed around blacked-out windows or under doors as the SEALs moved into position.
From his hiding place, Mariacher could hear the purr of the
diesel generator outside the warehouse that was their target.

Good. The enforced blackout was actually going to help.

He crouched in the darkness across the dirt road from the main gate of the warehouse, watching the two guards there through his night-vision goggles. Several empty fifty-five-gallon drums and disintegrating wooden crates had been dumped there, providing cover.

Osterlee was with him. Lehman—the best sniper of the team—was on the brick factory's roof next door, with Chief Bradley. Their job would be to take out the guard on the warehouse roof, then provide overwatch on the police compound. Raptor was elsewhere, with Abdul, Haji, and Khowst's anti-Taliban resistance.

"Blue One, Gold One," Bradley's voice said over Mariacher's M-biter headset. "We're in position. One tango on the roof. Clear shot."

"Copy that, Gold One," Mariacher replied. "Stand by." He glanced at Osterlee. "Ready, Charlie?"

"Ready, sir. But . . . you do all the talking, okay? My Arabic's not very good."

"Those guys look like native Afghans," Mariacher observed. "I doubt that their Arabic's very good either. But I'll carry the conversation."

"Thanks, Wheel."

They moved back from their hiding place and prepared for their approach, removing their night-vision goggles and wrapping their scarves about their lower faces. Their clothing consisted of nondescript items, some military, some local civilian—the grunge look tailored for Afghanistan. Both of them had their H&Ks slung over their backs, muzzles down, which would let them look nonthreatening when they approached. In their hands they carried green-painted boxes, provided by Abdul—the kind used to transport RPGs. Empty, the boxes were quite light. They held them cradled in their arms, however, which made them look heavy . . . and let them hold their Mark 11 pistols, with attached sound suppressors, cradled carefully out of sight between the boxes and their chests.

Before emerging, though, Mariacher opened the tactical channel on his M-biter. "Gold One! Blue One!"

"Blue One. We copy."

"Watch for your cue. We're coming out."

"Copy that."

Side by side they emerged from cover and crossed the dirt street, approaching the gate in the high chain-link fence and the two guards behind it—one directly behind the gate, the other perhaps twenty feet away, in front of the truck transport containers.

As they walked closer, the nearest guard flicked his cigarette away and motioned at them, a clear "stay back."

"We have these boxes for Khalid Shaikh Mohammed!" Mariacher called out in Arabic. He knew his accent was atrocious, but he doubted that these two would be able to tell the difference—if, indeed, they spoke Arabic at all. "Is Khalid Shaikh Mohammed here, please?"

The guard barked something in Pashto, probably a command to halt. The two SEALs continued to approach.

"Please, sir. Is Khalid Shaikh Mohammed here?"

"No here!" the guard barked in Arabic even more atrocious than Mariacher's. "Go! Now!" He began to unsling his AK.

"We were told to deliver these here!"

Had they been approaching an American military checkpoint, they would have been ordered to place the boxes on the ground and back away. These two didn't appear well versed in standard military procedure, however. The nearest guard unhooked the gate and swung it open, advancing into the street with an angry expression. The second man, guarding the truck container, snapped something in Pashto and walked forward.

"Do it," Mariacher said over the open tactical channel. With his left arm, he flung the empty RPG box, aiming for the guard's face. With his right, he brought up his Mark 11, triggering two quick, silenced rounds into the man's chest, a third into his throat. Osterlee dropped his concealing ammo box at the same instant, snapping up his Mark 11 and firing past the first guard's shoulder, hammering four rounds into the second man's chest before shifting his aim a bit higher and putting a round through his skull. The sudden twin volley of gunshots sounded like sharp, hissing chirps, no louder than the closing of a door.

Both guards were dead before they or the flying RPG cases hit the ground. Mariacher stepped forward, grabbed his man by the collar, and dragged him into the compound. Osterlee followed, holstering his pistol and pulling his MP5 into firing position.

"Blue One, Gold One," Bradley's voice reported. "Tango on the roof is down. The yard is clear."

"Copy. Cover us. We're going in."

They dragged the two bodies out of sight behind some rubble. Mariacher removed his NVGs from a pouch and slipped them over his face, and the dark-shadowed compound brightened into splashes of harsh-hued green.

The two SEALs started toward the warehouse.

Chapter 16

Mariacher hurried past the looming shadows of the truck containers, reaching the concrete side of the warehouse loading docks. Close by, the electrical generator rumbled as it continued to feed power to the building.

"Put 'em in the dark," he told Osterlee.

The other SEAL moved to the generator, and a moment later the sound clattered and died. The closest door to the generator was the one in front, just around the corner. With Osterlee watching his back, Mariacher crouched at the corner, watching the entrance, his MP5-SD aimed, a round chambered. A minute passed, then another, and finally the door opened and a man with a flashlight stepped out into the yard.

As soon as he was clear of the door, Mariacher squeezed off two rounds—the clicking chirps, if anything, quieter than the shots from his SEAL Mark 11. The beam from the flashlight danced wildly across the yard as the man stumbled and collapsed. Mariacher dragged the body back around the corner, then signaled the others. "Blue One. One tango down at the door. Entering the building."

Opening the front door, he stepped inside, H&K held shoulder high, the blunt length of the sound suppressor probing the darkness. By the green illumination provided by his NVGs, Mariacher could see that he was in a passageway with cinder-block walls and a cement floor. There were posters on the wall, but not enough ambient light coming through his night-vision goggles for him to make out what was on them.

Osterlee came through the door at his back. Together, moving in step, the two SEALs moved deeper into the building. They could hear cries now, of men calling to one another in the dark. He tried the knob of a door to the left—locked. He tried another to the right and it swung open.

Inside were two uniformed men, two desks, and several chairs and filing cabinets. The men each sat at the desks with the patient air of soldiers waiting for their superiors to sort things out so they could return to their work. Though they turned at the sound of the opening office door, they literally never saw what hit them. Mariacher put two rounds apiece into their brains at close range, then stepped back into the hall, gently closing the door behind him.

The next office along the passageway had one man who was in the process of striking a match over a candle. Mariacher took him down before he had a chance to cry out or reach for his sidearm.

A heavy door with a push-bar opened onto a large and mostly empty floor, the building's main storage area. A few stacks of crates and storage drums were piled up here and there, but the floor appeared deserted. A catwalk ran around the large room at the second-story level. Two guards on the catwalk died as Mariacher took aim and tapped them down with his H&K. Osterlee killed a third with his Mark 11.

The SEALs moved across the open room now, using crates for cover. At this point they were the only two people in the entire building who could see, but combat training died hard. If the lights came back on unexpectedly, it wouldn't do to be caught standing in the open.

Besides, Mariacher remembered the Russian NVGs worn by the al-Qaeda soldiers in the mountains. These guys were apparently police or militia—the distinction, actually, was fuzzy and depended on how you looked at it—and wouldn't be as well-equipped as the foreign volunteers of al-Qaeda.

A turbaned man with a long beard stepped out of a room in the back of the warehouse fifteen feet away, holding a flashlight. He didn't appear to be armed, but the light made him a threat. Mariacher shot him twice in the chest.

They'd been lucky so far, taking down eight of the warehouse's occupants without being heard. An instant later, however, the luck ran dry. Someone was up on the catwalk screaming something at the top of his lungs. Evidently, he'd come out of an office up on the second floor and stumbled over the body of one of the two sentries up there.

In seconds men began spilling out of various offices, shouting and calling to one another. Several flashlights appeared, the beams stabbing down from the upper floor, sweeping erratically back and forth.

"Blue and Gold, Blue One. They've made us! All weapons free!" He shot the screaming man, then pressed his weapon's mag release, dropping the almost empty magazine. He extracted a fully loaded magazine from a pouch and snapped it into place.

"Can't let the damned officers have all the fun," Osterlee said at his back. He'd been using his silenced Mark 11 pistol, not the more accurate MP5-A2, because his submachine gun did not have the integral sound suppressor of Mariacher's MP5-SD. Holstering the pistol, he brought his H&K

around to the front and raised it shoulder-high. Someone upstairs opened fire with an AK-47 on full-auto, spraying the
warehouse floor blindly. Firing quick, short, precisely controlled bursts, Osterlee killed the gunman and two of his
friends.

One group of Taliban coming from the north side of the
warehouse suddenly opened fire on more Taliban troops on
the south side. In seconds a savage firefight had erupted,
with screaming militiamen firing wildly into one another in
the darkness.

"We need some altitude," Mariacher told his partner as
stray rounds snapped above them and buried themselves in
wooden packing crates. "Let's get topside!"

A metal-rung stairway in the back led up to the second-
floor catwalk. The two SEALs raced up the steps one at a
time, each covering the other. The enemy resistance was en-
thusiastic but utterly blind. Those few Taliban militiamen
who'd managed to lay their hands on flashlights were the
first targets, and the survivors did not appear eager to pick
up the lights dropped by their dead comrades.

The firefight on the main floor died out as quickly as it had
begun. Survivors were now either clustering behind crates
near the big garage doors along the west wall or holing up inside their offices. Those would be the toughest ones to handle,
forcing the assault force to take them down one room at a time.

"Blue Team, this is Gold One."

"Gold One, Blue One. Go!"

"Good news and bad news, Wheel. Force Raptor is entering the compound."

"That's the good news. What's the rest?"

"We have Taliban air moving in. A single chopper. Appears to be circling."

"Is it a gunship?"

"Can't tell, sir," Bradley said. "It's a Hip . . . maybe the same one you said you saw earlier. Can't tell if it's armed, though."

"Pass the word to Raptor to get his ass inside here."

"Roger that!"

The helicopter was bad news. The numerous Hip variants made that particular aircraft the equivalent of the ubiquitous Huey slicks in Vietnam. Some were fitted out as cargo transports, as troop carriers, for medevac, as command aircraft, or for reconnaissance roles. Some had machine guns in the doors. Some were heavily armed gunships. The Hip-C could mount four UV-16-57 rocket pods on fuselage outriggers with a total warload of 128 rockets. The Hip-E carried 192 rockets in six pods, plus four Swatter or Sagger antitank missiles.

The aircraft he'd seen earlier had been a Hip-C, but at that range he hadn't been able to tell if it had mounted rocket pods or not. It might have been a stripped-down version, used for ferrying VIPs about in the rugged mountains of southeastern Afghanistan.

"Blue Team, this is Raptor," sounded over Mariacher's M-biter. "Check your fire and take cover! We're coming in! West side doors, south end of the building!"

"Roger that. Come ahead. We're clear. Watch for tangos by the garage doors."

"Copy. Fire in the hole!"

The two southernmost of the broad, sliding garage doors in the line down the west wall of the warehouse exploded inward as C-4 charges blasted them off their rails. Taliban police were hurled from behind their shelter or scrambled for cover. Half a dozen Afghan troops with flashlights rushed in through the openings, shooting down the survivors.

"Raptor, Blue One! Secure the main floor, but don't let them come in further!" None of Raptor's men would have NVGs, save for Raptor himself. If the anti-Taliban rebels started mixing it up throughout the building with pro-Taliban militia, the battle would swiftly become a free-for-all, the blind killing the blind.

"Got it, Blue One."

Mariacher was crouching on the catwalk fifteen feet above the main floor, giving him a superb view of the battle. He could see Raptor, easily identified by his NVGs, shouting orders to his darkness-hampered troops, bullying them into a perimeter from which they could control the entire main warehouse floor.

Thirty feet farther down the catwalk a door opened and a man stepped out.

For a slow-motion second Mariacher stared at the man and saw him staring back. He too was wearing night-vision goggles—a Soviet-made unit like the ones fielded by the al-Qaeda troops in the mountains—which gave him the look of a machine with glittering, hard, tube-mounted lenses above his full beard. The full import hadn't yet registered on Mariacher as he dragged his MP5-SD6 around to take aim. The man was holding a pistol, but rather than opening fire, he turned and began running the other way down the catwalk.

Just before Mariacher could acquire the running man in his sights, another door along the catwalk burst open and two Taliban officers with AK-47s rushed onto the catwalk, blocking Mariacher's shot.

He opened fire, but his selector switch was still set to single shot. Squeezing rapidly, he got off six or eight shots within a couple of seconds, the rounds snapping into both of the Taliban men . . . but his view of the guy with NVGs was momentarily blocked.

"Raptor, Blue One!" he yelled. "HVT on the catwalk, in the south!"

One of the Taliban officers slammed against the catwalk railing, doubled over it, then tumbled into empty air, falling to the cement floor below. The other crumpled to the steel grating of the catwalk, but slowly . . . slowly . . . and beyond, Mariacher saw a door on the south wall swinging shut. *Damn*!

"Blue One to Team!" he called. "Possible High Value Target. He's at the south end of the building, probably in a stairwell. He's wearing NVGs. Gold One! If anyone exits that side of the building, nail him!"

"Copy, Blue One. No sign of him yet. I see friendlies in the area, though."

"Roger that." Raptor would have deployed some of the anti-Taliban troops to set up a perimeter around the warehouse.

A savage explosion sounded from the warehouse floor near the anti-Taliban troops by the doors, and screams shrilled as light flared in Mariacher's NVGs. It took a moment to sort things out. In the northeast corner of the main floor, one Taliban soldier stood with an empty RPG launcher still on his shoulder, staring at a friend who was rolling on the cement in apparent agony. By the garage doors, a stack of splintered wooden crates were on fire. The flames had just transformed the battle, casting a bright, flickering light throughout the main warehouse area.

Raptor, crouched behind a fifty-five-gallon drum, shot the man with the launcher, then shouted more orders to his men, who were wavering now. It was clear enough what had happened. A Taliban soldier had just fired an RPG at the attackers, forgetting that the weapon had a two-meter backblast, which had just permanently blinded a careless buddy. The round had hit a stack of packing crates and set them ablaze. From his overhead vantage point, Mariacher saw two of Raptor's men down, and several who appeared to be wounded.

With light, however, Raptor's covering force could see what they were doing, and began moving deeper into the warehouse. Mariacher could hear shouts and gunfire echoing off the cinder-block walls below.

Within a few more seconds the fighting dwindled away. The only Taliban forces left were hiding inside closed offices and rooms.

"Blue One, Gold One!"

"This is Blue One. Go."

"The helicopter has touched down in the field next door."

That suggested that the aircraft was a transport, not a gunship. He thought about the HVT he'd just seen. Maybe the guy had radioed for an emergency evac.

"Can you hit it from your position?"

"Hit it, yes. Effectively, no. Range is about five hundred yards."

"He may be trying to pick up the HVT. You see anyone who could be him?"

"Negative, Wheel. Lots of friendlies. No one with NVGs."

Bradley and Lehman both were armed with SMGs. Typically, in close-quarters battle, a submachine gun firing 9mm Parabellum rounds had an effective range of fifty yards or less—some authorities dropped that figure to thirty yards. Like Mariacher, Lehman was packing an accurized MP5-SD6. The idea had been to be able to take out the guard on the warehouse roof silently from the brick factory's rooftop OP a hundred yards away. With the weapon braced and an expert marksman behind the sights, that effective range figure could be doubled or better . . . but the Parabellum cartridge was simply too low-powered to carry any accuracy at longer ranges.

Bradley was carrying an AKM, which had substantially harder punch at longer ranges, but it was not accurized. Too, even with night-vision devices, they would be hampered by the darkness at that range, and hitting anything important on the helicopter, like a fuel line or the pilot, at a range of half a kilometer would be entirely a matter of chance.

"Blue One, Gold One. Gold Two has the AK. He might be able to do something with it."

"Copy, Gold One. Just don't get the bad guys mad at you." If that Hip was a gunship, taking fire was a good way to bring down heavy-caliber retaliation.

He heard Bradley laugh. "Copy that, Wheel. Wouldn't want to make the bad guys angry at us now!"

They were beginning to take down individual rooms inside the warehouse. Osterlee and Mariacher stood against the wall to either side of a locked door leading off the catwalk. Mariacher pulled out an XM84—better known as a flash-bang—a slim tube with the charge visible through perforations in the canister. Nonfragmenting and nonlethal, it was designed for tactical situations such as this one.

Mariacher pulled the pin, holding the firing lever closed, and nodded to Osterlee, who stepped briefly in front of the door, raised his foot and kicked, hard.

A shotgun would have been a better choice for the maneuver, if they'd had one, but the thin door snapped back on dislodged hinges. Osterlee ducked back to the side, his back against the wall, as gunshots exploded from inside, followed by a torrent of angry Pashto. Mariacher released the firing handle and tossed the flash-bang inside. A moment later seven ear-splitting detonations went off within a second or so, accompanied by blinding, strobing flashes guaranteed to momentarily blind and disorient anyone looking at them.

Osterlee rolled through the open doorway, H&K at his shoulder, moving to the right inside the room, and Mariacher followed, moving left. A single, bearded, screaming man in fatigues was on his hands and knees inside, his AK on the floor and one hand over his eyes. Osterlee brought the butt of his H&K down on the back of the man's head. They needed a few prisoners out of this operation, at the very least, if they were going to get any intel at all. With the tango unconscious, Osterlee strapped his wrists together at his back with a plastic zip-strip, then picked up the AK. The prisoner would be safe for the time being. Together, the two SEALs exited the room back onto the catwalk and moved to the next door in line.

They entered four more rooms on the second floor and captured two more Taliban prisoners. On the lower floor, Raptor's anti-Taliban locals began opening other rooms. Sometimes they even took the occupants alive.

"Blue One, this is Raptor."

"Blue One, go."

"You'd better get down here. Something you should see."

Raptor sounded . . . detached, almost flat, as though keeping a tight rein on his emotions. Leaving Osterlee to maintain an overwatch from the catwalk, Mariacher trotted down the steps and followed Raptor's directions to one of the back rooms on the ground floor.

One of Raptor's men held open the heavy push-bar door. Several more guerrillas were inside. The room was perhaps fifteen feet by twelve, with a cement floor and a drain in the center. Along one wall were various pieces of equipment, including car batteries wired together in series, cables, wires, and alligator clips. There was a table with knives, saws, pliers, and other tools, and everywhere, everywhere, there was blood, lots of it. The air was almost unbreathably thick with the coppery smell of blood, mingled with the sour stinks of urine and vomit. Mariacher pulled his scarf into place over his nose and mouth and stifled the unpleasant twist in his throat and stomach.

There was worse.

Near the center of the room was a crudely made framework, with a man hung from a steel rod running horizontally five feet above the floor between two wooden uprights. The man was strapped into a tight ball, with his knees hooked over the rod and his head tied between his thighs. His legs were spread apart and his wrists were tied to his ankles. The victim was at first almost unrecognizable as a human being. The naked body was completely covered with blood, and a thick pool of partly clotted blood lay under the torture rack and was collecting sluggishly over the drain.

Mariacher steeled himself for a closer look. The victim's nose and ears were missing. So were his thumbs and several fingers, as well as his genitals. The open gash in his groin was still bleeding heavily, but a steady trickle rather than the spurts that marked a severed artery. Mariacher reached in and felt for a pulse at the man's blood-slick throat.

There was none.

What sick mind could have done this?

"My dad told me he'd seen torture once," Raptor said quietly. "By Noriega's thugs in Panama, just before Operation Just Cause. He never talked about it. I think it really bothered him. I used to wonder why he didn't talk about what he'd seen. Now I know."

Haji and Abdul both were in the room, at Raptor's side. "It is Hafez Tayed," Haji said. Somehow, Mariacher had been sure that that was the case.

"Get him down from there," he said. His voice was raw, his eyes burning.

"If they were still torturing him," Raptor said, "they might not have broken him yet."

"We don't know that," Mariacher replied. "Looks like he bled to death. They wouldn't have let that happen unless they were finished with him."

"Blue One, Gold One!"

"Blue One here. Talk to me."

"The Hip is revving up, Wheel. I think . . . yeah . . . it looks like someone is getting on board." Mariacher could hear gunshots now from outside, both through the open air and over the radio channel. "Chill is popping at them with the AK."

"Keep trying," he said. Then he added, "I'm going to try something." He looked at Raptor. "Someone fired an RPG at you. Did you see anymore?"

"More RPGs? Yeah. I think there's a box—"

Mariacher rushed out onto the main floor of the warehouse, followed by Raptor and the two rebel leaders. Near the northwestern corner of the room, where the RPG gunner had fired from, was a large open crate still containing several RPG rounds.

The launcher was the reusable type, not a disposable launch tube. Mariacher picked up the tube, slipped one of the rocket-propelled grenades into the muzzle, and made the wiring connection. Swiftly, he moved to one of the blown-open garage doors, facing the west.

He could just barely make out the helicopter in the darkness, half a kilometer away. The night was clear, and the moon gave some light; enough to see the Hip's overall shape. He could hear the engine revving harder. Behind him, gunshots banged from the brick factory roof.

SEALs train with many weapons, including those they might encounter in the possession of their foes. He raised the RPG's simple sight and estimated the elevation for a five-hundred-meter shot. "Anybody behind me?" he called.

"You're clear!" Raptor shouted back.

He squeezed the trigger, and with a loud *whoomp,* the grenade streaked into the night, its rocket engine showing as a bright star arcing higher, then burning out.

He counted the seconds. It was a long shot, but even a miss would result in a fairly big explosion when the grenade detonated. Shrapnel might sever fuel lines or hydraulics.

He counted to five . . . then to five again. The helicopter was lifting into the sky now. He could see the moonlight gleam along its fuselage, then glint off the cockpit.

Standard RPG rounds had a 4.5-second self-destruct fuse. That limited their range to under a thousand yards, but also guaranteed an explosion even if they missed their target. There'd been nothing, *nothing*.

The round had been a dud.

Which, he supposed, was not surprising. Russian munitions were not renowned for their reliability, and these rounds must have been captured by the Afghans no more recently than the end of the Russian war, twelve years ago. And in the intervening years, the Afghans . . . well, they weren't known for careful maintenance procedures.

But it was damned frustrating. Mariacher didn't know who the turbaned Afghan with the Soviet NVGs had been, but the fact that he had those goggles at all meant he was a person of some importance. Haji and Abdul had said that Qari Ahmadullah was in Khowst, and this satellite police facility would have been a logical place for him to have his headquarters. Mariacher was willing to bet that he'd been *that* close to nailing the chief of the Taliban's secret police.

The helicopter vanished above the rooftops of Khowst, headed north. Toward Zur Kowt.

A new round of yelling and screams sounded from inside the warehouse. Mariacher and the others returned to the back wall, where the guerrillas had begun opening more heavy doors. These were all padlocked on the outside. Inside the first one, the guerrillas discovered fifteen women packed into a bare, fifteen-by-twelve room. Most were naked. Most were bloodied and bruised, from torture and beatings. They huddled toward the back of their cell, clinging to one another and screaming in terror as their rescuers gaped awkwardly from the open doorway.

"Get those men away from there," Mariacher ordered. "Someone find some clothing, some blankets, anything. And get some first aid kits in here."

The nudity of some of the women and the general state of partial dress of the rest was posing an unexpected problem. During the decade when the Russians had controlled the cities, women in Afghanistan—in the Soviet-controlled urban areas, at any rate—had been well on the way toward adopting more or less Western ideas and fashions. Six years under the warlords and six more under the Taliban had drastically changed the mores of men and women alike. The far more conservative Islam of the countryside insisted that even a glimpse of a vaguely female form inflamed male passions in unclean ways and was cause for intense shame among women—hence burkas and blacked-out windows, and women beaten in the streets for wearing shoes that squeaked.

The prison keepers here, Mariacher noticed, hadn't been so finicky about what they saw, nor had there been any sign of police matrons. The rules, it seemed, were not evenly applied.

A pile of wool blankets and a number of burkas and other garments were found in a nearby storeroom. Mariacher entered the room with the pile, set them carefully on the floor, then backed out. He had Abdul call to them in Pashto from outside, telling them that they were free, that the Taliban militia had been defeated.

A moment later a single woman emerged from the cell. She was tall and, Mariacher was surprised to see, not wearing a burka or even a veil. Her hair was a very light brown, almost blond, and she had startlingly pale, blue eyes.

"You are American?" she said in surprisingly good English.
"Yes I am."

"Thanks be to God!" she exclaimed. Turning, she called to
the other women in rapid-fire Pashto. Turning to Mariacher,
she added, "We'd given up hope! Are the Taliban really gone?"

"For the moment," he told her. "We'll get all of you someplace safe . . . maybe see about getting you over the border
into Pakistan. We've chased them off for the moment, but
they'll be back, and soon."

The woman nodded and went back into the room. After a
time, other women began emerging cautiously, almost shyly.
Raptor and Haji began speaking to each, questioning them,
giving them first aid if necessary.

The other two locked rooms held a number of male prisoners. Abdul began screening them. Most were also nude, or
dressed in rags, and most had been badly beaten.

One was Ahmad Bhittani, the brother of one of Hafez's
wives.

Among the rescued women were Hafez's daughter and his
two widows. When they learned that Hafez was dead, their
cries cut to the heart of Mariacher's soul.

The anti-Taliban troops, most of them, were enraged by
the butchery of one of their own and by the barbaric treatment of good Muslim women. It was all Mariacher and Raptor could do to restrain the rage of some of them. Five
Taliban militiamen had been captured in the fight and left
tightly bound in various rooms with zip-strips. Some of the
anti-Taliban troops found the first one Mariacher and Osterlee had taken. He was just beginning to regain consciousness, and they began working on him with their knives. By
the time Raptor followed the bloodcurdling screams to their
source, the prisoner had been castrated and disemboweled.
The four surviving POWs were quickly brought downstairs

and placed under guard, with Osterlee watching the guards.

And there was yet more horror to come.

"We've found some more . . . prisoners," Raptor said, his voice grim.

"What . . . more Taliban?"

"No. People the Taliban were holding. Or, rather . . . *executing*."

Raptor led him outside to the front gate, to the large sheet-metal transport container sitting nearby. As he approached, he heard . . . What was that? That sound . . . where was it coming from? It took him a moment to realize that he was hearing something like a chorus of moans and muffled shouts coming from inside the cargo container.

Up close it was a chilling sound—muffled cries and groans, as though from a large crowd of souls in torment. In chorus, the voices sounded like a single, low moan that went on and on, punctuated now and again by louder yells, by despairing shrieks, or by the thump of fists against sheet-metal walls. If there was a literal Hell, Mariacher thought, filled with the tortured souls of the damned, it must sound like this.

"There are *people* in there," he said, his voice low but fierce. "In that container!"

Was that what the second sentry had been guarding . . . a kind of makeshift prison cell?

Two of the anti-Taliban troops were trying to prize the heavy padlock off the container's access door. Mariacher waved them off, drew his pistol, and fired two rounds into the lock, smashing the hasp. The door burst open. . . .

A dozen men and women in filthy rags tumbled into the open air, accompanied by a ghastly stench. The anti-Taliban rebels stood about, gape-mouthed, as though wondering what to do.

"Help them!" Mariacher yelled. "Abdul! Tell them to help!"

The first few prisoners were guided clear of the container, set down on the ground and given water. More were coming out every moment, some crawling on hands and knees, some staggering out upright, barely able to stand. Their escape was slowed by the corpses, dozens of them, most still jammed in tight, still upright, faces like scream-twisted hell masks in the beams of flashlights directed into the container's dark interior.

"What the hell is this?" Mariacher demanded.

"Yes," Abdul said. "The truck box. It is an execution."

"What?"

"An execution. For large numbers of people. It is more efficient than shooting them. They force them inside the box, many of them at a time. Perhaps a hundred. Perhaps two hundred. When they can push no more inside, they bolt the door. A few days in a metal box, out in the sun, with no food, no water, without space even to move or turn around or sit down . . . they die. The Taliban kill many Hazara this way. Whole villages sometimes."

"Hazara?" Mariacher asked. "What's that?"

"Another tribe," Haji explained. "Mostly from north of Kabul, but some live here in the south and east too. They are Shi'ite Muslims."

"But what did they *do*?"

Haji shrugged. "The Pashtun are Sunni Muslim. The Hazara are Shi'ite. You see?"

"No," Mariacher said. "I fucking *don't* see!"

"Perhaps you simply do not understand our ways."

That was for damned sure!

But the full truth was that he didn't want to. The horror of what he was seeing was unimaginable. There were parallels enough in Western history, though, and within Christianity. The doctrinal split between Sunni and Shi'ite—originally a difference of opinion over who was to succeed Mohammed as the head of Islam after his ascension to heaven—was roughly equivalent to the division between Catholics and the Eastern Orthodox Church over the authority of the Pope. For Mariacher, it was easier to think of the difference between Catholic and Protestant—and *that* bit of bloody-handed sibling rivalry had killed millions over the centuries.

But cramming people into shipping containers and leaving them to die in agony simply because they differed by a few points of religious doctrine raised images in Mariacher's mind of gas chambers and ovens. The Taliban hadn't quite achieved the sheer scope and scale of Hitler's death camps, but it certainly wasn't from lack of trying.

"I don't believe it," Mariacher said. "I had no idea the Taliban went in for genocide."

"Believe it," Raptor told him. "I'd heard they were doing this up north, especially in the regions with lots of Hazara. In August of 1998 the Taliban captured Mazar-I-Sharif. Reports said that between two and five thousand civilians were murdered, most of them ethnic Hazara. But I didn't know they'd started it down here too."

"The Taliban have used the Base to kill many, many Shia," Hadji said.

"They use al-Qaeda for a lot of the dirty work," Raptor agreed. "*That* is going to change."

Yes, a lot of things were going to change, Mariacher thought. At the moment, though, he wondered what difference it would make. Abdul had been so . . . so damnably matter-of-fact as he discussed the treatment of Shi'ite countrymen, as though it was a perfectly normal thing to lock people into a standing-room-only box and let sun and suffocation kill them.

He thought again about Raptor talking about fighting evil. *This* was evil . . . the very essence of evil.

After a moment, he began helping to pull people out of the container.

Chapter 17

Khowst Safe House
Paktia Province, Afghanistan
0245 hours, local time

The unveiled woman with the striking blue eyes was named Nooria Fahim. She spoke excellent English with a distinct Oxford accent, acquired, Mariacher learned, during four years at that school. Her eyes and fair hair, he decided, must be the genetic legacy of Alexander's men, from their occupation of this land over two thousand years before.

Mariacher and Raptor sat with her at the table in Abdul's house, which had been designated as a safe house for this evening's activities. The other SEALs were outside, keeping watch over the neighborhood—which was surprisingly, even uncomfortably, quiet after the pitched battle at the police facility on the eastern outskirts of the city.

The entire assault force had pulled out of the warehouse two hours ago, setting fire to the building as they left. Mariacher and the other SEALs had brought with them several canvas satchels stuffed with papers, maps, and documents.

There might be some useful intelligence to be gleaned from that haul.

Now, as the eastern sky glowed orange with the flames from the warehouse, the Americans were taking stock of the situation and preparing for the next step of their plan—to E&E clear of the city and head south.

Abdul alternated between hovering in the background and stepping outside to talk with members of the anti-Taliban militia. There was considerable division in the ranks just now over whether to flee Khowst for the mountains or stay put and fight. Abdul agreed that they needed to leave, but he had to talk with each of the Pashtun rebel leaders as they turned up on his doorstep.

At least there'd been no response from the Taliban, or even from the local police.

Not yet.

Nooria was an excellent eyewitness to the overall situation in the city, a mine of information on people, places, and beliefs. She was well-educated, the oldest daughter of one of Afghanistan's ambassadors to Great Britain in the 1960s, during the long reign of King Mohammed Zahir Shah. She'd actually grown up in England and gone to school there, and was a thorough-going Anglophile, unlike many of her countrymen.

She'd returned to Afghanistan—a country she'd until then known only through periodic visits—in 1973, when the king had been deposed by a military coup. Her hope was to return to England and go to medical school there, but the political reversal of her family's fortunes trapped her in Afghanistan. She had enough money to be relatively well-off, but was without the resources necessary to live or study abroad.

She'd worked instead as a medical technician in Kabul, and it was during this time, in the mid-seventies, when she began to wake up politically, as she put it.

"King Zahir Shah was actually quite a reformer," she was

telling them. "Starting in the early sixties, he began a campaign to modernize the country. He created a democratically elected parliament and a free press . . . things that were unheard of in most Muslim countries at the time. There was a lot of emphasis on equality and rights for women, and *that* was unheard of in Muslim countries too."

She took a sip of the tea prepared by Abdul's wife a short time before. Her hands, Mariacher noted, were thin and strong, but still trembling slightly after her ordeal in the Taliban prison. She set the cup down quickly.

"After the king was deposed, though," she continued, "things really started going downhill. The fundamentalists were gaining more and more of a voice in government."

"Didn't the king's cousin take over?" Raptor asked.

She nodded. "Lieutenant General Muhammad Daud Khan became president and prime minister, and he began reversing a lot of the reforms the king had instituted. In 1978, Daud was deposed by Noor Mohammed Taraki."

"Who aligned Afghanistan with the Soviet Union," Mariacher said.

"Yes. The next year, 1979, Taraki was killed in another coup and Hafizullah Amin took over. Three months later the Russians invaded Afghanistan on the pretext of stabilizing the government at the government's invitation. Amin was executed by Spetznaz commandos, and Babrak Karmal became president, a Soviet puppet. It was after the invasion that I met Meena."

"Meena?" Mariacher asked. "Is that a woman's name?"

"Yes. She only went by her first name, Meena. She founded the Revolutionary Association of the Women of Afghanistan—RAWA—and used it to try to stop the reversal of the new laws emancipating women. When the Russians came, she organized political protests and rallies, and tried to focus world attention on the plight of all Afghans under Soviet rule."

"I take it you're with this RAWA?"

"Of course!" she said, nodding. "I am a writer for a bilingual magazine Meena and RAWA started in 1981. My true calling. The magazine is called *Payam-e-Zan,* 'Women's Message,' and it is a rallying place for all Afghan women who wish to be free."

"Among those who were allowed to learn to read, anyway," Mariacher said.

"Literacy for women is one of our highest goals. When women learn for themselves that they don't need to accept the rule of the clerics—"

He made a sour face. "Which is why the fundies don't want women to read."

"Through *Payam-e-Zan,* Meena made many, many enemies, both among the communists and the Islamic fundamentalists."

"Huh. I was under the impression that women had it pretty good under the Soviets."

"In the cities, perhaps, things weren't so bad as elsewhere. Girls could go to school. Women could seek professional careers. But there has *always* been religious prejudice against women in this country, to one degree or another." She shook her head. "Anyway, I met Meena in 1978, as she organized a demonstration on the campus at the University of Kabul. To listen to her speak . . . it was wonderful. Amazing—the power, the intelligence, the dedication to her ideals, the *love.* I knew then I would follow her anywhere, do anything for her cause."

"That was before the Russians invaded. How bad was it for women back then?"

"Thugs in the pay of Burhanuddin Rabbani were going around the campus seeking out women wearing Western dress. They would throw acid on their exposed legs or faces."

"A moment," Abdul said, stepping forward into the lamp-light. "Burhanuddin Rabbani is a great man! He was a hero in the Soviet war and the leader of our government before the Taliban!"

"Burhanuddin Rabbani is a monster," Noori snapped. "He is as much an Islamic radical as any in the Taliban. He created the Jamiat-e Islami party to fight secularization in our country!"

"Now, now!" Abdul said, wagging a finger at her. "Girl, you should not speak of things you do not understand! You should realize that the devout followers of Islam are upset, and justly so, by women who display their bodies in violation of the holy Qu'ran." He looked her up and down, as though noting with stern disapproval her own lack of proper dress.

"Perhaps you should read your Qu'ran more carefully," Noori said. "The Prophet commands that women *and men* dress modestly. *Nowhere* does it command the wearing of the veil, or the burka! Nowhere does it demand that women be denied medical care or an education! Nowhere—"

"Whore!" He spat the word. *"You will not speak of Mohammed, His name be praised, in this fashion!"*

"Quiet! Both of you!" Mariacher said, standing suddenly. In another moment they were going to have another religious war on their hands, right here in this Afghan kitchen. "Raptor? Why don't you take Abdul outside for a moment and check on the preparations?"

"Right," Raptor said. "C'mon, Abdul."

"But this whore—"

"Come *on,* Abdul." That tone of voice permitted no disagreement or hesitation, not if the target expected to walk away with limbs intact. Abdul snarled something in Pashto, then preceded Raptor out the front door.

"What was that?" Mariacher asked.

"A rather foul name for women who don't know their proper place."

"Worse than what he called you in English?"

"Much worse." She shrugged. "It doesn't matter. Slanders don't matter unless you *let* them matter."

"Ah. I think I'm beginning to understand some of what you're fighting against, ma'am," Mariacher said.

"I doubt that. Your country is supporting the so-called Northern Alliance, is it not?"

"Yes . . ."

"And they are as rabidly fundamentalist as the Taliban! The U.N. still recognizes Rabbani as the legitimate head of government for this country, and he will fight any attempt to secularize Afghanistan. Don't you understand? Religious fundamentalism is the enemy of *all* of civilized humanity! You Americans, of all people, should know this after last September! And it's not just the fanatics within Islam! *All* narrow and single-minded all-or-nothing bigotry in the name of *any* god or ideology is the absolute enemy of justice, truth, liberty, and human dignity!"

Her fiery passion touched him. He didn't see much hope of her winning over a country of seventeen million people, though, when at least half of them were male fundamentalist fanatics. "You'll get no argument from me, ma'am," Mariacher told her. "But we'd better get ready to go now."

"Where are you going?"

"We are going south. The Taliban is going to be all over this city a few hours from now. We need to be gone. We're going to escort you and the other people we pulled out of that warehouse tonight across the border into Pakistan. You'll be able to apply for refugee status, get medical help, and figure out what to do next."

"I'm grateful for the help you've given us, Lieutenant. And I'm grateful for your helping the others. I already know what I am going to do next, however, and that certainly does *not* include going to Pakistan."

"I don't think it's a good idea for you to stay here."

"And who will stop me. You? Your commandos? Abdul and his army?"

Mariacher considered this. If Nooria was captured and tortured, she would tell her interrogators a lot about Task Force 5.

Or . . . perhaps not. He had the feeling that Nooria Fahim would die long before she gave the animals she hated so much as a single helpful word. The question was whether she would have any choice in the matter. The way those bastards had taken poor Hafez apart . . .

"Look, I can't stop you. I won't. But will you do us a favor? Me, and all the people we'll be evacuating?"

"If it is possible. I can't promise anything."

"None of us can. But I'd take it as a personal favor if you went into hiding for a few days, at least. Stay out of sight, until we can get these people across the border."

"You are afraid I will talk about your plans if I am captured."

"That's about the size of it. Yeah."

"I need to get to Kabul, but I will be doing my best not to attract attention. That is the most I can promise."

"You're going alone?"

She gave him a pained smile. "A woman alone on the road in Afghanistan? That's a good way to get arrested, don't you know. It's against the law for a woman to be out without a husband or an adult male relative. No, I'll be traveling with Ibrahium Azhar. He's one of RAWA's oldest supporters, and he's helped me travel incognito before. He was in the warehouse too, you see. He'll be posing as my father."

"I see. Why Kabul?"

"Some of my sisters are trying to organize a resistance there."

The way she said "sisters" made it sound like she didn't mean blood relatives. "A resistance? Against the Taliban?"

She sighed. "Against *all* fundamentalism. Before it's too late."

"What do you mean?"

"Soon . . . a week, a month . . . the United States will be here, in force. We all know this."

"Yes . . ."

"We welcome it, most of us. But the only way we can win true freedom is if a popular rising throws out the clerics and the fanatics. If Kabul is 'liberated' by the Northern Alliance, the women of Afghanistan will not be free. They will *never* be free, not until the religious fanatics are overthrown and a *secular* government is created."

"Whatever happened to this Meena?" Mariacher asked.

"She was martyred in 1987. An Afghani murdered her in Quetta, Pakistan, a man who was pretending to be a loyal member of RAWA. He was certainly working for KHAD, and may also have been in the pay of the fundamentalists."

If true, that was startling news. The communist-organized KHAD had had little in common with the Muslim fundamentalists of the country, their bitter enemies during the Soviet occupation. If they'd worked together to kill this woman, she must have posed a remarkable threat to them both.

But then, this Meena sounded like a remarkable woman.

"I'd better see to my men," he said. He stepped out into the night.

There was a lot he needed to think about, a lot to digest.

Two hours later a caravan departed the suburbs of Khowst, moving southeast across the valley floor toward the mountains and Pakistan. It consisted of the SEALs and Raptor, their gear carried on horseback, plus Haji and his men and a ragged army of both men and women—some of them anti-Taliban rebels, most of them people freed hours earlier from the police warehouse, which continued to burn against the eastern sky.

At the same time, a smaller group moved off toward the mountains in the northwest—anti-Taliban rebels who'd elected to remain in the Khowst area but knew it was healthier for them to remain out of the city proper for a time. Abdul led this latter group. Meena and her escort had already vanished into the night sometime earlier. "Good riddance!" Abdul had said in disgust. "That kind of woman is only trouble!"

Mariacher hadn't answered, but he was furious. Nooria and her "sisters" might well hold the key to Afghanistan's survival. The trouble was getting the men to listen.

Helicopters were circling to the east. Mariacher couldn't see them, but he could hear the clatter of rotors. There were heavier sounds as well, the rumble of heavy vehicles. Other armies were moving in the area as well.

After threading their way across a dry lake bed, they followed narrow footpaths as the land steadily rose—smugglers' routes known to Haji and his men that may well have been in use for centuries. By the time the sky grew light and the sun began pecking above the mountains to the east, they were well above Khowst, deep in the foothills below Zhawar Kili.

At this point, the SEALs and Raptor separated from Haji and the other Afghans. They were within a few miles of al-Badr II, a beehive of al-Qaeda and Taliban activity. Haji took the main caravan west, toward a series of trails and dry streambeds that would, he said, take them safely across the border to a Pakistani village called Miram Shah. The five TF-5 personnel, with two packhorses, turned east, skirting the valley that held the Zhawar Kili complex and making their way eventually to their well hidden base.

By sunset on October first, they were hunkered down in a

stone-reinforced pit covered over by a camouflage tarp. Their AN/PRC-117F satcom unit was set up, its cross-shaped antenna aimed at a particular spot in the southern sky where a communications satellite hung in geosynchronous orbit. The KY-99 crypto device was connected, and they had an open channel to Mother Goose himself—the code name for their operational control stateside, most likely somewhere in the Pentagon basement.

In the fading light, Chief Bradley was photographing documents with his high-resolution digital camera, using a cable from the camera to the KY-99 unit to upload each shot to Mother Goose. He'd gone through about a quarter of the papers they'd taken from the police building the night before. Most would have to wait for tomorrow. With luck, some of those documents pertained to HVTs on the Agency's hit list, and might give the SEAL operators an idea of where to go next.

Always there was that most urgent hope that the documents would lead them straight to Khalid Shaik Mohammed . . . or even to his boss, Osama bin Laden.

Mariacher was sitting on an outcropping nearby, overlooking the Khowst Valley below. Lehman and Osterlee were out in the night somewhere, setting up sentry alarms. Raptor came up behind him, silent.

"Need me?" Mariacher asked after a few moments passed.

"Nah. Everything's squared away. I was just wondering what's eating you."

"Why do you think I'm being eaten?"

"You've been moody and withdrawn all day. Thought it might have to do with what we saw last night."

"Ah. No. Well . . . mostly no."

"Want to talk about it?"

"Not really." He shifted position on the rock, pulling his

H&K closer. After a moment, he added, "You remember talking about fighting evil? The conversation we had in Pak a few days ago?"

"Sure."

"You really believe in all that stuff?"

"What stuff? Religion?"

"Yeah."

Raptor leaned against the boulder. "I guess I believe in something out there. Call it God, for lack of a better name. I don't believe in the devil or Hell or any of that."

"No?"

"Absolutely not. Any deity who would consign billions of people to an eternity of torture for the crime of being born in the wrong place or believing the wrong thing, well, that creature does not rate worship in my book. No more than the monsters who tortured Hafez Sayed to death."

"What about evil?"

"*That* I believe in. I've seen it."

"Me too. The question is what can be done about it."

"Seems to me, you and I *are* doing something about it."

Mariacher sighed. He'd been holding the depressive thoughts at bay for twenty-four hours now, but could not deny them any longer. What he'd seen in that torture chamber . . .

"Yeah, and the guy who was responsible for what we saw climbed on a helicopter and flew away. He *got away*! Right now I feel like you can fight evil and fight it and fight it, and after a while you realize that you're never going to get it all, that it's always going to be out there, just out of reach. That there's always some two-bit Hitler-wannabe somewhere, torturing or starving or shooting his own people to stay in power, or for ethnic cleansing, or for the glory of God, or whatever. You kill one and ten more spring up to take his place."

"It's worse than that," Raptor told him.

"How could it be worse?"

"After a while, if you're *really* dedicated to rooting out the evil and destroying it, you begin to realize that it's in here too." He tapped his own chest with a forefinger. "That's where it really lives, you know. Not in some concept of God or what pisses God off, but inside your own heart. Ordinary people—you, me, *anyone*—could end up wielding that knife, given the right circumstances."

"Thanks *so* much for the cheerful thought."

"Hey, what are friends for? But it's true. I read once they did a psychological study. They'd bring ordinary people into a room and give them a button. They were told that pushing that button zapped a volunteer in the next room with electricity, causing pain. They were told it was a psychological study. What they weren't told was that *they* were the subjects of the study, not the guy sitting in the hot seat next door. And what they found out was that *anybody* would push that button, even when they heard the 'victim' screaming. Especially if they thought the tester would think they were a wuss if they didn't. And a lot of people pressed the switch longer and harder than they had to."

"There's a difference between pushing a button and using a knife on a human being like . . . like that."

"Maybe. Not much, though. Like I said, the evil is in here." He tapped his heart again. "It's not just Noriega's thugs. Not just the secret police of some Third World shithole or the Taliban's interrogators. It's part of *all* of us."

"So you just can't win. Not in the long run." Mariacher reached down and pulled his canteen from its pouch. "You're saying we're all as bad as Qari Ahmadullah."

"That's where I have to disagree. We can win. Victory means holding out—doing what you know is right—one more day." He flashed a grin. "Ahmadullah's given in to the Dark Side. We don't have to do the same thing. We have the same tendencies, the same temptations, maybe. But we don't have to become him."

"To tell you the truth, I wouldn't mind seeing the bastard trussed up on a torture rack, just like Hafez. And I sure as hell wouldn't mind having him in my sights again."

"And when we have him in our sights, we take him down because that's our job, and . . . you know what? The world will be just a little bit cleaner when we do."

"Here's to then," Mariacher said, raising the canteen, then taking a swig. He offered it then to Raptor. "The trouble is," he continued, "that it's not that black and white. You heard Noori last night . . . this morning, rather. Remember how she tore into Rabbani? After you took Abdul outside, she was taking on the whole Northern Alliance. According to her, they're all religious fanatics, and they're all as bad as the Taliban. It sounds like we're going to kick one batch of bastards out and let another batch in."

"Maybe."

"Doesn't that bother you?"

"The way I figure it, next time around we're going to be here watching. If Rabbani tries the same shit—imprisoning women inside their own homes, or blowing up ancient statues—the U.N. and the U.S. will be down on his raggy ass so fast he won't know what hit him."

"Oh, come on, Halstead! The U.N. and the U.S. knew what was happening! I remember hearing about the Taliban winding back the clock to the Middle Ages here five years ago, at least! There was a drought here, and food shortages. Still are. And the world didn't do a fucking thing but pass resolutions and trade embargoes!"

"Which brings us to the right—or the evil—of telling other people how to run their lives. And whether the United States ought to be the world's policeman, judge, and referee. I'll tell you one thing Rabbani *won't* do if he gets into power."

"What's that?"

"He won't blow up any skyscrapers full of civilians in New York City . . . or protect people who do. And *that,* my friend, is why we're in Afghanistan. To get the fuckers behind 9/11."

"I'll try to keep that in mind."

But he remembered Abdul that morning . . . both his condescension and his anger toward Noori. The Americans trying to help ordinary Afghanis fight the monstrosity that had taken over their land also faced a monster that had taken over their minds. Abdul's convictions—that women were inferior creatures who had to be kept under lock and key, that they had no rights and deserved none, worse, that their inferiority was somehow ordained and approved of by God Himself— those convictions were shared by the majority of the men and even many of the women living in Afghanistan.

And not just Afghanistan, but in much of the rest of the Muslim world as well.

How did you fight that? "Winning hearts and minds" in Vietnam must have been a piece of cake compared to getting zealots to change attitudes engraved in stone since the seventh century or before, in a culture where even *thinking* about changing traditions or changing the way you thought about women was considered nothing less than heresy.

How did you fight something like that?

Was it even right to try to do so?

Raptor left to check on the perimeter security. Mariacher remained on the rock until the sky was quite dark, ablaze with stars.

We're here to get Khalid Mohammed and bin Laden and the others behind 9/11, he told himself. Nothing else.

But he still felt lost and empty.

Chapter 18

Monday, October 1, 2001, through Sunday, October 7, 2001

On the first day of October, Zahir Shah, the former king of Afghanistan, now an ancient man living in a comfortable exile in Italy, agreed with the anti-Taliban Northern Alliance to convene an emergency council, a first step toward creating a new government for the country. The Taliban, predictably, announced that the effort was doomed to fail.

On October 2, U.S. Defense Secretary Donald Rumsfeld flew to the Middle East to meet with the leaders of Saudi Arabia, Oman, Egypt, and Uzbekistan. The topic of discussion was to be the war on terrorism. Great Britain's Tony Blair announced that the Taliban must surrender the terrorists or surrender power, a demand the Afghan government again rejected.

Over the course of the next few days, the United States and her allies continued to marshal world opinion against al-Qaeda and the Taliban. The secretary-general of NATO said that the U.S. government had provided the eighteen members of the alliance with "clear and compelling evidence" of Osama bin Laden's responsibility for the September 11 attacks, while Great Britain made some of that evidence public, citing proof that bin Laden had spoken of "a major attack against America" before that date. Pakistan became the first Muslim country to agree that the U.S. evidence linking bin Laden to the attacks was enough to warrant an indictment. Washington announced that several of the terrorists involved in the September 11 attacks had also been implicated in the bombing of the USS *Cole* the previous year, and in the 1998 embassy bombings in Africa.

On October 5 one thousand U.S. troops were dispatched to Uzbekistan on Afghanistan's northern border. Colin Powell extended the financial sanctions already in place against al-Qaeda and twenty-four other organizations believed to be engaged in terrorist activities, and with links, real or potential, to bin Laden. The National Guard began patrolling U.S. airports, and Bob Stevens, a sixty-three-year-old resident of Florida, died of inhalation anthrax, the first U.S. anthrax death in twenty-five years.

On October 6, President Bush warned the Taliban that time was running out. He again demanded that they surrender the terrorists and shut down their operations in Afghanistan. In reply, the Taliban offered to free eight imprisoned foreign aid workers if the U.S. would halt what they called her "massive propaganda campaign" and promise not to target the Afghan people. The White House dismissed the offer, which seemed a transparent attempt to use hostages as bargaining chips.

And on the following day, October 7, the United States finally struck.

Monday, October 8, 2001

Al-Badr
Paktia Province, Afghanistan
2125 hours, local time

Mariacher lay on his belly in a shallow depression on the
ridgetop, peering through the sighting scope of the team's
SOFLAM.

Officially designated as the AN/PEQ-1A Special Operations Forces Laser Acquisition Marker, the SOFLAM was a
tripod-mounted tactical laser designator normally issued
only to Marine Force Recon units. This one, though, had
been supplied to Task Force 5 by the logistical arm of the
CIA for this op when the SEALs were still in Thailand. The
Company, it appeared, could come up with just about any
piece of military hardware desired on ridiculously short notice, and the SOFLAM was one of the best and most highly
portable laser designators on the market.

The unit weighed just twelve pounds—the entire system,
tripod, battery, and all, came in at under eighteen pounds—
and had an effective range out to five kilometers or more.
Right now this unit was bore-sighted with its AN/PVS-13
Laser Marker Night Vision Sight, or LMNVS, a device that
looked something like a megaphone attached to the top of the
SOFLAM. Mariacher focused in on the target first with the
NVS, then dropped his eye to peer through the SOFLAM's
eyepiece.

Everything was set—tripod locked tight, batteries hooked
up, the Off/Mark/Range switch set to Mark. Mariacher
pulled back on the TLD's reticule switch to illuminate it, then
twisted slightly to brighten the crosshairs. Another slight ad-
justment and the crosshairs were centered perfectly on the target, a squat, mud-brick structure set off by itself nearly a mile

away, and three miles from the main complex of al-Badr II.

The target had been identified earlier in the week as a radar and communications center, part of the network serving the entire Zhawar Kili complex. A radar dish was just visible against the night sky several hundred yards to the east, peering over the ridgetops toward Pakistan. So far, though, the Afghans had refused to switch their radar on. They knew— having learned by Iraq's experience during the Gulf War ten years before—that when defense radars were turned on, weapons like the U.S. Navy's AGM-88 HARMs—High-speed Anti-Radiation Missiles—were certain to arrive moments later, homing on the radar signals themselves.

The TAQs knew that American aircraft were in the area. They'd been sending up streamers of antiaircraft fire all evening, alternating long stretches of relative inactivity with brief periods of intense firing and the slow drift of brilliant white flares. There seemed to be no indication that they were aware of Americans on the ground, however, or to have guessed at the nature of the special package now headed their way.

"Sugar, Gray Ghost, Target acquired," Mariacher said, his words reaching both the other members of his team and the helmet headsets of a pair of U.S. Navy aviators somewhere over the mountains to the south. Out there in the night, a pair of Navy F/A-18 Hornets off the aircraft carrier USS *Kitty Hawk* was angling in low above the mountains, readying for the kill.

"You're sure you don't have a pharmaceutical lab there?" Bradley asked, the joke lightening, somewhat, the growing tension.

"I've got a lock on the chief radar operator's top button," Mariacher replied—a slight exaggeration. He could see a pair of guards outside the front door. The comment about pharmaceutical labs was a bit of gallows' black humor drawn from President Clinton's response to the al-Qaeda terrorist bombings of 1998.

"Gray Ghost, this is Sugar One, sixty seconds," sounded over Mariacher's headset. Green streams of triple-A continued to fire into the sky, but aimlessly, as though the gunners were firing blindly.

"Here they come," Mariacher said.

"'Bout damned time," Lehman replied. The SEALs were spread out along the depression. Nearby, several mujahideen anti-Taliban fighters lay on the slope, watching the sky nervously.

"Sugar One, ten seconds," the headphone voice reported. Then, "Ghost, Sugar One! Laser on!"

Mariacher triggered the SOFLAM unit, "painting" the target with laser energy that could be detected by the Warthog driver and the ordnance he carried. The spot of laser light was invisible to Mariacher, even through the NVS, but a moment later he heard the pilot announce "Spot!" He'd acquired the target. "Sugar One! Lock . . . launch!"

Mariacher found himself holding his breath, keeping his eye to the eyepiece, willing the incoming warhead to ride the laser light all the way down to the target.

"Sugar One . . . terminate." That meant the pilot had visually acquired the target and no longer needed the laser illumination. Before he could switch the laser off, however, the radar building erupted in a dazzling flash of yellow and orange light, a spray of burning debris, and a stage-lit billow of smoke mushrooming into the night sky.

The flash came first, the blast seconds later, a deep-throated slam of sound more felt than heard.

The explosion seemed to shock all of the Taliban antiair into silence. Seconds later, however, one of the gun positions opened up again, and soon others were joining in all across the valley. They still didn't seem to have a particular target in mind, but appeared determined to fill the sky with so much flying metal that they were bound to hit *something*.

In fact, the U.S. air assault on Afghanistan had begun with remarkably little fanfare or effort. The first wave consisted of just fifteen Air Force B-1, B-2, and B-52 bombers, twenty-five Navy strike fighters flying off carriers in the Arabian Sea, and fifty Tomahawk cruise missiles launched from British and American warships. The 1998 strike by seventy-five cruise missiles concentrated against the terrorist camps and training facilities at Zhawar Kili had been more intense. After all of the saber-rattling, the actual attack seemed a bit anticlimactic.

There were differences, though. When Clinton had ordered the strike against bin Laden's training camps in 1998, the attack was carried out entirely by cruise missiles—by robots, essentially, which were only as effective as the intelligence gathering and analyses that went into their programming. As it turned out, many of their targets had been abandoned, some just before the attack, some for many months. In some cases, the best intelligence on the targets was flat out-and-out wrong; the mistaken cruise missile attack against the pharmaceutical plant in Sudan was a case in point.

This time, however, there were teams with "boots on the ground," as the saying had it—advance elements of the CIA's Task Force 5, and several U.S. Special Forces A-teams or ODAs—Operational Detachments-Alpha—as they were now known. The Gray Ghosts had been in Paktia Province for a week, gathering data on Taliban positions, reporting on what they were seeing, and transmitting precisely determined coordinates for potential targets back to Washington, and now, along with other small units scattered throughout the country, they were painting specific targets for the inbound air strikes.

And there was another difference as well. Unlike the retaliatory attacks of 1998, these air strikes would continue,
relentlessly and unceasingly, until the job was done.

"Target destroyed!" Mariacher reported to the aircraft,
still invisible somewhere in the night. He was already loos-
ening the pins locking the tripod and swinging the
SOFLAM to the left, bringing it to bear on another target.

This structure was a long, low, single-story building inside
the walled compound, nearly a mile beyond the radar installation. For the past four days, the SEALs had watched large
numbers of armed men entering and leaving, sometimes
singly, often in large groups, and in the increasing chill of
Afghanistan's October evenings the building glowed
brightly all night under thermal imaging. The facility was almost certainly a large barracks housing al-Qaeda fighters or
recruits. Russian-made Zil trucks were parked along the east
wall, and a 30mm quad-mounted antiaircraft cannon had
been set up behind a sandbag barricade on the roof. The
weapon was contributing now to the streams of green tracer
fire streaming into the sky.

For most of the past week, the SEALs had watched the
building's occupants drilling, practicing on the firing range,
and going to classes. Many might be elsewhere in the compound, manning the guns, but a large number were still in
there. The tricky part was the location of the barracks. It was
planted almost directly adjacent to a smaller building with a
tall spire—the structure they'd identified as a mosque the week
before. While there was no question that the walled compound
was a terrorist training camp, there were Afghan civilians in
there as well, and a number of small structures that were probably private dwellings. The idea was to take out the obviously
military targets with as little collateral damage as possible.

Mariacher planted the targeting reticule squarely on the
double doors in the building's south wall, which was facing

the team's position two and a half miles away, then tightened the locking pins on the tripod. Another check on the reticule. "Sugar, Ghost," he said into the radio. "Target acquired."

A moment later he heard a naval aviator's dry voice in his headset. "Ah, roger, Gray Ghost. Sugar Two, sixty seconds."

The radar facility continued to burn, illuminating the cloud of smoke from beneath with a fierce, orange glow. A secondary explosion went off, first the flash, and a moment later a muffled thud. There must have been ammunition and fuel supplies stored in or near the building.

Mariacher ignored the spectacle, concentrating on the target picture in the SOFLAM's imager. The double doors in the barracks were opening and men were spilling out.

"Looks like they're evacuating," Osterlee said, watching through a night-vision monocular.

"Some of them are getting into the trucks," Lehman added.

"Are they gonna get clear?" Bradley wanted to know.

More and more men spilled out of the barracks, gathering in an unmilitary mob on the parade ground in front of the building. Even at this range, through the SOFLAM's ten-power magnification, Mariacher could make out details of dress and weapons. A few were carrying AKs. Most wore the black or dark-colored turbans favored by al-Qaeda fighters. From the way they were moving, Mariacher guessed that the majority were newbies—recruits and trainees. The armed ones were probably veterans and instructors; he could see them waving and shouting, trying to herd the mob into some sort of order. Drivers were starting up the trucks, and some of the recruits were climbing aboard. Apparently, the demolition of the radar site nearby had made someone over there decide it would be safer riding out the air attack in a less conspicuous place—a bunker, perhaps, or an underground stronghold.

"Sugar Two, ten seconds," the voice over Mariacher's headset announced. "Ghost, Sugar Two! Laser on!"

Mariacher briefly considered shifting the TLD's laser to the body of men, but immediately dismissed the idea. These first air strikes were primarily aimed at destroying the infrastructure of the Taliban and al-Qaeda military—SAM and radar sites, communications and control centers, munitions dumps, and bases such as this one. A secondary objective was to spread terror through the enemy's ranks. He kept the crosshairs on the double doors, which were again closed, and triggered the targeting laser.

"Spot!" the aviator called when his instrumentation acquired the reflected laser light. "Sugar Two, lock! Launch!"

The al-Qaeda recruits were moving off the parade ground now, clambering aboard the trucks. One truck had already backed away from the building and was turning. Its headlights were on, Mariacher noted, which didn't speak well of their air raid discipline.

Of course, with invisible laser beams and smart bombs, even a total blackout couldn't have saved them.

"Sugar Two . . . terminate."

The aviator had it. Mariacher released the trigger.

Through the scope, he saw the south doors open again. Two men wearing what looked like Russian military greatcoats and black turbans were emerging. They might be officers, possibly Taliban, probably AQ. *Damn!* Had opening the doors screwed the smart bomb's laser lock?

One of the men was walking down the flight of three steps, the other still in the open doorway when Mariacher caught just an instant's glimpse of motion, a blur on the scope . . . and the man still in the door vanished, as though swept away by an unseen giant's hand. The instant appeared to freeze in slow motion; the greatcoated man outside was turning, several al-Qaedas were turning as if to see what had happened to the disappearing officer. . . .

The wide-open doorway erupted in white light, and at the

same instant, windows all along the building's other walls lit
up, then hurled themselves outward. The second officer, on
the ground outside the door, was momentarily silhouetted
by the light, and then Mariacher saw him literally dissolve
as the blast engulfed him.

The roof, complete with its quad thirty triple-A mount,
lifted several feet into the air, then collapsed into the blast,
crumpling into fragments. Flame engulfed the trucks along
the south wall, and Mariacher watched men plucked off the
ground and hurled like wet rags through the air.

Secondary explosions detonated beneath one of the
trucks . . . then another . . . then three or four more as gas
tanks ignited. A moment later the sound of the strike reached
the watching SEALs and anti-Taliban militia, a distance-
muffled boom that continued to rumble and echo through the
mountain ridges and valleys.

The barracks walls were still standing, but the roof was
gone and the interior was ablaze. Trucks burned furiously,
and Mariacher could see several human figures burning as
well, some lying motionless on the ground, others, horribly,
thrashing about as the flames consumed them.

The Zil truck already under way had escaped the worst of
the blast, but it had slammed to a halt. AQ fighters were
scrambling out of the back and running for the sanctuary of
the mosque.

It was amazing to see the extent of the devastation in and
around the barracks, and to see the mosque with its minaret
still standing, apparently unscathed.

A number of AQ troops were on their feet now, apparently
dazed. One figure in particular would forever remain burned
into Mariacher's memory—the silhouette of a man against
the blazing barracks, his right arm clearly missing from the
shoulder down.

And in his left hand was a limp something that looked

very much like a severed arm. The figure was simply standing there, unmoving, watching the fire.

Or was the apparent dismemberment an illusion created
by the way he was standing? Mariacher couldn't tell at this
range. All he knew was that the thing the man held in his left
hand didn't look at all like a rifle.

"Target destroyed," Mariacher called over the open radio
channel. That was another advantage of having operators
boots-on-the-ground. They could give an immediate damage
assessment on the target. Somewhere back in the bowels of
the damaged Pentagon someone would be crossing a radar
facility and an AQ barracks off a carefully prepared list.

"Roger that Ghost. We are bingo fuel. RTB," one of the
aviators replied, meaning they were returning to their base.

They had just enough fuel remaining to get back to their
carrier, some six hundred miles to the south.

"Who was that masked man?" Osterlee joked. "And we
never even had a chance to thank him!"

Mariacher switched off the SOFLAM and unplugged the
battery pack. They would need to recharge the batteries before the next op. He noticed several of the Afghans standing nearby, talking excitedly among themselves and
pointing at him.

"Raptor?" he asked. "What's with our muj?"

Raptor had been with the anti-Talibans throughout the attack. He grinned. "I think they were impressed with the
show," he said. "They're talking about you blowing up buildings with your death ray."

"Death ray—what?" He was startled. "What death ray?
Oh."

He realized that to the Afghanis with the Task Force 5
team, it must have appeared that his SOFLAM had blown up
the two buildings from the top of this ridge, miles away from
the targets.

"Tell them the laser just guides the bombs released from our aircraft," he said.

"I did. I don't think they get it."

Mariacher shook his head. It didn't matter what the Afghan troops believed about American military technology. Who was it who'd said that any sufficiently advanced technology was indistinguishable from magic? Clarke . . . that was it. A British science and science-fiction writer. The line had been repeated so often everyone knew it, an apt and prescient aphorism for the twenty-first century. Smart bombs or death rays—either way, U.S. military technology was going to dominate this war.

The question was whether it would help the Americans achieve their goal, which wasn't so much simply winning as bringing bin Laden and the other AQ and Taliban leaders to justice.

He watched the burning buildings for a moment, two far-off, flickering spots of light to the naked eye. Killing the bastards amounted to justice, he supposed. He thought of the two AQs in greatcoats. Who had they been? What were their names?

Most likely he would never know.

"Pack up, gang," he ordered. "Let's get the hell out of here."

Sunday, October 7, 2001

Miramar Motel
Oceanside, California
2215 hours, PDT

They'd chosen the Miramar again for their tryst . . . what very well could be their *last* tryst, as Tangretti reminded himself. SEAL ops were by their very nature more dangerous than those of conventional military operations. Hell, sometimes SEALs didn't come back from *training* missions, and where he was going in another week or two was going to be a hell of a lot deadlier than training.

He was just glad he'd had the opportunity to see Marilyn again. His captain's mast punishment had not involved confinement to base, thank God. The lockdown late last month had been the result of a terrorist scare, one of a long string of false alarms, nothing more. The higher-ups were now being fairly liberal in their offers of liberty to enlisted personnel.

After all, for some this might be their last fling ashore.

So far, this had been a delightful fling, Tangretti thought. He and Marilyn were now sitting side by side in the motel bed. Both were nude after a long round of lovemaking, but for the moment, at least, their attention was not on one another but on the CNN broadcast coming through the television on the dresser opposite their bed. They were watching a replay of the televised address that the president had made a few hours earlier from the Treaty Room of the White House.

"More than two weeks ago," Bush was saying, halfway through his speech, "I gave Taliban leaders a series of clear and specific demands: Close terrorist training camps. Hand over leaders of the al-Qaeda network, and return all foreign nationals, including American citizens unjustly detained in their country.

"None of these demands were met. And now, the Taliban will pay a price. . . ."

"This is it," Marilyn said softly. "We're really at war with Afghanistan!"

His hand was resting on her thigh. He let it wander a bit, caressing. "Not Afghanistan, hon. We're after bin Laden and al-Qaeda . . . and, I guess, the Taliban because they've been protecting them."

"C'mon, it's all the same difference, right?"

Tangretti wasn't sure how to respond to that. It *wasn't* the same.

"Initially, the terrorists may burrow deeper into caves and other entrenched hiding places," Bush continued. "Our military action is also designed to clear the way for sustained, comprehensive, and relentless operations to drive them out and bring them to justice.

"At the same time, the oppressed people of Afghanistan will know the generosity of America and our allies. As we strike military targets, we will also drop food, medicine, and supplies to the starving and suffering men and women and children of Afghanistan.

"The United States of America is a friend to the Afghan people, and we are the friends of almost a billion worldwide who practice the Islamic faith."

"There!" Tangretti cried, pointing. "See? Just what I said! It's not the Afghans we're fighting!"

"The United States of America is an enemy of those who aid terrorists," Bush added, "and of the barbaric criminals who profane a great religion by committing murder in its name. . . ."

"Oh, get real, David!" Marilyn said, half bantering. "*Everybody* knows this is all about oil."

"What?" He pulled his hand back, startled. He was not "everybody," and he knew nothing of the kind. "What are you talking about?"

"Sure! Jack—Jack Fisher, he works with me at Jones and Galloway? Anyway, he was telling a bunch of us the other day how the oil companies are talking about putting an oil pipeline through Afghanistan now . . . you know, to reach all the oil in Uzbek—Uzibek . . . whatever. All those places over there that have names ending in 'stan.' The oil companies want to get that oil down to seaports in India or Pakistan, so we're invading Afghanistan so that we can control that oil."

"That," Tangretti said slowly, but with utter conviction, "is utter crap."

"Hey!" She pointed at the man on the TV screen. "Talk to his daddy! *He's* the big Texas oil baron, right? He's the one who took us to war against Iraq over oil. Now his son's doing the same thing in Afghanistan!"

"We're a peaceful nation," Bush said. "Yet, as we have learned, so suddenly and so tragically, there can be no peace in a world of sudden terror. In the face of today's new threat, the only way to pursue peace is to pursue those who threaten it.

"We did not ask for this mission, but we will fulfill it.

"The name of today's military operation is Enduring Freedom. We defend not only our precious freedoms, but also the freedom of people everywhere to live and raise their children free from fear. . . ."

"I don't buy it," Tangretti said, shaking his head. "If we wanted oil, why would we risk making every Muslim country in the world furious at us by invading Afghanistan?"

"Somebody asked Jack that. He said he didn't understand political realities. It's *all* about oil."

"We are going into Afghanistan to make it so bin Laden can't blow up any more Americans," Tangretti said. "That has nothing to do with oil."

"Well, of *course* they'd tell you that, silly!"

There was no way to answer that. He didn't have a high regard for Marilyn's ability to think for herself. Here was someone who would be unable to find "Uzbekistan," "Tajikistan," or "Kyrgyzstan" on a map, much less spell them, and somehow a conversation with her cronies at the office had made her an expert on international politics.

On the screen, Bush was talking about the need for patience, and of the possibility of sacrifices to come.

"Today, those sacrifices are being made by members of our armed forces who now defend us so far from home, and by their proud and worried families. A commander in chief sends America's sons and daughters into battle in a foreign land only after the greatest care and a lot of prayer.

"We ask a lot of those who wear our uniform. We ask them to leave their loved ones, to travel great distances, to risk injury, even to be prepared to make the ultimate sacrifice of their lives.

"They are dedicated. They are honorable. They represent the best of our country, and we are grateful.

"To all the men and women in our military, every sailor, every soldier, every airman, every Coast Guardsman, every Marine, I say this: Your mission is defined. The objectives are clear. Your goal is just. You have my full confidence, and you will have every tool you need to carry out your duty. . . ."

"He didn't say 'every SEAL'!" Marilyn exclaimed.

"He said 'every sailor.' I'm a sailor, Marilyn. U.S. Navy."

"If he's going to send in the SEALs, he needs to acknowledge it," she said. "The SEALs are the best we have! Right? The best of the best of the best!"

That again. Frankly, he was still concerned about Marilyn's fascination with him as a SEAL, rather than for himself. He'd wondered about that a lot in the past week and still wasn't sure what he thought about it.

"Of course," he said. "No question. But watch it! I know a few Marines who would disagree with you."

She punched him in the arm. "Oh, you!"

"Since September eleventh," the president said, moving into his concluding remarks, "an entire generation of young Americans has gained new understanding of the value of freedom and its cost and duty and its sacrifice.

"The battle is now joined on many fronts. We will not waver, we will not tire, we will not falter, and we will not fail. Peace and freedom will prevail.

"Thank you. May God continue to bless America."

The camera cut to a CNN news team and their inevitable dissection of the president's speech. Tangretti used the remote to switch the TV off.

"I thought that was pretty good," he said. "A good speech. Bush has been looking a lot more . . . I don't know, *presidential* since this all started."

"Jack says the whole terrorist problem is being manipulated by Bush. You know, to make him look good. He says the government might even have known about the attack ahead of time but let it happen."

"I thought it was supposed to be oil, not looking good."

"Well, yeah. That too."

"My dear, your Jack doesn't know shit."

"Yeah? Well, *I* know something." She put her hand on his crotch and began rubbing him, rough and aggressively.

"Ow. What?"

"I know I've got me a big, bad Navy SEAL here, and he is all mine for tonight!" She slid her legs out from under her, rolled onto her side and dropped her head to his lap. The two of them didn't say much—nothing coherent, at any rate—for another hour or so.

A long time later, though, Tangretti lay on his back, with Marilyn asleep, snuggled close with her head on his chest and his arm around her shoulders.

He didn't understand. He really didn't. America and Americans were at *war*. Technically, they'd been at war for several years, as al-Qaeda blew up American embassies and American warships and dragged the bodies of American soldiers through the streets of Mogadishu.

Overall, from what he'd seen, American civilians accepted the need to root out al-Qaeda, and even thirsted for vengeance for the World Trade Center and the Pentagon. They supported the military, unlike the situation on the home front during Vietnam. They were accepting long lines and searches at airports and other security checkpoints.

And yet, somehow, the events in Afghanistan simply didn't seem to touch them. The fact that there were people out there who'd literally danced in the streets at the news of September 11 and thousands of American dead was something they could not understand, something that didn't even penetrate their day-to-day thoughts and busy schedules.

Oil indeed. That was nicely remote; a theory that kept the enemy's blind and fanatical hatred at arm's length. You could nod sagely about oil companies and OPEC, and be scandalized at government conspiracies and rumors that gasoline prices would be rising.

You didn't have to think that there were people out there who wanted you dead.

And then again . . . maybe that was the point. He knew he would be face-to-face with the al-Qaeda enemy in a few more days, and he would be doing it so that Marilyn and Jack and a host of others could be free from fear . . . could be free to criticize Bush and his speech and the government and everything they stood for.

It was a good feeling, and the one with which he at last fell asleep.

Chapter 19

Monday, October 8, 2001, through Thursday, October 18, 2001

Throughout the following week, American and British aircraft continued to hammer targets throughout Afghanistan. Agreements had been struck with the governments of Uzbekistan, Turkmenistan, and Tajikistan in the north, and Pakistan to the south, allowing the use of airfields and logistical bases by allied forces. The use of bases in countries that had been part of the old Soviet Union was, alone, an indicator of just how radically, and in what an astonishing manner, the world had changed.

As for the actual prosecution of the war, events unfolded at what seemed a remarkably relaxed pace. In sharp contrast to the fire and fury of Desert Storm ten years before, allied aircraft flew only a few sorties each day, though the strikes were spread out through both day and night. On October 8, U.S. aircraft struck a SAM site outside of Kandahar, a Taliban headquarters facility at Mazar-I-Sharif, and eleven other targets.

At the same time, C-17 transports began dropping food packages over southern Afghanistan. Washington was desperate to prove to a watching world that this assault was not aimed at Afghan civilians. A week later USSOCOM aircraft began bombarding the country with propaganda leaflets as well.

By that time, though, American and British pilots were already complaining that Afghanistan was not exactly what they would call a target-rich environment, that there simply weren't that many targets on the ground to attack. Afghanistan's air force—a handful of old Soviet aircraft, many grounded for lack of parts—was annihilated within the first few days. There was little industry, little in the way of military infrastructure, and, as one observer put it, from the air, all of the country's dusty, mud-brick buildings looked pretty much the same.

Ironically, the one region with plenty of tactical targets deliberately not being hit was in the north of the country, along the border between Taliban forces and the Northern Alliance. President Bush had struck a deal with Pakistan's President Musharraf, promising not to use tactical air strikes against Taliban troops facing the Northern Alliance. Pakistan's government feared that if alliance fighters broke through in the north and swept down to take Kabul, it would reignite the old Afghan civil war, a conflict that might well spread to the country's neighbors.

Ominously, though, the war appeared to be on the point of spreading in other ways. A Muslim car bomb exploded in India, killing thirty-eight Hindus. In response, on October 15, Indian artillery opened fire on Pakistani positions in Kashmir. The U.S. State Department was in a frenzy to keep the situation from spiraling out of control. With both Pakistan and India possessing nuclear weapons, all-out war would have disastrous consequences.

Then, October 17, Israel's Minister of Tourism, a seventy-five-year-old right-wing hardliner, was gunned down in a Jerusalem hotel, revenge by the Palestinian Popular Front for the Liberation of Palestine for the killing of a militant

Palestinian leader. Israeli aircraft began plastering Palestinian positions on the West Bank. In the former Soviet Union, Russia's President Putin began moving against Islamic fundamentalist rebels in Chechnya, confident, apparently, that the world would no longer criticize Russia's policies in that region while America was bombing Afghan cities.

And, perhaps most terrifying of all, by the seventeenth U.S. citizens were being confronted by the very real specter of terrorist bacteriological warfare. An envelope containing a mysterious white powder and a crudely hand-lettered note was sent to the offices of Senator Tom Daschle, on Capitol Hill. The note read:

> 09-11-01
> YOU CAN NOT STOP US.
> WE HAVE THIS ANTHRAX.
> YOU DIE NOW.
> ARE YOU AFRAID?
> DEATH TO AMERICA.
> DEATH TO ISRAEL.
> ALLAH IS GREAT.

Thirty-one staffers in Daschle's office tested positive for contact with anthrax and were treated with antibiotics. Similar letters arrived at NBC's news offices in New York, and at the office of New York City's Mayor Giuliani. Anthrax spores were found in a mail sorting facility in Boca Raton, Florida, while suspicious letters and powder turned up at Microsoft offices in Reno, Nevada, and in several other countries, including Canada, Australia, France, and Germany. Among those testing positive for contact with the disease was the seven-month-old child of an ABC producer who'd visited the network's offices three weeks earlier.

The following day a postal worker in New Jersey and an aide to CBS anchorman Dan Rather both tested positive for the skin form of anthrax, bringing the total number of confirmed infections to six and of people exposed to the disease to perhaps fifty. The Bayer Company in Germany promised the delivery of 200 million doses of Cipro, an antibiotic specific for anthrax, within three months.

The major question was whether this biological warfare was part of a concerted al-Qaeda plot, the actions of a small number of domestic terrorists working in sympathy with Islamic fundamentalists, or something even more sinister.

America's retaliation for 9/11 continued, however, the pace now accelerating. American special operations units landed at the airfields at Dalbandin and Samungli in Pakistan, preparing them as logistical centers for operations into southern Afghanistan. In the north, special operations forces out of Uzbekistan were now operating openly with Northern Alliance commanders.

Meanwhile, Taliban broadcasts continued to refuse to hand al-Qaeda leaders over to the United States and triumphantly announced that both bin Laden and the senior Taliban leadership had escaped the attacks unscathed. Al-Jazeera television aired a speech by an al-Qaeda spokesman, Sulaiman Bu Ghaith, who warned Americans and Britons—especially Muslims, children, and all who opposed U.S. policy—not to ride planes or live in tall buildings.

On October 18, U.S. Secretary of Defense Donald Rumsfeld held a press conference at the Pentagon, announcing that victory in Afghanistan would require putting troops on the ground as well as bombing terrorist targets from the air.

Those military and paramilitary U.S. forces already on the ground in Afghanistan busily prepared for the coming invasion.

Friday, October 19, 2001

Sixty Miles Southeast of Kandahar
Kandahar Province, Afghanistan
2246 hours, local time

HM2 David Tangretti leaned back against the all-too-familiar hardness of the narrow seat, eyes closed, listening to the roar of the MH-47E's twin rotors overhead. Somewhere below, lost in darkness, the rugged desert terrain was slipping away as the helicopter thundered north.

The helo was an Army bird, one of the 160th SOAR's Nightstalkers, specially fitted out for a deep-penetration raid. The aircraft's nickname was the Dark Horse, and with the MH-53 Pave Low, was one of the best means Special Forces had available for inserting covert operations teams deep into enemy territory. The sixteen combat operators on board were a mixed team of 1st Force Recon Marines and Navy SEALs, code-named Osprey. They'd been training together now for months, and especially in the month since 9/11—in the California desert and the waters off San Clemente, in Panama and in the sere mountains of Nevada—learning to work as a team.

Their objective was nothing less than the capture or death of Osama bin Laden.

"So why the hell did they change the name?" Marine Sergeant Daniel Moore said, shouting to be heard above the rotor noise. His face, like the face of all of the Osprey operators, was masked, except for the eyes, by his black balaclava. He wore a night vision monocular, pushed back off of his face, pointing at the cargo deck's overhead like an off-center, high-tech horn. "I kinda liked 'Infinite Justice.' "

"Where you been, Moore?" Tangretti shouted back, grinning. "If we called it 'Infinite Justice,' the Muslims get pissed off because only God is infinitely just. 'Enduring Freedom' is something we can give the Afghans . . . not justice."

The name change had come through all the way back on September 25. The president's use of it during his TV broadcast on October 7 had made it official.

"Screw that!" Moore slapped his weapon, an M4-A1 "close-quarters battle weapon," as the carbine was now known. "Me and Betsy, here, we are justice incarnate!"

"Roger that!" Navy Chief Nofi said. "We are the fucking hand of God, and if the raggies are that hot to meet Him, we are here to oblige!"

Tangretti didn't add that infinite *anything* made him uneasy. It was possible to have too much of a good thing, after all. Anyway, the name "Enduring Freedom" had a good feel to it: a good solid ring. He wondered how the people tasked with dreaming up new mission names coped with keeping everybody happy, though, given the current climate of political correctness.

But he did like the idea of justice. "Bring them to justice, or bring justice to them!" he called out. The president had used that line in one of his speeches recently.

"Ooh-rah!" and *"Hoo-yah!"* echoed through the aircraft.

Turning in his seat, Tangretti could look over his shoulder through one of the MH-47's circular windows. There was absolutely nothing to see, however. They were skimming across the desert at 160 miles per hour with no lights . . . without even a moon in the sky to illuminate the desert below.

Team Osprey, along with other SOCCOM special operations forces, had flown by military transport to Oman, then by Sea Stallion out to the USS *Kitty Hawk*, cruising with her battle group just outside of Pakistan's territorial waters, and finally, yesterday, to a desert airstrip at Dalbandin, Pakistan.

This evening, at Dalbandin, they'd loaded onto two waiting MH-47s, packing themselves in with their gear, weapons, and two Desert Patrol Vehicles, lifting off into the night sky a little over an hour ago. He checked his watch, tugging back the Velcro light shield to read the self-luminous dial. Damn. They ought to be nearly to the LZ.

The MH-47's crew chief signaled from the front of the aircraft. "Ten minutes!" he yelled.

Yup. Getting close.

Lieutenant Fred Driscoll stood up near the front of the cargo deck, just in front of the DPV parked and chocked just aft of the cockpit. "You heard the man! Check your equipment! Check your buddies!"

SEALs and Marines gave their gear and weapons a final check, then turned and tugged at buckles and harnesses on the men to either side. A loose strap could trip a man at a crucial moment. A weapon snagged on an "Irish pennant," as a dangling tie was known, could delay a shooter for a critical—and fatal—half second.

The routine was similar to that carried out just before a parachute jump. Tangretti was glad this wasn't a jump, though for a time the idea had been discussed and even planned for. Night jumps into unknown terrain were never taken lightly.

In fact, if all was going according to plan, a group of 199 U.S. Army Rangers would be leaping into the night from four MC-130 Combat Talon aircraft some miles to the west, southwest of Kandahar. Their job was to seize an airstrip, code-named Rhino, which would become the operational center for U.S. Marine and SOCCOM forces in the area.

Elsewhere, special ops teams including Delta Force and Navy SEALs were now infiltrating the area around Kandahar on MH-47 Dark Horses and MH-53M Pave Low helicopters. The assault planners were working from what they called the shopping list—twelve different places in the region where the

subjects of a much longer list, of Taliban and AQ HVTs, might
be hiding. Osama bin Laden. Khalid Shaikh Mohammed. Mohammed Omar. Abdul Wakil Motawakil. Ubaidullah Akhund.
Qari Ahmadullah.

A *very* long list.

The idea was for the Delta and SEAL operators to swoop
in just ahead of the Ranger assault at Objective Rhino,
search each of the suspect bases and encampments, and bag
any HVTs they could find.

He turned in his seat again, searching the darkness. The
second MH-47 was out there somewhere with the rest of the
team and the other DPV, but he couldn't see it.

BM1 Randy Fletcher was squeezed in next to him, on his
right. "What's the matter, Tad? Nervous?" he asked.

"Screw you, Grandpa." Fletch had been ribbing him about
getting busted to second class, calling him "Newbie" and
"Tad," for "tadpole," the slang for BUD/S recruits. He, of
course had replied in kind.

"Don't sweat it. Nail Li'l bin Laden tonight and you just
might get your stripe back. Of course . . . that's assuming I
don't get to him first!"

"What, are you bucking for CPO?"

" 'Chief Fletch.' Yeah, I kinda like the sound of that."

"In your dreams, Gramps."

"So," RM2 Lawrence Karr said. "Whatcha guys wanna bet
Nighthawk's nowhere to be found and we're on a dry hump?"

"Bite your tongue, Kiddy," Chief Nofi said from his seat
in the back of the DPV. "That son of a bitch's got the landing
beacon. If we land and he's *not* waiting for us . . . guess who
has the beacon instead?"

"Five minutes, people!" This from Sergeant Major Drake,
the team's senior enlisted man. "Check your NVDs!"

Tangretti looked at the faces of the other men squeezed
into the thirty-foot length of the Dark Horse's cargo com-

partment, almost half of which was taken up by the thirteen and a half feet of the DPV. Many—not all, but many—were combat-hardened; like him, veterans of Desert Storm. Those who hadn't seen combat, though, had still been through the toughest combat training anywhere in the world. The expressions on their faces registered various emotions—boredom, excitement, introspection, premission banter, taut waiting—but all looked confident and *ready*.

He reached up and pulled his NVD down over his face, adjusting his balaclava around it. The unit was a monocular AN/PVS-14 Night Vision Device, which could be handheld, mounted to a face mask or helmet, or attached to his weapon. By wearing a monocular over his right eye—his shooter's eye—instead of a full set of night-vision goggles, he left the other eye free. All of the Osprey team members were clad completely in black, from balaclavas and CQB harnesses to Nomex pants and boots.

"One minute out! Pilot says he's acquired the beacon! Stand by!"

Those last sixty seconds dwindled away with unexpected speed.

He felt the Dark Horse slow, then turn slightly to the left. This was the touchy part, the moment when you found out if the enemy had known you were coming and was waiting for you with antiaircraft missiles, ZSUs, heavy machine guns, and RPGs. There was nothing more vulnerable than an incoming helicopter loaded with troops. The special danger in an op like this one was that the pathfinders—the guys out there guiding you in to the LZ—had been captured. If the enemy knew when and where the helos were coming in, maybe even what passwords and call signs to use . . .

It was better not to think too much about that.

The ramp was already lowering as the MH-47 drifted toward the ground. "Go-go-go-go!" Driscoll was shouting, waving them on. Bent almost double beneath his massive pack, Tangretti fell into line and moved aft, trotting down the ramp and dropping the last step to the gravel. He cut to the right, just like in the practice simulations, running hard, legs pumping, then threw himself down flat, his H&K MP5-A2 searching the darkness. Behind him the DPV revved its four-cylinder engine and lurched forward.

There was no sign of a waiting enemy. In the distance, the second MH-47 couched down, ramp lowering. Around him the rest of the team completed the defensive perimeter, with the Desert Patrol Vehicle and its three-man crew taking up its station in the middle. At his back, the helicopter barely lingered after the last man cleared the ramp before lifting again into the night and banking toward the south. A moment later the second Dark Horse lifted off as well, leaving the team on the ground.

They had plenty of air support still, however. It was too high to be heard, but somewhere out there was a Specter gunship.

The thought was remarkably comforting, now that they were down and alone in the night.

Well, not quite alone. Through the green glow of his night-vision monocular, Tangretti could see a lone man approaching them, hands up. "Osprey!" he heard over his M-biter headset. "Nighthawk!"

"New York!" Lieutenant Driscoll snapped, a challenge.

"Payback!" came the response. A moment later the man entered Osprey's circle.

He seemed an unlikely sort of person for an encounter such as this—short, not fat, exactly, but not lean and training honed either. He wore night-vision goggles and an incongruous black cowboy hat and was chewing on an unlit cigar.

Nighthawk, Tangretti knew from the mission briefing, was a

CIA officer—one of dozens who'd been operating in-country for the past month. He would have already scouted this area, hooked up with friendly locals, chosen the landing zone, and used an infrared landing beacon to guide in the MH-47s.

"Welcome to Afghanistan, boys!" Nighthawk said.

Driscoll stood up and shook the man's hand. "Lieutenant Driscoll. Osprey team."

"Name's Dugan," the man said, grinning. "Sean Dugan, but y'all can call me 'Tex.' I'm with the Company."

The man's casual attitude was a bit unnerving, Tangretti thought, completely out of place out here in the Afghan desert.

He just hoped to hell this CIA cowboy knew what he was doing.

West of Zur Kowt Training Camp
Paktia Province, Afghanistan
2259 hours, local time

"This," Raptor said with heartfelt sincerity, "has all of the makings of a cluster fuck."

Mariacher had to agree. The two SEALs had worked their way as far forward as they could, but the path—which Abdul insisted was the only way around the Zur Kowt camp—was occupied at the moment by a ZSU, a Zenitnaya Samokhodnaya Ustanovka, which was Russian for Antiaircraft Self-Propelled Gun.

Not good.

"Where the hell did it come from?" Mariacher asked.

"Kabul, probably. That's where most of the Taliban's heavy stuff is . . . there, or up on the northern front. Someone here must've got nervous and brought the thing down for antiair support."

The ZSU had originally been a Soviet weapon, the Shilka

ZSU-23-4. It had a squat, round turret mounted atop a PT-76 chassis, with four 23mm cannon quad-mounted in the turret. An unknown number had been captured by the victorious mujahideen after the Russians abandoned the country.

Though primarily an antiaircraft weapon, those cannon were deadly against infantry, and lightly armored or unarmored vehicles as well; able to engage targets, while stationary or moving, out to a range of perhaps three kilometers.

"Soviet tactical doctrine deployed those things in pairs," Mariacher said, "two hundred meters apart. Think there's another one?"

"I doubt it. The muj aren't keen on Russian doctrine, and they don't have that many Shilkas. Besides . . . where the hell else are they going to put one?"

Raptor had a point. The Shilka completely blocked the narrow road—hardly more than a goat path—that had led the SEALs up the south face of the mountain. The road continued across the top of the ridge and off toward the northern slope. The ground was rugged—all boulders and cliff and even some patches of snow from a brief shower the night before. Unless another ZSU was set up on the east side of the Zur Kowt ravine a mile or so away, which seemed unlikely, this one was unsupported.

Unsupported by more armor, that is. Through night-vision binoculars Mariacher could see several dark-turbaned gunmen sitting on top of the sandbags that walled in the ZSU's position. He couldn't tell whether they were Taliban or al-Qaeda, but they were armed—one held an RPG—and there were undoubtedly more of them out there, well hidden. Their beards were shorter than most Taliban wore them; they were probably either AQ or foreign jihadists, volunteers from Pakistan or, possibly, from the former Soviet SSRs to the north.

Mariacher pulled back behind the boulder sheltering them. "They've got a sweet position," he said. "Overhead camouflage too. I'll bet they set up there hoping our aircraft would hit the training camp."

"That's what it looks like to me," Raptor said, continuing to study the enemy position through his binoculars.

The Shilka was emplaced behind a horseshoe barricade of sandbags, and had layers of camouflage netting stretched overhead, held above the massive Gun Dish radar by wooden poles. It was positioned on top of the mountain immediately west of the deep, steep-sided ravine that sheltered Zur Kowt. Some facilities—mud-brick buildings, gun emplacements, and what looked like a firing range—were located on the ravine's floor, on either side of the road running from Khowst, to the south, up the mountain pass north toward Kabul. Other structures appeared to be built into the sides of the ravine, and the SEALs had already spotted and marked a number of cave entrances.

This whole region was riddled by caves and whole cavern systems. The base they could see was a fair-sized one; what they couldn't see, hidden underground, was probably much larger.

"We won't be able to get behind them, Mark," he said. "The back door is going to be wide open."

The Gray Ghost component of Task Force 5 had been in the area for several days now, reconnoitering, marking target positions with their GPS units, and transmitting tactical information back to the World. Raptor and the four SEALs had hooked up once more with Abdul and his anti-Taliban fighters. And, together with the Pentagon mission coordinators—code-named Mother Goose—they'd begun to formulate a plan.

Tonight, the night of October 19 and 20, U.S. special ops forces were staging a massive raid. Most of it was aimed at targets in the area around Kandahar, a little less than three hundred miles to the southwest, but Task Force 5 and the

Gray Ghosts were hoping to take part as well. Intelligence provided by Abdul and his people suggested, with a very high reliability, that Khalid Shaikh Mohammed and Qari Ahmadullah both were holed up at Zur Kowt.

There was a singular difficulty with this objective, however. Zur Kowt was a village located in a mountain pass, running northwest-southeast through the mountains between Khowst and Gardez. A mostly paved road—rare for Afghanistan—actually connected the two cities, albeit by a winding, indirect route.

Which meant that if Task Force 5 and their anti-Taliban allies came charging up from the south, Mohammed and any other HVTs in the Zur Kowt camp would simply hightail it out of town toward the north.

Abdul had promised the SEALs that there was a way to sneak around behind the enemy base, bypassing the mountain ravine by using a smuggler's track unknown to anyone but the locals. Two of the SEALs, plus a small band of mujahideen fighters, could sneak around the camp and position themselves to ambush anyone fleeing toward the north.

Unfortunately, the ZSU was completely blocking the trail. As Mariacher had already observed, its position suggested that it wasn't deliberately blocking the path so much as it was lying in ambush for American aircraft. Bombers, helicopter gunships, even cruise missiles attacking the camp would have to fly up the ravine from the southeast. The Shilka was in a perfect position to shoot down any attacker that got within three kilometers of the place. Its radar—code-named Gun Dish by NATO—was superb, and would even let it successfully engage something as small as a cruise missile.

"We can take it out," Mariacher said, thinking aloud. Back at their camp outside of Khowst they had a couple of M136-

AT4 rocket launchers. An 84mm rocket would make short work of a ZSU.

"Yeah, and as soon as we do, we give away the game," Raptor pointed out. Destroying the Shilka would alert every Taliban and terrorist fighter in the area. Certainly, an assault team wouldn't be able to kill the Shilka and then make it into position northeast of Zur Kowt in time to catch any HVT runners.

Alternatively, they could try to sneak up and take out the Shilka quietly. That was not an appetizing idea. Those AQ gunmen were there precisely to prevent such an attempt, and the vehicle commander would be in radio contact with his base. There was no way to guarantee getting close enough to take out all of the bad guys with silenced weapons—including those buttoned up inside the vehicle—without having the base alerted.

It seemed an insoluble problem.

"Let's get back to camp," Raptor said. "We need to consult with Mother Goose."

Silently, they backed away from their hiding place and began making their way back down the steep path through the darkness.

Zur Kowt Training Camp
Paktia Province, Afghanistan
2312 hours, local time

Davlot Iskanderov stepped outside the concrete-reinforced entrance to the main cave. Ventilators kept the air moving inside, but the cavern interior was always so close, so stinking of human sweat, urine, garlic, onion, and the spicy *sambosa* sauce these people loved to ladle over their lamb. He drew in a deep breath, enjoying the clean, cold mountain air.

It was quiet. That, of itself, made him uneasy. So far, Zur Kowt had been spared the American air strikes that had been blasting Afghanistan for the past thirteen days, but every day there'd been the rumble of bomb and cruise missile strikes across the valley, at Zhawar Kili, and beyond the mountains to the northwest, in the area around Gardez. Tonight there was nothing—nothing within earshot, at any rate. The Americans certainly hadn't given up.

He glanced up at the mountainside overlooking the valley to the west. He couldn't see it, but somewhere up there the Shilka he'd ordered brought down from Kabul lay in wait. If the Americans did get around to trying an air assault on Zur Kowt, they were in for a very nasty surprise. He had people up there with Stinger antiaircraft missiles too, as well as heavy machine-gun emplacements on both sides of the pass. Any pilot trying to make a bombing run would be tracked by the Shilka's radar and handily brought down by fire from half a dozen hidden positions.

Overall, the Afghan defense was holding well. The Northern Alliance had made no headway at all during these past two weeks, even with the American air effort, which, weirdly, had been deployed at targets everywhere in the country *except* the northern front. Strategically, it made no sense at all, and that meant there was almost certainly politics behind it.

That could only be to the Taliban's advantage.

In fact, Taliban morale had been increasing, if not soaring. After almost two weeks, they were as strong as ever—stronger, actually, with the influx of foreign volunteers. The Americans, so feared after the demonstration of their resolve and technical prowess ten years ago in Kuwait, were proving to be a paper tiger after all.

It was possible they would keep up the air attacks for another week or two, then declare that they had punished the Taliban enough and go home.

But Iskanderov didn't believe that for a moment.

They're coming, he thought. And they'll be coming in a night like this . . . when it's quiet and the men are off their guard.

He wondered. Should he sound an alert, just in case? He didn't want to sap the men's wills through too many false alarms.

Still, a middle-of-the-night exercise, a drill, wouldn't hurt, and it might help.

He was definitely feeling uneasy.

Yes, a drill would be just the thing, and maybe a patrol or two, probing down the valley toward Khowst. . . .

Chapter 20

Hada Compound
Fifty Miles Southeast of Kandahar,
Kandahar Province, Afghanistan
0015 hours, local time

By Tangretti's watch, it was just past midnight. It had taken them an hour to get sorted out and moving—twenty-four SEALs and Force Recon Marines, along with about thirty anti-Taliban militia and Tex Dugan all crowded into six ancient, fume-belching Zil army trucks. The two DPVs had already been deployed ahead with the remaining six Ospreys, reconnoitering the ground leading up to the eastern edge of the Hada Hills.

The Hada Hills—the Afghans called them De Hadi Ghar—were a cluster of hills and eroded valleys rising some nine hundred meters above the surrounding plain. Kandahar was located at the northeastern edge of an enormous, flat desert plateau known generically as Rigestan. North, lay the towering, snowcapped peaks of the Shah Maqsud Range; south, the lower but still rugged Kwaja Amran Range, part of the chain of mountain ranges and ridges along the border with Pakistan.

Between the two lay a series of valleys running toward the northeast all the way to the cities of Ghazni and Gardez, and almost the whole way to mountain-locked Kabul. The De Hadi Ghar rested in the mouth of that valley passage, isolated and insular, fifty miles southeast of Kandahar. At the eastern end of the Hada Hills, tucked away on top of a broad, flat ridge overlooking a paved road running southwest toward Chaman and the Kojack Pass, just over the border into Pakistan, lay Objective Gazelle, a fair-sized walled compound believed to be one of several used by both Mohammed Omar and by bin Laden himself. Tangretti had studied satellite photos of the place. The walls enclosed a small village—eight or ten buildings, some of which were quarters, some storage facilities, some, possibly, classrooms or training areas. There was also a mosque, and several low guard towers overlooking the surrounding valley.

What he didn't know was why they were going in this way, from a distance, and on foot. Or, rather, he knew why the planners had done it this way. The question was, *why?* Objective Gazelle looked like a perfect target for a Son Tay operation—so named for the POW-rescue raid launched by Army Special Forces outside of Hanoi in 1972. In that op, helicopters swooped in and touched down inside the compound, delivering their load of raiders with stunning surprise and ferocity.

The powers-that-were, however, had wanted to use local assets. That meant hooking up with Nighthawk and his tame mujahideen first, and that had to take place far enough away from the objective so the bad guys didn't see or hear the helicopters coming.

Tangretti questioned whether they needed the mujahideen on this op. How much of that was practical and how much political? There was a lot of scuttlebutt back at Coronado about how paranoid the Defense Department was about American casualties. They wanted this to be a surgically clean and neat war, most of it fought from the air, and with

their anti-Taliban surrogates doing most of the actual muck-
ing about with the enemy on the ground.

Wars were rarely neat. This one certainly wasn't going to
be. The Secretary of Defense had finally admitted the other
day that ground troops would have to go in, and all Tangretti
and his fellow SEALs had to say about that was: "About
freaking time!" Most of the effort would be expended in the
north, alongside the troops of the Northern Alliance, but
USSOCOM had decided that a lightning, large-scale raid in
the south, at Kandahar and a few other select locations on
the shopping list, offered U.S. forces their best hope of nabbing bin Laden and his cronies before a major ground war
drove them all underground.

Lieutenant Driscoll, sitting on the bench opposite Tangretti, was trying to talk with one of the mujahideen fighters
through his Phraselator. He held the PDA-sized device up to
his mouth, pressed the touch screen and said, clearly, "How
much longer?" Pressing another point on the touch screen
made the device spit out a brief, barking phrase in Pashto.

The effect among the several mujahideen fighters was elec-
trifying. All of them wanted to have a look at the talking box
and try it out. Only with difficulty was Driscoll able to get one
of them to actually answer the question . . . which it then trans-
lated into English. "Five minutes. Maybe ten. God willing."

And they still wanted to examine the translator.

The Phraselator was a neat gadget. Tangretti and the other
Ospreys had trained with it back in California. It had been
invented, actually, by a team led by former Navy SEAL Ace
Sarich, and was being developed by Applied Data Systems,
using voice-recognition software from Voxtec. Its memory
included between five hundred and fifteen hundred phrases,
in as many as ten different languages. The units issued to the
Osprey team could recognize and translate phrases in
Pashto, Dari, Urdu, and Arabic. Besides being stocked with

useful phrases you weren't likely to find in a Berlitz language guide—like "Stop or I'll shoot"—it was intended to help battlefield medics and doctors treat Afghan wounded, and for troops faced with mass surrenders, like those that had caused such logistical problems during Desert Storm.

So far as Tangretti was concerned, the Phraselator could have been straight out of *Star Trek*. The technology certainly seemed like pure magic to the Pashtun tribesmen riding on the truck.

Ten minutes to the objective? How close were they going to go in by truck? Too close and the element of surprise would be lost. Too far and Osprey could spend the rest of the night hiking around in the desert.

He got his answer a few minutes later when the line of trucks pulled over to the side of the road and lurched to a halt. The DPVs were waiting up ahead. They'd found a path up the ridge that would bring the strike force onto the crest right below the target compound's east wall.

Half an hour later Tangretti lay on his stomach, southeast of the compound, studying the objective through night-vision binoculars. The compound itself was hidden behind the nine-foot wall that completely encircled the place. He could see a single gate in the south wall, which appeared to be standing open. He knew from satellite photos that there was a north gate as well, but he couldn't see it from here. He saw no guards; not by the gate, and not in the squat guard tower that barely rose higher than the southeast corner of the wall.

The place looked deserted. No lights. No fires. No noise. No movement.

"What now, Wheel?" he asked Driscoll over the tactical channel. "We go up and ring the doorbell?"

"Teams of four," Driscoll's voice replied softly in his ears. "You guys know the drill. Just like we rehearsed it. Fireteams Bravo and Charlie, take the south wall. Alfa will

hit the south gate. Delta, Echo, Foxtrot, over the east wall.
Golf and Hotel, you have overwatch. Everyone stay low, stay
out of sight. Do not engage until the order is given."

"This is Nighthawk. What about my people?"

"Stay put. Keep an eye on the north gate and don't let
anybody leave. Move when we tell you to. Everybody clear?
Okay. Now . . . *go!*"

Tangretti was in Fireteam Delta, along with Fletch and
two Marines: Gunnery Sergeant Eakins and Sergeant Tomajczk. Silently, they moved forward, angling toward the east
wall. The ground was broken here, with plenty of large boulders and stunted, twisted trees to provide cover. The builders
of the fortresslike compound had wanted to keep an eye on
the road running through the valley below, not the ground
immediately surrounding the compound, so it was a fairly
simple evolution to reach the wall unseen.

Once there, Eakins and Fletch stood face-to-face, gloved
hands linked. Tomajczk planted his boot on the proffered
step, grabbed the top of the wall, and chinned himself up.

"Delta Three, on the east wall," they heard over their radios. A moment later a rope uncoiled down the nine-foot
wall. Tangretti grabbed it, placed a boot against the bricks of
the inward-sloping wall, and started climbing.

"Fox Two," he heard. "On the wall."

"Bravo on the south wall. All clear."

"Echo One, on the wall."

"Alfa, at the gate. One tango in sight."

So there *was* someone home. Tangretti had begun wondering if the compound was deserted.

"Charlie, in position."

Tangretti reached the top and rolled over onto the parapet.
The wall was about three feet wide at the top, wider at the
base, and had a walkway inside, where Tomajczk had braced
himself, boots to the wall, holding the line.

As Fletch started up the wall, Tangretti took a careful look around. Through his monocular he caught a glimpse of something . . . yes! In the nearest watchtower, at the southeast corner of the wall, he could make out the turbaned head of a man, just visible inside. He appeared to be hunkered down inside the guard tower, which was about six feet square but only rose about four feet above the rest of the wall and was invisible from the ground. The muzzle of a weapon stuck up vertically beside him. He appeared to be asleep.

"Delta Four," he said, identifying himself. "I'm on the wall. I have one tango in the southeast tower. Looks like he's asleep."

"Delta Four, Alfa One," he heard Driscoll's voice. "Copy. Take him out."

"Copy."

Leaving his H&K slung over his shoulder, Tangretti drew his Mark 11 SIG Sauer and carefully worked the slide, chambering a round, then thumbing off the safety. The tango was about fifteen yards away . . . a long shot for a pistol. Tangretti decided to move all the way up to the tower, to take down the guard at point-blank range and make sure there wasn't another guard inside with the first.

He'd only covered a third of the distance, however, when a long burst of automatic fire opened up from the north wall, shattering the nighttime silence.

An instant later other weapons joined in, all from the north side of the compound, accompanied by yells and a weird, high-voiced ululation: a tribal battle cry. The tango in the guard tower leaped to his feet, fumbling with the PKM machine gun beside him. He was looking toward the north gate, past Tangretti and to his right, and didn't appear to have seen the SEAL, now only ten yards away.

Tangretti had no choice. Bracing his pistol in two hands, he dropped into a firing stance and squeezed off three silent rounds. The tango staggered backward into the tower's parapet, hands clawing at his throat. Tangretti advanced, firing twice more as he moved, putting both rounds into the man's skull.

He vaulted the low wall into the guard tower. The dead guard was alone, sprawled against one side with the machine gun beside him. "Delta Four! One tango down, southeast tower! I'm in the tower!"

"Copy, Delta Four. Provide cover fire."

"Roger that!"

He heard shouting in Pashto from beneath his feet. A wooden trapdoor in the guard tower floor suddenly flew up; Tangretti put two rounds into the head that emerged. Then, as the second tango dropped clear, he pulled out one of the two fragmentation grenades he was carrying, yanked the pin, and sent the small iron sphere down the opening before kicking the trapdoor shut.

There was a loud, ringing blast and the door snapped open again. He kicked it shut once more, then picked up the PKM, which was propped up against the inside of the tower wall.

The weapon had a bipod on the muzzle, and was belt-fed from a 250-round metal box at his feet. He dropped the bipod onto the tower wall, dragged the bolt back, checked the safety, and began looking for targets. He first checked the other tower, at the northwest corner of the compound, but could see no activity there at all. Near the center of the compound, however, two men emerged from a long, low building, both carrying AKs. He dropped the muzzle of the PKM, but before he could get them in his sights, one of the men stumbled and fell, followed an instant later by the second.

"Charlie One! Two tangos down, center compound!"

"Alfa One! One tango down, south gate. We're coming through."

He glanced at the south gate but couldn't see the Ospreys of

Fireteam Alfa. They would be sticking to the shadows as much as possible, not charging headlong through the open gate.

But that appeared to be exactly what was happening at the opposite side of the compound. Half a dozen men were streaming through the north gate, firing wildly, their AKs on full auto. Tangretti couldn't see what they were shooting at—he doubted they had a clear target. They were simply emptying their magazines into buildings, walls, the air, and, for all he could see, each other.

Damn it all!

More mujahideen fighters came through the gate, and Tangretti could see Tex Dugan now, striding forward in his incongruous black cowboy hat and night-vision goggles, carrying an M4-A1. The anti-Taliban Afghans were already moving from building to building, breaking in, then emerging, sometimes with one or more people stumbling ahead of them with arms held high, more often alone.

The whole fight was over in less than five minutes. Some of the SEALs and Marines began assembling on a broad field near the compound's center. There were a number of prisoners—fifteen of them, men and women both—who were found inside various buildings in the compound. None had been armed. In fact, all were wearing long nightshirts or gowns, which appeared to be sleepwear. It was possible they were all civilians who just happened to be living here, though the team would take no chances. They shoved and prodded them all into two rows, kneeling, hands behind their heads, while Fletcher and a Marine staff sergeant began using plastic zip-ties to secure their hands behind their backs. Several of the women were sobbing, and all of them, men and women both, appeared terrified and dazed. Dugan and one of his mujahideen began roughly searching the prisoners one at a time, eliciting shrill cries from the women and harsh, rapid-fire protests from the men.

Driscoll stormed toward the group, furious.

"What the fucking hell were you thinking of, mister?" he bellowed at a startled Tex. "What do you mean charging in like that?"

"Do *not* speak to me in that tone of voice, *mister!*" the CIA officer shouted back. "This is my operation!"

"And *I* am in tactical command! Your failure to control your locals alerted the enemy before we were ready, and could have cost us lives, not to mention the mission!"

"Look, Lieutenant," Dugan said, apparently backing down. "It was a misunderstanding. A mistranslation, that's all! I told Faisel to wait until we got the command to go. He thought I said to go . . . and his men started running and shooting before I could stop them. I had no choice except to go with it, okay?"

"*Not* okay," Driscoll said. "Either keep your men under control or get the hell out of *my* operation!" He pointed at the kneeling prisoners. "Also, you will *not* touch the prisoners!"

"Searching prisoners is an intelligence operation, damn it! That's *my* job!"

For a moment Tangretti thought the SEAL lieutenant was going to deck the CIA man, but a sudden burst of automatic gunfire echoed through the compound. SEALs, Marines, and mujahideen scattered, some dropping to the ground, others ducking for cover. The shots were coming from up high, from the direction of the minaret that rose beside the compound's mosque.

"Shooter!" Eakins called over the tactical channel. "Shooter in the minaret!"

"Bravo One," another voice said. "I've got him."

A single sharp, ringing crack interrupted the chatter of an AK firing full-auto, and instantly the minaret was silent again.

"Tangretti! Fletcher! Check that damned mosque!" Driscoll was glaring at Dugan, because several of the anti-Taliban mujahideen had entered the mosque, then emerged moments later. Clearly, they hadn't carried out a thorough search.

"Aye aye, sir!" Tangretti snapped. "C'mon, Fletch."

They entered the dark mosque carefully, rolling through the open doorway one at a time. Tangretti saw one pair of boots sitting just outside the door, and remembered having read somewhere that good Muslims took off their shoes before stepping into a mosque's holy grounds. Did that mean only one shooter inside?

Or only one shooter who was a good Muslim?

The building appeared completely deserted, however. A spiraling staircase ran up the minaret tower, accessed through a door in the back of the building. Weapons at their shoulders, the two SEALs leapfrogged cautiously up the stairs, around and around, and finally emerged at the top, in a narrow box with four large windows. Two loudspeakers were mounted on the walls, through which the muezzin could call the faithful to prayer.

A bearded man lay on the floor next to his AK-47, barefoot, a quarter-sized hole directly above his right eye, and the back of his head missing. There was a lot of blood and brain splattered across the walls and floor.

"Delta Four," he called. "Tango is dead. Minaret is secure." He then added, "Great shot, Bravo One!"

Bravo One was Staff Sergeant Benjamin McConnell, one of two Marine snipers attached to Osprey. His position had been on the south wall west of the gate, where he could cover the rest of the assault.

The next half hour was spent thoroughly searching the entire compound, going through each building. They were searching for more holdouts, but were also on the lookout for maps, papers, computers, notebooks . . . anything that might yield useful operational intelligence.

There wasn't a lot. One building on the north side appeared to have been the headquarters. There was a radio on a table inside, and a separate office with desk and chairs. On the walls were several garishly colored posters featuring Osama bin Laden's face, together with crudely drawn cartoons of skyscrapers with passenger planes crashing into them. Tangretti couldn't read the Arabic script but could guess the tone of the message.

There was a filing cabinet against one wall. Alert for the possibility of booby traps, the team pulled the drawers open from across the room, using lengths of stiff wire, but it was empty. So were the desk drawers. In fact, it looked like the place had been cleaned out in something of a hurry.

In the end they had five dead AQ fighters and fifteen prisoners. Nine of the prisoners were male, and some, possibly all, were also AQ or Taliban. To judge by the nightshirts and nightgowns, all appeared to have been sleeping when the assault went down. Searching them posed something of an embarrassing political problem. The men were stripped, then kept lying facedown on the ground; the women were approached in a more genteel fashion, quickly but carefully patted down from neck to ankles, checking for weapons or documents that might be hidden under their gowns. Within this culture, Tangretti thought, with their strict views on body and sexual taboos, body searches were akin to rape, but there was nothing that could be done about that. However, none had weapons or papers or other identification on them. They segregated the prisoners, male and female, in two carefully searched buildings, and kept them under guard. They would be flown out and back to Dalbandin for interrogation.

"Osprey, this is Rat One." The radioed voice was Chief Nofi's, coming from one of the two desert patrol vehicles still somewhere outside the compound walls.

"Rat One, Osprey One," Driscoll replied. "Go."

"We got company, Wheel. Looks like seven trucks and a

couple of technicals, on the main road from Big K. ETA . . .
thirty minutes."

"Roger that, Rat One. Keep them under surveillance. Enterprise, Enterprise, this is Osprey. Do you copy?"

"Osprey, Enterprise," a new voice replied. "Go ahead."

"We have a target for you, Enterprise." Driscoll described
the convoy Nolfi had reported. Nolfi broke in when he was
done, giving precise GPS Plugger coordinates, bearing, and
range.

"C'mon," Driscoll said. "We should be able to see from
the north wall."

A few minutes later several of the team's members, a
handful of mujahideen, and Tex Dugan all stood on the compound's northern wall. To the northwest, a faint glow could
be seen against the sky, possibly the lights of Kandahar—
"Big K"—and possibly fires from the Ranger assault, which
must be under way by now. There were no other lights, no
sign of anything moving in the night.

"What are we looking for?" Dugan asked.

"Tell your muj to keep watching out that way," Driscoll
replied. "I want them to see this."

"Osprey, Enterprise. Target acquired. Enterprise locked
and loaded."

"Roger that, Enterprise," Driscoll said. "Take 'em down!"

"Firing phasers."

A solid bar of intense, orange-white light sprang into
view, reaching from the sky at a forty-five-degree angle
down to the ground. A moment later two lesser streams of
fire snapped on as well, from close alongside the first beam,
intermittently flickering and converging with the solid beam.

The unfamiliar sight startled the mujahideen fighters on
the wall. They jabbered to one another in Pashto, and several
pointed in excitement.

The beams moved together, the upper end drifting through

the sky, the part on the ground apparently anchored in place. The display, several miles off, was completely soundless. Only a few seconds later did they hear anything—a sharp, far-off buzz-saw sound, followed by a hollow rumble.

Explosions flashed and flared on the ground. The ground end of those light beams was moving now, sweeping from left to right. More explosions flashed, like strobe lights going off, and several fires could be seen, burning brightly against the dark.

"Enterprise" was one of the AC-130U Specter gunships assigned to the Kandahar raid. Based on a four-turboprop C-130 transport, Specter carried a 40mm cannon, a 105mm howitzer, and a 25mm high-speed Gatling gun, all mounted on its port side like the side-firing cannon of a nineteenth-century man-o'-war.

The bright beam of light—a cascade of tracers from the Gatling gun firing so quickly they blurred into a single ray—certainly had the appearance of some sort of death ray from a science-fiction movie. The cannon fire, while rapid, still appeared as distinct shots, but the watchers could see each round flashing from the sky to the ground one after the other, erupting in bright, snapping bursts on the ground. An orange fireball was rising now from the ground, as fuel or an ammunition store exploded and burned.

After a few seconds the death ray and cannon fire ceased. "Osprey, Enterprise," came the dry voice. "Target destroyed."

"Roger that, Enterprise. Thanks for the assist."

"Don't mention it. We're here when you need us. Enterprise out."

By now the excitement among the Afghan tribesmen was spreading, as several of the mujahideen on the wall hurried down to talk in agitated tones to their kinsmen below. That display of American firepower and technology had certainly had an effect on them.

"Might help morale a bit," Driscoll explained, watching. "And maybe it will get them to take our orders seriously!"

"Don't count on it, Lieutenant," Gunnery Sergeant Eakins said. "We can't trust 'em. No discipline."

"We work with what we've got," Driscoll replied. "Okay people! Finish up with the document search! I'm calling in our ride out of this hole!"

Hole, Tangretti reflected, was right. A dry hole.

Their search for IIVTs at Objective Gazelle had come up dead empty.

Saturday, October 20, 2001

South of Zur Kowt Training Camp
Paktia Province, Afghanistan
0219 hours, local time

"So, when the hell are we supposed to hear something?" Raptor said.

Mariacher shrugged. The two were in the camo-netted hole that was serving as the Ghosts' HQ and communications center, hidden away among the rocks and boulders in the valley below Zur Kowt.

"Mother Goose just said to sit tight," Mariacher replied. This felt uncomfortably like the situation in Kuala Lumpur— watching an enemy target with a wide-open back door and orders to just watch and do nothing. *Wait one.*

"They can sit tight on this and rotate," Raptor snapped, holding up his thumb. "Those people have their heads so far up their asses they use their belly buttons as navel observatories."

"Roger that. Shall I call them again?"

"Nah. When they want us to do something, I'm sure

they'll tell us . . . and yell about how we're late and screwing up the schedule."

Down the hill and to the right a truck rattled up the Zur Kowt valley road. From here, through his night-vision goggles, he could see eight or ten Afghans in the back, all armed. The vehicle was followed a moment later by a "technical"—a civilian pickup truck outfitted with an RPD machine gun pintel-mounted in the back, with three riders. Technicals had first been encountered in Somalia, where the warlords had used them as cheap, light armor. The Afghans appeared to have picked up the idea . . . possibly through the al-Qaedas, who'd been operating out of Somalia at the time.

The two vehicles, obviously either Taliban or AQ, drove past the Gray Ghost position and vanished up the road, toward Zur Kowt.

The Gray Ghosts were positioned at the bottom of the valley, just west of the road, in a stretch of rugged terrain that descended in boulders and escarpments down from the mountains and onto the northern rim of the plain around Khowst. The other three SEALs were all about thirty yards uphill, behind the low, stone walls that marked the foundations of a cluster of long-vanished buildings, probably burned during the Russian war. Abdul and about fifty mujahideen fighters were with them, hunkered down and clearly impatient with the delay.

Mariacher was close to declaring the mission a wash. They could not charge straight up the valley into the teeth of the defenses they knew must be in place up there. And they couldn't go around—not by any path known to the local mujahideen, at any rate.

The only alternatives appeared to be trying to find another path over the mountains, having the SEALs try to work their way up the valley silently and without triggering any alarms, or breaking off and retreating.

Mariacher didn't like the idea of just giving up. Damn it, Khalid Shaikh Mohammed was up there. Abdul had told them that the AQ leader was seen at Zur Kowt just yesterday.

Green Tiger. He *wanted* that man. . . .

The question was whether Mother Goose was going to come up with a new idea, and with time enough before sunrise that they had half a chance of pulling it off. The next question was whether Mother Goose could come up with something viable. Running an op like this one—long distance, micromanaging things from the Pentagon basement—was a scary thought to any experienced field operative. Like General Beckwith, the Army Special Forces commander during the hostage-rescue attempt in Iran, Mariacher retained the right—one not written in any set of orders or regulations—to develop "communications difficulty" if he didn't like the orders. President Carter had been micromanaging Eagle's Claw from the White House basement, ordering Beckwith to proceed with the mission after it had already turned sour.

Only the commander on the ground, in the thick of things, could best judge what was possible . . . and what was not.

In fact, if Mother Goose didn't get back to him within the next ten minutes—

Gunfire ripped through the night, a clattering racket of AKs fired full-auto.

Mariacher exchanged a despairing glance with Raptor. "I'll go check," Raptor said. He slipped out from under the netting and was gone.

"Gray Ghosts!" Mariacher called over the tactical channel. "Ghost Leader! Sitrep!"

"Ghost Leader, Ghost Three!" Bradley replied. "Looks like a raghead patrol, coming down the valley. Our muj opened up before we could stop 'em!"

Mariacher sighed. "Copy. On my way."

It promised to be a *very* long night.

Chapter 21

Mariacher reached the defensive perimeter as gunfire crackled and snapped through the night. There was a sudden flash from overhead, and then a pair of flares hung in the night sky like savage white stars.

Bradley and Osterlee knelt behind a stone wall, loosing short, controlled bursts at the enemy as they showed themselves—turbaned figures in mismatched uniforms moving in the harsh light of the flares fifty meters beyond the wall. Mariacher saw one figure scrambling up on top of a house-sized boulder, apparently looking for a good sniper's position. He took aim with his H&K and lightly tapped the trigger once . . . twice . . . then again, and the Afghan fighter tumbled back off his perch, his arms pinwheeling.

The other attackers already seemed to be fading back up the valley.

"How many were there?" he asked Bradley.

"Not sure, sir. Eight or ten. I think it was a patrol, coming down the road." He looked disgusted. "We were gonna let 'em pass, but one of our muj decided he needed some fucking target practice!"

"Gray Ghost One to Ghost Three. Chill-Phil! Where are you?"

"To your right, Wheel," Lehman's voice came back. "By the road."

"What's happening?"

"Looks like the bad guys are pulling back! Wheel! Our muj're going after them!"

"Raptor! Ghost One! Where's Abdul! Can you get the locals in line?"

"Working on it, Lieutenant."

The next several minutes were confused and chaotic. Half a dozen anti-Taliban fighters vaulted the walls and sprinted forward, as Raptor, joined a moment later by Abdul, screamed at them in Pashto. That was *all* they needed: for Abdul's people to run smack into a cross fire farther up the valley.

Mariacher stood there for a moment, looking. He couldn't see the training camp from here; it was out of sight a couple of milcs up the road, tucked away among the rocks and hidden by a kink in the valley.

So what the hell did they do now? The bad guys knew they were here, and any chance at surprise had just been lost.

Still, there was a way they could use this shift in the situation. "Raptor! You're in charge. Tell Abdul you're in charge, and order him to make his people stand down!"

"Aye aye, Lieutenant," Raptor said, reverting for a moment to his old Navy training and courtesy. "What are you doing?"

"Getting back to the satcom. We need to update Mother Goose." *And, just maybe, find a way to make this thing work.*

Ten minutes later he squatted in the communications center, holding the headset to his ear. The AN/PRC-117F had been set up in the hole, with the cruciform antenna on the ground outside, pointed at the southern sky.

"Gray Ghost, Mother Goose," he heard. "We have backup on the way, call sign 'Osprey.' What we need to know is . . . can you take out the ZSU you reported earlier?"

"Affirmative, Mother Goose," he replied. "What do we have inbound?"

"We have directed a Dark Horse at the Kandahar op to redeploy to Zur Kowt. Pickup is scheduled for . . . ten minutes from now. The distance is 230 miles. That means the Dark Horse's ETA is approximately ninety mikes, or 0400 hours, your time. But it is imperative, repeat, imperative that you take out the ZSU before they reach the area."

"I copy, Mother Goose." He did a fast set of calculations. It would take an hour, maybe an hour and a quarter, just to reach the ZSU's position. It was going to be close. He checked the luminous dial of his watch—0241 hours. "Mother Goose, we should be in position to hit the ZSU at 0400 hours. We'll pass the word when it's done."

"Roger that, Gray Ghost. Good luck."

"Ah . . . Mother Goose, just so you know. These mountains are rugged. It's possible the hostiles have more ZSUs up there, or machine guns, that we haven't spotted."

"Copy, Gray Ghost. We'll tell them to be careful."

"Roger that, Mother Goose. Gray Ghost, out."

Minutes later Lehman, Osterlee, Bradley, and Raptor showed up at the HQ. Mariacher was already breaking out a pair of M136-AT4s from the mound of canvas bags they'd dragged up on horseback days before.

"You wanted to see us, sir?" Bradley asked.

"Yes. Here's the deal." He told them about his conversation with Mother Goose.

"So . . . the Dark Horse is going to set down north of Zur Kowt?" Lehman said. "Sweet."

"Yeah," Bradley said, "except that the hostiles know we're coming. If there are any HVTs in the camp, they're getting ready to take off right now. By the time Osprey gets here, they'll be halfway back to fucking Kabul!"

"I don't think so," Mariacher told them. "Look . . . all the bad guys know so far is that there's a hostile force down here. Were any of you spotted in the firefight just now?"

"I don't know," Bradley said. "Probably not."

" 'Probably' is good enough for me. Raptor . . . I want you to take direct charge of Abdul and his people. Don't press the attack, but let 'em know you're down here. I want our friends up the valley to think they've got a band of anti-Taliban rebels raising a ruckus down here."

Raptor nodded. "Lots of noise, shouting, shooting, that sort of thing."

"Exactly. Hold their attention."

Both Raptor and the SEALs were dressed to deliberately blend in with the locals as much as possible, with gray or brown patterned scarves wrapped around their faces, although Raptor still had his Jack Daniel's ball cap. Both Mariacher and Bradley were wearing their scarves draped as *ghutras,* with strips of cloth tied in the back serving as makeshift *igaals.* Their uniforms by this time were as mix-and-match as those of their adversaries—combinations of BDUs, blue jeans, pullovers, and desert camo jackets—and all had been letting their beards grow since before the start of the mission. From a distance they might well be Arab volunteers or al-Qaeda. So long as they were *kept* at a distance, the occupants of Zur Kowt had no reason to believe that there were any Americans in the attacking force.

This was a warrior culture, one that put a lot of stock in

personal bravery and leading from the front. Chances were, Mohammed and any other HVTs would stay put until they *knew* American Special Forces were about to move in on them. They might well be seen as cowards if they fled a minor skirmish with mere local rebels, something warriors could never afford if they wanted to maintain control over their troops.

A very great deal depended on what Taliban and AQ leaders here had heard about what was going down in Kandahar tonight. They might be more nervous, more likely to bolt and run, if they knew that American forces were abroad, searching for them.

Raptor, of course, was the natural choice for staying with Abdul and his rebels. He spoke the language and he had a good rapport with them. The four Gray Ghosts, however, would make their way back up that goat track west of the valley and take out the ZSU. Afterward they would have to guide in the incoming Dark Horse and meet their back-door reinforcements.

He finished giving his men their instructions.

Saturday, October 20, 2001

Zur Kowt Training Camp
Paktia Province, Afghanistan
0245 hours, local time

Colonel Iskanderov scowled at the al-Qaeda fighter before him. "You don't *know* if there are Americans with the rebels?"

"Colonel Khan . . . if there were Americans with these bandits, how would we know? My men reported no unusual weapons among the enemy . . . and no death rays."

"For the last time, Yusufzai," Iskanderov snapped, "there is no such thing as an American death ray!"

Ismail Yusufzai looked away, and his fists clenched. Iskanderov's lack of an honorific and his tone of voice were deliberately insulting, and the Pashtun tribesman was clearly weighing whether to challenge his authority. Iskanderov, seated at his desk, kept his right hand on the pistol in the top drawer, out of the man's sight. If he was foolish enough to attack . . .

Evidently, Yusufzai was not that foolish—or that head-strong. He gave the slightest nod of his bearded head. "As you say, Colonel Khan."

"The Americans use laser designators to guide their smart bombs. They are not 'death rays.' "

"Yes, sir."

Iskanderov sighed. There were Americans in the area. The Pakistani ISI man had given him full details on the American CIA team and their crossing into Afghanistan weeks ago, and the report had been confirmed by the interrogation of the anti-Taliban leader at the end of September. Even more telling, Qari Ahmadullah had told him about the men he'd seen assaulting the satellite police station outside of Khowst several nights ago.

He didn't like Ahmadullah, but he respected the man's training. His description of the handful of people leading the rebel assault—with silenced weapons, sophisticated night-vision gear, and flash-bang grenades—clearly was based on a glimpse of American Special Forces commandos . . . Delta Force or Navy SEALs, most likely. That, together with Ahmadullah's report from the interrogation of Hafez Tayed, suggested at least the presence of a small American team in the Khowst area.

For weeks now the Taliban-controlled areas of Afghanistan had been full of wild rumor and speculation. American CIA agents had been reported everywhere from Kandahar to Mazar-I-Sharif, moving through the countryside with suitcases filled with currency, bribing Taliban officers and anti-Taliban rebels alike and trying to organize a resistance movement against the government in Kabul.

There were also absurd stories spreading everywhere about American commandos with their "death rays," high-tech weapons that obliterated anything they were aimed at. The locals appeared unable to grasp the idea of laser designators or of airdropped weapons that homed on painted targets. All they could see was that when Americans aimed the devices at a building, that building promptly exploded in spectacular fashion. The rumors grew with the telling, and the result was a deterioration of morale within the Taliban forces.

And tonight a new dimension had been added to the rumors. He'd received a string of radio alerts from Kabul. The first, from al-Qaeda informants with the Pakistanis, had warned of possible American attacks aimed at capturing Taliban and al-Qaeda leaders. During the past couple of hours, there'd been confused reports from Kandahar, less than three hundred miles to the southwest. It was too early yet to sort fact from fantasy, but *something* clearly was going on out there. The reports spoke of paratroopers, of helicopters landing in the night and disgorging American soldiers, of several Taliban and al-Qaeda compounds raided or captured.

Those reports were . . . disquieting. Possibly, the Americans were launching the ground phase of their war. Possibly, they were engaging in raids to capture al-Qaeda leaders. If they were striking Kandahar, it was at least possible they would strike here as well.

"I need to know if there are American agents with the attackers," he told Yusufzai. "We should also reinforce our antiaircraft detachments on the mountain top. If there are Americans, they will seek to destroy them, so they can bring in air strikes against this camp."

"The attackers in the valley below are rabble," Yusufzai said. "With Allah's help, we will drive them away with ease."

"Then do so. But I also want another platoon of your best troops on top of that mountain."

"Yes, sir." The man hesitated.

"What is it?" Iskanderov demanded.

"I was wondering, Colonel, about my request. For a transfer to the Northern Front. Allah, bless His name, knows there is no honor in fighting these . . . these bandits."

Iskanderov looked at the other man for a long, cold moment. Since the air attacks had begun, morale among the rank-and-file Taliban and al-Qaeda fighters had been shaky. Meanwhile, morale had been improving among fighters stationed in the north, where American air attacks were notably few. More and more Taliban forces had been moving to the northern line—or requesting that they be moved. Those requests could be because they wanted to fight . . . but it was more likely they wanted to avoid the attention of the American bombers.

"This," he said at last, "is not the time to speak of transfers. You will defend this base in the holy name of Allah. You will defend it whether the attackers are bandits or the entire American army. And I will *not* tolerate cowardice in the face of the enemy, whoever he is. Is that clear?"

Yusufzai's eyes grew large at the implied insult. He opened his mouth for an angry retort, then thought better of it. "It is clear, Colonel Khan," he managed to say.

"Good. Keep me informed. You are dismissed."

The man whirled and stalked from the office, furiously angry.

Let him be angry, Iskanderov thought. It might keep him

on his toes. He picked up the phone on his desk and punched a number.

"Yes." The heavy voice was that of Khalid Shaikh Mohammed, in his office farther back in the cave complex.

"It's me, sir. You should make preparations to evacuate."

"Ah. The Americans are here, then?"

"I don't know, sir," Iskanderov replied. "But we should assume that they are. It sounds as though they are indeed raiding locations near Kandahar. Do you have any news yet of al Barq?"

Arabic for "Lightning," *al Barq* was the code name designating none other than al-Qaeda's leader, Osama bin Laden.

"Safely within al Mawa."

"God be praised." *Al Mawa* was another code name, this one meaning "the Refuge." It referred to the underground fortress complex at Tora Bora, a mountain fastness on the border sixty kilometers to the north. Bin Laden had been taken there as soon as al-Qaeda's Pakistani informants learned the Americans might be raiding Kandahar this night. It would take more than a helicopter raid to get him out of *there*.

"Allah willing, when should we leave?"

"Not yet. I just want to be ready. One of our patrol encountered rebel forces at the mouth of the valley, and there has been some fighting. If this is an American raid, I want you safely with al Barq. But there is no need to evacuate yet."

"Very well. God willing, I will be ready."

Iskanderov hung up the phone. *God willing.* Such obscene pap. God had nothing to do with it. It was he, Iskanderov, who was responsible for the smooth and efficient running of al-Qaeda forces in the Kowst region. The running would have been more efficient still if he'd had full control of the Taliban forces as well, but that simply had not been feasible politically. The Taliban listened to him and considered his suggestions because they needed al-Qaeda's trained military might. But they continued to carp and squabble, and were rarely able to agree on anything.

In time . . . God willing . . .

He snorted and returned to reading the reports out of Kandahar, trying to make sense of what was going on there.

West of Zur Kowt Training Camp
Paktia Province, Afghanistan
0355 hours, local time

The four SEALs had made their way rapidly back up the trail, hugging the rocks as they scrambled up a path at times nearly invisible, even through their night-vision optics. Now, they'd spread themselves out along the ridgetop, facing the ZSU behind its sandbag parapets some two hundred yards away.

Mariacher studied the position for a long while through his NV binoculars. Several Taliban troops were still gathered by the sandbag barrier. He could also see someone standing on top of the ZSU's huge, flat turret, just behind the quad of cannon aimed up at the layers of camo netting.

He checked his watch: 0355 . . . which meant that Osprey should be close if they were on schedule. The Gun Dish radar on that ZSU could track an aircraft six miles out and detect it at twelve. There was no time to lose.

"Chill?" Mariacher said to Lehman. "You're our best shot. You want to take it?"

"Best shot with a rifle, Wheel. I'm not sure I qual'ed on this thing."

"Sure you did. We all did."

"Yeah, but I bribed the instructor." But he took the M136, balancing the tube over his right shoulder and taking aim.

The M136-AT4 was the U.S. Army's standard-issue

shoulder-fired light antitank weapon, a one-shot disposable launch tube weighing just 14.8 pounds and measuring forty inches in length. The fin-stabilized rocket cartridge could fly for over a mile, but in combat that was reduced to an effective range of around three hundred yards. Its shaped-charge warhead could penetrate over fourteen inches of armor.

Since the thickest armor on a ZSU's hull was around six-tenths of an inch, it should have been no contest. All Lehman needed to do was hit the thing.

The problem was, the target was almost completely masked by the sandbag wall. An impact on that barrier would be wasted; the rocket had to strike the vehicle's armor for the shaped charge to penetrate it.

Lehman took his time setting up the shot. A few yards to his right, Bradley held the second M136; if Lehman missed, he would fire the second rocket.

And after that, there were no more. They would have to try to work their way close enough to disable the thing with grenades or improvised munitions.

"Clear," Lehman said, squinting through the night sight attached to the tube.

Mariacher took a check around. No one was behind either shooter, nor were there obstacles like boulders or trees close enough to reflect the hot gas from the rocket motor. These launchers were the AT4 CS variant, the CS standing for "Closed Space," which meant you could fire them from a room or a bunker without worrying about the hundred-meter back-blast frying you. Even so, you didn't want to be too close to the ass end of one of those things when it cut loose.

"You're clear."

"Engaging . . ."

Lehman squeezed the trigger, and the four-pound rocket whooshed from the tube. For a second only it was visible by its own exhaust, a bright, yellow-white star swiftly streaking through the darkness toward the target. . . .

Hit! The rocket missed the sandbag wall by inches and struck the ZSU on the hull, just below the joining with the turret. There was a flash and a loud boom, followed an instant later by a second, much louder detonation that sent the turret with its four rapid-fire cannon spinning end over end through the night sky, along with at least one body and myriad burning fragments of the camouflage netting. Orange flame lit up the surrounding landscape like a bloody dawn. Thousands of rounds of 23mm ammo continued cooking off in a spectacular display of pyrotechnics.

"Move!" Mariacher snapped over the M-biter channel, as Lehman pulled the detachable night sight from the empty tube and tossed the expendable launcher aside. The four SEALs backed away and began working to the left, trying to get around and above the ZSU's position.

The explosion had taken down a number of Taliban troops, but others were emerging now, as if from holes in the earth. Several were firing, blindly and wildly, into the surrounding night. Mariacher could hear shouted orders and counterorders, mingled with the shrill screams of men in agony.

They moved to the left as far as they could go, then began pushing forward. A lone tango emerged from the darkness, weaponless. Mariacher shot him down with three quick taps on his H&K's trigger. Lehman and Osterlee opened fire on several running, brightly illuminated figures behind the burning ZSU, cutting them down. They reached the sandbag barrier a moment later, slipped over, and made their way past the furiously burning vehicle on their bellies. There was no other way around, and remaining upright would make them as good a target as the Taliban militia.

With luck, the enemy would interpret the explosion as an attack by an American stealth aircraft—an F-117 or a B-2—the only aircraft that could get within a few miles of a ZSU undetected. By the time they'd worked their way out of the illuminated area, all of the Taliban troops were dead or had fled.

"Osprey, Osprey, this is Gray Ghost," Mariacher called.

There was no response. They must still be out of radio range.

"Raptor, Ghost One," he called instead.

"Raptor. Go."

"Target destroyed. Pass the word to Osprey and Mother Goose." Raptor was manning the satcom gear back at their camp, and would be in communication with both the incoming helicopter and the Pentagon.

"That blast lit up the whole valley, boss," Raptor replied. "Looked like a freaking volcano. I'll pass the word."

"Thanks. Ghost out."

"Luck, Ghost. Raptor out."

A quick survey of the area on the mountaintop behind the ZSU emplacement turned up no additional threats. They did spot the tail end of a military truck, however, bouncing its way down the trail—which had expanded to a small and deeply rutted dirt road—toward Zur Kowt.

"Should we engage?" Osterlee asked, shouldering his H&K.

"Negative," Mariacher said. "They're too far . . . and if you miss, they'll know there are troops up here."

"That's probably the Zoo's logistical tail," Bradley added. ZSUs typically were accompanied into battle by a truck carrying extra ammunition for their shell-hungry cannons.

It looked like a number of Taliban troops were clinging to the back of the vehicle, clearing out of the area. That was good news in several ways. The road was narrow, between cliff up and cliff down, which meant the SEALs had to stick to the road for the next mile or two—never a good idea if there's a chance the enemy is looking for a good ambush site. The odds were, however, that if there were any more emplacements or troop concentrations along this stretch of road, the truck would stop when it encountered them, if only to pass on news of what had happened. The SEALs were able to move openly and quickly until the terrain began to open up, descending in a broad and gentle slope toward the mountain pass below and in a steeper ridge of bare rock rising to the west. The higher they went along the ridge, the more frequently they encountered patches of snow— sometimes deep, but isolated and easily skirted.

"Here," Mariacher said at last, raising a fist. "Brad? You have the beacon?"

"Right here, Wheel."

Bradley placed an IR strobe on a barren and windswept stretch of open rock. The device flashed a steady, pulsing beat of light visible for many miles, but only on infrared wavelengths. The incoming Dark Horse crew would see it, but no one else. The SEALs then spread out, taking positions that gave them a good view of the entire surrounding area.

Just seven minutes later Mariacher heard a new voice over his headset. "Gray Ghost, Gray Ghost, this is Osprey One, Do you copy, over?"

"Osprey One, Gray Ghost. Copy. Beacon deployed."

"Gray Ghost, wait one . . ." There was a long pause as the invisible and still inaudible helicopter circled, its pilot searching for the landing beacon through his night optics. "Gray Ghost, Osprey. I have you. We're approaching from two-nine-five, eight miles out."

Moments later the SEALs could hear the far-off *whup-whup-whup* of a large helicopter inbound. The MH-47E, black-painted and running without lights, materialized out of the night suddenly, a black shadow against the stars that swiftly expanded into a fifty-foot-long bulbously nosed monster, settling to earth beneath its two huge, fore-and-aft rotors.

The rear ramp was already lowering, and black-clad men were spilling out, followed by a squat, open little vehicle that looked like an armed and armored dune buggy, with three men on board. Mariacher approached, hands raised. "New York!" he called out.

"Payback!" was the reply as one of the men detached himself from the rest. "Lieutenant Mariacher? DevGroup?"

"That's me. Seconded to Task Force 5 at the moment."

"Lieutenant Driscoll, SEAL Team Three."

They shook hands. "Welcome aboard, Lieutenant."

"Thank you. You're up to speed, I'm not. You have operational command."

It was important to establish who was in charge from the start. Both Driscoll and Mariacher were lieutenants, and it was bad military practice to have two men giving the orders. Driscoll would maintain direct control of the men on his team, but Mariacher, who knew the situation and the area, would be in overall command.

"Thanks." His eyes widened as another man approached—wearing a black cowboy hat. "Jesus! Diamond!"

"Hey, Mynock," Sean Dugan said in his best expansive, Texan drawl. "Small world, ain't it!"

It sure as hell isn't good to see you, Mariacher thought, but he held his tongue. "What's *he* doing here?" he demanded of Driscoll.

"Picked him up when we landed outside of Kandahar," Driscoll said, sounding a bit apologetic. "He's been . . . working with the locals."

"I insisted on tagging along," Dugan told him. "There might be papers—intelligence—to pick up here, or high-ranking prisoners who will need identifying and special handling. The Agency *is* going to have a piece of that."

"Like hell!"

"May I remind you, Lieutenant," Dugan said patiently, "that Task Force 5, to which you are currently assigned, is a CIA-run asset? My turf. My rules. Got it?"

"Got it." There was no fighting the inevitable. But he didn't have to like it. "Just stay the hell out of the way. My turf is the military end of things. Got *that*?"

"Sure. No prob, pardner."

"Okay." He turned to Driscoll. "Our objective is about five kilometers in that direction." He pointed southeast, into the Zur Kowt valley. "We need to set up across the road in the pass above the objective to keep the bad guys contained."

"Right. Situation?"

"Local forces are engaged at the southern mouth of the valley. We hope the bad guys think it's *just* locals, and not us. The destruction of their antiaircraft battery up here a few minutes ago might have woken them up. If we move fast, though, we can still slam the rear door on them."

"We'd better hump it, then." He turned to his men, who were forming up outside of the Dark Horse's rotor sweep. "Okay, men! We're moving!"

Gray Ghost and Osprey together numbered thirty-four SEALs and Force Recon Marines, plus one tag-along CIA officer. A section of ten Osprey personnel would stay on the mountainside, deployed around the helicopter, which would stay put unless threatened by the enemy's approach, ready to get the team out of Dodge.

The rest slipped off into the darkness, moving downslope.

Chapter 22

North of Zur Kowt Training Camp
Paktia Province, Afghanistan
0445 hours, local time

The air under the clear night sky was bitingly cold with a stiff northerly breeze. In places, patches of snow had drifted to a foot or so in depth. Most areas, however, windswept and barren, consisted of bare rock, and progress down the slope was rapid. The road was clear, though in places melting snow had turned it to mud, which in the cold was slowly gelling to the consistency of unpleasantly viscous molasses. They soon came to the truck, stuck in a mud hole and abandoned, the doors of the cab still hanging open.

They proceeded more cautiously after that, for the Taliban troops they were following now were on foot and might stop to set up an ambush. In another twenty minutes they reached the outskirts of Zur Kowt.

The village itself was a tiny straggle of mud-brick and adobe buildings, little more than huts, sprouting from rock and mud along either side of the road coming up the valley from Khowst. The single multistory building was obviously a mosque, with its attendant minaret.

Just below the town proper the valley narrowed, its walls growing steeper as the road hugged the western bank of a deeply cleft streambed. The compound identified as an al-Qaeda training camp was located beyond the southern outskirts of the village, in a wide spot in the valley. Stairways appeared to have been hewn up the faces of the cliffs to both sides, with ledges and cavern entrances visible about halfway up. Through night-vision binoculars, several sentries could be seen standing on ledges or on the top of the mountain, silhouetted against the eastern sky, which was showing the first, faintest hints of the coming dawn.

In the distance, echoing up the valley, gunfire crackled and snapped. Raptor and Abdul were still at it.

"We'll set up here," Mariacher decided, pointing. "Along that gulley . . . behind those boulders."

"We could get inside the camp, you know," Dugan pointed out.

"Maybe. But our job is to stop any HVTs who might come up this way. I want to keep open our line of retreat, and if we put the village at our back, we might get a nasty surprise if the villagers decide to come out and help their Taliban brothers."

Mariacher was disturbed by Dugan's presence. His failure to keep the back door shut during the Kuala Lumpur op had let one HVT escape already, and Mariacher didn't like the idea of civilian interference in a purely military op.

When this was over, he was going to see about having a long talk with that guy. He still wanted answers about what had gone wrong in Malaysia.

With the SEALs and Recon Marines in place, they had good coverage of the road north of the village. Two Marines slipped out on their bellies and returned half an hour later, after having planted several claymore mines to either side of the road and in the streambed farther down the hill, covering that approach.

After that, and a call back to Raptor, all they could do was wait.

Below the Zur Kowt Training Camp
Paktia Province, Afghanistan
0538 hours, local time

Mark Halstead—Raptor—former Navy SEAL and current CIA paramilitary operator, had just about had all he could stand. "In Allah's name," he screamed in Pashto, "stand and fight!"

He'd just received word from Mariacher that the backdoor team was in place. All that was necessary now was to kick down the front door and announce themselves. Abdul's Pashtun tribesmen, however, had other ideas. They'd been lying among the ruins at the bottom of the valley, firing blindly at Taliban and al-Qaeda positions above them, but now, in groups of two or three, and without orders—*against* orders—they were trickling toward the rear. They'd been eager enough to fight earlier, so eager they'd opened fire on that Taliban patrol without orders. Now, though, they seemed bent upon leaving.

"It will be light soon!" Abdul told him with an expansive shrug. "Those people up there are Pashtun, like us, yes? My men have no desire to face their cousins like this!"

"I thought the words for 'cousin' and 'enemy' were the same in Pashto!"

"One set of words, yes."

Raptor decided to risk all, knowing that what he said next could easily get him shot. "What is it? Are your men *cowards*?"

Abdul's ample eyebrows snapped together in an impressive glower, but then, surprisingly, his face relaxed. "No, Raptor. Not cowards. But Pashtun tribesmen can put a bullet through the eye of a man at six hundred meters! They have the high ground! Courage does not require us to face slaughter!"

So far Raptor had been less than impressed by Pashtun marksmanship. He decided not to press the issue, however. "Look . . . everything is in place!" he told Abdul. "Get your people to wait just a few more minutes, okay?"

"How many minutes?" Abdul demanded.

Raptor peeled back the Velcro cover over his watch. "Ten minutes. No more. After that, you can all leave . . . unless you decide not to!"

"Unless we decide not to? What do you mean?"

"Just stop your men from leaving! And watch!"

With considerable effort, Abdul bullied and chivied his men—most of them, at any rate—into stopping their retreat. Raptor saw their sullen looks, heard their angry murmuring. Several were bringing up the horses they'd ridden from Khowst, dozens of the small, scraggly-looking beasts. He would need something spectacular to turn this around.

Fortunately, and thanks to Mother Goose, he had something spectacular.

At least, he *would* have, in a few more minutes.

"Raptor, this is Enterprise," sounded over his headset. "Do you copy, over?"

"Enterprise, Raptor! Thanks for joining the party!"

"Glad to oblige. What do you have for us?"

Raptor looked at the mujahideen warriors gathered behind him. Many were already mounted on horseback, ready to leave. Reaching to a holster slung from his combat harness, he unclipped the cover and removed his light saber.

Officially, the device was an AN/PEQ-4 Medium Power

Laser Illuminator, or MPLI. Ten inches long and three in diameter, with several buttons and keys inset in its black plastic case, it did have the look of the handle of a light saber out of the Star Wars movies.

The output of this device, though, was in the infrared wavelengths. It was visible to troops with night-vision equipment but invisible to the unaided eye. It had a range of up to ten kilometers, though it was only effective out to about two kilometers close to the ground, and less in broken terrain such as this.

Essentially, it was a very large, very powerful laser pointer, a big brother to the laser pointer pens used by speakers giving talks or by cat owners tormenting their pets. Powered by six AA batteries, it was a Class 4 laser, which meant that at close range it could burn paper or human skin. The safety notes in the manual warned that it was a weapon, and never to be pointed at anything you didn't want destroyed.

Raptor climbed up on top of the stone foundation of a long-vanished building, struck a heroic pose, and aimed the pointer at the cliffside above, far up the valley. The focus knob could widen the beam to a floodlight or narrow it to an intense spot. He'd dialed it down to create a five-degree cone, which was now glowing against the top of the eastern cliff face just above the Zur Kowt camp.

Through his NVGs he could see the aim point. Slowly, he moved the laser pointer, "snaking" the red point back and forth to attract the attention of the AC-130U pilot somewhere overhead. A moving spot was easier to see than a stationary one. The difficulty was that the spot would only be visible to the pilot from certain angles on approach.

"Enterprise, Raptor," he said. "Laser on. Do you have it?"

"Negative, Raptor. Wait one."

Raptor maintained his pose, continuing to illuminate the

top of the cliff. Gunfire rattled overhead from the direction of the camp, but nothing was coming close enough to force him to seek cover.

A minute passed.

"Is there something we are supposed to be watching for?" Abdul said finally.

"Just watch," Raptor replied. "This takes a few moments."

The Pashtun tribesman looked up the valley but could see nothing, of course, without NVGs. The murmuring among the other anti-Taliban troops was increasing in volume and in anger. Raptor heard the clip-clop of hooves as several of the fighters began riding back down the valley.

"Okay, Raptor! This is Enterprise! Spot! I have your target at zero-niner-one!"

That meant that Enterprise was somewhere to the west, to be able to see the laser light to his east. It also meant that the pilot would have to swing south a bit in order to put the valley on his left side.

Another long minute passed. The Pashtun tribesmen, clearly, were fed up. "This is senseless!" Abdul snapped. "You are doing nothing with that . . . toy!"

"Just wait." He could hear the far off drone of the Specter gunship now, beyond the mountainside to the west. "Doesn't Allah counsel patience?"

"You would do better not speaking of what you do not understand!" Abdul was angry. The drone of the Specter's turboprops was louder now, clearly audible. Several of the mujahideen had stopped and were looking up at the sky. The gunship, high enough above the valley to present an extremely small silhouette, was invisible in the still-night sky.

"Raptor, Enterprise. Illuminate your target."

"Roger that," he replied. He moved the laser pointer off the mountainside and toward the main body of the al-Qaeda camp, "roping" it. With his free hand, he twisted the focus

knob, opening the beam to a forty-five-degree cone. The
laser light reflected skyward toward the gunship was more
diffuse now, but also covered a much larger area. Buildings
and boulders would be interrupting parts of the beam, but
enough was painted that the gun crews onboard the Specter
could see the valley compound clearly picked out in a
yellow-green IR glow.

"Enterprise, firing phasers!" the pilot said with cheerful
nonchalance.

Mariacher jumped off the wall. "You guys might want to
cover your ears," he told his audience as he took his own
advice.

"What?" Abdul demanded. "What are you talk—"

The night sky exploded in dazzling flame and the shrill
crash of Armageddon.

North of Zur Kowt Training Camp
Paktia Province, Afghanistan
0552 hours, local time

The SEALs and Marines had been able to see the laser
pointer's signature against the rocks through their night-
vision monoculars. When the light had roped down the side
of the canyon's eastern cliff side, then grew dimmer and more
fuzzy, Mariacher simply said, "Look out! Here it comes!"

The stream of high-speed Gatling gun rounds struck the
center of the valley below the village like a lightning bolt, like
a solid shaft of orange light spearing into the valley's depths.
With a cyclic rate of 1,800 rounds per minute, the Specter's
GAU-12/U Gatling cannon, which bore the name Equalizer,
delivered 25mm shells on-target at the incredible rate of thirty
each *second*. The ammunition was a mix of PGU-20/U armor-

piercing incendiary and PGU-22 high-explosive rounds. The effect was mind-numbing, awe-inspiring, and very, very noisy.

The Equalizer's shells struck in a cascade, detonating in a torrent of light and sound. The main part of the terrorist camp was out of sight down the slope from the Osprey's position, but a fountain of flame erupted from behind the intervening boulders and terrain. API rounds struck rock and bounced high into the air, burning as brilliantly as flares as they arced high into darkness or ricocheted back and forth from one side of the canyon to the other. HE rounds detonated on impact, shattering mud-brick and adobe buildings, exploding vehicles, and sweeping men and animals out of existence in an eye-blink instant.

Once, seventeen years before, when he was a child of ten or so, Mariacher's parents had vacationed in Hawaii. There, on the Big Island, he witnessed an eruption of Mauna Loa, the largest active volcano on the planet. This—the fountain of fire, the arcing flares of spent rounds—reminded him forcefully of that unforgettable sight.

The ground shook beneath Mariacher's stomach and legs as he stretched full-length on the muddy floor of the streambed. The noise, a high-pitched shriek, part tearing metal, part dying beast, assaulted the senses, was *felt* as much as heard. He plugged his ears with his fingers and opened his mouth wide, riding out the storm of sound.

After a small eternity—a few seconds or so—the gunship's other two weapons added their voices to the din. The 40mm Bofors cannon fired one hundred rounds per minute—almost two shells per second—while the big 105mm howitzer slugged away at a more stately pace, firing once every ten seconds or so. At Mariacher's side, Bradley was screaming something at him.

He couldn't hear a word.

Below the Zur Kowt Training Camp
Paktia Province, Afghanistan
0552 hours, local time

Mark Halstead crouched behind the wall, fingers in his ears,
as the torrent of hellfire flashed out of deep, predawn sky
and exploded within the Zur Kowt canyon. The effect on the
mujahideen with him was dramatic. Most simply stared,
open-mouthed, at the spectacle. Others followed Raptor's
example and took shelter behind the wall. A few, already on
horseback, bolted and ran, though whether deliberately or
because their horses had spooked was impossible to say.

The gunship trained its fire first at the lower end of the
training camp, then walked it slowly north, almost to the
edge of the village, sweeping that savage beam of destruction back and forth, from one canyon wall to the other. When
the 40mm Bofors and the howitzer joined in, they began
hammering at specific targets—concentrations of troops,
vehicles parked along the road, buildings, even rock ledges
and cavern entrances where these were exposed enough to
the sky that the gunners could see them.

The gunners, some twelve thousand feet above the valley
floor, possessed an almost magical array of thermal and
night-vision imaging systems, magnified on their targeting
monitors to allow surgically precise placement of their fire. At
one point a heavy machine gun opened fire from the top of the
eastern cliff, though its target was far out of reach. The stream
of Bofors fire almost casually walked out of the valley, across
bare rock in fast-popping puffs of smoke, and obliterated the
emplacement before sweeping back to continue dealing out
death and devastation within the close confines of the canyon.

The barrage lasted all of ten seconds, then switched off
with a suddenness as startling as the initial blast of sound.
Mariacher's ears were ringing. He stood up, along with the

mujahideen warriors who'd taken shelter with him. For a handful of seconds the valley was profoundly silent . . . and then the men broke into a wild chorus of cheers and screams and bellowing shouts, raising clenched fists and shaking their weapons in the air. *"Allah akbar! Allah akbar! Allah akbar!"* The cries proclaiming God's greatness rang across the valley and echoed off the cliffs.

Abdul stood nearby, staring at the cliffs above, then turning to stare at Raptor. Impulsively, the Pashtun leader lunged forward. Raptor almost countered with a block-and-strike that would have crippled the man, but checked himself at the last instant when he realized Abdul was simply trying to embrace him.

He let Abdul bear-hug him for a moment before pushing the man back a step. "Okay, okay," he said. "You're welcome!"

Abdul turned and shouted at his men in Pashto, and was answered by a thunderous chorus of cheers.

And suddenly the anti-Taliban army was surging forward, some on foot, but most on horseback. "Abdul! What the devil are you doing?"

"Allah has opened the way!" was his reply. He raised his AK overhead, brandishing it. "We will *take* that camp . . . now!"

Now it was Raptor's turn to stare in open-mouthed astonishment, this time at the sight of an honest-to-God cavalry charge in this, the first year of the twenty-first century. The mujahideen horsemen were spread out across the valley, straddling the road, galloping ahead like the cowboys in some old, black-and-white western movie.

Gunfire cracked and echoed down the valley, the horsemen opening fire on nothing in particular. Raptor couldn't tell if there was any answering fire from the tangos. After that demonstration of sheer, raw firepower, he doubted there would be.

With his army now vanishing up into the canyon, Raptor

decided he'd better move fast if he wanted to stay with it. He signaled a couple of mujahideen who were still mounting up nearby. One gestured, offering his horse with a broad, toothy grin. Raptor swung into the saddle, checked his slung H&K to make sure it was easily accessible, and urged his mount forward.

Mark Halstead, CIA paramilitary and former Navy SEAL, galloped into battle on horseback.

North of Zur Kowt Training Camp
Paktia Province, Afghanistan
0555 hours, local time

When the gunship's weapons fell silent, Mariacher and the other team members rose slowly, checking the terrain around them with a sense akin to dazed wonder. Though he'd worked with them in training, Mariacher had never been this close to the sharp end of a Specter gunship before, and the experience was both exciting and humbling, and a little terrifying as well. As it was, the Osprey team had been a bit closer to the kill zone than he liked. From twelve thousand feet, twenty-some SEALs and Marines looked pretty much like local mujahideen. The Specter gunners would have constrained their fire to the immediate area illuminated by Raptor's light saber, but even so, and even though the Ospreys had deployed a flashing IR beacon just before the attack to mark their position as friendly, the chances of a friendly-fire incident here had been unpleasantly high.

The canyon appeared lifeless, filled with a thick haze of smoke and an almost suffocating silence.

"Shouldn't we go down and look?" Dugan said. Somehow, in the past few moments, he'd lost his cowboy hat.

"Negative," Mariacher said, sliding his NVGs up and back

on his head. The sky was now considerably lighter than it had been even a few minutes ago. Dawn came on swiftly up here in the mountains. "We stay put and watch the back door."

"There!" a SEAL said, pointing. "Looks like a runner!"

Mariacher spotted the figure and raised his binoculars to his eyes. The man might be Taliban militia, AQ, or a civilian; there was no way to tell. He had neither a weapon nor a turban, and despite the chill air wore only a knee-length *shalwar kameez*. He was running like a track star, head back, beard streaming over his shoulder, knees and elbows pumping.

A second runner appeared, following the first . . . and then two more. A moment later a Zil army truck bounced up the road from the base. The vehicle must have been sheltered from the firestorm in a cave or bunker. It appeared none the worse for the attack, but the driver was coaxing every scrap of speed possible from the relic, clashing gears as he accelerated over the crest of the hill and into the village. A number of men were packed into the back of the truck, clinging to the side rails to keep from being bounced out.

"Do we take them, sir?" one of the Ospreys asked.

Mariacher nodded. "If they come out of that camp, we assume they're hostiles. Bradley? Take out that truck."

Chief Bradley nodded and rose to a kneeling position. He was still carrying the remaining M136-AT4, which he balanced over his right shoulder. "Clear aft?"

"You're clear! Fire!"

Bradley paused a moment, lining up his shot. The range was a couple of hundred meters and the target was moving fairly quickly. It also kept vanishing behind the individual buildings that made up the town of Zur Kowt.

The truck emerged from the north side of the village, running almost broadside to the American ambush now. Leading the target slightly, Bradley squeezed the trigger. The rocket gave a shrill whoosh and launched itself at the truck, streaking low across snow, mud, and bare rock. For a moment Mariacher thought Bradley had miscalculated and that the missile would miss. It connected with the truck, however, almost all the way to the back. Another foot and it would have missed.

The blast flung TAQ soldiers into the air and sent the truck into a hard, slewing skid. The driver almost recovered, but then the vehicle bounced and flipped, hitting on its right side and rolling two or three times along the road. The gas tank ruptured, then exploded, sending a ball of orange flame and greasy black smoke mushrooming into the sky.

SEALs and Marines opened fire together, picking targets carefully and knocking them down with short, controlled bursts. One of the Marines was packing an M249 Squad Automatic Weapon, and he was using it like a sniper's rifle, squeezing off two- and three-round bursts simply by controlling the pressure of his gloved finger on the SAW's trigger. Once the fleeing TAQs realized they were under fire, they began to scatter, some dropping to the ground, some running back down the hill into the camp, some fleeing up the far slope of the valley beyond the town.

A sharp bang sounded from farther down the streambed. Some TAQ personnel had just blundered into the watchdog claymore the Marines had set there. The M18A1 claymore was a curved, rectangular case containing a charge of C-4 packed behind seven hundred steel balls set into a plastic matrix. When the charge was triggered, the device became in effect a giant and devastating shotgun, shredding anything downrange with a storm of high-speed ball bearings. Another claymore went off a moment later alongside the road, and that was enough to turn the TAQ route back upon itself. The entire action lasted less than a minute.

As the area fell silent again, Mariacher realized he could hear steady and vigorous firing coming from down the valley.

Raptor must have begun his assault. The gunfire was mingled, however, with a steadily growing roar . . . a chorus of many voices cheering or raging—it was impossible to tell which.

"Hey, Wheel?" Lehman said. "I'm wondering if we're going to get any more action way up here."

Mariacher took a look at the sky, then at his watch. Sunrise here would come at 0628 hours . . . another twenty minutes. The sky was swiftly growing lighter almost minute by minute. The valley and the village both were still in deep shadow, but even without NVGs, visibility was now clear in all directions.

Visibility meant enemy gunmen could see them. They had pretty fair cover here, in the dry streambed, but the longer they stayed in place, the likelier it would be that a TAQ force might spot them and try to encircle them.

Besides, SEALs operated best on the offense. It would be better to keep moving.

"Okay, people!" he called. "Stay out of the town. Stay spread out. Lets make for the crest of the ridge."

The objective he'd singled out was the spot in the road where the valley came up and over a hump just south of the town and above the terrorist camp. From there they would have a better view down the canyon and be able to better support the anti-Taliban militia coming up the valley.

Moving in fireteams of four, the Ospreys began leapfrogging south.

Below the Zur Kowt Training Camp
Paktia Province, Afghanistan
0610 hours, local time

For Raptor, the moment was one of surreal strangeness. He'd ridden horses before, but never with an eye to riding one into combat. Up ahead, Afghan horsemen urged their mounts to leap a low wall of brick and piled-up sandbags that until minutes ago had been the lead defensive position for the TAQ forces. He decided not to try anything as sophisticated as jumping. It was enough, for now, just to manage to stay in the saddle as the wiry, short-legged beast beneath him clattered up the road at something more than a trot but less than an all-out gallop.

The wall had blocked off the southern mouth of the canyon completely except for the road itself, where a small guard shack had been set up to monitor traffic coming up from Khowst. He guided his horse through the opening and into a scene of shocking devastation.

The guard shack was . . . simply and startlingly *gone,* with no piece of the structure left larger than a man's finger. Sandbags had been strewn carelessly about, the canvas shredded, the contents spilled. Mud-brick structures had been pulverized, leaving little behind but piles of rubble. The frame of a truck rested next to the western cliff, burning furiously, the blackened husk of the driver still seated at the wheel.

Several other fires were burning here and there, the oily smoke staining the glow of the clean, predawn sky. Weapons—mostly AKs, but a few RPGs and machine guns as well—lay scattered across the ground, mingled with completely random abandon with papers, canvas satchels, bricks, unidentifiable bits of machinery, canteens, and other items of personal gear, broken glass, chunks of wood, and such bizarrely out-of-context items as the back half of a bicycle and a completely whole, undamaged china teacup.

It took a few moments for Raptor to begin to see the more grisly remnants of the Specter attack. Somehow, at first, it was as if his brain blocked them out or couldn't comprehend just what it was he was seeing. Liberally mixed with the rubble, however, were not bodies, but *pieces* of bodies, most little more than scraps of bloody meat. Some were more recognizable, however . . . an intact foot still wearing a sandal, a hand still wrapped around the grip and trigger group of an AK-47, a six-foot length of bloody intestines, and even a head, *just* the head, bearded, still wearing a dark blue turban, and with eyes wide open in what looked like an almost comical expression of bewilderment.

Ahead, the cavalry charge had come to a halt, and the anti-Taliban mujahideen began to dismount. His own horse shied suddenly, backing away from a smear of gore in its path. "Easy there, girl," he said, trying to steady the mare. He swung off and dropped to the ground, leading the animal by its bridle.

Here and there, oddly, a few corners of the compound had been left relatively untouched, by chance or by the geometry of canyon walls and shifting lines of sight from the circling Specter gunship. Several buildings were intact, along with some fifty-five-gallon drums, a pile of supply crates, and even a civilian pickup truck. A cave entrance, framed with bricks and sealed shut by a heavy wooden door, could be seen in the shadows beneath a rock overhang. As complete as the destruction was outside, most of this base would still be untouched, protected deep underground.

To finish the job, they would have to go inside, to face the devil within his lair.

Chapter 23

East of Zur Kowt Training Camp
Paktia Province, Afghanistan
0630 hours, local time

Tangretti moved carefully along the edge of the cliff, a sheer drop of perhaps fifty feet to the rubble-and-debris-strewn floor of the canyon. The DevGroup SEAL officer, Mariacher, had led them to the hump on the valley floor below the village, then ordered flanking parties of six men apiece to move off to the sides and out along the canyon's rims in order to secure the cliff tops to either side. From up here he had an exceptional view of the terrorist camp—correction, of what had once been the terrorist camp—below. The destruction wrought by the Specter gunship had been complete and uncompromising.

He glanced up. The Specter was visible now in the morning light, a tiny, black, cruciform shape still circling a couple of miles overhead. The AC-130U would continue to orbit the area until the raid was complete. A comforting thought.

The DPV was moving down the debris-cluttered road now,

followed by the ten men who hadn't been assigned to one of the flanking parties. Tangretti could also see a number of mujahideen locals—ten or twelve of them, perhaps—picking their way up the road, leading horses by their reins.

The battle appeared to be over, the enemy annihilated. He could see the openings of several cave entrances among the rock ledges on the opposite cliff, to the west, however, and knew there were almost certainly terrorists and their allies hidden belowground.

"Hey, guys!" Fletcher called. "Take a look at this!"

Thirty yards from the side of the cliff, two members of the party had found the remnants of an antiaircraft gun position. A ring of sandbags had been more or less flung apart, and a Russian-made DShKM heavy machine gun, with its two crescent-shaped shoulder rests, was lying on its side, together with the toppled ruin of its tripod. Three bodies lay there as well . . . no, not three. Only two. One body had been ripped into roughly equal halves, though with all the blood and spilled intestines, it was tough to tell what was what.

Tangretti looked away for a moment, took a breath, then made himself look back. He'd seen death before, in Kuwait, but he didn't think it was possible to ever become used to the savage mutilation caused by modern munitions and weapons systems. The coppery tang of blood was thick enough in the air to taste.

Fletch hadn't been calling him over to view the carnage, however. Behind the sandbag gun position was what looked like the mouth of a well, a depression in the bare rock surface of the ground, centered by a three-foot-wide circular hole lined with bricks. A piece of plywood lay partly over the opening, but it had been shoved back enough to reveal the black entrance hidden beneath.

"Whatcha guys think?" Fletcher asked as Tangretti, Tomajczk, Eakins, Karr, and McConnell all gathered around. "This might be the *real* back door."

"One of them, anyway," Tangretti said. "That looks like it might be a *karez* entrance."

"I doubt that," Eakins replied. "Wrong kind of terrain. But it might be a ventilator shaft."

They'd been briefed on various tunnel systems they might encounter in Afghanistan. During the Soviet war, the mujahideen had become masters at constructing underground fortresses. A *karez* was a long underground irrigation tunnel used to carry water to farmland. Vertical access tunnels, or wells, were spaced along the main waterway, anywhere from a few yards to a hundred yards apart. According to CIA reports, mujahideen fighters had used the *karez* tunnel systems extensively to hide from Soviet/DRA forces, store supplies, and as bases for their campaigns, and civilian populations had taken shelter in them as well.

As Eakins had suggested, though, this wasn't a likely place to find an irrigation tunnel, high atop a mountain ridge and far from anything resembling agricultural land. There obviously was a fair-sized cave complex here, however, and the Afghans reportedly improved those systems, digging out new chambers and connecting tunnels, ventilation shafts, and secret exits.

That well at the top of the ridge might be an access tunnel or a ventilator shaft to an underground maze of caverns, corridors, and rooms.

"So, what do we do?" Tangretti asked. "Seal it with C-4? Or go down there?"

"We need to check this with the wheel," Fletcher said.

He used his M-biter to put in a call to Driscoll.

Zur Kowt Training Camp
Paktia Province, Afghanistan
0630 hours, local time

Iskanderov strode into the big meeting room.

This was normally a classroom for al-Qaeda trainees, though Iskanderov and other high-ranking members of the organization occasionally used it for planning sessions and briefings. During the Russian war, a narrow passage through the rock had been laboriously widened with jackhammers, creating a roughly circular space ten meters across with a low and uneven ceiling braced, in places, by massive timber supports. Naked lightbulbs strung along the ceiling provided generator-powered light.

The walls were unevenly decorated with posters in Arabic and Pashto, many showing Osama bin Laden's face, despite the prohibition among strict Muslim fundamentalists against any depiction of the human face or form. Some of the Taliban brothers, he knew, disapproved. Most al-Qaeda fighters were a bit more flexible in their approach to the will of Allah. And the leaders—most of them—were bluntly pragmatic.

They were waiting for him when he entered, seated in a circle at the far end of the chamber—ten men with dirty faces and haunted eyes. Khalid Shaikh Mohammed, with a suitcase and an AK-47 at his side, looked up. "We should have left hours ago!"

Iskanderov nodded. "Yes. I underestimated the scope of the enemy assault. It appeared to be nothing more than a raid by Afghan rebels."

"But what are we going to *do*?" Mohammed wailed.

"My brothers!" one of the fighters cried. His fatigues were ripped and thickly coated with drying mud. He'd lost his turban, and his face was streaked with blood. He stood up, brandishing his AK. "My brothers . . . there is nothing to fear! Allah, blessed be His name, is with us!"

"Yes, yes, Jaish," Major Qadi said. "Of *course* He is—"

"No!" the man shouted, shaking his head wildly. "No, I mean He really is with us! Isn't that right?" He turned, looking to two of the other fighters for support. "Salam! Mohammed! You were there! It was God's hand!"

"What happened?" Iskanderov said, taking a seat on the stone floor with the others.

"My brothers and I," Jaish cried. "We were on guard outside, in the valley, when the American Satans fired their death ray! The blast picked us up and flung us across the road . . . but we were unhurt! And then . . . and then . . . I looked up, and I could see the bullets raining down upon me! I thought, I thought . . . Allah! If it is your will that I die, then let me die for you and your cause. And I could see the bullets sweeping to the side, changing direction as they flew! It was the hand of Allah, hovering above me, deflecting the bullets and sparing my life!"

"It is true!" one of the others exclaimed. "We were there! We all were spared by God's hand! He shielded us from the American death ray, then protected us from the bullets! Great is His name!"

"There *is* no death ray," Ismail Yusufzai said. He gave Iskanderov a hard look. "Is that not right, Colonel Khan?"

"I'm sure you thought God was protecting you," Major Qadi said.

"You have no right to speak to me as though I were a child, Pakistani dog!" Jaish yelled, rising to his feet, his voice shrill and a bit unsteady. "I know what I saw! What we all saw! We are protected by the hand of Allah, the mighty, the merciful . . . and if we flee now, He will judge us!"

"You are quite right, Jaish," Iskanderov said, holding up a hand. "God is on our side, and He will protect us! It is written, in Surah 22.38, that surely Allah will defend those who believe, and surely Allah does not love anyone who is unfaithful or ungrateful."

"We are under God's protection!"

"Yes," Iskanderov told the agitated fighter. "And now, you and the men with you shall show the world God's greatness!"

Superstitious nonsense, he thought even as he calmed the man. Strange things happened in battle, with men saved—or killed—by the slightest shift of chance and happenstance. Optical illusion and perspective—or panic—could make a stream of tracer rounds appear to magically bend away.

What he *did* know was that if Allah had indeed protected these three in the hellstorm outside, He'd done a remarkably poor job of protecting everyone else caught in that rain of destruction, blood, and death. Iskanderov didn't know how many fighters had just died in the ten seconds or so the camp had been under fire. Likely, no one would *ever* know. The American weapons had left precious little remaining for burial, with flesh, blood, and random body parts scattered across the valley floor so thickly it was difficult to walk without stepping on something that once had been human.

If that was an example of God's infinite mercy, Iskanderov wasn't sure submission to the Divine Will was worth the price.

"Are you saying everyone killed outside was an unbeliever?" Qari Ahmadullah asked, echoing Iskanderov's own thoughts.

Mohammed pointed at Iskanderov. "The colonel has said it! God does not love the unfaithful!"

"And perhaps too it was His desire that they become holy

martyrs, because He loved them so much," Iskanderov said.
"Listen to me. There is no time for arguing among ourselves. Major Qadi! Are your people ready?"

"What remain of them," the Pakistani ISI man said. "Yes."

"You three," Iskanderov said, turning to Jaish. "Go with
the major. Join his men. Now is not the time to worry about
the failings of our brothers or why some are chosen and
some not. You must fight the invaders. You must become
holy martyrs yourselves, if need be, to buy precious time.
These men . . ." He pointed at Mohammed and Ahmadullah. "These men *must* remain alive and free, in order that
they may continue leading our brothers against the Americans. It is God's will."

"Allah akbar!" several in the room cried.

"Allah akbar! Brothers! Here is what we shall do!"

Zur Kowt Training Camp
Paktia Province, Afghanistan
0632 hours, local time

"I have some people up there," Mariacher said, pointing to
the top of the cliff on the valley's east side, "who've found
an entrance of some sort. We might be able to use that."

Raptor nodded. "Tunnel-rat work."

The tunnel rats had been Army personnel during the Vietnam War, men chosen for their small stature and their
bravery—some said it was their insanity—to descend into
the caves, tunnel complexes, and spider holes used so successfully by the VC and North Vietnamese. It seemed an ax-
iom of modern warfare: When the enemy controlled the sky,
you took your men, your supplies and weapons, and even
your women and children underground—safe from bombs,
safe from prying eyes in the sky.

"I don't like that," Driscoll added. "We don't have the manpower. Or the time. And it would be asking our boys to walk right into a trap."

They were crouched behind a boulder, together with several of the Marines and SEAL personnel, outside of what they all agreed must be the main entrance to Zur Kowt's underground complex. A quick survey of the compound area had turned up three entrances at the valley floor level—two on the east cliff, one on the west.

The west cliff did not appear to be very extensive. Bradley's flanking team had found no sign of ventilator shafts or tunnels at the top, and a brief exploration of the main opening turned up boxes of ammunition and some narrow shafts leading to the ledge openings halfway up the cliff, nothing more.

On the east side, however, one of the major openings was the entrance to what appeared to be a fair-sized motor pool, with tires, spare parts, a technical mounting a heavy machine gun, and two Zil trucks. Two tunnels led off from that cavern, one to the south, one to the east, deeper into the mountain. Neither of those had been explored yet.

The second eastern entrance was this one, a nine-foot-high opening recessed into the rock face, framed by cemented bricks and plaster. The entrance was open. When a Marine had approached minutes earlier, however, a long burst of machine-gun fire opened up from the darkness inside. The shots missed wildly, but it was proof that someone was inside, and that they were willing to argue with anyone who wanted in.

"I think we should seal the entrances," Raptor said. "Toss in enough C-4 to bring it all down on top of them—or to collapse the outer tunnels, anyway. Let 'em rot in there."

"No!" Dugan exclaimed. He shifted a bit, peering up and over the boulder to take another look at the main entrance. "The fact that they're defending this position instead of just heading for the hills means there might be some HVTs holed up in there."

"First," Mariacher said, "these *are* the hills. And some of them *did* try to run. We just didn't let 'em."

"Oh, there's no doubt there are HVTs inside," Raptor added. "Our locals picked up some pretty convincing leads."

"Bin Laden?" Dugan asked. Mariacher could almost see his mouth watering.

"No. He's not been seen in these parts for several months. But the Taliban's head of intelligence may be in there. There's also another man—possibly a Russian or a Tajik— who's been giving military advice to the TAQs lately. We don't have a name on him yet. We also think Khalid Mohammed is in there."

"Then we can't just seal them up! We need to capture them if we can."

"Why?" Mariacher said. "So you can ship them off to Mactan, or wherever, and torture them?"

Dugan gave him a sharp look. "What the hell is that supposed to mean?"

"I was just wondering about those tangos we captured in Kuala Lumpur. Remember them? The ones you turned over to the Filipinos?"

"We saw the aftermath of a TAQ torture session a couple of weeks ago," Raptor told the CIA officer. "It wasn't pretty."

"No," Dugan said. "No, I guess it wasn't. Let me ask you this, though, Lieutenant. If torture could have exposed bin Laden's plot, if it could have prevented 9/11 . . . would it've been worth it?"

"I don't know," Mariacher replied. "All I know is it's *not* worth it if we become no different than the people we're fighting."

"And all I know," Dugan replied, "is that the real world

isn't clean, neat, or fair. Extreme circumstances require extreme measures."

"You know," Mariacher said, "I'll bet that's exactly what the Germans said when they elected Hitler."

"Enough, you two," Raptor snapped. "You want to argue philosophy, sign up for a USAFE course."

"I hate to pull rank," Dugan said, "but I'll remind all of you that this is an Agency operation. As the senior Agency man on the ground, *I* am in charge. Do we need to take this up with Mother Goose?"

Mariacher glanced at Raptor, who folded his arms and gave a small shake of his head.

"Don't look at him," Dugan added. "He's a CIA contract employee. And for the duration, so are you. Task Force 5 consists of CIA Special Action Teams. That means you're *my* team. Is that clear?"

"Clear. But I'll remind *you* that these men are my responsibility," Mariacher replied. "I won't let you throw them away on some harebrained scheme."

"Noted."

In fact, Mariacher knew he was on damn thin ice. Technically, he was only in command of the Gray Ghosts, with Raptor as his CIA contact with the native Afghans. He'd assumed command of Osprey as well when Driscoll offered it to him, on the grounds that he had a better grasp on the local situation.

But Driscoll's team was part of a CIA op as well.

He just wished it were possible to *trust* the guy.

"If Mohammed is in there," Dugan was saying, "we're going to get him out. One way or another. *You* people are the experts. Any ideas how we can do this?"

Great, Mariacher thought. He's in charge, but we have to do the thinking.

The problem was how to assault what might well be an

underground fortress, but without having it turn into a very
expensive frontal assault.

"Okay," he said. "I have a suggestion."

East of Zur Kowt Training Camp
Paktia Province, Afghanistan
0635 hours, local time

". . . and they did it time after time," Tangretti said, warming
to his topic. They were lying on top of the cliff, a few yards
from the shaft opening and the ruined triple-A position. The
attack had stalled while the officers on the valley floor decided what to do. It was always the same: Hurry up and wait.

"Every damned time the Marines went ashore on a differ-
ent Pacific island," Tangretti continued, "they'd find this sign
set up on the beach, facing out to sea. 'Welcome U.S.
Marines!' And it would be signed by one or another of the
UDTs. So you see? The Marines aren't the first ones in. It's
Navy frogmen, and nowadays that means the SEALs!"

"Fuck you, squid," McConnell replied, but he was grinning
as he said it. There'd been near constant banter pitting the
SEALs against the Marines ever since they'd started working
together in California, months ago. Most of it had been good-
natured. As Tangretti had just been saying, it was a rivalry that
went all the way back to the Underwater Demolition Teams in
the Pacific during World War II. "The way I see it, those guys
were honorary Marines. Now, if you ask me—"

"Watch it!" Tangretti yelled, bringing up his H&K. The
wooden sheet that had been covering the well opening was
sliding back, a hand reaching up from underneath to move it.
At Tangretti's shout, the hand snapped back into the opening, but an instant later a turban emerged, followed by a
man's head and shoulders and the AK-47 he was holding.

He never had a chance to get the weapon clear of the opening, however, Tangretti fired a short burst, which combined with the volley of automatic weapons fire from the rest of the SEALs and Recon Marines. The man's head snapped back, then exploded. Corpse and rifle vanished back down the hole.

Tangretti crossed the five yards of open ground to the tunnel opening, pulling out a hand grenade and twisting the cotter pin free as he moved. He tossed the grenade down the shaft, then fell flat, covering his head.

Three seconds later there was a sharp, hollow-sounding crack, and the rock transmitted a bit of a kick to his chest. Complete silence followed.

"Okay," Tangretti said. "Anybody got a light saber?"

"I do," McConnell said.

Carefully, the two approached the rim of the opening, while the others hung back a short distance, weapons at the ready. A smart enemy—if anyone was alive and conscious down there after the grenade—might position himself at the bottom of the shaft, ready to fire up at the silhouetted head of anyone foolish enough to look down into it from above.

However, the possibility that anyone in the tunnel would risk a second grenade coming down the shaft, or be thinking that quickly, wasn't likely. McConnell chanced a quick look over the rim, ducked back, then looked again, using an AN/PEQ-4 to illuminate the shaft's interior.

Tangretti pulled his night-vision monocular down over his right eye, took a deep breath, then rolled to a point where he could simultaneously aim his weapon and look down the shaft. The laser, shining at infrared wavelengths, was invisible to the naked eye. Through his monocular, however, the shaft was brightly lit . . . almost too brightly lit, since the beam turned the haze of smoke and dust in the tunnel into a shining, nearly opaque fog.

He could see to the bottom, however. The shaft was round

and appeared to descend for perhaps thirty feet. A wooden ladder was bolted to the interior and seemed to go all the way down. It also looked as though there was a side tunnel or opening about halfway down.

All the way at the bottom he could make out what looked like a pile of dark rags. It took him a moment to realize that it was the body of the TAQ he'd shot. After the grenade had landed on it, what was left was not easily recognizable as human.

"You see the side tunnel?" McConnell said. "North side?"

"Yeah."

"That could be trouble."

The concussion of the hand grenade, detonating in a tightly enclosed space, might have killed or stunned anyone in that side passage.

Or possibly not. There was no way to know how long that passage was or whether there were jogs in the tunnel that would protect people hiding down there. The same went for the main tunnel all the way at the bottom.

"Damn it, we're going to have to go down there."

"Fuck that!" McConnell said.

"We were told to sit tight," Fletcher added.

"Sure," Tangretti said, "and while the brass and the spooks argue, we could have the whole damned TAQ army come storming out of there. We should at least put a plan together. Close assault and CQB."

"Agreed," Gunnery Sergeant Eakins said. "I'll go. I need one more. Volunteers only."

"Me," Tangretti said. "Hell, it was my idea."

"We're all volunteers," Fletcher said. "Take me. I outrank this bastard."

"C'mon! This is my chance to get my stripe back!"

"Right," McConnell said. "The question you gotta ask yourself is why you want it in the first place."

"Osprey Two, this is Gray Ghost," a voice said over their headsets. "Do you copy?"

"This is Osprey Two," Eakins said. "Go ahead!"

"Listen, guys," the voice said. "This is Lieutenant Mariacher. Does it look to you like you could get a team down that hole you found up there?"

"We're already on it, sir," Eakins said. "Just give us the word."

They began discussing the situation.

Tangretti continued to stare down the hole, ready to open fire if anything moved.

Once, when he'd been a kid growing up in southern California, he and his best buddy had been playing at an old mining site. They hadn't known that at the time. To them, it was just a sere bit of southern California hillside scheduled to be turned into a shopping center. But they'd found a mine shaft, squared off with heavy, rotting timbers and partly closed over by two-by-fours. Mark, his buddy, had dared him to go inside.

He had, and he'd gotten stuck.

Not *badly* stuck, but his jeans snagged on a protruding nail, and the opening had been too narrow for him to shift to one side and free himself. For ten long minutes he'd hung there, unable to go down, unable to go up, until Mark managed to pry some more boards away and help him scramble clear. He managed to cut himself on the nail coming up, which had, of course, meant tetanus shots and a lecture from his father.

He hadn't tried climbing down wells or mine shafts ever again. The one thing he could say about the incident now was that he hadn't panicked.

But now, as he stared down into this one, he could certainly feel panic's stirrings.

Zur Kowt Training Camp
Paktia Province, Afghanistan
0638 hours, local time

Mariacher nodded to Dugan, who was not plugged in to the communications net. "Okay. They're getting ready to send some people down to flush them."

"That's great!"

"Let's hope we think so after they get in there. I don't like this, Dugan. This is a raid, not an invasion."

"This is a CIA operation. The whole reason we're in this damned country is to capture bin Laden and the rest of his gang and bring them to justice."

He wondered if justice wouldn't be as well served by blowing up the whole damned mountain. Still, looking at the problem strategically—the big picture—it made sense to capture any high-ranking TAQs they could find. Interrogating them would lead to the capture of others, and, just maybe, to stopping another 9/11.

He hated to admit it, but Dugan was right.

"Driscoll?" he said. "We'll need a team to go in from this side."

"On it."

"Abdul? Where the hell is Abdul?"

The Pashtun rebel was with several of his men, picking through the debris left by the Specter attack. When someone told him Mariacher was looking for him, he hurried over.

"My friend!" Reaching out, he took Mariacher's hand, holding it tightly. "My army is yours to command!"

Mariacher gently extracted his hand from Abdul's grasp. "We're going to flush those bastards out of their caves," he said.

"You . . . you are going *into* the caverns?" Abdul took Mariacher's hand again. "That is most dangerous!"

He glanced at Dugan. "Well, we don't have much of a choice. Here's what we need." Pulling back his hand, he stooped, picking up a sheet of stiff paper lying with the wreckage on the ground. From one side, the sleepy gaze of Osama bin Laden watched from between two Manhattan towers in flames. The other side was blank. He pulled out a pen and sketched quickly. "Here's the canyon . . . we're here. Okay?"

"Okay!"

"The caverns go back into the mountain in this direction." He sketched in several lines, running east, northeast, and southeast. "We don't know how far back these go. But it's a fair bet that there are some openings along here." He indicated the southern edge of the mountains, east of the canyon and facing the city of Khowst. He drew another line, a semicircle, blocking those presumed exits.

"I want you to string your men out along here. When we go in, the TAQs will either fight or they'll run. If they run, I want your men to catch them. You understand?"

"Absolutely, my friend! You can count on us!" Impulsively, Abdul grabbed Mariacher, pulled him close and kissed him.

"Looks like you've got a friend for life there, Mynock," Raptor said, grinning.

Mariacher checked to make sure Abdul was out of earshot. He was eagerly hurrying away to pass on the orders to his men. "I wish they treated their women as well as their boyfriends," he replied, wiping his mouth with his sleeve.

"Maybe I should be with them," Dugan suggested.

"I want you here with us," Mariacher said. "You're the one who wanted to interrogate live HVTs, right?"

"We won't have HVTs to interrogate if the damned raggies let them get away," Dugan replied. "Or if they kill them!"

Mariacher almost made a sharp retort, but bit it off. He neither liked nor trusted the CIA man, and he didn't care for the man's arrogant attitude toward the locals. But now wasn't the time for a confrontation. "Mostly, I want our friendlies out of the way," he said.

"He's right," Driscoll said. "They're eager enough, but not disciplined in a fight. A few hours ago I watched a bunch of them disobey orders to charge a TAQ compound while my team was in the process of infiltrating it." He shook his head. "Gave the whole show away."

"I don't know," Raptor said. "I'm kind of curious about how they'd manage a cavalry charge inside a TAQ tunnel!"

"I'm more concerned about what *we're* going to do in those tunnels," Driscoll said. "We don't know how extensive the tunnel system is, and we don't know how many tangos are in there. I agree with what Tex, here, said earlier. If they're still fighting after getting nailed by a Specter gunship, they're protecting something—or some*body*. I think we should blow every tunnel entrance we can find and get the hell out of Dodge."

That was certainly the safe play. "We'll go in prepared to do just that," Mariacher told them. "Our entrance teams go in just far enough to get an idea of the layout in there. Follow-on teams will plant explosives inside the tunnels, so we can blow them if we have to pull out." He continued to sketch out his plan. As he talked, a thuttering growl sounded from up the valley, and a moment later they saw the MH-47 flying just above the cliff tops, headed toward the eastern side of the canyon. Mariacher had suggested earlier that Driscoll bring the rest of the Osprey strike force over to join Osprey Two on top of the mountain. That would give them the manpower they needed to sweep the area for more tunnels and to provide backup for the tunnel entry team.

"Everybody clear?" he said at last. "Okay. Let's do it."

He glanced at the sky. It was full light now, though the

valley was still in deep shadow. It wouldn't be long before Kabul started reacting to last night's raids. There were plenty of hostile forces within fairly easy reach of Zur Kowt, including Gardez, just over the mountains, and Khowst, to the south. They had to wrap this up and be out of here within the next couple of hours.

And to hell with what the Agency had to say about it.

Chapter 24

"Right," Gunnery Sergeant Eakins said. "Everybody ready?"

"Good to go, Gunny," Tangretti said. The other men chorused agreement. A hundred yards to the east, on a flat shelf of rock, the MH-47 was unloading its cargo of men and equipment.

He looked past the helicopter, at the sun just peeking above the snowbound mountain peaks to the east. What he was about to do, he decided, might well be the toughest thing he would ever do . . . and that included BUD/S and the whole damned SEAL program.

Gunfire cracked and banged in the distance, down in the valley. The assault was beginning.

"Okay," Eakins said. "Here goes."

Eakins and Tangretti were lying next to the well-shaft opening. Tangretti had prepped for his entry by securing a climbing rope to his combat harness. He'd stripped off all the equipment bags and spare gear, leaving nothing to snag on the way down. He'd also attached the AN/PEQ-4 to the rail mount on his H&K, like a flashlight. It was a flashlight, in fact, but one that illuminated only in infrared.

The Marine, meanwhile, was holding a block of C-4 to which a hand grenade was tightly wired. A detonator cap had been added, just to make certain, but the grenade blast itself ought to trigger the plastic explosives. As Tangretti shined his IR flashlight down the shaft, Eakins looked over the rim for one last check, then twisted out the cotter pin and released the arming lever before dropping the improvised munitions into the tunnel mouth. "Fire in the hole!"

Literally fire in the hole. Both men rolled back from the opening, arms over their heads and necks. They heard the package strike bottom, and then a second later a column of flame erupted from the opening with a ringing, savage blast.

Part of Tangretti's mind hoped that the blast would be too much, that it would actually collapse the tunnel. If it did, Osprey Two's role up here would be done. But as the smoke from the shaft opening cleared, the structure was still intact. The only question was for how long. The blast could well have weakened it badly.

Well . . . he would find out. He pulled his monocular into place and checked to make sure it was working. "Climbing!" he called, and slipped over into the opening head first.

There was a rappelling technique, originally developed by the British SAS and later much beloved of Hollywood, where the climber secured his line and went over the side of the cliff or building, walking facedown instead of the more traditional—and safer—faceup. The technique was generally considered useful only for show; there were few times when that kind of cowboying was tactically appropriate.

In this case, though, it *was* appropriate, though there wasn't enough room for a true rappel—bouncing down the shaft with his feet, as though standing horizontally. He had to trust his teammates—Fletcher and Tomajczk—who were braced a few yards back, holding his climbing rope. They'd rigged his harness so the center of pull was below his center of gravity, close to his butt. This way, he could hang head down as they lowered him and aim the IR beam from his light saber down the hole. With his night-vision monocular, he'd be able to see if any TAQ bad guys decided to make an appearance at the bottom.

The C-4 blast should have killed or stunned everybody up and down the horizontal tunnel for quite a distance, and taken care of any ambush or booby traps they might have had in place. Still, Navy SEALs did not become old, retired Navy SEALs by underestimating the enemy. Despite the danger of weakening the tunnel walls and ceiling, it was important to make sure there were no surprises waiting below.

Five feet. Then ten. They lowered him slowly, paying out the line as he descended. He found he could brace his feet against the underside of the rungs on the ladder next to him, pushing gently against the support from the climbing rope, giving himself a measure of control.

When he opened his left eye, all he could see was complete darkness. When he opened his right, the shaft was revealed in shades of green and yellow.

"Hold up," he said over the open mike at his lips. The line stopped paying out, and he dangled for a moment, head down.

SEAL training included long practice at firing from any and all positions, however unlikely. His head, now, was just above the opening of the cross shaft some fifteen feet beneath the surface. Though the C-4 should have taken care of anyone in that tunnel as well, it was best to approach it cautiously.

The thought of the word "cautious" and what he was doing right now almost made him giggle out loud. The stress must be getting to him, he decided.

He positioned himself, using his legs against the ladder and the tunnel wall. "On my mark," he said, "give me a drop of two feet and secure." He brought his H7K to his shoulder, the muzzle just above the opening of the side tunnel. "Mark!"

He dropped two feet, jolting to an uncomfortable halt, head and shoulders now dangling in front of the side tunnel, his weapon aimed into the tunnel, sweeping it with infrared light.

Empty. "The side opening appears to be a room," he told the others over his M-biter. "It's clear." He took a deep breath of acrid, smoky air. Now for the hard part. "Start paying out. Take me down."

Foot by foot they lowered him down the shaft. The air was growing warmer and closer, thick with the burn of smoke. The lower ten feet of the ladder were gone—destroyed, presumably, by the clearing blast. His boot scraped against the side and a sudden shower of loose rocks, some as big as his fist, tumbled past his shoulders and head and clattered onto the rock floor below.

If anyone was waiting for him, they knew he was coming.

With his head just above the opening into the horizontal tunnel at the bottom of the shaft, he called for another halt. This was the trickiest part of the operation, and by far the most dangerous. There was only one of him, and the tunnel ran off in two directions, toward the east and back toward the west and the main entrance to the underground facilities. It was entirely possible for him to drop in facing one way—and be shot in the back by someone waiting for him in the other direction.

In saner CQB situations, operators used dental mirrors or fiber optics to peer around corners. He didn't have any fiberoptic gear, however, and mirrors didn't reflect infrared the way they did visible light. He would have to chance dropping in, trusting the effectiveness of the C-4, and hope that any bad guys waiting for him would not have NVGs.

"At the main tunnel," he reported. He turned to face the east, the part of the tunnel leading deeper into the mountain. "On my mark, drop me three feet and secure."

He took another steadying breath, then tried not to cough on the smoke burning his lungs. This bungee-jumping in slow motion sucked, he decided. For several interminable minutes now the blood had been rushing to his head, pounding behind his eyes. He just wanted this over. "Mark!"

The rope went slack and he dropped, then jerked to a breath-jolting halt, dangling head down from the ceiling of the main tunnel. His IR beam swept bare rock walls and stacks of wooden crates, the nearest ones smashed by the explosion. Hundreds of rifle cartridges had spilled across the rock floor.

The instant the image registered in his brain, he twisted hard, kicking with his feet and turning in place to face west. More rocks came loose, pelting him, but he steadied himself, sweeping the western part of the tunnel with invisible light.

More boxes, scattered everywhere. And sandbags. And a DShK heavy machine gun, toppled over backward in a tangle of ammo belt and tripod legs.

And *bodies* . . .

He was already tapping the trigger of his H&K, firing short bursts into every human body he could make out against that cool green glow. "Tunnel clear!" he announced. "Take me down!"

The rope lowered him farther, until he could get his legs clear of the vertical shaft, brace a shoulder on the floor, and scramble upright, weapon still pointed down the tunnel. The passageway was fairly large, a good six feet high and perhaps eight wide, with wooden cross-braces and supports spaced every few feet.

Reaching around to his back, he released the carabineer from his combat harness. "I'm down. The blast loosened some rock, but the walls look like they're holding. I'd kind of like some company down here!"

"On the way," Eakins replied. "Move clear!"

Tangretti took a closer look at the machine-gun position. There were five tangos sprawled in various contorted positions. They'd obviously decided the Americans might come down the shaft, and had prepared a surprise welcome.

C-4. The SEAL's friend. "Get your ass down here, Gunny."

Zur Kowt Training Camp
Paktia Province, Afghanistan
0702 hours, local time

Mariacher clapped Bradley on the shoulder. "You're clear!"

Gunfire barked and chattered, echoing off the canyon walls. The Marines and SEALs had opened up minutes ago, and were continuing to direct a tremendous volume of fire at the main entrance to the caves. Loudest and most insistent was the M50 machine gun mounted on the DPV, with which Chief Nolfi was hammering at the entrance. The tango machine gun that had fired on them earlier was far enough back down the tunnel that it didn't have a wide field of fire. The DPV had been positioned well outside that kill zone, which meant Nolfi couldn't fire on the TAQ machine gun directly, but he *could* send a stream of 7.62mm rounds slamming into the tunnel wall just inside the entrance at an angle, sending ricochets screaming deeper into the mountain.

That volume of gunfire would at the very least make the tangos take cover, which allowed Bradley to rise from behind the boulder directly in front of the tunnel mouth—and squarely in the enemy's field of fire—with one of Osprey's M136-AT4s on his shoulder. He squeezed the trigger, and the rocket hissed sharply, the white-hot flare of its exhaust streaking into the tunnel entrance.

The warhead was designed to penetrate light armor, but the charge was powerful enough to serve in a minor bunker-busting role as well. They didn't have to breach anything, just stun or kill any bad guys waiting inside. All they needed was a minimum ten-yard flight path so the warhead could arm itself en route.

There was a flash and a sharp report. Smoke puffed from the opening.

"Cease fire! Cease fire!" Mariacher called. "Assault team . . . *go!*"

Four men—Lehman, Osterlee, and a couple of Marines from Osprey, Moore and Carruthers—had been positioned to either side of the tunnel, well back from the entrance. They ran to the entrance now, peered around the corner with their NVGs and light sabers, then rushed inside.

"Alfa One, Osprey!" he heard. "Tunnel entrance secure."

"On our way!" He rose from cover as Bradley dropped the expended launch tube.

"Better living through superior firepower," Bradley quipped.

"Yeah, but now it's a fucking knife fight."

SEALs were not designed for a stand-up slugfest. For most missions, simply having to fire a weapon meant that the mission had failed. For those times when close-quarters battle was called for, the SEAL strategy was to employ literally overwhelming firepower, from their own weapons and from all available air and artillery support, to put the opposition down and put him down hard.

For the most part, frontal assaults were out of the question. SEALs were too valuable to throw away in an attack against a prepared position. Every SEAL had studied the classic cluster-fuck at Paitilla airport in 1987, during Operation Just Cause in Panama. SEALs had been deployed on that op like infantry, for a mission that could have been accomplished by a two-man sniper team half a mile away—taking out Noriega's private jet. The SEALs had walked into a trap, caught in the open by Panamanian troops hidden inside a hangar. At the end of it, the mission had been accomplished . . . but four SEALs were dead, the highest single-mission combat loss for the Teams to date.

He was determined that *this* op would not become another Paitilla.

Zur Kowt Training Camp
Paktia Province, Afghanistan
0712 hours, local time

Tangretti moved down the tunnel cautiously—a left step forward, his right foot up to his left, another left foot, right foot to his left . . . a stealthy bit of choreography that kept him always perfectly balanced, his H&K at his shoulder. Eakins was behind him, covering him, and Karr and Tomajczk were a few paces back, covering the rear. Two more Marines had also descended the vertical shaft and were guarding the eastern end of the tunnel now, while two SEALs placed explosives against the tunnel walls, enough C-4 this time to collapse this entire underground complex.

Now, though, they needed to see how far into the complex they could probe.

Gunfire sounded from somewhere up ahead. Osprey One must be knocking at the front door.

A few yards farther along the passage a smear of light threatened to overwhelm his monocular's optics. With his unaided eye he saw a dogleg in the tunnel ahead, with light spilling from it. These tunnels were normally lit by incandescent bulbs strung along the ceiling. The clearing blast had taken out most of the bulbs along this part of the passageway, but evidently they were still working around the corner.

At least that meant he could use a dental mirror this time instead of leaping out into the open.

He signaled a halt with a raised, clenched fist, then carefully extracted the mirror from a Velcro-sealed pocket. Extending the mirror past the bend in the tunnel, he was able to make out bright light . . . and movement.

He studied the tiny reflected scene for a long moment. The worst thing that could happen now was mistaking the assault team from the main entrance for bad guys and scoring an own goal.

Black turbans. Beards. And them someone shouted an order in Pashto.

At his feet, Eakins lay full-length, using his own mirror to study the Taliban activity around the corner. "Osprey Two, Osprey Two-one," he whispered over his radio. "Multiple targets around the corner, to the south."

The rock walls blocked their communications with the outside world, but the signal would carry to everyone along the corridor's length. The guys at the shaft could relay information if necessary.

Carefully, Eakins rose to his feet, then tapped Tangretti twice on the shoulder. Tangretti nodded, pulled out a flashbang, pulled the pin, and tossed it around the corner.

Someone shouted a warning, a shrill, wailing cry . . . and then a dazzling chain of flashes and sharply ringing concussions detonated in the narrowly confined corridor. The overhead lights went out, shattered by the blast, and an instant later Tangretti and Eakins swung around the corner, weapons aimed.

This branch of the passageway ran for five or six yards before opening into a larger room. TAQ militia stood there, brightly illuminated by the IR beams from two light sabers, but clearly both blinded and deafened by the flash-bang. Tangretti picked a target and tapped off two rounds, semi-auto, shifted aim and fired two more. At his side, Gunny Eakins loosed burst after burst, as Taliban and al-Qaeda fighters shrieked, ran, staggered, collapsed, died. . . .

Tangretti moved forward, still firing.

Zur Kowt Training Camp
Paktia Province, Afghanistan
0714 hours, local time

The front door assault team had entered the main tunnel without incident, passing the wreckage of the machine gun that had been blocking the entrance, and two bodies. Mariacher took a moment to check one of the bodies for papers or ID; the guy's face was beardless—he wore a Saddam-Hussein-style mustache, but his chin was bare.

He found a wallet with a military ID. The plastic card—though covered in Arabic script—sported the image of a flag—a green square with a vertical white bar to the left, and a white crescent and star against the green field. As he'd suspected—Pakistani.

The other body was clad in a ragged *kameez* and sported a beard as long as Mariacher's forearm—almost certainly Taliban. Twenty yards deeper into the mountain, they passed a side tunnel headed north, toward the motor pool chamber, and continued on, leaving a Marine there to keep it under observation. Fifteen yards more they came to a T in the corridor. To the left, the north, the passageway opened into a large room. Someone had blocked the entrance, however, with crates and fifty-five-gallon drums. Gunfire cracked from the barricade, sending rounds whining off rock walls.

Mariacher signaled for Sergeant Moore, who was carrying an M4A1 carbine with an M203 mounted under the barrel. The Marine was just getting into position to fire when Mariacher heard the hammer blow of a flash-bang and saw the strobing flicker of light reflected off the rock wall in front of him. An instant later he heard the sharp reports of H&K gunfire, which were quite distinct from the deeper-throated roar of the AK.

"Osprey One, Osprey Leader!" he called. "Check your fire! I think we just found Osprey Two!" He motioned Moore away from the corner. The M203 fired a 30mm grenade that would have blasted down the barricade, but he didn't want to risk shredding Osprey Two with flying splinters. Instead, he tossed a flash-bang of his own around the corner to the left, while Moore did the same to the right.

Seconds later both detonated, and then Mariacher, Raptor, and Moore rolled around the corner. Mariacher and Raptor headed left, toward the barricade, while Moore guarded the right branch of the tunnel. The barricade was a flimsy affair, with only one defender visible. Raptor took the man down with a burst from his AK, and both men charged the barrier, slamming against it, sending crates spilling into the room beyond.

The lights were still on, casting weirdly shifting shadows across rock walls. A small group of men had gathered here, barricading the doors in a desperate last stand. One man on his knees behind the makeshift barrier clutched at his eyes, screaming. Mariacher put a bullet behind his ear, then swung his weapon up to fire into a small, struggling group at the back of the room.

Another figure rose suddenly at Mariacher's left, a *familiar* figure, clutching at the grip of a tripod-mounted RPD machine gun and trying to aim it at the invaders despite blood streaming from his ears . . . and then Raptor triggered his AK, slamming the man back from the weapon and into one of the wooden posts supporting the rock wall at his back.

Perhaps a dozen more figures groped about in the glare of dangling lightbulbs, some just beyond the boxes, the rest toward the back of the room. Raptor and Mariacher opened fire on the closest ones, cutting them down one after another. The ones in the back were falling as well . . . and then the ones still standing were throwing down their weapons and holding their hands high, screaming something shrill in Pashto.

Black-clad figures, hooded, with monoculars over their right eyes, were emerging from a doorway in the back. "Check fire! Check fire!" Mariacher called. "Osprey Two, this is One! We have you in sight!"

"We see you, Osprey One."

The last three tangos huddled at the center of the room, still blinking against the leftover dazzle in their eyes from the flash-bangs. Mariacher and Raptor, followed by Lieutenant Driscoll, more SEALS, some Marines, and Tex Dugan, all pushed past the barricade and entered the large chamber.

Mariacher went to the man sprawled behind the machine gun, rolling him onto his side, looking at his face.

Major Qadi.

Raptor pushed his night-vision goggles back on his head. "You two!" He signaled to the Marines, then pointed toward a third door in the back. "Watch that entrance!"

"Mark? . . ." an incredulous voice called out, heard both over the radio circuit and the ear. "Mark *Halstead*?"

"*Tangretti? . . .*"

An instant later the assault team was treated to the unlikely spectacle of a Navy SEAL and a CIA Special Action operator embracing in the center of the room, pounding one another's backs.

Mariacher looked at the astonished Driscoll. "You know, I think our boys may be picking up bad habits from the locals."

Zur Kowt Training Camp
Paktia Province, Afghanistan
0716 hours, local time

Tangretti pulled back from Halstead, looking his old friend up and down. "I had no idea you were out here."

"Same here. Small world, huh?"

"Good to see you again, bro."

"Yeah, me too . . . but we'd better stop meeting like this. We're embarrassing our lieutenants."

Tangretti laughed. "Not to mention the Marines."

The unexpected encounter with Mark Halstead—his boyhood friend and a fellow SEAL until he'd left the service a few years ago—had left Tangretti almost giddy. Damn it . . . what were the odds?

Well, he decided, maybe the odds weren't that long after all. They were both hunting for the same people. He'd known Halstead was working for the Agency and was overseas *somewhere*.

One fact of military life continued to amaze him. The Navy was a tight little world all its own, and the SEAL community smaller and tighter still. It was astonishing how, over the course of ten years or so, the same people kept popping up at new duty stations or on new deployments as their paths kept crossing yours.

A bright flash startled him. Dugan had pulled out a digital camera and was taking pictures of dead terrorists.

"Back to work, bro," Halstead told him. "We need to get this place secure and get out of here."

"Roger that," Tangretti said.

"Just one thing."

"What's that?"

"I thought your dad told you never to go poking around in holes in the ground ever again?"

Zur Kowt Training Camp
Paktia Province, Afghanistan
0717 hours, local time

The room apparently had been used as a classroom or for indoctrination. The walls were decorated with garishly colored posters, some showing bin Laden's face, the World
Trade Center and crashing airliners, others just covered in
bright passages of Arabic script. There was a single folding
table next to piles of books—Qur'ans, probably—and, most
alarmingly, a number of eight-by-ten color photographs on
the table that had the feel of a tourist's vacation snapshots:
the White House, the Capitol, the Smithsonian Air and
Space Museum, a long line of people waiting at the foot of
the Washington Monument, more crowds standing before
the Wall of Names in the Vietnam War Memorial.

A kind of al-Qaeda shopping list . . .

"Hey, Lieutenant?" one of the Marines standing by the third
door in the room called to him. "Sir, you should see this!"

An instant later a savage explosion rocked the chamber.

Zur Kowt Training Camp
Paktia Province, Afghanistan
0717 hours, local time

Iskanderov heard the explosion echoing down the underground passageways behind him and smiled. The American
raiders, evidently, had found one of the little surprises he'd
left for them to find . . . one of their own claymore mines,
left over from the Russian war, when their CIA had been
funneling so many deadly little toys to the mujahideen with
Pakistani help. The blast, with its shotgun effect constrained
by the narrow tunnels, would be deadly.

He hoped it had killed many of them. At the very least, it would discourage pursuit.

Iskanderov was in a cement-walled passageway so low he had to bend nearly double to negotiate it. There was no light, but he didn't need light to see. The tunnel was smooth and straight.

Originally, this had been a natural channel through the rocks. When the Afghans had built the Zur Kowt complex, they widened it to serve as a drainage conduit. In the spring, melting snow could flood some of the lower storerooms. This tunnel channeled the water down to the foot of the mountain, letting it flow into a streambed on the northern rim of the Khowst Plain.

The tunnel served admirably as an emergency escape route from the compound. Iskanderov had sent Mohammed and Ahmadullah on ahead, while he set up the claymore outside the door to the classroom. They would be able to bypass the American commando force entirely, make their way into Khowst, and there begin to assemble a counterstrike.

In fact, he had already decided that it was time to abandon not only Zur Kowt, but Afghanistan. This raid would be only the beginning. American special operations forces would soon be everywhere in the country. Bin Laden, Omar, and the rest might continue to hide in caves along the Pakistan border, or they might slip into Pakistan and from there make their way to al-Qaeda cells elsewhere in the world. Iskanderov planned to go back home, back to Tajikistan, where his contacts with the drug pipeline and the Russian mafia would let him shift his fortune back into the former SSRs. There were empires to be won there, with the Islamic revolt in Chechnya. *Empires*.

The gently sloping tunnel leveled off, and a moment later Iskanderov stepped out, blinking, into hard morning sunlight.

"There he is!" a voice screamed in Pashto. "Grab him!"

Rough hands seized his arms and the back collar of his jacket and he was forced to his knees.

"Wait!" he cried. "Wait! I am your brother!"

The men around him, clearly, were anti-Taliban militia. There were five or six of them, well-armed, and with horses. The Americans must have set them to guard this area south of the mountains.

A hand lifted his chin, and a bearded man locked eyes with him. "*You* are no brother," the man said, before spitting into his face. "With those eyes? You are not Pashtun!"

"I have money! I can pay you well!"

"That," his captor said, "has already been taken care of."

The man stepped aside. With growing horror, Iskanderov looked past him to see Mohammed and Ahmadullah standing among some other Afghan tribesmen. Mohammed shook the hand of one, then climbed onto a horse held by another. Ahmadullah looked back at Iskanderov, gave him a sardonic smile, then gestured with a good-natured salaam.

Go in peace.

"Wait!" he called. "What are you doing?"

"Those men are wealthy and they are brothers," his captor said. "They told us you have been using the holy name of Allah, may His name be blessed forever, to further your own ends." He grinned. "They also told us your name is Iskanderov, that you are a filthy Russian! So you are going to stay with us. . . ."

"No! Wait! You can't do this to me!"

Khalid Mohammed looked at him from horseback for a moment, his expression showing uncertainty. Then he shrugged, looked away and turned, urging his mount toward the south and Khowst. Ahmadullah clambered onto another horse, then laughed aloud.

"Tell the Americans they will never find us!" he called . . . in Russian.

A rifle butt slammed against Iskanderov's face, sending him sprawling.

"You filthy Russian dog," one of the Pashtuns standing over him said. Iskanderov heard the steely snick of a blade being drawn, saw the gleam of sunlight on a sharply honed knife.

He began screaming. . . .

Zur Kowt Training Camp
Paktia Province, Afghanistan
0745 hours, local time

"They *what*?" Mariacher was furious. "Who told them to do that?"

Dugan spread his hands. "No one. It's . . . their way."

Mariacher looked up at the hard, blue sky overhead, fists clenched in frustration. They'd moved out of the underground complex after they'd found the booby trap at the inner tunnel entrance, while small teams continued to explore the complex. " 'Their way' is going to cost us this war, damn it! Tell Abdul I want to talk to him!"

"It won't do any good," the CIA man replied. "They're Pashtun, remember."

Raptor was sitting on a boulder nearby, allowing Tangretti, who'd turned out to be a Navy corpsman as well as a SEAL, to wrap a bandage around his head. All of them were lucky to be alive. A Marine had spotted a trip wire stretched across the entrance to the third tunnel leading out of the classroom. He'd called Mariacher over, and, when he indicated it using the muzzle of his rifle as a pointer, he evidently triggered *another* tripwire, an invisible one—probably a simple photoelectric cell set up just beyond the tunnel entrance.

By extraordinary good fortune, no one in the assault team

had been killed. Both SEAL and Recon Marine training emphasized the need to stay out of doorways that hadn't yet been secured. The claymore's detonation had shredded the timbers supporting the doorway and shotgunned a swarm of deadly steel balls into the classroom, but the door itself had served to keep the blast tightly focused—and no one was standing in its path. Only Raptor, who'd been several yards back from the door and just to one side, had been hurt—as a wood splinter tore his scalp just above his left eye. The bleeding wound looked a lot worse than it was.

"He's right," Raptor said. "Their code of Pakhtunwali is a hell of a lot more binding to them than any allegiance they might owe us."

"But they *let the bastards escape*!"

According to Dugan, a couple of anti-Taliban fighters had arrived at Zur Kowt a few minutes ago with news that they'd captured a man—they claimed he was a Russian—in a dry creek bed to the southeast. Further questioning had elicited the astonishing news that they also encountered several Pashtuns escaping from the underground complex, but that they'd been released.

"They were our brothers!" the mujahideen bearing that unwelcome news had explained through Dugan's Phraselator. "They said they surrendered and that they wanted to change sides, and so we let them."

Mariacher wondered if the Phraselator had been working right. It just seemed too incredible a story to be believed.

At least the assault force had the "Russian," though apparently his captors had been pretty rough with him. He might well have information that would lead to the capture of the others.

"Where is the Russian now?" Mariacher asked Dugan.

"They're bringing him in. I guess he's bleeding pretty

badly." He nodded toward Tangretti. "Maybe he can patch him up."

"I'll do my best," Tangretti said. "There," he told Raptor. "Good as new. And maybe that'll teach you not to poke around in holes in the ground either!"

An hour later Mariacher watched as the last of the Marines and SEALs moved up the ramp into the waiting MH-47 helicopter. The rotors were turning. It was time to leave Zur Kowt . . . and Afghanistan. Their next stop was Dalbandin, Pakistan.

The CIA man was next to him.

"Dugan . . . tell me something."

"Sure. If I can."

"What happened in Kuala Lumpur? How did Green Tiger get away? You told us you had the back door covered. Was there another way out of that building?"

Dugan hesitated, as though struggling with whether to answer. Then he sighed. "It was my bad," he said. "I told you guys to hold off while I put together my own team to go in and grab him."

"Why? I mean, we *had* the bastard!" He held out his hand, palm up. "We had him right *here*!"

And now Green Tiger was on the prowl once more.

"Well, you know how it is. I needed a victory, a really flashy victory, to show to my boss back at Langley, you know?" He made a face. "They stuck me out there on the ass end of nowhere to get me out of Langley, you know. Office politics. I'd stepped on some toes." He shrugged. "It happens. Anyway, a hit team—like the one that tried to cap you boys in the hotel room—showed up and scattered my assault team. Turns out they hit you guys at the same time. And in all the confusion, Mohammed got into a car waiting for him in a back alley and made his getaway. Had a private jet waiting for him at the airport."

"Son of a bitch! You let him get away because of office politics?"

"Hey, it happens." He gave a careless shrug. "Don't worry. We'll still get him. We'll get *all* of them!"

But Mariacher wasn't so sure. He'd seen wars ruined by politics before.

Moments later the MC-47 lifted up above the mountain valley. Mariacher was watching through one of the cargo deck windows when Driscoll pressed the switch on a radio control and the whole east side of the canyon appeared to lift out from the rest of the mountain, then collapse in a billowing pillar of dust and smoke. Other blasts joined in from the west side of the valley as dozens of explosive charges planted by the SEALs detonated, collapsing Zur Kowt's caves and tunnels.

Gaining altitude, the Dark Horse circled toward the southwest and began picking up speed.

Chapter 25

Kabul
Kabul Province, Afghanistan
1610 hours, local time

They were dancing in the streets.

Mariacher, Tangretti, and Mark Halstead stood on the sidewalk along a street jammed with people—happy, wildly celebrating people: men, women, and children alike. Music blared from boom boxes and cheap Pakistani transistor radios, music that had not been heard on Kabul's streets for six years. Many of the men were now beardless, or else sported neatly and newly trimmed mustaches and beards. A circle of men had formed in the middle of the street, and they were holding hands and dancing, while other men, and a few women, stood nearby and clapped out the time.

The capital city of Afghanistan was officially liberated the day before, and the population had been celebrating enthusiastically ever since.

"What do you think, Tangretti?" Mariacher said, leaning

close to the other SEAL so he could be heard over the din. "You think the folks back home should see this?"

"Where's CNN when you really need 'em?" Tangretti shouted back.

Mariacher clapped his friend on the back. Tangretti had been a bit down earlier. A few days ago, at the new special ops base south of Kandahar, he'd managed to put a call through to his girlfriend back in the States. Apparently the news there was all about continued American bombings in Afghanistan, hundreds of civilian deaths, and the fact that American forces hadn't been able to catch the senior leadership of either al-Qaeda or the Taliban. Tangretti's girl appeared to be having second thoughts about the relationship.

He seemed to be bouncing back, however. It was tough to stay depressed in this atmosphere of unrestrained jubilation.

The war wasn't over yet, not by a long shot. But the Taliban was now out. The Northern Alliance was in.

Afghanistan, most of it anyway, was free.

The tide had begun turning when U.S. air attacks started hammering Taliban and al-Qaeda positions facing the Northern Alliance. By the end of October earlier political concerns about having the alliance take Kabul had been set aside. Almost at once the Taliban began disintegrating, fleeing the front or surrendering in large numbers. The Northern Alliance, though slow to move at first, swarmed south.

On November 11, Mazar-I-Sharif—considered the strategic city in the north—fell to forces led by General Rashid Dostum, forces that included volunteers from the regular army of Uzbekistan. Dostum's Afghan contingent, which had changed sides several times already, proceeded to slaughter six hundred Taliban soldiers as they surrendered.

Washington, hoping to avoid a similar slaughter in Kabul, directed the force that had belonged to the assassinated former Northern Alliance commander, Masoud, to take Kabul. That force, comprised largely of Tajiks, negotiated with Taliban troops and reached an agreement with their leaders, letting them use the main roads south.

On the night of November 12 the Taliban quietly slipped out of Kabul. Americans would not be among the first to enter the city—not officially, at any rate. That distinction would be reserved for the Northern Alliance.

Even so, a pair of Russian-made helicopters slipped into the outskirts of the city late that evening, bearing teams of CIA Special Action operators who moved to secure a number of embarrassing documents that linked various U.S. officials with the Taliban. There were a large number of skeletons in the Agency's closet, it seemed, some going back to the days when they'd helped Pakistan create al-Qaeda.

A Russian team entered as well, setting up shop at the former U.S. Embassy. They had their own agenda to carry out, and wanted to send a clear message to the United States that they would not be left out of affairs in this part of the world. The terror war in Chechnya, it seemed, not to mention Islamic insurrections all across south Russia, had also been orchestrated from Afghanistan.

On November 13, Northern Alliance forces formally entered Kabul, with a pair of Russian Mi-24 helicopters repainted in Afghan colors flying cover. Numerous nearby cities fell to Dostum's forces, as the slaughter of Taliban troops continued. In the south, near Kandahar, money liberally spread by the CIA purchased an anti-Taliban insurrection. Intercepted radio communications from Mullah Omar indicated that morale and discipline within the Taliban army were on the point of complete collapse.

And now, just twenty-four hours after Kabul's liberation, a handful of U.S. Special Action teams, Special Forces, and Navy SEALs were in Kabul. Army Special Forces units had accompanied some of the Northern Alliance troops; the others had arrived by helicopter from Pakistan or from the *Kitty Hawk,* in the Arabian Sea.

There was a special urgency in this. The first S.A. teams into the city had uncovered some disturbing documents during their covert housecleaning two days earlier. In their hasty departure from Kabul, al-Qaeda personnel had left behind some papers indicating that bin Laden's network was actively attempting to acquire nuclear weapons, possibly with help from Pakistani scientists. A few days before, on November 10, Pakistan's largest newspaper had published an interview with bin Laden in which the al-Qaeda leader claimed that al-Qaeda already possessed nuclear and biological weapons, and that they would not hesitate to use them against America.

The threat was being taken *very* seriously. CIA and special ops forces converged on the city to follow up on related leads and to try to get an idea of the shape and scope of the threat. It was tough to do anything, though, when the entire city appeared to have gone insane.

Sean Dugan had contacted Halstead and Mariacher specifically the evening before. It seemed there was a woman who wanted to meet with them, a woman who might have some information for the Americans. Halstead and Mariacher had duly flown in early that morning from the USS *Kitty Hawk,* by way of Dalbandin. Tangretti had gotten permission to come along, "riding shotgun," as he put it. He and Halstead had been spending a lot of time catching up.

The Americans started when full-auto gunfire cut loose from nearby. "It's okay," Tangretti said as they turned to face the shots. "It's just some idiot firing his AK into the air."

"People can get killed that way," Mariacher replied. "What goes up has to come down!"

"Yeah," Halstead added. "The Taliban's laws have been

repealed, but not the law of gravity. I remember there were some people killed in Kuwait that way too."

The crowd in the street gave way—reluctantly—to an ex-Russian T-54 tank piled high with cheering, waving Northern Alliance troops.

"So, Lieutenant," Tangretti said. "Where's this girlfriend of yours?"

"I don't know. Dugan said she'd meet us at this corner . . . wait a sec. I think that might be her!" He waved.

A tall woman across the street waved back. As soon as the tank with its entourage had passed, she began to make her way toward them. She was accompanied by a much older, bearded man, who carried a battered attaché case.

Nooria Fahim, the lady of the striking pale blue eyes, smiled at them. She was not wearing a burka, though she was wearing an *abaya*—a long outer robe—and a *hijab*—a triangular scarf worn over the head, draped to veil her lower face.

She spoke rapidly to her escort, who nodded and replied in Pashto. Then she turned to the Americans. "This is my friend, Ibrahium Azhar," she said. "If anyone should ask, he is my father."

Raptor said something in Pashto, and the man beamed, nodding.

"This . . . demonstration is in *your* honor, you know," she said.

"I don't think so, ma'am," Mariacher replied. "Looks to me like it's in honor of *freedom*." He turned, introducing her. "Ms. Fahim. You might remember Mark Halstead, though he was going by the name of 'Raptor' at the time."

"I remember you well . . . Raptor. Good to see you again."

"The pleasure's mine, Ms. Fahim."

"And this is David Tangretti. Tangretti . . . Nooria Fahim, of the Revolutionary Alliance of the Women of Afghanistan."

"Enchanted," she said, the lilt of Oxford thick in her voice.

"Pleased to meet you."

"So, how's your revolution coming?" Mariacher asked her. "It looks like things might be improving."

"That," she said, "remains to be seen. A few of us have discarded the burka. But attitudes and prejudice are not changed overnight, even by a liberating army."

"I see you still don't go out on the street without an escort."

"No. Too many people don't understand." She looked thoughtful. "It would be like *your* women suddenly walking naked through the downtown of one of your cities. It would shock good Christians. Perhaps make them angry. And it would . . . shall we say . . . inflame the passions of the men who saw them."

"Sounds like an idea," Tangretti said.

"Stow that, mister," Mariacher snapped. He gave Nooria an apologetic look. "Don't mind him."

She let the comment pass. "It may surprise you, but most Muslim women wear the veil because they *prefer* to. They'd rather not deal with men's lust."

"If you say so. The idea is that you're free now. You can do what you want."

"Up to a point." She looked around. "But . . . perhaps we should get off the street. I know a small sidewalk café that has reopened already."

Afghans, it seemed, were as much possessed by the entrepreneurial spirit as the inhabitants of Pakistan's Northwest Frontier. With the departure of the Taliban, businesses of every kind had been blossoming throughout the war-shattered city.

Mariacher hoped the boom would continue. He'd also seen signs of the wrenching poverty here—women and children begging in the streets . . . or offering to sell themselves.

The five of them sat around a table on the dusty street, watching the celebrations. Mariacher was pleased to see several kites tugging at their strings high above a park toward the north. Afghans—the children especially—adored kites, but they'd been against the law for six years, in some places longer. A whole new generation of children had been born and reached kite-flying age without ever having seen one of the magical devices.

They were learning now, from fathers and older brothers.

"So, Ms. Fahim—" Mariacher began.

"Please, call me Nooria."

He nodded. "And I'm Ken. Sean Dugan said you had something for us, but you wouldn't talk to him."

She smiled. "Mostly, I wanted the chance to see you again . . . Ken. To know you were all right. And to . . . thank you."

"Like I said, it wasn't me. Your people did most of the work."

"Nonsense. The Northern Alliance would not be in Kabul now if not for what you Americans did."

"I thought you didn't like the Northern Alliance."

"I don't. But they're better than the Taliban. A little, anyway. And we have hope now. A chance at a truly democratic government." She spoke with Ibrahium. He nodded, and set the attaché case on the table, opening it. Nooria extracted a manila envelope. "I'm sure you will know how best to use this," she said.

Mariacher untied the string sealing the flap and opened it. Inside were black and white photographs of several men, a map of a town, and several sheets typewritten in English. His eyes widened as he read the first few lines.

"We certainly do. Thank you."

"I heard about your . . . problem at Zur Kowt. I thought, perhaps, this would make up for that."

"It'll help a lot. I still haven't forgiven Abdul Hafez for that, you know."

She shrugged. "What you Americans don't understand is that war—the blood feud of *badal*—is a way of life here, and has been since long before the time of Alexander the Great. An enemy is an enemy, until he suddenly switches sides. We've been seeing a lot of that lately."

"Yes, we have."

It was true. The Northern Alliance troops seemed to be in constant contact with their Taliban opponents. They'd negotiated that deal for moving down the road to Kabul. There were dozens of reports of wholesale defections by Taliban troops, with those soldiers welcomed with open arms by their former enemies. There were also reports of bloody massacres, of course, especially by Dostum's Uzbeks ... but that seemed to be rooted in ancient hostilities between very different tribes. Among the Pashtun, the word for "cousin" was the same as the word for "enemy," but that could just as easily be put another way. The word for "enemy" was the same as the word for "cousin."

And members of the family could always be forgiven, then welcomed into heart and hearth under the ancient blood obligations of Pakhtunwali.

The system seemed to work for the Afghans, but it was confusing, and damned frustrating, for the Americans. More than once in the past month Afghan prisoners had been released by their Afghan captors before they could be questioned. There were suspicions that some Taliban leaders were being protected in Pakistan, despite Pakistan's outraged protests to the contrary—those ancient blood ties among Pashtun, once again, stronger than the bonds of nationality.

Mariacher still felt a white fury over Mohammed and Ahmadullah claiming they were changing sides, handing over some money ... and walking right through Abdul's lines.

Damn it all! They'd risked so much ... and lost the prize.

But maybe not all of it.

Mariacher glanced through the photos once more. "Thank you. Is there anything we can do for you, in exchange?"

He couldn't see through her veil, but her eyes revealed her smile. "You can continue helping us, my people. We're grateful. More grateful than we can say. But also . . . we're afraid."

"Afraid? Of what? I don't think the Taliban will be coming back any time soon."

"No." She turned, looking toward the street where another Northern Alliance tank was clattering past the cheering throngs. "No . . . but I am afraid of *them*. Someday, you Americans will be gone. And then *they* will determine how best to interpret God's word."

Mariacher remembered what Nooria had told him about the thugs at the University of Afghanistan in the 1970s, long before the Taliban, throwing acid on women's bare legs and faces. And, too . . . he'd already heard some disturbing reports coming from the north, from areas already liberated by the alliance. There were stories of women who'd thrown off the burka and adopted Western dress being accosted, humiliated, even beaten and raped by Northern Alliance troops, by Islamic zealots, or by members of the new police militias.

It might well be a foretaste of what was coming. It might well be that Enduring Freedom, so far as Afghanistan's women were concerned, was not so enduring after all.

He looked at one of the young women dancing in the streets. She wore an *abaya,* but no veil. Sure enough . . . several of the men, and even a few veiled women, were watching her with dark, even hostile looks.

"I don't know what we can do, Nooria," Halstead told her. "We're not allowed to set policy. Your people have to come up with a government that works for you."

"I ask only that you not forget us," she told him.

Her eyes glistened with tears.

Thursday, December 27, 2001

Outside Naka
Paktika Province, Afghanistan
2205 hours, local time

Halstead lay on his stomach, peering through the SOFLAM's sight. Mariacher was next to him. The rest of the Special Action team was spread out across the hilltop in a perimeter, invisible in the darkness.

"Raider One, ten seconds," the headphone voice reported. Then, "Raider One! Laser on!"

Halstead triggered the SOFLAM unit, painting the target—a particular single-story adobe house, one of five in a small compound on the outskirts of the tiny village of Naka.

"Raider One, Ghost One," he said. "Laser on."

"Spot!" the voice said. "Raider One . . . locked on. Launch!"

For a moment the night was silent.

Then, *"Damn!"*

"What is it, Mynock?"

Mariacher pointed to the left. "See that guy? That's Red Cobra! That's our pigeon! Pulling that motorcycle out of that shed! He's going to get away!"

Halstead picked up a pair of night-vision binoculars and focused on the man. It was tough to see at this range but . . . yeah. Enough light was spilling from the shed that Halstead could make out his features.

It sure looked like him.

For a moment Halstead considered shifting the aim of the

SOFLAM. Doing so would deflect the aim of the incoming bomb. But there were other considerations as well, other HVTs. And they didn't dare risk another miss.

He kept the laser designator aimed at the house, the original target.

The man, the HVT, was on the motorcycle now. Halstead heard the purr of the engine, far off. The Special Action team was too far to take him down with an H&K or AK. With a Barrett .50 they might have managed it. But the rules for this op were to stay out of direct combat, paint the target, and watch the bombs fall.

Come on . . . come on . . .

It was heartfelt prayer. Willing the bomb to hit . . .

The information Nooria gave them in Kabul had led the CIA to begin surveillance on the tiny village of Naka, here in the north of Paktika Province, sixty miles west of Khowst. The house in the valley below belonged to Maulvi Ahmad Taha, a former Taliban commander and the governor of Kunar province. Intelligence developed since Nooria had met with them suggested that a meeting of Taliban leaders would take place in this house tonight. Taha's two sons, both Taliban subcommanders, were there. Mullah Abdul Salam Rocketi, a former Taliban military official in Jalalabad, was supposed to be present.

And the meeting had been called by none other than the HVT designated Red Cobra—Qari Ahmadullah, the Taliban's Minister of Security.

Ahmadullah was leaving the compound, riding the motorcycle to safety. Several bearded men were exiting the main house as well now.

Had the SEALs been spotted? An alarm given? There was no way to tell.

"Ghost One, Raider One," the voice said. "Laser off."

They were committed. Mariacher switched off the laser designator.

"You know," Mariacher said, "this Rumsfeld Doctrine shit really sucks."

"Give it time."

"We should've landed a team, gone down there, kicked the door in, and rounded 'em up. Enough of this damned sneaking-peeking."

"When you're Secretary of Defense," Halstead told his friend, "then you can make the rules."

In fact, though, he agreed. The so-called Rumsfeld Doctrine envisioned a clean war, a surgical war, where America's enemies were brought to justice . . . but where American military personnel were not subject to risk.

In Halstead's mind that was just plain crazy. He was all for reducing risks for the men and women who faced them—and some of the new high-tech wrinkles of modern warfare, from unmanned aerial surveillance drones to stealth aircraft to laser-guided ordnance to the brute-force punch of 15,000-pound Daisy Cutter bombs were nothing short of astonishing.

But bin Laden had made this war *personal* with his attack on New York City. It was sheer foolery to imagine that the payback could be carried out by proxy.

Or without combat loss.

The seconds dragged. . . .

And then the house exploded, every window blowing out an instant before the walls disintegrated in a white glare of destruction. The men close by the house were gone in a literal flash. A second later the motorcyclist veered sharply, then was swept from the road by an unseen giant's hand.

The initial blast was silent, but seconds later the noise reached the watching SEALs—a deep-throated boom that echoed across the valley.

And then other houses were engulfed by separate blasts. The attacking aircraft, unseen, unheard, had dropped a whole string of bombs, the first one guided by the SOFLAM beam to Taha's house, the others following, scattering, annihilating the entire compound.

Overwhelming, irresistible firepower.

More explosions. Bricks and sections of wall rained across the road, as orange flame and smoke billowed into the night. Mariacher picked up his binoculars and tried to find Ahmadullah, but there was no sign of him.

"Raider One, Ghost One," Mariacher said. "Mission accomplished. Target destroyed."

It was time to go home.

Epilogue

Tuesday, January 1, 2002

Ground Zero
Lower Manhattan
1340 hours, local time

After carrying out the raid to find and target Qari Ahmadullah, the SEALs had extracted by helicopter and returned to the *Kitty Hawk*. Two days later they were stateside once more, being debriefed at a CIA secure facility at Camp Peary, near Williamsburg, Virginia. Saturday, December 29, they'd been granted a week's leave—a bit of time off for the New Year. They had orders to report back to base—SEAL Team Three headquarters in Coronado for Tangretti, and Dev-Group's headquarters at Virginia Beach for Mariacher. There would be more debriefings then . . . and then more missions.

The war continued.

On New Year's Eve, David Tangretti and Ken Mariacher had flown to New York City on a half-drunken whim, to see in the New Year in Times Square. The next day they made a pilgrimage, waiting in line for hours, but filing at last onto the observation platform.

The structure had been opened only yesterday. Tourists

and New Yorkers had been lining up ever since, coming to see . . . coming to pay homage.

Mariacher and Tangretti leaned against the railing, looking out over the vast, jagged, wreckage-rimmed caldron that was Ground Zero, all that remained now of the twin towers of the World Trade Center and several other buildings destroyed by the collapse. The crater gaped below them, vast and cold. A policeman had told them during their wait that the fires smoldering in the wreckage had finally been declared extinguished just two weeks ago, on December 19. Those fires, after burning for ninety-nine days, had been the longest-burning commercial fires in United States history. On December 20 the last remaining WTC structure had been taken down.

The city—and the country—prepared to rebuild.

"So . . . what do you think, Lieutenant?" Tangretti asked. "Are we going to get the bastards?"

Mariacher folded his hands as he leaned on the railing. "The problem is, we could've gotten 'em already, and never know it." He sighed. "And, aw, hell. If we kill them, there's always more to take their place."

The reports out of Afghanistan lately had not been encouraging. Early in December, U.S. intelligence sources and satellite intercepts of cell phone calls had finally pinpointed bin Laden and his major supporters in a rugged stretch of the Malawa Mountains on the Pakistan border, a place called Tora Bora. American warplanes pounded the region incessantly for weeks, and then, in accordance with the Rumsfeld Doctrine, anti-Taliban Afghan troops had been sent in.

Astonishingly, and to the Coalition troops' horror and anger, the friendly Afghans had allowed hundreds of their opponents to pass through their lines to freedom after a series of negotiations. Two hundred TAQ bodies had been found in the mountains—mostly killed by the air attacks— and about sixty were arrested. The prisoners turned out to be more Pakistani troops newly arrived to join the great jihad, and had no connections with al-Qaeda at all.

Osama bin Laden, with a $25 million reward on his head, had not been heard from since . . . but there were conflicting reports. He was dead, sealed inside a cave. He was alive, smuggled across the border into Pakistan by well-paid sympathizers. He'd escaped to his old haunts in Saudi Arabia or the Sudan. He was sick, dying of kidney disease. He'd been granted refuge in Iraq or Iran.

In Afghanistan, the war continued. The first American combat death had occurred on November 25—Michael Spann, a CIA officer killed in an uprising by TAQ prisoners in a fortress poorly guarded by Northern Alliance troops. Kandahar fell early in December, amid reports that thousands of Taliban fighters had slipped through Afghan lines. Increasing Coalition frustration with the Northern Alliance's apparently casual prosecution of this war was swiftly leading to the Rumsfeld Doctrine's end.

On December 22, Hamid Karzai, a Western-educated Pashtun, assumed control of a provisional Afghan government, promising that his priority would be peace and stability.

Three months after 9/11, the face of the world had changed. A crater gaped in the heart of New York City's financial district, marking the spot where nearly three thousand innocent lives had been snuffed out in an instant of sociopathic-religious insanity. Halfway around the world, a government had been driven from power and freedom restored to an enslaved people. Allah alone knew if that freedom would endure.

And the fear of further attacks continued to haunt Americans.

With the death toll now at five, the anthrax letters remained a mystery, deeper now than before. Five different laboratories had tested samples recovered from Capitol Hill, and all had linked them genetically to a strain held in U.S. Army biowar stocks. How had foreign terrorists gotten hold of them? Or, perhaps a more chilling possibility, was it an inside job, one unrelated to al-Qaeda save circumstantially, carried out by persons unknown, for reasons unknown?

More pressing were the rumors within military and government circles about nuclear weapons in terrorist hands. Already, open speculation was circulating throughout Washington about Saddam Hussein's possible role in the 9/11 attacks, about Iraq's open determination to acquire weapons of mass destruction, and about the possibility of invading Iraq to save the West.

Tangretti remembered a briefing session months ago, and the incredible idea of the United States taking on the entire world at once.

The idea was still impractical, but the possibility that a nation still bleeding from the wounds inflicted upon it might actually try such a thing no longer seemed so far-fetched.

"Three thousand people dead," Mariacher said beside him. "How do you put a price on something like that? How do you exact vengeance?"

"You're not saying we should let them go!"

"Of course not. And it's not about revenge. The president was right in one of his speeches, you know. The fanatics have launched a war against civilization itself. *Our* civilization, anyway. The damned fundamentalists are the world's new barbarians, ready to destroy, to tear down, to kill anything or anyone they don't like or don't understand or that doesn't fit their narrow, Middle Ages mind-set. We've *got* to fight back, or they'll run right over us."

Tangretti brought his fist down on the railing, striking hard enough to hurt. "Damn it! It's like this was Pearl Harbor for World War Three."

"I think it was. The war actually started earlier—maybe

with the *first* bomb attack here—but if this was America's wake-up call, then, yeah, it was."

"I'm not sure it did wake us up," Tangretti said, angry.

Mariacher chuckled. "You still pissed about your girlfriend?"

"Huh? Nah. Last time I talked to her on the phone, she was marrying an investment broker. Someone named Jack."

"That sucks."

"Not really. Damned SEAL groupie. She . . . didn't understand. I wonder, sometimes, if *anyone* understands."

"Do you? Look around."

Tangretti turned his head. The new observation platform was thronged, and a long line still waited outside. They could only let people in a few at a time.

He saw men and women in business suits under open winter coats. Teenagers in baggy pants, their ball caps on backward. Mothers with children. Couples. Grave men in the uniforms of police and fire fighters—the new American heroes. Latinos. African-Americans. A bearded man in a turban, the woman on his arm in a *sari*.

The expressions on their faces ranged from stolid to angry, from tightly controlled to tear-streaked sorrow.

From meditative to determined.

Yeah. They understood.

They knew they were a nation at war.

There *would* be a reckoning.

And the SEALs would be there to see it through.

Afterword

This is a work of fiction, based on real-world events. As of this writing, in the spring of 2005, the war in Afghanistan continues, as does the larger, global war on terror. Many of the names mentioned, the characters described, are real.

Qari Ahmadullah was the Taliban's Minister of Security. On December 28, 2001, he was reported killed by an American air strike in the village of Naka.

Khalid Shaikh Mohammed, the number-three man in al-Qaeda and the head of that organization's propaganda arm, has been solidly linked to planning for the failed Operation Bojinka—which actually existed and failed as described—and to the attacks of September 11. He conspired in a failed attempt to bomb American Airlines Flight 63 in December 2002, and in the murder of Daniel Pearl, a reporter with the *Wall Street Journal* kidnapped in Karachi late in January 2002. In May of that year he dispatched José Padilla to Chicago, reportedly as part of a plot to detonate a "dirty bomb"—conventional explosives laced with radioactive material—somewhere in the United States. Mohammed was also linked to fertilizer-bomb attacks against nightclubs in Bali and the U.S. Embassy in Karachi.

He was also suspected of being either an asset or an agent for the Pakistani ISI.

In March 2003, Khalid Shaikh Mohammed was captured—reportedly, if unconvincingly—by the ISI without the assistance of Western authorities. He was turned over to American custody and has been held since for ongoing interrogation at an undisclosed location.

The U.S. Navy SEALs continue to serve with distinction in the Afghanistan theater. By the end of July 2002, SEAL teams had already taken part in twenty-three combat operations, forty-five recon missions, the underwater inspection of twelve suspect merchant ships, and provided direct ground tactical support for 150 air strikes. In January 2003 a platoon from SEAL Team Three inserted into Zawar Kili on an operation that was supposed to last twelve hours. Nine days later, after numerous retaskings, they extracted, having survived by killing local livestock. Zawar Kili had been abandoned by al-Qaeda, but Team Three nevertheless returned to their base near Kandahar with eight captured terrorists and hundreds of captured weapons and documents discovered in a vast maze of seventy caves beneath a six kilometer-square of mountainous terrain. Nearly one million pounds of ammunition and military equipment were found and destroyed in that operation.

Later that spring, operating with a team of Danish commandos, a SEAL detachment out of Kandahar was responsible for capturing one of bin Laden's principle lieutenants, Mullah Khairullah Kahirkhawa.

During these ops, they were credited with the deaths of 115 enemy combatants and the capture of 110 more, at a cost of two Navy SEALs killed and two wounded.

Courage. Duty. Honor.

The SEAL legend continues.

H. Jay Riker
Spring 2005